SHE COU███

Rhun grabbed East███████████████████er face was crushed aga███████████████████s gripped her tightly. "Oh, Eastra, I'm so sorry you had to suffer such torment and degradation. I have thought sometimes that it might have been better if I had not saved you, if you had perished in the flames, innocent and pure."

She could not hold back now. His words had touched the raw wound inside her. Shoving him away with all her might, she shouted at him, "Aye, then I would not be soiled in your eyes—a contemptible slave girl! Although I have told you otherwise, I know you think my master bedded me, that I am a whore in truth! That's why you shy away from me and avoid my gaze! You're like all the others!"

He looked at her as if she had struck him. She swallowed, wondering if she had gone too far, if he would erupt with anger to match her own. But his voice when he spoke was tense and sorrowful. "Forgive me. I didn't mean to hurt you. I want nothing more than for you to be safe, from me and every man." He took a ravaged breath, then reached out. His big fingers grasped one of her braids and stroked it, softly, lovingly. "I see the pain inside you, and it troubles me. But it does not diminish . . . what I feel for you. If only you were not my hostage and kin of my enemy, I would love you in a heartbeat. I would make you mine . . . forever."

Gazing at Rhun's intent, rapt face, Eastra felt her anger dissolve and fall away. This man *was* different from the others. When he looked at her, he did not see a slave; he saw into her soul. She gave a little cry and reached out for him. He gathered her into his arms; his mouth came down on hers. It was far beyond tenderness. It was exquisite, shimmering need—liquid fire. Their bodies and souls as one . . .

BOOK YOUR PLACE ON OUR WEBSITE AND MAKE THE READING CONNECTION!

We've created a customized website just for our very special readers, where you can get the inside scoop on everything that's going on with Zebra, Pinnacle and Kensington books.

When you come online, you'll have the exciting opportunity to:

- View covers of upcoming books

- Read sample chapters

- Learn about our future publishing schedule
  (listed by publication month *and author*)

- Find out when your favorite authors will be visiting a city near you

- Search for and order backlist books from our online catalog

- Check out author bios and background information

- Send e-mail to your favorite authors

- Meet the Kensington staff online

- Join us in weekly chats with authors, readers and other guests

- Get writing guidelines

- AND MUCH MORE!

**Visit our website at
http://www.kensingtonbooks.com**

THE
DRAGON
PRINCE

Mary Gillgannon

ZEBRA BOOKS
Kensington Publishing Corp.

http://www.kensingtonbooks.com

ZEBRA BOOKS are published by

Kensington Publishing Corp.
850 Third Avenue
New York, NY 10022

All Kensington titles, imprints, and distributed lines are available at special quantity discounts for bulk purchases for sales
promotion, premiums, fund-raising, educational or institu-
tional use.

Special book excerpts or customized printings can also be created to fit specific needs. For details, write or phone the office
of the Kensington Special Sales Manager: Kensington Publishing Corp., 850 Third Avenue, New York, NY 10022. Attn.
Special Sales Department. Phone: 1-800-221-2647.

Zebra and the Z logo Reg. U.S. Pat. & TM Off.

First Printing: January 2002
10 9 8 7 6 5 4 3 2 1

Printed in the United States of America

To my children, Moira and Thomas,
who represent a modern blending of Celtic and Saxon.

Prologue

Southeast Britain, A.D. *528*

He couldn't breathe. The helmet he wore was suffocating him.

"Rhun, this way!" someone called.

He forced himself to move forward into the burning Saxon village. All around him, men were setting fire to the timber dwellings. A woman with yellow braids darted out of one of the huts. She saw him and screamed. Before Rhun could move, another warrior pursued her into the haze of the smoke. There was another terrified cry, then no more.

Rhun took a deep breath. His first raid. He hadn't known it would be like this. When he joined Arthur's army, he had imagined himself riding into battle on a sleek warhorse, the red dragon of Gwynedd shining proudly on his shield.

The image faded as he straightened and started toward the center of the village. There was a sound behind him. He whirled and saw another woman. She held a gleaming Saxon battle-ax, and her cobalt eyes shone with hatred. He stared at her, wishing he knew her language, some words to reassure her he did not mean her harm.

She raised the axe, and Rhun's muscles responded instinctively, moving his heavy broadsword in an arc to block the deadly blow. Iron grated against iron. The axe spun out of her hands and landed behind her. Her expression turned to one of dread.

"Go," he said. He motioned with his sword. She hesitated, then turned and ran.

Rhun relaxed his stance, breathing heavily. After a moment, he started toward a large timber structure near the center of the settlement. He approached the building and used his sword to push aside the hide door. Tense with caution, he bent his head and entered.

Light from slit windows and a smokehole in the roof illuminated a large living chamber, furnished with stools and benches around a main hearth. Rhun observed that the furniture was well made; the fabric hangings on the wall richly colored and luxurious. A sense of relief washed over him. This must be the Saxon chieftain's dwelling. If he could find treasure here, he would have an excuse to transport it back to camp and leave the killing behind.

There was a wooden chest in the corner of the room, decorated with hammered bronze strips. Rhun shifted his sword to his left hand, then went and opened it. The chest was filled with straw. He reached in and felt around. His fingers closed around a cold, hard object, and he lifted out a heavy gold drinking cup. Two stags, their eyes of garnet, encircled the vessel. The beasts looked so real he half expected them to come to life and spring away.

A faint sound made him pause and listen. He replaced the cup and started toward the back of the room. A low doorway led to an adjoining chamber. He ducked and entered. The floor was covered with woven mats; a large wooden bed filled the rest of the room. Carved horse heads adorned the four corner posts. They were so beautifully crafted, Rhun could not help going over and tracing one of the polished shapes with his free hand. If the Saxons were truly crude savages, how came they by things like this?

Another muffled sound froze him in place. His gaze

swept over the chamber and came to rest on the narrow space between the wall and the side of the bed. Sword at the ready, he edged around the bedposts. A bundle of crimson cloth was wedged beside the bed. Squeezing into the narrow space, he reached down to examine it. It appeared to be caught on something heavy. He laid his sword on the bed and used both hands to yank hard.

The cloth gave way, and a cat flew out of the space, hissing its fury as it churned across the bed. He watched it streak out the door, then leaned down once more. All he could see was masses of pale hair. At first he thought it was another animal. Then he realized a delicate hand was clutched protectively over the tangle of flaxen hair.

He jerked back. If he left now, no one would ever know he had found anyone here. Then he thought of the fires. Eventually this building would be put to the torch like the rest. The child or woman or whatever he had glimpsed would die a horrible death.

Bile rose in his throat. His orders were to kill every Saxon he found. Godless savages, Cador called them. He said they bred like hares, and if they and their offspring were not wiped out, in another generation they would control all of Britain.

Rhun picked up his sword with trembling hand. If he failed in his duty, Cador would never recommend him for the Companions, Arthur's elite warband. He took a deep breath and prepared himself to make the killing thrust. His eyes watered; his mouth worked. Blessed Jesu, he could not do it!

He flung his sword back on the bed and clenched his hands into fists. If he failed as a warrior, so be it. He had joined Arthur because his cause seemed a noble one. They fought for freedom and safety for their own people and to preserve the Christian faith against the marauding pagan hordes. But the Blessed Savior would not want him to kill an innocent child. It went against everything honorable, everything Rhun believed in.

He started to retrieve his sword, but even as he did so,

the Saxon leaped out of hiding and tried to scramble over the bed. Reacting instinctively, he reached out and grabbed a handful of hair. His breath caught as he jerked the girl around. She was exquisite—her skin as pale as buttermilk, her eyes as pure and blue as the summer sky. Against the tawny furs piled on the bed, she appeared to glow. He stared at her, unable to move.

She was very young. He doubted she had even reached womanhood. He could not kill her, and yet what could he do? If he left her, she would perish in the flames. But if he allowed her to flee, some other warrior might find her, someone who might not consider her too young for rape and defilement. Killing her was the most merciful thing he could do. And yet . . .

If only she would not look at him so. Her eyes were desperate, pleading. They seemed to reach inside him and twist something until it ached.

He exhaled through his teeth. He had to save her. Releasing her hair, he grabbed her by the garment she wore and dragged her across the bed. She relaxed in his grasp, like a kitten in its mother's mouth.

He let go of her and bent to retrieve the piece of fabric she had used to shield herself. It was a cloak, fashioned of densely woven crimson wool. He tossed her the cloak and tried to indicate she should wrap herself in the garment. She watched him in puzzlement.

He motioned impatiently to the doorway. They did not have much time. At any moment, some other soldier might come searching for booty.

At last she seemed to understand and gather the cloak around herself. He reached to arrange the fabric so it hid her hair completely, then retrieved his sword and sheathed it.

She watched him with a look of trust that unnerved him. At over four cubits in height, most men considered him a giant, and with his helmet and full battle gear, he must present a terrifying aspect. What did she see in his face that made her acquiesce so easily? Was it because he was

young, only seventeen years this spring? Or did she somehow guess his thoughts and know he was incapable of hurting her?

A shout outside reminded him they should not linger.
He picked up the girl and wrapped the cloak more tightly
around her, concealing her face. Then, taking a deep breath,
he carried her out.

"Did you find the chieftain's treasure?" Cian, another
young soldier, demanded as soon as Rhun stepped out of
the dwelling.

"Aye. I bundled up what I could, but there is plenty
more." Rhun jerked his head. "Go inside and see. There
is a chest full of fine metalwork and plate in the main
room. Perhaps you can use one of the wall hangings to
carry it."

"What is that?" Cian motioned to Rhun's burden.

"A harp." For the past few seconds, he had tried frantically to come up with an explanation for the strange-
shaped bundle in his arms. "I mean to take it back to my
father's bard. That is, if Cador allows it."

"A harp?" Cian frowned. "I didn't know the Saxons
cared for music or poetry. I thought they were——"

"Crude savages? Aye, I did also. But once you see the
things in there, you will know they have as much love of
beauty as our people."

Cian started toward the door, then hesitated. "You found
no one inside? You're certain I will not be ambushed?"

"Only a gray striped cat. I would look out for that one."

Cian's face split into a grin beneath his helmet. Then he
disappeared into the doorway.

Rhun hurried past the burning huts and storage buildings
toward the forest beyond the village. It was slow going.
The smoke was thick; he could hardly see. He struggled
on, trying not to breathe the noxious haze. His metal helmet
grew hot, and sparks stung his bare arms. At least his boiled
leather jerkin would not burn. Nor would the wool of his
trews or the girl's mantle catch easily.

At last he reached the cool, shadowy stand of oaks. He

kept walking. If he remained close to the village, one of
the other soldiers might see him.

The forest closed around them. The air grew fresher and
was filled with the sweet perfume of growing things. He
finally paused in a little glen. In a gap between the trees,
purple loosestrife and golden broom grew in wild profusion
on the forest floor. In this tranquil place, it was easy to
forget the destruction and violence he had left behind.

He gently unwrapped the girl and set her on her feet.
Her head reached only to his chest, and he wondered how
tall she would be when she was a woman grown. Then he
wondered if she would live that long. How would she survive? She could not live alone in the forest, and it did not
seem likely any of her kin would be left to aid her.

For a moment, he considered taking her home to his
father's fortress in Gwynedd. Then he realized if he did
so, she would end up a servant. Living in that fine timber
dwelling, she was likely the Saxon chieftain's daughter
or granddaughter, a princess of sorts. She deserved to be
free.

He sighed, staring down at her. In the dimness of the
forest, her silvery hair shone like sunlight on a waterfall.
Her delicate form and magical coloring made him think of
a wood sprite. Maybe the fairies of this wood would find
her and make her one of their own.

He half smiled at his own foolish thoughts. He didn't
believe in fairies, no matter that his stepmother, Rhiannon,
teased him it was only because he had not yet met one.

The girl smiled shyly back at him, her expression making her appear even lovelier. He thought he could stay there
and look at her forever.

But he could not. The longer he waited, the more likely
someone would find them. He knew many men in his troop
would not hesitate to rape or murder the girl, despite her
youth. She was a Saxon, the enemy.

Once again, Rhun wondered what he had gotten himself
into. He had sworn a soldier's oath to Arthur, vowing to
fight Britain's enemies. Now he defied his orders and set

one of the hated Saxons free. *But she is female and a child,* his mind screamed. Then he thought of all the British women and children who had perished at the hands of Saxon raiders, or been brutally enslaved. Where was the right in this thing? All he saw was the pain and suffering of innocents.

He closed his eyes and said a silent prayer. A voice inside him seemed to answer. Rhiannon said the voice was his true spirit. The priest said it was his conscience. Either way, he could not deny it.

Opening his eyes, he looked again at the Saxon. He nodded to her. "Go," he said. He gestured toward the wildwood beyond. "Go in peace, and may God be with you."

Her eyes beseeched him, as if instead of fearing him, she clung to him for safety and reassurance. It made a lump form in his throat.

He grew angry. She made a mockery of his soldier's oath, his bright dreams of glory and honor. Why could she not simply leave him be? He forced his face to sternness. "Go!" he shouted.

She gave him one last helpless look, then moved like a deer into the forest, soft-footed and graceful, a splash of light against the shadowy green.

Rhun sighed. His decision to be a warrior, to fight for God and Britain, had once seemed so clear and true, but already it was tainted. The voice inside him spoke again. It told him this moment of harsh reckoning was only the beginning.

One

Britain, near Londinium, A.D. *541*

The Saxon longhouse was brightly lit, with oil lamps set in recesses along the walls and a steady fire glowing in the main hearth. British and Saxon warriors sat on stools and benches around the room and eyed each other warily.

"We have come here today to speak of peace, a lasting peace for all of Britain." Arthur, the high king, opened the discussions in a calm, ringing voice. Rhun ap Maelgwn, seated beside him, thought how royal and noble his commander appeared. Arthur had the dark coloring and high-browed, strong-featured countenance of his Roman grandfather Ambrosius, and the commanding presence of a man descended from emperors.

But Cerdic, the Saxon leader, was equally imposing. He sat as tall and broad-shouldered as Arthur, and with his tawny gold hair and thick, powerful neck, he looked much like the gold-maned stallion on his battle shield. Watching Arthur, his pale blue eyes were as cold and forbidding as the western sea.

"Would any of us here argue that the cost has not been great these past years?" Arthur continued. "Both sides have lost good men and loved ones. Worse yet, these many years and many lives later, is the fact that very little has been

settled, despite the bloodshed. It is time for a truce. Time
for us to sit down and apportion the land between us, before
we destroy it altogether." He made a graceful motion with
his hands, and the ruby eye in the eagle ring he wore
gleamed blood red in the firelight.

He paused and Bridei, Rhun's brother, repeated his
words in Saxon. Then Cerdic spoke, his voice sounding
harsh and guttural after Bridei's musical tones.

When he was finished, Bridei translated. "Cerdic says
he has thought much the same thing, that Briton and Saxon
have fought until the whole island is red with blood and
all the women weep in grief. He agrees it is time to put
aside weapons and to settle the matter with words and reason."

As Bridei finished the translation, he smiled faintly.
Rhun could not help wondering if Cerdic had spoken quite
as eloquently as his brother made it appear. He would not
put it past Bridei to have altered the Saxon's response to
give it a more dramatic phrasing. His younger brother was
oftentimes too clever for his own good.

Rhun shot Bridei a warning look. Bridei's smile widened
and his dark blue eyes sparkled with amusement. Rhun
shook his head, then directed his attention to his commander once more.

Some of the tension had left Arthur's face, and he looked
less careworn and grim, more like the soldier to whom
Rhun had first sworn over ten years ago. Back then, there
had been an inspiring fire in Arthur's gray eyes, a ringing
conviction in his voice. The years and their losses had
dimmed the fire, although it was not yet quenched. "I'm
pleased we can meet as equals and speak of these things,"
Arthur said. "This is a great day for both our peoples."

Cerdic looked to a far corner of the room and nodded
to a servant standing there. The woman came forward with
a tray full of small gold cups. Cerdic spoke again and
Bridei translated. "Let us share a cup of mead to com-
memorate our resolve this day."

Rhun watched Cerdic's face, searching his cunning, wintry blue eyes for some hint of his thoughts.

The woman picked up two of the cups and handed them to Cerdic and Arthur. Rhun's gaze followed her as she retrieved more cups and passed them around. Only once before had he seen hair the silvery, flaxen shade of the serving woman's long braids. The memory triggered a sharp pain in his gut. It had been over ten years since he carried the Saxon girl through a burning village to the dubious safety of the forest. What were the chances she had survived, alone and helpless as she was?

The Saxon had been on his mind nearly every day these past years. Sometimes at night, he lay on his bedroll and closed his eyes, conjuring the image of her glowing beauty. She seemed to represent something good and true, and the thought he had rescued her brought him satisfaction, if not peace of mind.

He hoped the act helped atone for all the blood he had shed as a soldier, the suffering he had caused. War was much uglier and less glorious than the idealistic youth he had been could ever have imagined. Even if the cause was a righteous one, the means used to win it were so brutal and cruel they left a permanent stain upon a man's soul.

The woman reached him and held out a cup. Rhun smiled at her, thinking how very fair she was. Their gazes met for a moment, and he experienced a pang of longing. It might have been *her,* these many years later. This woman had the same fine features, the same luminous skin and clear blue eyes.

She handed him the cup, then abruptly turned away and hurried back to the tray. Rhun watched her, wondering if his bold stare had offended her.

He continued to observe her as she carried cups to the other men. She wore a gown of fine blue linen embroidered in yellow and rose at the hem and neck, and a gold girdle around her waist. No serving woman would possess such finery. Could she be Cerdic's wife? She was younger than the Saxon chieftain by a score of years or more, but maybe his first wife had died.

When all the cups were passed around, Arthur and Cerdic exchanged formal toasts. Rhun hardly listened. His attention was focused on the woman, who had retreated back to the corner of the room. He could swear she was staring at him, and he felt acutely aware of her also, as if her gaze had set his flesh ablaze. Why should she affect him like this? Unless . . .

His mind whirled with the incredible possibility she truly might be the Saxon girl he had rescued so many years ago. Had she recognized him in that brief moment when he smiled at her?

Astounding that they should see each other again, that she could have survived and ended up in Cerdic's household. Was she kin of his? Or wife? The idea repulsed Rhun. It did not seem right that such a delicate, ethereal creature should be forced to share the bed of a ruthless barbarian like Cerdic.

Yet it seemed likely. What else would she be doing in Cerdic's longhouse? If she were his daughter or other female relative, she would be wedded to some other man by now. Saxon girls married young, the better to breed many warriors. It was not so different among Rhun's own people, the Cymry. It was not uncommon for girls of fourteen or even thirteen winters to be wed, although his father refused to discuss whom his sisters Annwyl and Elen might be matched with, and they were fifteen and seventeen already.

Rhun repressed a sigh. It was good to know the girl had not perished as he had feared, that she had been rescued and lived to womanhood. But it troubled him to see her in these circumstances. He almost wished he had been left with only a memory. Then he could imagine her living among the forest fairies, her bright beauty indestructible and eternal.

The toasting finished, Arthur sought to begin discussion of the details of the truce. But Cerdic was not quite ready to leave the past behind. He began a long recitation of all he had suffered at the hands of the British. He told how nearly all his kin had been killed, his mother and wife and sons and daughters murdered.

His words opened raw wounds for the British, who had suffered their own soul-wrenching losses. Arthur sought to turn the conversation to the future, but Cerdic stubbornly resisted. Rhun could sense his fellow soldiers growing angry, and both sides shifted restlessly, their hands reaching unconsciously for their sword belts, searching for weapons that were not there. Rhun was glad Arthur had insisted everyone entering the longhouse leave all swords and knives in a pile by the door.

Perhaps the woman also sensed the growing tension, for she stepped forward with a bronze ewer and, moving lightly around the room, began to refill everyone's cups. Rhun watched her more closely this time, more and more certain it was she, the Saxon he had saved those long years ago. He also observed Cerdic's reaction to the woman. Surely if she were the chieftain's wife, he would nod or look at her. But Cerdic took no more notice of her than he would any servant.

Cups filled, they made more toasts, and the mellow warmth of the mead seemed to dispel some of the tension in the room. Arthur brought up the idea of exchanging hostages to provide surety for the truce, and Cerdic appeared amenable to the idea. Rhun's thoughts turned back to the woman. He'd made up his mind he must speak to her somehow, if only to tell her how pleased he was his worst fears for her had not come to pass.

The discussions dragged on, hampered by the need for Bridei to translate everything and the cautious, tense nature of the occasion. At last, Cerdic called for a break, and Arthur agreed. It was decided the Britons would return to their camp outside the village for the night and talks would resume in the morning.

As everyone rose, Rhun looked for the woman. He was disappointed when he did not see her. Had she gone to a private area of the dwelling? Or slipped out a back entrance and vanished altogether?

Bridei came up beside him, and the two men gathered up their weapons and walked out of the longhouse together. "By Llud's silver hand," Bridei swore, "I'll be glad to get back to camp and have a cup of wine and some food. I'm starving. I've never fancied mead. Give me good Gaulish wine any day."

"The woman who served us," Rhun said. "I wonder where she went?"

Bridei raised a brow. "I've never known you to be taken with a pretty face, and certainly not when it belongs to one of the enemy."

"God willing, there will soon be peace between our peoples," Rhun said irritably. "Besides, I only want to talk to her."

"Talk to her? Have you forgotten, brother, that you don't speak Saxon?"

"Maybe she knows a word of two of Briton, and I am not completely without understanding of her language." *Once before we met and understood each other,* he thought. *We needed no words then. Why should we need them now?*

Bridei shook his head. "I suppose it had to happen sometime—that your loins would get the better of your wits. Just be careful, brother. As one who is experienced in these matters, I can tell you that dallying with royal-blooded maidens can be a dangerous business, even when they are *not* our enemies. If you recall, only a day ago you said this truce might be the answer to all Arthur has fought for these past years. Take care you are not the one who ruins your idol's dream."

"I would never do anything to jeopardize this truce!" Rhun retorted hotly. "And furthermore, I have no intention of dallying with this woman. Indeed, I suspect she is Cerdic's *wife.* I would be risking much more than peace for Britain if I were foolish enough to pursue her!"

"Cerdic's wife?" Bridei made a face. "Seems a shame a hoary old goat like him should have such a comely lass warming his bed. But to the victor go the spoils. He probably killed her father to have her. He's a savage bastard. I think pious, noble Arthur has overreached himself this time. Cerdic may agree to a truce, but he'll break it as soon as it becomes inconvenient."

Bridei's words aroused a gnawing bitterness inside Rhun. Had he saved the Saxon only to doom her to a grim, onerous life, married to a crude man who scarce seemed to notice her? *If she were my wife,* he thought, *I would not have her serve my enemies like a slave. I would dress her in finery and jewels and seat her by my side like a queen.*

As the two men walked out the gate of the timber-walled palisade, Bridei continued his questioning. "If you know you can't have her, why do you want to speak to this woman?"

Rhun pressed his lips together. He was not about to tell Bridei the tale of his rescue of the Saxon girl all those years ago. Although he did not regret his actions, he had disobeyed a direct order. Cador had later been chastised by Arthur for his brutality in killing women and children during the raid, but that did not entirely excuse Rhun's defiance. He had no desire to reveal to Bridei—cynical, opportunistic Bridei—his long ago breach of honor.

"You aren't going to tell me, are you? I guess I'll have to find out my own way." Bridei grinned, alerting Rhun that his brother had some mischief in mind.

Rhun gritted his teeth as he headed toward his tent. Why had God seen fit to give him a brother like Bridei? He was like a flea that burrowed beneath a soldier's jerkin, biting and irritating, but never causing any real harm a man could complain of. Yet he loved his brother and was proud of his talent for languages and his ability with words. Besides acting as interpreter, Bridei served as Arthur's bard on campaign. His skilled fingers could make a harp sing, and his facile tongue composed bawdy soldier ditties and heartbreaking tributes to fallen warriors with equal grace.

Rhun sighed. Bridei's sly, slippery nature was the least

of his worries today. He had to find a way to speak to the Saxon. If he did not, he would never know peace.

He is here! I have found him! I stood so close to him I might have touched his hand! Eastra's heart pounded as she hurried through the encampment. It did not seem possible. Yet she knew there could not be two men in Britain with such kind, beautiful eyes, eyes that had looked at her with such tender pity, eyes that had stolen her heart all those years ago.

His build and coloring were the same as she remembered. His shoulders might be a touch broader, his long-limbed body more heavily muscled, his burnished gold hair a bit darker, but he was a man in his prime now, and such changes were only to be expected.

A tremor rushed down her body. For so long, she had dreamed of him. Now he was here, not an arrowshot from her uncle's longhouse. She could scarce breathe, she was so excited.

Eastra cast a quick glance over her shoulder and slowed her pace as she neared the back entrance of the palisade. She must not be seen. If would be disastrous if Cerdic discovered she went to meet a British warrior. He would probably use the incident as an excuse to refuse the truce, and the vicious fighting would continue indefinitely.

Eastra's eyes filled with tears. How she hated war. It had cost her everyone she loved and taken much of her youth and all her innocence. Sometimes it seemed all she had left was her memory of a young warrior who took pity on a terrified child. As huge and fiercely clad as her rescuer had been, she had never feared him, not from the moment she had looked into his blue-gray eyes and known this was a man incapable of cruelty.

Nor could she forget the way he had looked at her when they were in the forest. His expression had been beyond tender, almost worshipful. Although many men had taken note of her since then, none had ever made her feel the way the young warrior had. He was special, wonderful. She had to speak to him. She had to tell him what he meant to her. And she did not have the patience to wait for him to return to her uncle's encampment the next day. She would go to him now.

But how to find him? She spoke the British tongue fairly well, but it would be risky to approach the enemy camp. Her uncle might have spies there. In fact, he undoubtedly did. Cerdic was treacherous and unprincipled, at least in regards to the Britons. He bore them a bitter grudge for killing his family, and somehow, someday, he would get his revenge. Eastra suspected the truce was only a temporary arrangement so he could rest his warriors and give his client thanes a chance to plant their crops and rebuild their villages.

She spotted the British camp, situated a short distance away among a grove of trees. Arthur ap Uther had not brought many warriors with him. It would be easy for Cerdic to encircle the camp with his troops and kill them all. But that kind of treachery might be too heinous for even Cerdic to contemplate. Eastra hoped so.

She slowed her pace, creeping through the thick underbrush, which was greening rapidly in the warm spring sunshine. Buttercups, violets, and wood anemone bloomed everywhere. How would she find him, she wondered, one Briton among many? He appeared to stand high in Arthur's favor. He must be an important man, one of the British leader's most trusted warriors.

She took a deep breath as she neared the camp. Many of the tents had colorful pennants planted in the ground outside their doorways, the battle devices of the men within. In the center of the camp, Eastra saw Arthur's banner, rippling purple silk, portraying a huge bear with an eagle flanking it. At one time, Cerdic had said, Arthur carried a dragon on his banner and his shield, the symbol of his father's lineage. But in recent years he had changed to the bear, for Artoris, his birth name, and the eagle, representing the might of Rome.

The thought of the dragon jogged Eastra's memory. Had not the young warrior who rescued her also carried a dragon on his shield, red on white? A rush of excitement filled her. If only he had not altered his symbol in the intervening years. If she could spot his device, she might be able to sneak into his tent without being seen.

She moved cautiously, slowly circling the camp, straining her eyes for a glimpse of crimson and white. Bees and mayflies buzzed around her, and her linen gunna clung to her skin and snagged on brambles and bushes. She thought of returning to Cerdic's palisade and changing into old clothing. But she wanted him to see her like this, looking like a princess, not a serving girl.

On her second circuit of the camp, she finally spied it. Not a large banner, and quite tattered and worn, but mostly white and with a red dragon emblazoned upon it. Viewing the rather bedraggled pennant, Eastra considered this was not a man who cared much for the trappings of power. A practical man, a man who relied on his formidable size and striking appearance to intimidate his foes, rather than showy display.

She sighed heavily. Not a hundred paces stood between her and the object of her quest. What if he didn't remember her? He might have rescued many other children in the intervening years. But she didn't think so. He could hardly stand so high in Arthur's favor if he spent his time *aiding* Saxons, rather than killing them.

Determination made her press forward. She had to speak to him. If nothing else, to tell him how his act of kindness had given her courage and hope, the will to go on when her life seemed impossibly hopeless and bleak. All those years when she was a slave girl, almost less than human.

Then, five years ago, Cerdic had found her and rescued her. He offered her a life of luxury and comfort, but she was no happier. There were many among Cerdic's household who looked upon her as hopelessly devalued by her years as a British thrall. She might be a princess because Cerdic called her one, but she would never be accepted by his womenfolk.

She took a cautious step toward the dragon banner snapping in the breeze, then squared her shoulders and stepped more boldly. She would hold her head high, and if anyone stopped her, she would say she brought a message from Cerdic. If Cerdic had spies in the camp, it would take them some time to discover her claim was only a ruse.

She saw two soldiers on the way there. They gave her startled glances, then nodded politely. *I am a princess,* she thought. *I have every right to walk freely on Saxon lands.*

She approached the tent with the tattered white banner, and, taking a deep breath, ducked inside.

He sat sprawled on a worn cowhide, cleaning his armor. Her first thought was to wonder why he did not have a body servant perform such tasks for him. Then her eyes adjusted to the dim light and she simply drank in his glory.

It was not only that he was handsome, golden-skinned and fair like her countrymen, with well-made features and a manly form. It was some other quality he had, a gentleness about him even the fierce trappings of a warrior could not obscure. Seeing him now, wearing only a tunic, he appeared so magically beautiful, like a god. And so much like the youth who had rescued her all those years ago.

Her heart melted. She wanted to reach out to him, to have those strong arms close around her once more, making her feel safe and protected, as she had not felt since the last time.

But she did not approach him, was not quite that brave. He watched her, stunned. Then, when his surprise faded, he frowned. "You should not be here," he said. "It's not safe."

She wanted to laugh. For if she was not safe with him, where was she safe? Had the years affected him so little he had not yet learned security was not a roof overhead nor a full belly? It was not even knowing her kinsman and protector was likely the most powerful Saxon on this side of the eastern sea. None of those things made her feel safe. Only he had done that, all those years ago.

He rose as much as he could, given his size. It clearly would be impossible for him to stand inside the small tent. "I'm sorry, I don't speak much of your language." He frowned in thought, as if searching for words, then gave up and gestured to the tent entrance.

"I'll not go," she said in his tongue. "I've come to speak to you."

"You speak Briton." He looked amazed.

"Aye, although a different dialect than the one you use. I was a slave on a villa in the south. They spoke a mixture of Latin and Briton, and their speech had a different cadence than the language you use."

"You were a slave?" His expression altered to one of horror.

"Aye." The bitterness rose up inside her. Would he also shun her? "Five years past, Cerdic found me and took me into his household."

He closed his eyes, and she could not guess what he was thinking or feeling.

When he opened them again, he appeared calmer. But there was a distance between them now. Eastra suppressed a sigh. She should have known he would not be any different than the others. How many men had expressed an interest in her, only to change their minds when they learned of her past? Never before had she cared. In fact, it was a relief. She did not want to be any man's wife, his chattel. She valued her freedom too greatly.

But this man, she could not deny she sought his regard. It was like a dagger in her gut to see the distress in his eyes when she told him she had been a thrall.

She almost left then. But despite her pain and disappointment, she could not bring herself to give up.

He spoke again. "I'm sorry. I had hoped you would be rescued by your people, that they would keep you safe. But . . . at least you are alive. And still beautiful." He smiled at her, although it seemed forced. "When I saw you in the longhouse today I thought that only once before had I ever seen a creature so radiant and fair. I have never forgotten you."

But you want to now, she thought, *I can see it in your eyes.* The anger rose up inside her. She bit her lips to keep from weeping.

"I would like to speak with you, but . . ." he glanced again toward the tent opening. "I think it would be wisest if we went elsewhere to do so."

She nodded, still paralyzed by heartache.

He donned a leather jerkin and his swordbelt, then escorted her out of the tent. She followed him as he walked rapidly through the camp. The few soldiers they saw stared, then looked quickly away. She decided it must be courtesy and respect for this warrior that made them behave so discreetly.

As they approached the forest, her mind was filled with the memory of him carrying her through the burning settlement to the sanctuary of the woods. But this time he did not carry her. Indeed, he took care not to touch her.

When they had gone a little way into the tangle of foliage, he stopped and turned to face her. "Do Cerdic's men patrol this area?" he asked.

"I don't think so," she said. "He feels secure behind the walls of his palisade. Besides, he trusts Arthur's honor. He has no concern that the British will attack."

The warrior nodded. "Then we should be safe here. For a time."

She took a deep breath, thinking about what she wanted to say. She started to speak just as he did. They both stopped, then laughed.

He gestured graciously. "You first. You are the one who sought me out, although I must say I had made up my mind to have speech with you before this peace council was over."

"I don't know what to say," she said. "I have thought

about this day for so many years, and now . . . now it is here and I can't seem to find the right words." She gazed up at him. "My name is Eastra. What is yours? What have you been doing these past years?"

"I am called Rhun ap Maelgwn. I have served in Arthur's army since the day I last saw you."

"It seems you have risen high in Arthur's favor if he seats you at his right hand in meetings."

His mouth twisted wryly. "Not so high. Arthur has other captains. But of all of them, it is me he wishes to have at his side when the talk is of peace rather than war."

"That is because you are an honorable man, and he knows you will advise him to be fair and generous in his dealings with his enemies."

"Maybe. Or it could be he knows I won't lose my temper, no matter how Cerdic might provoke me. I am generally slow to anger and quick to forgive." He smiled. "Many men count my good nature a flaw and advise me I will never be a strong leader because of it."

Eastra could not help sighing. "Deliver me from hottempered men. My Uncle Cerdic is often rash and unreasonable."

A strange look came over Rhun's face. "Cerdic is your uncle?"

"Aye."

Rhun gave a hearty laugh.

"What amuses you?" she asked.

He shook his head, beaming. "I can't tell you how relieved I am. I thought Cerdic was your *husband*. I was in dread we would be found together and he would not only abandon all thought of a truce, but geld me as well." He laughed again. "Although I doubt he would be pleased to learn you had speech with one of his enemies, at least the transgression is not quite so outrageous."

"Why did you think I was wed to him?"

"I could think of no other explanation for your position in his household. I thought surely if you were his daughter or niece, you would be wed and gone by now." His mirth faded. "Are you a widow? Is that why you live in Cerdic's household and serve his guests?"

She shook her head. "I am unwed."

His expression grew puzzled, then he nodded slowly. "Cerdic must value you a great deal, that he will let no man take you to wife. My father is like that. I wonder when he will ever let my sisters wed."

Eastra looked at the ground. "You misunderstand my circumstances. I think Cerdic would be pleased to match me with one of his thanes, but none of them will have me, and Cerdic would never let me marry a sokeman or serf."

"Not have you? How can that be? You are by far the most exquisite woman I have ever seen, among my people *or* yours. Surely your father's clients are not blind."

"You forget." She heard the bitterness in her voice and, for once, did not try to hide it. "For five years I was a British thrall. All my people think I am defiled because of it."

His voice was tight. "Did you serve as your master's . . . concubine?"

"No! He never touched me! In truth, my owners were not cruel. They treated me well, but like a servant, a *nithing.*" Her eyes stung with tears as she remembered the feeling of being no more important than one of the hounds who slept at Gaius's hearth.

He reached out and touched her arm. "I'm sorry. It pains me to know you suffered. I have thought many times that rather than leaving you alone in the woods, I should have taken you back to my father's fortress in Gwynedd. But you would have been a servant there as well, and it might have been no better for you."

She shook her head. "If you were there, it would have been better. If I could have been with you, I would not have cared that I was a slave."

Their eyes met, and Eastra felt all the years of longing and dreaming filling up her insides until she could scarce breathe. He was here, in front of her, her rescuer, her brave, kind warrior. He was real and alive and even more beautiful than she remembered. She wanted to throw herself into his arms, to have him hold her not as a man holds a child, but as he holds a woman. She wanted him to kiss her and caress and fill her body with his own flesh.

The moment stretched on. She lost herself in his eyes, their stormy blue-gray depths. She could not speak nor move, only wait breathlessly, hoping he felt what she did, that he wanted her as badly as she wanted him.

But then he stepped back, and his expression grew anguished. "We cannot do this. There can be no future for us. Cerdic would never allow it. If we are found together, your uncle will use it as an excuse to call off the truce." He shook his head, and his eyes glittered, as if with tears. "It's enough that I have seen you, that I know you are alive and safe. I will carry this moment in my breast, and it will content me the rest of my days."

He turned away. Eastra took a great choking breath. He could not leave her now. She could not bear it! She reached out to touch him, then froze as she saw another man standing in the shadows. A Briton. If they were caught, better it be by his people.

Rhun spoke first. "Bridei, damn you, how long have you been standing there?"

The man smiled. He was startlingly handsome, with hair as black as ebony, deep gentian blue eyes, and features fine and graceful enough to be a woman's. Abruptly, Eastra recognized him as Arthur's interpreter. "I've been here a while," he said. "Long enough to be quite intrigued."

Rhun strode toward the man and took him roughly by the arm. "You're going to forget you ever saw us. She's Cerdic's niece, not his wife, so there is no dishonor in my speaking with her. But even so, none of the Saxons can know about this. It would ruin everything."

"Aye." The man called Bridei still smiled, a shrewd smile. "I suppose it could. Not the least of which is your saintly reputation. Maybe your cock is not made of wood after all."

Rhun made a hissing sound through his teeth. "Hold your tongue! She is yet a maid!"

Bridei rolled his eyes. "Oh, aye, but for how long with you around?"

Eastra would not have believed it, but Rhun's face grew red and he clenched his hands into fists. It looked as if her gentle-natured warrior was on the verge of pounding Bridei's face into the dirt.

Bridei appeared unconcerned that he might be attacked at any moment. He gave a cheery laugh. "Relax, brother, I'll not betray you. Oh, no, there is much more sport in keeping your secret and watching how this tale turns out."

Rhun glared at Bridei. Eastra said, "You are brothers? I can't credit it. In truth, you look nothing alike."

At her words, Bridei raised his raven-dark brows. "We're as different as night and day. Rhun outdoes the angels with his purity and goodness, while I possess neither attribute. My brother is also chaste, dutiful, and serious, while I"— he paused for emphasis and gave her a wicked grin—"am lewd, careless, and as lighthearted as a boy. Rhun wins the admiration of warriors and kings, but who do you suppose the women fancy?"

Eastra could not help herself. She laughed. The fate of all of Britain and both their peoples might hang in the balance, and yet this man jested.

Rhun frowned, and Eastra quickly quelled her mirth. Bridei might be amusing, but it was his brother who held her heart. "I'm sorry," she said. "I didn't mean to anger you."

Rhun shook his head. "Never could you anger me. It's not possible."

The tension between them built once again. It seemed they could not look away from each other, that their souls were bound together like links forged in a chain.

Bridei broke the spell. "Well. As fascinating as it is to observe this tender tryst, I have to agree with Rhun. Cerdic strikes me as a hot-tempered sort. If we are found, he likely would not be satisfied with cutting off my brother's balls and would also try to divest me of mine. In the interest of all the maidens who would be grievously affected by such a loss, I must insist the two of you bid each other farewell, at least until the morrow."

Two

"Where did you meet *her?*" Bridei asked as the two men left the woods and started back to camp.

"None of your business," Rhun retorted. His insides churned as he thought of Eastra being enslaved. At least she had survived and was now free and living among her countrymen. Yet she did not seem happy. Her beautiful blue eyes had shone with pain when she told him no Saxon would have her for a wife. Had he saved her only to have her endure a life of misery?

"I could make it my business," Bridei said. "I'm sure Cador or any number of Arthur's officers would be interested to know you are acquainted with Cerdic's niece."

Rhun observed the canny expression on his brother's face and swore loudly. "Why must you always seek to make trouble?" he demanded.

Bridei shrugged. "It's more interesting that way. Indeed, this whole matter is very intriguing. I saw how that woman looked at you—as if you were some sort of god come to life."

"If you must know, I . . . helped Eastra when she was a child."

"Helped?"

"All right, I rescued her," Rhun said angrily. He did not think his brother would betray him, but he might cause trouble in his relentless quest for the truth. It seemed better to give him at least part of the story. "It was many years ago, and I was young and impulsive. She was merely a child, of no threat to anyone. I carried her out of the Saxon settlement we were attacking and left her in the woods. Apparently, she was captured and made a slave, so it's hard to say if rescuing her was the wisest course after all."

"Ah, and ever since then, she has dreamed of you, her noble hero."

Rhun grimaced. Eastra's obvious adoration was disquieting. The worshipful expression on her face, the sense she was willing to do almost anything for him, aroused feelings he did not know how to deal with. Being so close to her lush, golden beauty had conjured some very unnoble thoughts in his mind. He wanted to hold her, to taste her full, rosy lips, to—

"I can guess what you're thinking, brother, and although she's an exquisite woman, I doubt bedding her would quite be worth having your ballocks cut off. Cerdic is a ruthless savage, and she is, after all, his niece."

"I was not—"

"Of course you were," Bridei interrupted, one dark brow cocked in amusement. "If you want this woman, you're going to have to arrange to meet her under some other circumstances. While I care little enough for Arthur's treaty, I do feel an obligation to keep my older brother alive. After all, have you not rescued *me* time and time again?"

Rhun gave a snort. Bridei attracted trouble as a field of meadowsweet attracted bees. Almost since Bridei was a baby toddling around their father's fortress, Rhun had been getting him out of scrapes. He seemed to have an infallible sense of how to infuriate their father, the famed warlord Maelgwn the Great. Rhun was always arguing that Bridei was merely being playful and mischievous, that he meant no real harm. But as the years passed and Bridei failed to curb his careless, rather selfish behavior, Rhun began to wonder if his brother were not somehow lacking in moral character. There was always a cynical edge to his words, a hint of malice in his teasing.

"Don't worry, your assistance will not be necessary," Rhun told him coldly. "I will have no more private conversations with Princess Eastra. I'm simply relieved to discover she is alive and safe."

"Hmm. I don't think this woman intends to let you get away so easily."

He glanced at his brother. The smug, mocking look on Bridei's face irritated him unbearably. "I'm going to meet with Arthur and the others and discuss plans for tomorrow. You can come or no." He strode off briskly, not giving Bridei time to answer.

It was a relief to take his place in the circle of warriors as they sat around the fire eating the food Cerdic had provided. Rhun heaved a sigh as he accepted a thick chunk of boar meat. This was where he belonged, among Arthur's Companions. For over ten years he had fought alongside these men, shared jests and wagers. He would not forget the common vision they shared—to preserve Britain for their own people and to drive the marauding Saxons back to the sea.

Of course, that vision was now altered. They all knew in their heart of hearts there was no way to rid the land of the invaders altogether. Some families in the settlements along the Saxon Shore had already lived in Britain a generation or more. There was no way to force them out now. Arthur and his men could only hope to contain the invaders to the eastern and southern fringes of the island, which was exactly what this treaty with Cerdic was about.

Cador ap Cadwallon was speaking now. "The only way to make certain Cerdic keeps his end of the bargain is to take hostages. Only if he knows the lives of his countrymen hang in the balance will he consider keeping the peace."

"Hostages." Arthur stroked his chin thoughtfully.

"The hostages must be either from among Cerdic's trusted thanes or his personal household, someone whose life he would be unwilling to sacrifice."

The other men nodded at Cador's words. Rhun took a swallow of wine from the skin the men were passing around, then wiped his mouth. He tried to focus on the conversation as the men began to discuss other aspects of the treaty—how much land they would cede to Cerdic and whether the other Saxon leaders would accept Cerdic as speaking for all of them—but his thoughts kept wandering. Poor Eastra. The past years had scarred her. While her ethereal beauty remained untouched, there was such pain in her eyes. He wanted to help her, but knew he could not. Indeed, it would be better if he never saw her again. Her allure was too strong, too intense.

Odd, but he'd never felt this way about a woman before. He'd shared his bed with several over the past years, but usually discovered they cared not for him but for who he was. As Maelgwn's oldest son, he was heir to the kingdom of Gwynedd. And as one of Arthur's trusted officers, should their cause prevail, he was likely to end up ruling other portions of Britain as well. Although he'd never particularly aspired to be a king, he knew strong leaders were necessary to bring peace. The difficult part was the loneliness and the sense that people treated him differently because of who he was. He hated the women who sought to pleasure him merely in the hope of improving their own status.

Of course, when he wed, it would be primarily to form a political alliance. That was what marriage was about for a prince. Even his father had married for the sake of politics, although it had ended up being a love match. Knowing his own destiny, Rhun knew he could not afford to be mooning over a woman like Eastra.

He released a sigh, then sought to turn his attention back to the business of Arthur's council.

Eastra shifted restlessly on her straw pallet, then rose and wrapped a shawl around her shift. Leaving her bedchamber, she crept out into the courtyard of the abandoned Roman villa that Cerdic had made his fortress. His men had used the stones from the original buildings, combined with timber, to build the palisade wall, and constructed a traditional longhouse where the main dwelling had been, but much of the rest of the complex they had left alone. The stonework around the longhouse was crumbling, the vegetation overgrown and wild, but there were still vestiges of the lovely garden that had once existed there. White and yellow roses grew in profusion around a tumbled down wall, and a plum tree bloomed next to the remains of a fountain, sending the soft perfume of its blossoms into the night air.

A sense of desperation gripped her as she paced on the uneven stone pathway. For near all her life, she had been powerless—first as a child, then as a slave, and now as a woman in her uncle's household. She was sick to death of having her life ordered by others. Having found the man she had dreamed of for so many years, she was not going to lose him once again. In a day or two, this meeting between Saxon and Briton would be finished and all the warriors would return to the lands they claimed for their own. But she was not going to let Rhun ap Maelgwn simply walk away. When he left, she would go with him.

She'd thought on the matter every moment since their conversation in the forest, and she'd decided what she would do. During the last part of the discussions, hostages had been mentioned. If she were one of those hostages, she would be able to go with Rhun. Although she doubted he would guard her himself, she would at least have a chance to speak to him some more, to convince him that despite the conflict between their peoples, they were meant to be together.

Now all she had to do was persuade Cerdic to go along with her plan. How should she do it? She must not appear overeager, or he would become suspicious of her motives. It would have to be a casual offer, made while he was in the midst of discussion with his thanes. In the morning, before the Britons returned to the council meeting, he would gather them around him and plot strategy. She would be there, moving about unobtrusively, serving them food and drink. When the subject of hostages came up, she would quietly suggest herself.

It was a bold, daring scheme. The idea of it made her heart pound with trepidation. But she was determined. This might be the only chance she would ever have to be with the man she loved.

The gods favored her—or at least Freya, the goddess of love did, she thought the next morning as she arranged pieces of bread spread with butter and honey on an ornate gold tray and prepared to take it in to her uncle's council. As she left the kitchen shed and approached the longhouse, she could hear the men discussing who the hostages would be. It was clear from their hesitant, uncomfortable tones that they all knew if Cerdic broke the truce, which was likely, the hostages' lives would be forfeit. No one among them wanted to risk his life or his close kin's life.

Her hands trembled as she carried in the tray. How could she dare speak to Cerdic when he was meeting with his thanes? But she had to. She had to be bold.

She moved around the room, serving each man, smiling cordially at them if they bothered to look at her. As always, some of the men cast admiring glances her way. They lusted for her, she knew. But they did not want to wed her, only take her for a leman.

Her heart pounded faster as she approached Cerdic. He would take no notice of her; to him she was less important than that of his hunting hounds. She paused next to his huge, carved wooden chair. "Uncle," she said in a trembling voice. "I would serve as hostage to the Britons, if you would wish it."

His head jerked around and his pale eyes regarded her with terrifying intensity. She wondered how any man dared face him in battle, so ruthless and paralyzing was his gaze. "You? Why would you do that?"

She licked her lips and spoke the speech she had rehearsed. "I want this truce to last. I am tired of war, of seeing everyone I care for die or be enslaved. I will do anything to bring peace." Cerdic knew how much she abhorred battle and killing. Her words were heartfelt, even if they did not exactly tell the truth.

He said nothing for a time, and neither did any other warrior in the room. The seconds passed, counted out in her heartbeats. Cerdic glanced around at his men, then back at her. "Leave us," he said.

She placed the tray on the table and walked out with as much poise and grace as possible. In the antechamber, she paused. If she were a dutiful, obedient niece, she would go to the kitchen and fetch more ale, instead of standing near the door and listening to them decide her fate. But years of being powerless had taught her to glean what knowledge she could.

She could catch only bits and pieces of the discussion, but it was clear they viewed her suggestion favorably. "Close family member . . ." and "don't have to give up a warrior." and "Arthur . . . soft . . . might not kill . . . a woman." That was Cerdic speaking, making it clear that as hostage, her life would be in the hands of the Britons' leader.

Eastra took a deep breath. What if her scheming cost her life? If she were the hostage and Cerdic broke the truce, she would die. But surely Rhun would not allow that. He stood high in Arthur's favor, and he had saved her life once already. Besides, would not dying be almost preferable to the life she lived now, as a princess in name and a *nithing* in fact? She had no future, nothing to look forward to except growing old. Never to marry, have a home of her own, bear a child—what sort of life was that?

She squared her shoulders and hurried to the kitchen. When Cerdic sent for her to tell her his decision, she would have the ale ready.

* * *

"No! He can't offer her as their hostage! It's barbaric! What sort of man involves a woman in war?" Rhun paused to take an anguished breath. When he looked around the room, he saw Arthur and the rest of his fellow Britons were staring at him in shock. Across the table, Cerdic folded his arms across his chest and gave Rhun a look as cold as the north wind off the mountain peaks of Gwynedd.

Bridei broke the stunned silence. "Obviously, Cerdic *is* a barbarian. That's the whole point of exchanging hostages." Then he turned to Cerdic and spoke in Saxon.

"What did you say?" Rhun demanded when Bridei finished.

"I told him you were displeased to have a woman involved in men's business."

Rhun opened his mouth to angrily dispute Bridei's comment, then remembered himself. Bridei was being diplomatic, explaining things so the Saxon savage would understand and not take offense. Besides, Rhun decided, seeking to calm himself, he should not have spoken out so emphatically. It was Arthur's place to politely decline this ridiculous offer.

Rhun looked to his commander. Arthur was frowning, which relieved him. He did not like the idea of a female hostage any better than he did.

Arthur said, "I think this is a matter we must discuss in private."

Bridei translated for Cerdic, who nodded, then rose from the table, gesturing to his fellow warriors to do the same. He spoke in his gutteral language and left the room, his thanes trailing after him.

"How can we trust they won't put a spy by the door to listen?" Cador asked angrily.

"If they understand Briton, they already know what we think," Bridei pointed out.

"No, they know what *Rhun* thinks." Cador turned to

him, his face tight with resentment. "What was the point of that outburst? It's not your place to discuss the terms of the truce with Cerdic."

"I'm sorry. I forgot myself," Rhun said tightly. He disliked Cador. In his obsession with the cause of ridding Britain of the "heathen Saxons," Arthur's secondary commander had done many cruel and awful things. What was the point of saving Christian Britain, Rhun had more than once mused aloud, if a man lost his own soul doing it?

"Rhun has a point," Arthur said quietly. "But I actually think it works to our advantage. Cerdic is proposing to give us only one hostage as surety against his honoring the truce. That means we only have to offer up one ourselves."

"But we cannot accept a woman as hostage!" Rhun exclaimed. "What if Cerdic breaks the truce? Do you want to be the one to order her death?"

"But she is his niece," Bedwyr pointed out. "I can't think he would willingly sacrifice his own kin."

His own kin, but worthless to him anyway, Rhun thought bitterly. Eastra had made it very clear that because she had been a slave, she was considered unmarriageable, and therefore useless in helping Cerdic form political alliances. But he could not say that. Then he would have to explain the circumstances of how he knew her.

Arthur stroked his jaw. "I take this as a sign Cerdic is serious about seeking a lasting peace. I must match his bold gesture with one of my own. I have no blood kin, save Mordred. What think you of offering him as our hostage?"

No one spoke, but an uncomfortable tension filled the room. Mordred was not popular among Arthur's captains. Some among them even doubted the young man was really Arthur's bastard son. All they had was Arthur's stone-faced pronouncement it was true. Rhun could sense the other men weighing and analyzing Arthur's proposal. If the truce were broken and Mordred killed, that would be one way to be rid of him.

Rhun felt he should argue against Arthur's choice. Mordred was a cunning and slippery man. Putting him into the hands of the enemy seemed like a dangerous idea. But at least if the truce were broken, clever Mordred might be able to make some arrangement with Cerdic to save his own skin. And if Mordred did not die, Eastra was safe.

Rhun's stomach churned with anxiety at the thought of Eastra's being a hostage. It was almost worse than her being a slave. But he did not think he could prevail against Arthur in this matter.

"Mordred is in Londinium." Arthur's mouth twitched in disgust. "Probably wenching and dicing his life away. I will send you, Bedwyr and Tristan, to fetch him. As soon as he is here, the exchange will be made."

"And then what?" Cei asked. "Where will the woman be held?"

"At Camlann with Guinevere?" Cador suggested.

Arthur shook his head. "I don't want to be forced to leave a large force there to protect my queen. So far, the Saxons have not seen fit to attack our settlements, but that could change if we make them too enticing as targets."

"Where, then?" Cei asked again.

"It should be somewhere far enough away that Cerdic's forces would have to travel a long distance through enemy territory to free her," Bedwyr said.

Arthur nodded.

"I have an idea," Bridei said. "What if we took her back to my father's fortress in Gwynedd? Then the Saxons would have to journey all the way across Britain to claim her. Once in Gwynedd, they would be very conspicuous among the mostly dark-haired Cymry."

"And would your father accept responsibility for a hostage?" Arthur's eyes glowed with bitterness. He had never gotten over Maelgwn's refusal to join their cause. Since he had no fear of them taking over his territories and no quarrel with whatever gods they chose to worship, Maelgwn always said he saw no point in waging war against the Saxons. Rhun resented his father's attitude, but was powerless to influence him.

Bridei shrugged. "I don't think he would care one way or another. My father takes very little interest in politics these days."

Rhun shot his brother a hostile look. He wanted to argue against Bridei's plan, but he could not think of a good reason to oppose it.

"An excellent suggestion." Arthur nodded approvingly. "I will charge Rhun with the responsibility for taking her to his father's fortress at Deganwy."

"Me?" Rhun exclaimed. "But am I not needed with you, to fight if the truce does not hold?"

"I will expect you to return as soon as you have seen to the woman's safety," Arthur said.

Rhun bit down hard, torn between conflicting emotions. He did not want Eastra to be the hostage, but if the thing was decided, perhaps it was better if he were the one to protect her—unless the truce was broken and Mordred killed. A wave of terror washed through him. What would he do if his commander ordered him to kill her?

He must not think about that, Rhun told himself. Cerdic must be at least partially sincere in his desire for peace, else he would not have agreed to the truce. And barbarian or no, he surely was not so coldhearted that he would allow his niece to be killed unless his enemy did something truly treacherous.

He was jerked from his thoughts when he heard Bridei say, "I will go with my brother. I can translate for them—since it's doubtful that the woman speaks the British tongue."

Rhun glared at his brother, wondering at his intentions in making this offer. To make trouble, no doubt. That seemed to be Bridei's purpose in life.

Arthur nodded. "Once this truce is arranged, I will not need you as interpreter. And some other bard can be found to entertain the troops."

Bridei grinned broadly.

Arthur sent a man to call the Saxons back into the meeting room. The final details of the hostage exchange were arranged. Then the Britons left the settlement and went back to their camp. Although Rhun itched to speak to his brother and give him a piece of his mind, he had to keep company with Arthur for a while longer. They discussed what supplies and additional troops might be needed to transport a woman such a distance. Rhun convinced Arthur that a small party of experienced warriors would be sufficient to guard them. After all, he argued, they would be traveling through their own territories and not subject to attack. His real reason for declining a larger escort was because he did not want one of Arthur's other officers around in case his previous acquaintance with Eastra came to light.

Finally, Arthur dismissed him. Rhun went to find Bridei. He discovered him seated around a cookfire with several of the other men. "Ah, my brother," Bridei said as Rhun approached. "Join us in celebrating the truce." He held out a wineskin.

"I would speak to you alone."

Bridei shrugged and stood up. He took a few more gulps from the wineskin, then passed it to the man beside him. Rhun strode off into the darkness with Bridei trailing after him.

"Aren't you going to thank me?" Bridei chortled as soon as they were out of earshot of the others. "I've arranged for you to spend some time with your ladylove. And Gwynedd is clear on the other side of Britain. That should give you plenty of time to—"

"Hush, damn you!" Rhun jerked around, his voice taut. "You know I'm not pleased with any of this. I don't want her to be a hostage. It's too dangerous. At least if she stayed in Cerdic's camp, her life would not be at risk!"

"But you said yourself she was unhappy here."

"Unhappy, aye, because she is held in poor regard by her own people. Now she is to be a hostage, and far away from anything familiar to her. It's not much better than being Cerdic's servant—or being a slave, for that matter!"

"Ah, but with you as her captor, she might be content," Bridei sniggered.

"By the Cross, I'm sick of your disgusting innuendoes! You act as if I mean to bed her as soon as we are out of sight of Arthur!"

"Well, aren't you? If you're honest with yourself, that is."

"Of course not!" Rhun sputtered. "I have more honor than that! I wouldn't take advantage of any woman that way, let alone one under my protection."

"But what if she wants you to? I'm not blind, brother. I saw how she looks at you. She would lie with you in a heartbeat. You have only to find a safe—"

"Stop!" Rhun grabbed his brother by the front of his tunic and gave him a violent shake. "I won't have you impugn her virtue, you lewd, disgusting bastard!"

"Hah! You see, I'm right! You would not get so angry if you did not care for her!"

Rhun twisted the fabric of his brother's wool tunic, wishing it was Bridei's neck he was wringing. But he realized the angrier he became, the more his brother would taunt him. The only way to deal with Bridei was to refuse to rise to his bait.

Slowly, he loosened his grip. "I'm not like you," he said coldly. "I do think about someone other than myself sometimes. There are a dozen reasons I should not lie with the Saxon. But even if there were not so many arguments against it because she is a hostage in my care, I would still not do it. She is a princess of her people, not a whore or serving girl. The only man fit to take her to bed is the one who takes her to wife."

"But you said she is unlikely to be married because of her years as a slave."

Rhun took a deep breath. For every argument he came up with, clever Bridei would find one to refute it. Already, he could feel a part of himself weakening. Eastra had said herself it was doubtful she would ever wed. Why should she not know some happiness in life? If she truly wished for him to love her . . .

Nay, he could not think like that. She might want him now, then hate herself later. Besides, he had a duty to Arthur's cause. His commander would expect better of him than to become involved with a hostage.

He shook his head. "My vow to Arthur must come before everything else."

"Of course," Bridei said, still grinning.

Three

Eastra placed the gold and garnet neckpiece around her neck, then lifted the polished bronze mirror to gaze at her reflection. The dozens of stones in the heavy piece shone like drops of blood in the lamplight as she perused her image. Sighing, she lowered the mirror. Her plan had succeeded, but even so, her stomach fluttered with anxiety. What if she were wrong about Rhun ap Maelgwn and he cared nothing for her? She was delivering herself into the hands of the enemy, and, having heard many tales of the Britons' ruthlessness and barbarity, she was more than a little uneasy. Cerdic was right that she should go to them in all her splendor, decked in jewels and finery, so they would know she was valuable to him and that if she were abused or wronged in any way, he would avenge her most cruelly.

Of course he would avenge her, she thought bitterly. Not because he cared for her as his kin, as a living, breathing woman, but because she was a symbol of his pride and power. She had been reduced once again to an object, a piece of property. Which was the reason she was doing all this. She believed that to Rhun ap Maelgwn, she was more than an object, that he saw her as a woman and cared for what she felt.

But what if she assumed too much? What if he had no real interest in her? It had all happened so fast. She'd had no time to speak to him, to tell him her plan and watch his reaction. And now she was trapped, trapped in a plot of her own making. She adjusted her best gunna, smoothing the saffron-colored fabric embroidered with flowers on the bodice and sleeves, then left her sleeping chamber.

Mordred was brought from Londinium, and the hostage exchange took place in the open area outside the Saxon fortress. A faint queasiness spread through Rhun's stomach as he watched Arthur's bastard son walk to meet the enemy. Mordred moved easily, almost nonchalantly. His lean, graceful build reminded Rhun of Bridei. Like Bridei, Mordred had a cunning, handsome face that appealed to women, but made men wary.

Rhun had observed the meeting between Arthur and his son the night before. Mordred had behaved in his usual manner, mocking and scornful of his father, his words edged with sarcasm and hostility. And yet he'd agreed to serve as hostage. Even he could not defy the high king of Britain. But what sort of hostage would he be? Could they trust him not to conspire with the enemy? Arthur seemed sure of his son. Maybe he had some sort of hold over him no one else knew about. Rhun hoped it was true.

As Mordred reached the Saxon contingent, Rhun saw Eastra step forward, staring straight ahead. A bodyservant leading a heavily laden packhorse followed behind her. With the rich buttery shade of her gown and the heavy gold jewelry at her neck, her fair skin and silvery-blond hair, she was as dazzling as the sunrise. Rhun heard the other men's indrawn breaths and knew a moment of fierce possessiveness. He would keep her safe! No man would touch her!

But by what right did he claim the role of her protector? Was it because Arthur had charged him with the responsibility, or because he felt in some way she already belonged to him? A dangerous notion, and one that could easily lead him to disaster. He must not forget his allegiance to his commander, the solemn oath he had sworn. That oath must come before any feelings he had for Eastra.

He saw she was walking directly toward him. He frowned and shook his head faintly, trying to indicate it was Arthur she must present herself to. Gradually, she shifted course and approached the high king with a cool, regal grace. Arthur greeted her with a bow, then said, "Princess Eastra, no matter what you may have heard about us, we are not crude savages. As long as Cerdic honors the truce, I promise you will be safe and well cared for."

Bridei, standing a little behind Arthur, immediately translated his words into Saxon. Eastra looked puzzled, and Rhun wondered if she had not realized the implications of being a hostage and was unsettled by the threat implicit in Arthur's words. But then she spoke in clear Briton, and he understood what had surprised her. "I speak your language," she said. "I have no need for anyone to translate for me."

Arthur looked surprised, then nodded. "I'm pleased to learn you know our tongue. Perhaps you will not feel so lonely and isolated during your stay with our people." He motioned to Rhun. "This is Rhun ap Maelgwn. He will take you to a fortress where you will be safe."

Rhun bowed. As Eastra met his gaze, he struggled to keep his face expressionless. Arthur said, "Rhun, escort Princess Eastra to the cart she will ride in."

"Please." Eastra put up her hand in an imploring gesture. "I would rather ride astride."

"It's a long journey." Arthur regarded her intently. "You might well be more comfortable in a cart."

"Nay, I would rather ride."

Rhun was impressed by her stubbornness, and also relieved he would not have to stay to the back of the army train with the slow-moving wains and other baggage. He smiled at her, then thought better of showing such warmth. He was not supposed to know this woman.

Arthur motioned for one of the young armor bearers to

come forward and take the lead of the packhorse from the Saxon servant. Then he turned to Bedwyr, his captain of the horse. "Find her a mount. Some beast with an easy gait, but enough spirit to keep up."

Bedwyr nodded and hurried off.

Arthur motioned across the field to Cerdic, indicating with a formal salute that the hostage had been accepted. Cerdic motioned back. Then the Saxons seemed to swallow up Mordred as the mass of warriors moved back to the fortress. Beside Rhun, Cador muttered an oath. "I don't like it. I can't help feeling we have offered the seawolves a willing spy rather than a hostage."

"Watch your tongue. Remember the woman." Cei motioned with his head toward Eastra.

Cador barely spared a glance for her. "She may speak our tongue, but she's naught but a helpless female."

An angry retort rose on Rhun's tongue, but he bit it back. Let Cador ignore her and think her of no account. She would be safer that way.

Everyone began to move off. Arthur motioned to Rhun. "Wait here until Bedwyr brings her horse." To Eastra he said, "Is there anything else you require, princess?"

She shook her head.

As soon as Arthur left, Rhun moved nearer to Eastra and spoke in a low voice. "Do you mean to travel wearing all your finery? Would you not be more comfortable in a plainer, looser garment?"

"Cerdic bid me dress as a princess."

"But did he not also provide you with a bodyservant to help you dress and care for your needs?"

"He offered one, but I declined it."

"Why?"

"Having been a slave, I'm not comfortable with having some other woman forced to wait upon me."

"That's generous of you, but I still fear you will find it awkward traveling with an army camp. Who will comb out your hair and aid you in dressing?"

He was sweet to worry for her, Eastra thought. In truth,

she had not thought ahead to such matters. Cerdic had not offered her a bodyservant, although she thought he would have provided one if she had asked. But she had not asked. Her mind had been too focused on her plan to find a way to stay as near to Rhun as possible. Fortune clearly favored her in that Arthur had chosen Rhun to serve as her guard.

"I'm certain I will manage," she said. "I do have plainer clothing in my pack."

Rhun nodded curtly. "I will fetch it. Then we will have to find some place for you to change." There was more than a hint of exasperation in his voice. As he walked away, Eastra bit her lips. She had not done well in angering him.

"Don't mind him." She turned at the sound of a familiar musical voice. Bridei stood a few feet away, smiling at her. "He's always a bit ill-tempered in the morning."

Eastra regarded Rhun's brother with wariness. He appeared to have made a jest, but she could not tell for certain. She wondered what Rhun had told Bridei about her.

"What I mean to say is that he is not really angry at you," Bridei said. "It's Arthur he's wroth with."

"Why?"

"Because he did not want Arthur to find you acceptable as a hostage."

Her heart sank. She had hoped Rhun would be pleased with the arrangement. Apparently, she was wrong to think he cared for her.

"Ah, princess, don't look so sad. It's not what you think. I believe my brother dreads your company not because he mislikes it, but because he likes it all too well." Bridei's grin deepened and the skin around his blue eyes crinkled with mirth. Eastra found herself blushing. It was almost as if this man could read her thoughts. She stared at him, not knowing how to respond.

"Here he comes now," Bridei said. "Smile at him and, I assure you, he will regain his good nature in a heartbeat."

She turned and saw Rhun approaching. Remembering Bridei's words, she smiled tentatively. Rhun's face did seem to change, as if some of the tension left it, replaced by a brief look of longing that made her heart twist in her chest. He paused a few feet away, holding her pack. "I have brought your things." His voice sounded out of breath, although he did not appear winded. "There's a stand of trees to the left where you can change. I will stand guard."

"Do you need any help, brother?" Bridei's voice was mocking.

Rhun shot him a hostile look. "Come." He motioned for Eastra to proceed him. She obeyed, wondering what there was between Rhun and his brother.

As she walked toward the stand of beech and oak, she became nervous and unsettled. Rhun was so close. If she turned around and reached out, her hand would graze his body. But she dare not do such a thing. Even if Rhun desired her, they could not act on it here, not within arrowshot of his commander and her uncle. There would be plenty of other opportunities for them to be alone on their journey. And if, as Bridei said, Rhun truly felt something for her, his hunger would only deepen and intensify the longer they were together. For now, she would appear maidenly and demure.

She turned her head to ask, "Where is the place we are traveling to?"

"We're taking you to my homeland, called Gwynedd."

"Gwynedd?" They had reached the trees. She finally deemed it seemly to turn around and look at him.

"Aye. My father's fortress is there. You will be safe under his protection."

"Is it very far?"

He nodded gravely. "On the other side of Britain."

They had a long journey ahead of them. There would be plenty of time to convince Rhun that the fact she was a Saxon and he a Briton was not such an obstacle after all.

She took her pack from him and went off in the trees to change. Carefully removing the gold and garnet necklace and her earbobs, she wrapped them in some clothing in the bottom of her pack, then unfastened the matching girdle from around her waist. As she pulled the heavily embroidered gunna over her head, a feeling of relief washed over her. The gold jewelry around her neck had felt as confining as she imagined a slave collar might feel. She would be much more comfortable in her loose, faded blue gunna, and she was grateful to Rhun for suggesting the idea. Now that she was away from Cerdic and the rest of her countrymen, she could finally act like herself.

She had learned to ride as a child, practicing on a shaggy, dappled gray pony her father had procured in a raid. Not many of her people were comfortable on horses, but she had always found riding pleasurable. It had turned out to be a useful skill as she traveled from fort to fort with Cerdic's camp. She did not have to endure the endless jostling in a cart at the back of the army train like the other women did, but could ride near the front. Cerdic was pleased with her skill because he said it made her seem more royal, and because it kept her near him where he could have her serve his thanes.

Now she would ride beside Rhun. She knew many of Arthur's warriors fought on horseback and that the Britons were famed horsemen. The fact she could ride might make her seem more like a woman of his own people.

She changed her embroidered linen shoes for a pair of soft leather sandals, then smoothed her hair. Hurriedly stuffing everything into her pack, she started off toward where Rhun was waiting. She did not want to delay him any longer than necessary.

It was every bit as bad as he had feared, Rhun thought as he waited for Eastra. Her mere nearness was enough to make him into a nervous, witless fool. At this moment, when he should be thinking ahead to their journey and the possible dangers awaiting them, he was instead imagining Eastra undressing a few paces away, his mind wandering unwillingly to visions of her naked body, her creamy, perfect skin, the lushness of her womanly form.

He shook his head, trying to expel the images from his thoughts. He was *not* what Bridei believed him to be—a lust-maddened beast. What he felt for Eastra was a sense of protectiveness and responsibility, and his intentions toward her were noble and Christian. He meant to keep her safe and make her ordeal as a hostage as pleasant as possible. Although he might heartily wish Arthur had not assigned him this task, now that it was done he must do his duty to the best of his ability.

"I am ready." Her soft voice interrupted his thoughts. He turned and smiled at her. Nay, she did not need ornate garments or gold adornment to make her look like a princess. Even in plain garments she was stunning. Her unbound hair, braided at the temples to keep it out of her face, flowed over her shoulders like pale, shimmering silk. Her face was like a flower, delicate, perfectly formed. He motioned with his head, wanting to take her hand, but not daring to touch her. "Let us go back to where the others wait."

Due to the lateness of the day, they did not get far out of Saxon territory before Arthur called a halt. They made camp on a rise of land—the better to defend themselves in case the Saxons planned some treachery, as Cador put it—then sent a party of men down into the vale below to fetch wood for the cookfires and water. Rhun found Eastra a sheltered place near the supply carts. He spread out the blanket from his pack, then bid her sit down. "I will bring you food shortly," he said, then left her.

After sending his armor bearer, Arwistyl, to obtain a portion of the stew and a loaf when it was ready, Rhun made his way to the center of the camp where Arthur and his officers, the Companions, were gathered. Bridei was squatting down near Arthur and speaking quietly to the high king. Rhun joined them.

"I would like to believe Cerdic is sincere in his desire for peace, but based on past experience I cannot depend on it." Arthur spoke in a quiet, serious voice, and in the firelight, his handsome, kingly face appeared tense. "I think it's wisest that we remain vigilant and ready for war. What concerns me most is that the Saxons might use this summer of peace as an opportunity to bring more warriors from their homeland across the sea. We need to alert our spies in the east to watch the coast."

Cador nodded thoughtfully. "We should also send an envoy to Londinium. With all the ships that sail in and out of that place, they might hear something of what is happening across the Eastern Sea."

"An excellent idea," Arthur said. "But who do we send?"

"I could go," Bridei offered. "I know several merchants in Londinium."

"But I need you to go with Rhun to Gwynedd," Arthur said. "The plan was for you to be part of the princess's escort."

"She could come with us to Londinium first. It's only a day's journey to the south."

Rhun stared at his brother. What was Bridei planning?

Arthur frowned. "It seems very odd to take a hostage on such a mission."

"Not so odd," Bridei said. "Who knows? Seeing her, knowing we have some hold over Cerdic, might sway some of the traders into helping us."

"But what if she intends to spy for Cerdic?" Cei asked in concern. "Then she would know our plans."

"I would not involve her directly when I met with the merchants." Bridei favored Cei with a withering look. Cei was a solid, loyal officer, but not the cleverest of men. "Rhun would guard her while I went about my business." He looked around the gathering. "Many of these merchants are wary of soldiers, of all things having to do with war. I am the man who can convince them this is not merely Arthur's battle, but something every man in Britain who values his freedom to earn his livelihood should be concerned about."

Arthur looked to Cador. Despite Cador's excesses in past

campaigns, all the Companions knew the high king depended heavily on his judgment.

Cador shrugged. "I can't see any harm in the plan. Cerdic will certainly never expect us to take his niece into the south. By the time he learns she is there, the business will be finished and they will be on their way to Gwynedd." He turned to Bridei. "And I agree that our silver-tongued bard is the man for this task. If anyone can convince the greedy merchants of Londinium there is some reason for them to support our cause, it is him."

Arthur let out his breath. Then, as an afterthought, he turned to Rhun. "Have you any objection?"

What could he say? He could not guess his brother's scheme. "I have no objection," he answered.

Eastra sat in the back of the supply cart, dangling her legs as she watched the night sky turn from purple to blue-black. Around her, spread out over the hillside, campfires gleamed into light, like stars reflecting those above in the heavens. She tried to eat the stew that the young soldier had brought her—Arwistyl, he said his name was. Although the pottage was savory and well-seasoned, she had to force each bite down. She could not help thinking about the fact she was surrounded by her enemies.

After every mouthful, she paused as the lilting cadence of the British tongue came to her ears from every quarter of the camp. Although she could understand most of what they said, the unfamiliar rhythms of their language seemed foreign and somehow threatening. All her life she had heard tales of the treachery and cruelty of the Britons, and during her childhood she had experienced their brutality firsthand. She had lost her mother and her brother in one of their raids. Although she had not seen their deaths, she could not help imagining her loved ones lying in the dust with the reeking smoke around them, their blue eyes staring sightless and bright red blood oozing from their wounds.

But during that same raid, Rhun had rescued her, carrying her out of the longhouse to the freedom of the forest. He had hidden her from his fellow warriors, clearly disobeying orders to save her. Having done that so many years ago when he was but a fledgling warrior and she only a child, surely he could be trusted with her life even more now. He was a powerful, important man among his people. He sat at Arthur's side and shared in his council meetings. And she was a woman, not a scrawny child. She could make him desire her, make him look at her with longing as other men did.

She sighed and dipped a piece of the bread into the stew. Bannock, they called it, a flat unleavened mealcake cooked over a campfire. Filling, substantial food, although plainer and coarser than what she was used to in Cerdic's household. But she had never traveled with her uncle when he went to war, and this was the food of an army on the march.

Again, her stomach twisted. She had risked everything to be with Rhun. What if she had made a mistake?

"Why did you do that?" Rhun asked his brother as they walked away from the gathering of Arthur's Companions. "Now we are bound to go to Londinium, prolonging our journey all the more." He turned and grabbed Bridei's tunic. "Are you plotting some mischief? Because if you are—"

"Peace, brother." Bridei soothed. "I have no devious intent. Arthur needs a man to go to Londinium, and I'm the obvious one. As for taking the woman"—he shrugged— "why should she not see a bit of the country before she is shut up in our father's fortress?"

"She's a hostage, Bridei! Not some sort of . . . of . . . of guest we are showing off the choice parts of Britain to!"

"Do you want her to be miserable? To feel like a prisoner, a kind of game piece in this contest between Cerdic and Arthur? I thought you cared about her."

"I don't care about her! That is, I do, but I can't act on

those feelings. I have to deal with her as I would any other hostage."

"Oh, so that is why you argued with Bedwyr about what horse she would ride, making sure she had as fine a mount as any of Arthur's Companions?"

"That was simply a practical consideration. She must have a decent horse if she is to keep up with us. Besides, she is a woman and royalty. I can't treat her as I would a rough fighting man."

"My point exactly. She's a woman and has lived a pampered life—at least since Cerdic rescued her and made her part of his household. What does it hurt to take her to Londinium with us and enjoy ourselves for a time?"

"Enjoy ourselves?" Rhun gave his brother an aghast look. "What are you talking about? You're going to Londinium on a sensitive diplomatic mission. This is not a matter in which we should find pleasure!"

"And why not?" Bridei asked. "Why should we be wretched and gloomy every moment? This battle between Saxon and Briton has been going on since before I was born—before you were born, in fact. Why must our lives be grim and cheerless because Arthur ap Uther and Cerdic Hengistson both seek to rule Britain? They are like two hounds fighting over a bone. Neither will give in until they are dead—or until this whole island is ravaged and ruined."

"The cause we fight for means that little to you?" Rhun asked bitterly. "Do you really want to end up a Saxon slave, to see our people wiped out?"

"They can't enslave every man in Britain. Nor are they likely to kill us all, either. I don't see why we can't live side by side, as the Romans and our people once did. The Saxons are farmers. They care nothing for the highlands where our people live." Bridei grimaced. "Although I despise having to admit it, I fear for once our father is right. This war is a futile waste of effort and lives."

"But the Saxons are barbarians! Heathen devils who worship loathsome gods. We must fight for the Christian cause, for light and truth in this time of darkness!"

"So you believe," Bridei said. "But I do not. I hardly think the Christians possess any sort of special claim on all the light and truth in the world. Many of them have done terrible things, things I doubt the Christos would have condoned, at least from what I know of His teachings."

Rhun took a deep breath and fought for composure. He should know better than to argue with his brother. Bridei was always able to twist things, to prick at his doubts and make him uneasy and unsettled with the beliefs he had honored all his life. "Perhaps I should tell Arthur how you truly feel about things," he said coldly. "Perhaps then he would be less eager to send you to argue his cause among the merchants of Londinium."

"Oh, I will be persuasive enough with them, do not doubt it." Bridei raised a dark brow and his eyes grew ironic and amused. "The thing is, I don't have to believe what I say in order to be convincing. Even now, can you be certain what I've just said is really what's in my heart? Perhaps I was just playing with you, trying to see if I could make you angry." He burst out with a brilliant smile. "And, as always, I have succeeded. Your passion and sincerity are going to be your undoing, big brother."

"I would rather be a fool who wears his convictions on his sleeve than a heartless wretch like you!"

"Heartless? How am I heartless? Who have I hurt?" Bridei shrugged. "I don't wield a sword. I don't kill and maim. I would say I'm actually more kindhearted than you are."

Rhun shook his head. It was hopeless. Bridei was like a slippery eel, too elusive and cunning to ever be trapped. "I suppose if we're going to Londinium, we must make plans," he said, changing the subject. "Consider what supplies to take and what sort of escort we will need."

Bridei nodded. "The smaller the escort, the better. We don't want to appear on the streets of Londinium with a band of spear-toting warriors. A few men only. They can act as our servants while we play the role of fun-loving noblemen out to explore the city."

"And what of Eastra? How will we explain her being with us?"

"Anyone can tell by looking at her she is Saxon. Except for the merchants—to whom we might possibly reveal her true circumstances if it appears to aid our cause—we will tell everyone else she is your leman."

"My leman? That's appalling! An insult to my honor and hers!"

"Perhaps, but can you think a better explanation for her being with us? One that won't alert the Saxons in Londinium that we are holding one of their women as a hostage?"

Rhun clenched his jaw tight. He hated how Bridei was always able to make what he dreaded most seem like the best possible course of action.

"I will go see about the escort," Bridei said. "That way you can return to your ladylove and make her comfortable." Although Rhun could not see his brother's expression in the darkness, he knew he was grinning.

"Princess Eastra?"

She gave a little gasp at the sound of his deep voice behind her. Then she sat up in the cart and turned around to see Rhun's tall form, the sunkissed strands of his hair glinting in the light from the torch he carried. A sense of deep relief washed over her. "Oh," she said. "You startled me."

"I'm sorry. I wasn't certain this was the right cart. Arwistyl should have brought you a torch so you would not have to sit in here in the dark."

Rhun sounded angry as he fastened his torch to a spear shaft and stuck it in the ground. Eastra thought about the young soldier who had brought her the food—his soft, unformed features, the sprinkling of freckles across his nose. She did not want Rhun to punish the youth. "Arwistyl brought me something to eat and treated me with every courtesy," she said quickly. "I'm certain he got busy with other things or he would have come back with a torch."

"Not likely," Rhun grumbled as he dug in one of the saddle packs lying near the cart. "He's probably off somewhere playing knucklebones and drinking wine right now." He straightened suddenly and turned toward her. "I wanted to come and tell you—our plans have changed. Instead of setting out for my homeland, tomorrow we will travel to a place called Londinium."

She could sense the tension in his body. "Is something wrong?" she asked. "Is there going to be a battle there?"

"Nay. Arthur and the rest of the army aren't going. Only you and I and my cursed brother. And a small escort, of course. It's not safe to travel anywhere in Britain these days without a troop of fighting men."

Rhun and Bridei had obviously been arguing again. She hoped their conflict had nothing to do with her. She did not want to be responsible for coming between Rhun and his close kin. The ties of family were too precious to forsake for any reason—certainly not for a woman who was by rights their enemy.

"I have heard of Londinium," she said. "My father used to go there to buy trading goods. Years ago it was." As always, she knew a pang of grief at the thought of her family and her lost childhood. "Is that why we are going there? To purchase trading goods?"

Rhun didn't answer immediately. Then he said, "Aye, that is it. There are some things I would like to buy to take back to Gwynedd to my father and stepmother."

She had thought he would say they were buying supplies for Arthur's army. It surprised her to think they would make such a journey simply to purchase gifts for his family. "Are you fond of your stepmother?" she asked.

Rhun nodded. "She is a gentle, loving soul, and has always treated me like I was her own. My own mother died when I was not yet a man, so I have always appreciated her kindness. Besides, she makes my father happy, and he has endured so much tragedy and suffering in his life he deserves to know some peace in his later years."

The way he spoke of his family brought tears to Eastra's eyes. She thought of all she had lost, and the ache that filled her was almost unbearable.

"There is one thing," Rhun said, breaking into her gloom. "While we are in Londinium, we must give some explanation for why a Saxon woman is traveling with us. Bridei has come up with an idea, but I don't think you will agree to it. If his plan distresses you, rest assured I will not insist on it, but will find some other means to explain things."

"What is his plan?"

Rhun took a deep breath. "He wants me to say that you are my leman."

His leman. With any other man, the idea would distress her, but with this one—wasn't this what she truly wanted, to have Rhun love her and take her maidenhead? "I have no objection," she answered.

"You don't? But . . . perhaps you don't understand. Men will think that I . . . that we . . . that we share a bed, that we are intimate."

"I know what it means," she said. "Is it considered so shameful among your people for a man and a woman who are not married to lie together?"

"Nay, I suppose not. My own mother was my father's leman, so I can hardly condemn it. But the Christian priests say it devalues the woman, that it's a barbaric, dishonorable practice."

She looked intently into his deep-set eyes. "It's a plausible tale, is it not? And if you and I know the truth, what does it matter what the people of Londinium think?"

He nodded, but she could see he was still uncomfortable with the idea. She wondered at his unease. Was he embarrassed by the thought that people would believe he had a Saxon lover? Or did the fact she had been a slave distress him? She thought back to Bridei's playful words. He had implied Rhun desired her. Could she believe Rhun's brother?

Rhun cleared his throat. He was staring at her, something he'd vowed not to do. But it was so hard not to take delight in her pale, glowing beauty. He cleared his throat. "Is there anything else you require for the night?"

"Are you leaving?"

"Nay, I will sleep beside the cart. But I wondered if there wasn't something else I could do to make you more comfortable."

She shook her head. "I've plenty of blankets and sheep-skins to sleep on, and I ate my fill earlier."

"Well, good night."

He got his bedroll from his saddle pack and spread it out on the ground. He had not wanted to bother with having Arwistyl pitch his tent, especially since it looked to be a clear, warm night. He settled himself in his bedroll and looked up at the stars. Soft rustling sounds came from the cart beside him. Was she uncomfortable, despite her assurances she had plenty of blankets? Was that why she seemed to toss and turn?

He thought of her, so close, so very close. It almost seemed he could smell her, some fragrance that clung to her skin from when she had last bathed. But maybe it was only the honeysuckle and clover growing on the hill, casting their sweet scent into the breeze. Whatever it was, it made his heart squeeze in his chest and his loins tighten. He sighed. A fine summer night, with all thoughts of battle and war forgotten. Despite the army camp around them, it seemed as if there were only the two of them—man and woman, dreaming beneath the starlit heavens.

Four

They set out the next day under a bright blue, cloudless sky. Rhun and Bridei rode side by side at the front of the traveling party with Eastra a little behind them. Bringing up the rear were five warriors clad in mail shirts. Three of them had dark hair and swarthy skin, while the other two had flame-colored tresses. There was enough of a resemblance between the darker men that Eastra wondered if they were brothers.

Her mount was a beautiful reddish brown mare. She had never ridden such a regal beast, and she found the mare's gait to be smooth and graceful. As they rode out of the army camp, where everyone was busily preparing to march, Eastra's spirits soared.

Ahead of her, Rhun and Bridei spoke quietly, obviously discussing the journey ahead of them. After a short while, Rhun fell back to ride beside her. "It's not too long a journey. By nightfall we should be within sight of the city's walls."

"Have you ever been to Londinium before?" Eastra asked.

"Aye, several times. It's an amazing place. There, Saxons, Britons, and men who still call themselves citizens of Rome all live side by side, engaged in a common cause."

"Which is?" Eastra prompted.

Rhun grinned. "They are merchants, and that makes

them view politics and war differently than the rest of us. They are loyal and devoted to only one thing—*pecunia*."

"*Pecunia?*"

"It's a Roman word for wealth . . . gold . . . cattle . . . coins."

"You sound critical of them," Eastra said. "But it seems to me they are more sensible than other men. Why spend your time killing? Why not live in peace as the merchants do?"

His smile faded. "The merchants need only a small shop in which to ply their trade, but most men need land. Land to raise crops on, as your people do. And for Britons, land to hunt on and to graze our herds and flocks."

She gestured to the broad green expanse of hills around them. "It seems to me there is plenty of land here. Enough for both your people and mine."

Rhun raised a brow. "Do you think your uncle is a man inclined to share?"

"Nay," Eastra answered.

"Well, neither is Arthur, nor are many Britons. In our minds, it's a simple thing. We were here first, so we have the better claim."

"Is that why *you* fight?" she asked. "Because you are greedy for land?"

Rhun looked at her, and his expression changed. "Nay, that is not why I fight. My people live in the hills, a land too rugged for farmers like the Saxons."

"Then why do you fight for Arthur?" She knew she should not argue with him and behave so disagreeably, but this was a thing that had troubled her for years. Why should so many people suffer—women, innocent children—all because of men's stubborn greed?

He did not answer her for a time, and she grew worried she had made him angry. Then he spoke in a slow, thoughtful voice. "I first swore allegiance to Arthur because I believed the priests and holy brothers, like Gildas of Llandudno, when they said that the Saxons were heathen barbarians and any man devoted to the Christian cause must fight to drive them back into the sea. That was what sent me to Arthur's camp. But then, in the next few years, I came to know him as a man and a king. I saw he had a vision for Britain no man had ever had before. He wants to unite the whole of the island, to finally end the futile squabbling between tribes and chieftains that has always made us vulnerable to our enemies. It's a glorious, valiant dream, one that was irresistible to a youthful warrior, the man I was a few years ago."

"And now?" she asked.

"I'm no longer certain Arthur's dream is possible. In times of crisis, aye, then the chieftains will rally around and fight side by side. But as soon as the threat has passed, they go back to their petty disputes, recalling old grudges, insults made to their fathers' fathers." He grimaced. "My people have a kind of blindness that way. No matter that the Christos teaches us to forgive our enemies, most of my countrymen believe the opposite—that a man's honor depends on vengeance, and every slight to him or his tribe must be repaid. I think sometimes it is the curse of our race."

He has pondered these matters a great deal, she thought, observing his intent, serious face. He met her gaze and smiled suddenly. "My father says he worries about me because I think like a priest, rather than a warrior. That I am not ruthless and ferocious enough."

"Well, I think it is wonderful you are not ruthless and ferocious," she said emphatically. "I have lived most of life around men like that, and I do not like them." She hesitated, then asked, "Is your father like my uncle, then?"

Rhun cocked his head. "My father? When he fights, I know he is as pitiless as any man. But his heart is tender, and he does not really think like a warrior, either. For the love of a woman, he nearly gave up his kingdom—not once, but twice." He nodded at Eastra's amazed look. "When his first wife died, he mourned so deeply that he renounced his title and power and went to live in a priory for several years. Then, later, when there was opposition to his relationship with Rhiannon, my stepmother, he told his chieftains he would remain wed to her even if it cost him everything he had fought to regain."

Eastra was encouraged. If Rhun's father was a man who would put a woman before his ambitions, then perhaps . . ."It sounds as if your father and you are much alike," she said breathlessly.

Rhun gave a laugh and turned around to gesture for Bridei to ride forward and join them. "Bridei, tell her, tell her *exactly* how well I get along with our father. How *much* we are alike."

Bridei cocked a brow sardonically. "Well, they are both tall giants of men, and they have blue eyes, but I would say those are about all the traits the two of them share."

"Truly?" Eastra asked.

"Truly. You will see when we reach Deganwy. Every moment they are together, they will argue. Of course"— Bridei's mouth quirked—"they still have more in common than Maelgwn and I. As far as I can tell, the only traits the two of us share are the blue eyes."

"You do not get along with your father, either?" she asked.

"Rhun and he might argue all the time, but Maelgwn still believes his firstborn is the most noble and admirable of men. While I . . ." Bridei shrugged. "He thinks I inherited all the evil traits of his line—which are many."

"It's not as if you've never given him cause to doubt your honor," Rhun said.

Bridei shrugged, then met Eastra's gaze, his vivid blue eyes mocking and self-depreciative. "So, you see, I am the evil spawn, and Rhun the saint. But remember, saints have their drawbacks. Much of the time, they are so unholy grim and serious, the rest of us can hardly stand to be around them. Here we are, riding out on this fine, glorious day, and all my brother can do is talk of politics and honor." He winked. "I can tell you such is not my idea of how to entertain a beautiful princess. If I were him, I would seek to make you laugh and be merry." He grinned again, then suddenly began to sing. It was a playful tune, about a man courting a maid and all the outrageous, absurd tasks he promised to perform in order to win her love.

Bridei's voice was rich and deep, and Eastra felt spellbound as she listened. As the vibrant melody echoed across the hills around them, she could almost feel her worries and concerns falling away. When he had finished, she said, "That was wonderful. Are you what your people call a bard?"

"Not a true one," Bridei answered. "I was never willing to undergo the rigorous training to learn all the sagas and heroic tales an official bard must know. It takes near a score of years for that." He smiled. "But Arthur sees fit to keep me around anyway. He knows I have the means to gladden his men's hearts when they are heavy or to compose a satisfying tribute when one of their own is lost. I believe he counts me as useful, in my way, as any of his Companions."

Eastra glanced at Rhun. He nodded. "My brother has a way with words. Although I think if Arthur had any idea what mischief he sometimes causes, he might not be so pleased to have Bridei in his army train."

"What mischief?" Bridei asked, his face a mask of innocence. "I have no idea what you're talking about."

Rhun rolled his eyes, and Eastra looked from one man to the other. How different these two brothers were, not merely in looks, but in the way they saw things. She could not help being drawn to Bridei's lighthearted nature. After the harshness of her life, his playful outlook was as appealing as a burst of sunshine among the clouds. But she admired Rhun as well, for his thoughtfulness and kindness.

But there was certainly more than admiration in her feelings for him. Being near him aroused a deep yearning. His tall, well-muscled physique and gold-streaked hair reminded her of her countrymen, and yet he was different, his eyes a deeper, grayer blue, his features finer, his hair darker and slightly wavy. The subtle strangeness of his appearance aroused and attracted her. Never before had she met a man she desired to lie with, to have him touch her and put his mouth against hers. But she felt that way with Rhun. And the longer she was near him, the more intense those feelings became.

Caught up as she was in her thoughts, she did not notice the change in the landscape right away. They had left the rolling hills and moved down to a small valley. The grass and vegetation here grew lush and deep, a more brilliant green than she'd ever seen before, and there were strange shaped mounds scattered here and there. A sense of desolation hovered in the air, and when she saw a blackened, half-burned tree with blackbirds on the barren branches, she experienced a strange, uneasy feeling, a vague sense of recognition. Then she caught a glimpse of the waving heads of the grainfield and knew. Her body went rigid and her throat seemed to close up. It was as if a cloud had passed over the sun, and the world was suddenly cold and bleak.

"Jesu." She heard Rhun swear, and knew he had also guessed what they had come upon. "Eastra," he said. "I'm sorry. I didn't know this was here. I was merely taking the most direct route."

Eastra shook her head, unable to respond. Every patch of green made the gorge rise in her throat. Was there a body hidden in the tall vegetation? The crumbling skeleton of one of her people? A child or a woman left to lie where they were butchered?

She glanced around, blinking away tears. Not all of the longhouse had burned, and she could still see its faint rectangular shape in the tall grass. And the furrows of the grainfields, abandoned how long now—one season or two?—were still discernible.

"It looks like there was a village here," Bridei said. "I wonder what happened?" His voice came to Eastra's ears as if from far way.

"They were burned out, probably by a British patrol," Rhun answered.

"Saxons?" Bridei asked.

"Aye. You see where the longhouse was? And the way they plowed their fields in straight, even lines? Unmistakably Saxon."

"What happened to the people?" Bridei asked.

"Eastra," Rhun said. "Do you want to stop?"

She shook her head violently, the tears blinding her.

"I'm sorry," Rhun said again. "I wish you did not have to see this. If it helps any, know that these days Arthur forbids his patrols to kill women and children. Those who lived here have probably moved north, or nearer to the coast."

"Do you truly believe that?" she asked in a shaking voice.

Rhun sighed. "I want to, but I cannot promise it's true."

At last they reached the edge of the ruined settlement. Eastra took a deep breath, torn between conflicting emotions. Seeing the cruel handiwork of the Britons made her feel like a traitor to her people. How could she have willingly offered herself as a hostage? How could she have deliberately chosen the company of her enemies?

She glanced at Rhun. His face looked grieved, his jaw set with grim resignation. It had disturbed him to see the lingering aftereffects of bloodshed and war. Did it remind him of when he rescued her? Those many years ago, he had not been part of the senseless slaughter, but instead hid her from his fellow soldiers and carried her to safety. Her anger faded. He had saved her life. He was not like his countrymen. She could not believe he was.

They rode on. Although some of the luster had gone from the day, Eastra felt her turmoil easing. She was here because she wanted to be here. With Rhun. He was like no man she had ever known. She could not let him vanish from her life once again. She urged her mount closer to his. "How long will we spend in Londinium?" she asked.

"A few days. It depends on how long it takes us to purchase supplies."

"What sort of things will you buy?"

Rhun did not immediately respond to her question. He

gave Bridei a look, and Bridei answered. "We will purchase wine, of course. And perhaps Samian ware, leather goods, and fabric. We can get those things from the merchant ships that sometimes come to Deganwy, of course. But the quality and selection will be better in Londinium."

"But if we buy wine and pottery, we'll have to have a cart to transport it in," Rhun said, frowning. "I don't want to be slowed down with a baggage vehicle. I say we buy nothing too heavy or cumbersome, nothing that can't be carried on a packhorse."

"Whatever you wish," Bridei said. "How we travel to Gwynedd is up to you."

Eastra saw Rhun's jaw tighten. She wondered what had angered him. Was it simply that his brother rubbed him the wrong way? The two of them always seemed to be disagreeing.

After a time, Rhun pulled his mount to a halt and pointed to a tall stone marker in the distance. "There's a mile marker for the old Roman road. We can follow it all the way to Londinium."

They rode to where he pointed. There, glinting white as bleached bone, was a broad, level stone trackway. "The going will be easier now," Rhun said. "The Romans built their roads well. See, the pavement has hardly crumbled even in the hundred years since the legions left."

"It must have taken many, many slaves to build this," Eastra said as they set off down the road, the horses' hooves echoing loudly on the stones.

"It was not built by slaves, but by the troops themselves," Rhun answered. "The Romans were disciplined men. Their footsoldiers knew how to dig and build as well as fight. It was part of what made them so successful. They would conquer a territory, then immediately build up forts and settlements to secure it before moving on. Once all these things were in place, it was almost impossible for the native people to defeat them. Then the Roman soldiers intermarried with the local women, and before you knew it, the conquered tribes had become like the conquerors, seduced to the pleasures of Roman living."

"Is that what happened to the Britons?" Eastra asked.

"For the most part," Rhun answered. "My people, living up in the wild highlands, never really adopted Roman ways. And there were other tribes, scattered here and there, who retained the speech and livelihood and ways of their ancestors. When the legions left and the first wave of barbarians washed over Britain, many of those who called themselves citizens of Rome were killed or driven from the country. That left us, the original tribes of Britain, to defend it."

"The barbarians? Is that how you speak of my people?" Eastra asked.

"Those first invaders *were* barbarians. They did not come to settle the land, but to rape and pillage and slaughter. They did not bring their womenfolk or their families. They came and took what they could carry in their boats and destroyed the rest, and then they left." Rhun gave her a look of helplessness. "It was over a hundred years ago, long before our time, or even that of our grandsires. The Saxons and Jutes and all those seafaring warriors from the lands across the eastern sea, they especially liked to attack the priories and holy places, and that set the Christians against them. They have always denounced the invaders as savage men who worship foul, bestial gods."

"And do you think *I* am a barbarian?" Eastra asked.

"Of course not! Nor do I think that of your uncle, Cerdic. I have seen how your people live, the exquisite jewelry, the woven goods and furniture your artisans craft, the order of your households, the efficiency of your farming techniques. In many ways I admire your people, and think there is much we Britons can learn from them."

"But you believe we worship foul, bestial gods," she pointed out sourly.

Rhun shrugged. "Many of my people worship gods and goddesses other than the Christos. At one time, that bothered me a great deal. But I have gradually come to terms with it. I no longer think it matters so much what god a man or woman calls holy, but what is in their heart, what sort of person they are. I have known Christians who have done vile things, things at least as bad as any barbarian. And then there is my stepmother, a devotee of the Great Goddess, and one of the kindest and wisest people I've ever known."

"Besides." Bridei joined the conversation. "If he thought you were a bestial barbarian, he would not have rescued you all those years ago." He lifted his dark brows knowingly.

Eastra looked at Rhun. She was rather surprised he had told his brother about that incident, especially given the tensions between them. In a way, it troubled her, as if he had shared a secret that was supposed to be between the two of them.

"I had to tell him," Rhun said, as if guessing her thoughts. "Otherwise he would have pestered me relentlessly, or started asking questions of the other men." He shot Bridei a hostile look.

"What have I done now?" Bridei demanded. "Here I am, trying to help you win over this woman, to convince her you are not like most Britons. I'm certain she has heard many awful tales about *our* race—that we are monsters who eat Saxon children for breakfast." He looked at Eastra expectantly.

She nodded. "The most horrifying tale I was told is that you Christians have a ritual where you drink blood and eat human flesh."

Rhun gave her a shocked look. "That's not true! Only wine and bread are consumed during the Sacrament. The blood and flesh are merely *symbolic* of our Lord's sacrifice."

"Still, you must admit, it sounds gruesome," Bridei said. "Savage enough to frighten the barbarians themselves."

"I know now that it's not true," Eastra said. "But to a child—well, you can imagine how much we feared and hated the British."

"And yet, when I rescued you that day, you came to me willingly," Rhun said softly. "How could you have dared to trust me with your life? How did you know I was not going to 'eat you for breakfast,' as Bridei put it?"

"I saw something in your eyes. I knew you would not hurt me."

They stared at each other. Eastra could feel the emotion welling up inside her. She had trusted this man with her life all those years ago. And in this moment, she gave him the rest of her heart.

Although it was difficult, Rhun forced himself to tear his glance away. When Eastra looked at him like that, he felt all his will, all his reason, slipping away. It was as if Bridei and the other men did not even exist, as if it were only he and she in the world, their souls touching.

It was sort of an enchantment, he thought uneasily as they rode on down the Roman road. A dangerous enchantment. He had to remember his duty, his purpose in being with this woman. She was a hostage, Cerdic's kinswoman. Although every fiber of his being told him he could trust her with his life, he dared not succumb to his feelings. Reason said he did not really know her. She might be a spy for her uncle, using her beautiful face, her sweet, guileless countenance, to pry secrets from him.

He must be on his guard. Damn, it was difficult! Especially with Bridei around, talking easily and comfortably, as if they were on a pleasant ride with one of their sisters in the mountains of Gwynedd, rather than on a sensitive diplomatic mission, accompanied by a woman who was kin of their fiercest enemy!

She had some hostility toward the Britons, that was obvious. He'd heard the anger in her voice when she spoke of how his people had slaughtered hers, seen her face change and grow remote and stricken as they passed the burned-out Saxon hamlet. Although he believed she truly cared for him, that she would not do anything to hurt him personally, her resentment and hostility toward his people might still cause her to undermine the cause he fought for.

He wanted to curse aloud. Bridei had entangled him in this wretched mess. If not for Bridei, Arthur might have appointed some other man to guard Eastra. Of course, then he would always worry how she was being treated. What he truly wished was that Arthur had refused to accept her as hostage altogether. There should have been no question that a woman was not acceptable, even if she were Cerdic's kinswoman. Why had Arthur done it? Because it gave him a chance to offer up Mordred as his own hostage? An opportunity to get his troublesome son out of the way?

Rhun repressed a sigh. No point agonizing over what was already done. He must get through this the best he could. Keep Eastra safe, accomplish their mission, make the long journey to Gwynedd—and all the while, try not to lose his heart to his captive. It was going to be the most difficult fortnight of his life.

"What would you like to purchase in Londinium?" Bridei asked Eastra after they had ridden in silence for some distance. "Is there some luxury item you've always coveted? Perhaps a finely made necklace to wear around your slender, white throat? Or a length of silk cloth to make a gown that matches your sky blue eyes?"

She smiled at his flattering words. "I brought no coin with me, so if I did find something I liked, I would not be able to buy it anyway."

"Oh, but Arthur has given us plenty of gold to defray our expenses on this journey. I'm sure he would not begrudge you some of it. After all, Arthur did advise us to treat you with all the respect and honor due a princess. For that matter"—Bridei gestured to Rhun—"I'm certain my brother would gladly purchase anything you desire. So be thinking of that which cannot be obtained in your own territories."

"I will do that," Eastra said, laughing. Then she looked at Rhun and, seeing his somber face, wondered what troubled him. Had his brother's teasing brought on his dour mood, or something else? Only a short while before he had looked at her with a tenderness that took her breath away. Now he seemed distant and wary.

She focused her gaze on the road ahead of them, wondering whether things were going to be like this the whole way across Britain.

As they neared Londinium, they began to see farmsteads here and there. Most were in the traditional British style of a few thatched timber buildings enclosed within a thorn hedge, but some had rough stone buildings, the masonry obviously salvaged from some ruined villa nearby. Although pigs rooted in the ferny ground of the forestlands and shaggy cattle and golden white sheep grazed in the meadows, they saw few people. It seemed likely they were in hiding.

But gradually, they met other travelers on the road—a black-bearded, red-nosed tinker with a cartload of goods, a farmer and his family with a wheelbarrow full of cabbages and a handcart piled high with leeks, turnips, and other vegetables, a pair of holy brothers on mules. The travelers regarded them with suspicion at first, but when Rhun greeted them cordially, they seemed to relax. As they passed them, one of the holy men urged his mule close to Rhun and asked for news.

Rhun told him of the truce with Cerdic. The man—who had a fiery red tonsure and fierce dark eyes—nodded in satisfaction. "I'm glad to hear there might be peace for a time. I have traveled much of Britain this past year, preaching of Our Lord and ministering to the sick and downtrodden. I have found suffering and devastation everywhere. Near as bad, some people say, as when the Saxons raided and burned a hundred years before."

"Where are you headed now?" Rhun asked.

"From Londinium I hope to find a merchant ship to take me to Gaul. From there I travel to Rome. If you have no objection, Brother Anselm and I would like to follow behind your troop the rest of the way into the city. I'm certain I will encounter other dangers on my pilgrimage, but I would as lief not be killed by marauding Saxons before I even cross the eastern sea."

"Have you seen many Saxons in your travels?" Rhun asked.

The brother shook his head. "No warriors. Only traders, old men, women, and children. You can always tell they are Saxons because of their coloring." His gaze moved to Eastra, probing and hostile. "Speaking of which, I might ask you, young warrior, why does one of Arthur's soldiers travel with a woman of the enemy close at hand?"

Rhun opened his mouth, but it was Bridei who answered, "She's a prisoner," he said smoothly. "We're taking her to the slavers market in Londinium."

Rhun made a faint outraged sound and Eastra felt her cheeks grow hot. But the holy brother nodded in satisfaction. "No doubt you will fetch a high price for that golden-haired Saxon witch. Then you can use the wealth you earn toward the cause of driving the rest of her kind back into the sea. Ungodly bastards!"

Eastra gritted her teeth. She would not let this man make her feel shamed. She would not!

She looked at Rhun, who also appeared distraught. Bridei spoke casually. "I thought the Church was opposed to slavery. Or did I hear wrong?"

The holy brother's expression went sour. "Aye, that is the Church's official policy. But I believe we must use every weapon at our disposal in this desperate battle to save Britain from the barbarian hordes."

"Since you are obviously so uncomfortable in the presence of one of those 'barbarians,' I think it would be best if we traveled separately." With those words, Rhun nodded to Eastra, then urged his horse into a trot. Eastra dug her knees into her own mount to catch up with him. A few seconds later, the rest of the troop joined them.

"Narrow-minded fool!" Rhun said hotly. "I have half a

mind to go back and confiscate his mule in the name of
Arthur's cause. I wonder how he would like *that!*"

"Relax, brother," Bridei coaxed. "Remember our purpose for this journey and our mission in Londinium. It was
reasonable for him to believe we share his prejudices
against Saxons. That was exactly what I hoped he would
think when I said Eastra was a prisoner. But you, you cannot let a lie stand for even a second, can you?"

"I saw no danger there," Rhun said. "No reason to lie,
to make up that crude, disgusting story about Eastra. You
know what he was thinking, that we mean to sell her for
a bedslave, and that we have all had her already!"

"And what does it hurt to let him think that? It's a plausible explanation for her presence in our troop. If she is a
slave, a captive, then she becomes invisible. No one would
think to guess she is kin of the most feared Saxon warlord
in Britain." Bridei looked at Eastra, his raven dark brows
level over his piercing blue eyes. "Perhaps it hurts your
pride to think of yourself as a slave, but it might well save
your life."

She nodded slowly. "Bridei's right. I should not care
what that man thinks of me. He is obviously ignorant and
embittered." She turned to Bridei. "If you think it best to
tell everyone I am a slave, I have no objection."

"I thought we were going to say she is my leman," Rhun
protested. "That sounds a little more dignified, at least."

"When we reach the city, the story that she is your leman
will better serve. But for now, on the road—I don't think
those holy men would have understood."

"No, probably not," Rhun said furiously. "But I would
have liked to make them understand!"

"What were you going to do?" Bridei asked. "You can
hardly strike a holy man. And if you tried to defend Eastra,
he would undoubtedly have complained to everyone he met
that King Arthur's Companions are not the noble Christian
heroes they have been portrayed to be, but Saxon-loving
whoremongers. Frankly, that is not the sort of gossip we
need right now."

"I don't dispute that." Rhun sounded resigned and weary. "But . . ." He sighed. "I mislike this whole business. This journey is not a fit venture for any woman, let alone a princess!"

"And yet here we are." Bridei said. "We can worry about proprieties and hurt Arthur's cause, or we can make the best of things."

Rhun still looked angry, but he said no more. And as they neared the outer edges of Londinium, Eastra also began to forget the holy man's rude words in her interest in the things she saw.

They entered the city through a towering gateway of stone, and all around were the remnants of old, tumbled down stone buildings. She could see newer structures, some of them in the Saxon style, with high roofs supported by arched beams and timber walls, others with red tiles on the roofs and walls of white plaster in the Roman fashion. And here and there was a round dwelling that looked distinctly British, with bracken-thatched roofs and rough timber walls.

It was like a village, only much bigger, Eastra thought as they continued down the paved roadway. The people she saw seemed to be as varied as the buildings. On one side of the trackway, a plump woman with butter-colored braids, ruddy cheeks, and a white apron over her gunna threw out grain for her chickens and geese. On the other side, a thin, dark-haired, barefooted girl balanced a dusky-skinned toddler on one hip and a full pail of water on the other. But Eastra was truly unprepared for the sight of two huge men with skin as black as soot carrying a curtained box. As they passed by, a woman suddenly opened the curtains and leaned out of the box, speaking in a shrill, peevish voice. Eastra did not recognize the language, but guessed it must be Latin.

"Ah," Bridei said, as the woman and her servants passed by. "A fine Roman matron out for a bit of fresh air."

"And the men carrying her?" Eastra asked. "Where are

they from? I've never seen anyone with skin that color before."

"Probably from Nubia," Bridei answered. "It used to be a province of Rome." He smiled. "You truly can find anything in the world in the city of Londinium."

"Have you been here often?" she asked him.

"Now and then. Arthur has a few contacts here, and he sometimes sends me to get news on what's happening on the eastern shores."

"Spies?" Eastra asked grimly.

Bridei smiled. "Nay, certainly not. They are all merchants and seamen, and as Rhun said, they care about their profits, not politics. I'm certain they share information with your people as well as ours."

As they traveled deeper into the city, they passed several large stone structures, now falling to ruins. The sun crept low in the west, shining like a bright copper disc. It cast a lovely rosy glow over the tall pillars and graceful archways of the remains of a massive building. "That used to be the basilica," Rhun said.

"It's beautiful," Eastra said. "Hard to imagine something so fine and elegant could be fashioned out of stone."

"The Romans were great lovers of beauty. They liked the things around them to be pleasing to the eye. Their passion for art was almost as great as their passion for power."

"And comfort," Bridie put in. "They were obsessed with ease and luxury and cleanliness. You will understand when you see the baths. Huge structures, with vast pools for bathing in. Some of them had heated water, some cold."

"How did they heat so much water?" Eastra asked.

"Very ingeniously. The water flowed over heated rocks and gradually filled the pools. They also had special rooms where the water was heated until it formed steam. They would stand in the steam until they began to sweat, then jump into a pool of cool water."

"And they did this all merely to get clean?" Eastra asked.

"There was more to it than that," Rhun responded. "The important men would go to the baths together and while they were in the pools or the steamrooms, they would talk about war and politics and trade. It was a kind of meeting place. Almost like your people or mine might gather around a hearth."

"The Romans seem very strange to me," Eastra said.

Rhun nodded. "I have thought so, too. In many ways, your people and mine are more alike than either of us are like the Romans."

"You think we are alike?" Eastra asked in surprise.

"I can see many similarities between us. We both love war and heroes and fighting. We both have great loyalty to our leaders and our own races. We both love beauty, but of a different kind than the Romans. Most of our people live in small settlements, rather than in large cities like Londinium. We also live close to the land, acutely aware of the passing seasons and our dependence upon the earth for sustenance. We both favor bright colors and ornamentation in our clothing, and use animals as symbols of our might and power. Cerdic fights beneath the standard of a white stallion, while Arthur goes into battle with a bear and an eagle emblazened on his shield."

"Your standard is a dragon," Eastra said.

"The dragon is the symbol of the Cymry, our tribe. My father is even called 'the dragon of the island' by some men."

"Why a dragon?" she asked. "It's not a real beast, is it?"

Rhun smiled, his white teeth flashing. "Of course it's real. When we reach the mountains of Gwynedd, I will show you its lair."

Eastra looked at Bridei, trying to decide whether Rhun was teasing. Bridei quirked a dark brow. "A beast so many believe in *must* be real."

Eastra regarded him dubiously, then laughed. Rhun was right. There were many similarities between Saxon and British. Here she was, spending time with two men who by rights should be her enemies and enjoying herself immensely.

By the saints, she is beautiful when she smiles. Rhun felt intense longing wash through him. The fading glow of the sunset caught the pale gilt of Eastra's hair and tinted her smooth skin a warm golden shade, making her appear so breathtakingly beautiful his chest ached with yearning. He wanted to lean from his horse across the short distance between them and kiss her lips. He wanted to hold her lithe body in his arms as they stood in the waning rays of the sunset and feel the night fall like a soft, dark mist around them. Most of all, he wanted to send Bridei and the other men away so he could show her the delights of Londinium by himself.

A golden Saxon witch, the holy brother had called her, and in a way, she was. She had enchanted him, ensorceled him. Or maybe she was a fairy, one of the Shining Ones who came into the worlds of mortals and stole away a chosen one to bide with them beneath the hollow hills.

What strange fancies this woman aroused in him. Here he was, in one of the largest settlements in Britain, and his thoughts were lost in the mysteries of the wild hills of his homeland. He shook his head, trying to remember that the shadows were growing long, and they still had not found a place to spend the night. He turned to Bridei. "Is there an inn around here that would welcome men from Arthur's army?"

"Any of the inns would welcome us—if we offer enough coin," Bridei answered.

"But we need hosts who are discreet, who will not gossip about our business in Londinium," Rhun reminded him.

"I know of a place, although it's not an inn," Bridei said. "It's this way. Toward the river."

Five

She could sense the river nearby, smell the rich, sweet scent of water and decaying vegetation, hear the rustle of wings and the faint squabbling noises of the ducks and herons and other water birds as they settled down for the night among the reeds. It reminded her of the fens and marshlands of South Seax, where she had lived as a child until her tribe moved farther inland in search of richer farmland.

It was nearly dark, and she wondered how Bridei could find the way as he led them down the narrow, twisting byways. And then, suddenly, she saw blazing torches set on tall poles illuminating a large complex of buildings, and the smell of the river was blotted out by the odors of burning pitch and food cooking. A man, obviously a guard of sorts, came forward to ask their business. Bridei spoke to him in a quiet voice. In a few moments, servants came to help with the horses and baggage. Rhun and Bridei dismounted; then Rhun came to help her off her horse.

"What is this place?" she asked as she slid down on stiff legs.

"Some friend of Arthur's," he answered. "Bridei had only to speak the name of the high king and we were bid welcome."

They were led into an entryway lit by oil lamps. The light danced on the walls, making the images of men and beasts there spring to life. Eastra gazed in amazement. She had seen mosaics and frescoes before, but never ones so detailed and lifelike. The panther depicted on the one wall seemed ready to leap out and attack them.

"This way," a servant said, and they were escorted down a hallway and around a corner to another room. There were more paintings on the walls, red tiles on the floor, and several lamps set about the room on tall bronze prickets. In the center of the room, a man with thinning auburn hair and bulging blue eyes reclined on a delicately carved wooden couch. Around him, also on couches, were three women, two much younger than the other one. They all wore flowing, light-colored garments, and the women's hair was arranged in elaborate curls and plaits like the Roman women Eastra had seen in painted scenes.

Bridei executed a graceful bow. "Aurelius Silurium. I bring you greetings from Artorius Rex."

The man bowed back. "Welcome, Bridei ap Maelgwn, Prince of Gwynedd. I am honored by your visit to my humble dwelling." He motioned to Rhun and Eastra. "Who are your companions, that I might greet them properly?"

"My brother, Rhun ap Maelgwn and"—Bridei hesitated a moment—"Eastra."

Rhun bowed, and Eastra did the same, although she felt tense and unsettled. Without a title before her name, everyone would think her Rhun's leman, a foreign woman who had thought to improve her lot by sharing her enemy's bed. Although she had agreed to the deception, she half regretted it now.

"We were about to dine," Aurelius said, "but we will wait for you to wash and make yourself ready to join us." He motioned to one of the younger women. "Calida, take Lady Eastra to the women's quarters that she might change her garments and refresh herself."

"I have clothing in my pack," Eastra said.

"But not, I think, anything in the Roman style," Aurelius replied. He motioned once more to the younger woman, who got up from the couch and approached Eastra. "Come," she said.

Eastra followed her down the hallway to a small room. Like every other part of the house, there were several oil lamps lighting the room and the walls were of some dazzling white stuff painted with colorful pictures of flowers and birds. The birds, depicted in the motion of flight, seemed to be flying around the room. Calida gestured to a tall chest. On it sat a red Samian ware basin and bronze ewer. "You can wash there. I will have a servant bring a towel and some clothing." She turned to go.

"Wait," Eastra called.

The woman—she was really little more than a girl, Eastra decided, although the elaborate hairstyle made her seem older—turned and stared at her. Eastra could not read the expression in her eyes. Was it impatience? Distaste? It did not matter. She had agreed to this part and now she must play it. "Thank you," she murmured.

The girl left. Eastra poured some water in the bowl and swished her hands around in it, watching the dust of the road settle in the bottom of the basin. In a short while, a female servant appeared bearing a towel over one arm and a garment over the other. Eastra nodded to the servant, wondering if she were a slave. She was dark and small.

The woman lay the garment on the bed, then brought Eastra the towel. "Thank you," Eastra said. "You do not have to stay, if you have other duties to attend to."

The servant shook her head. "I must help you dress and fix your hair."

She did not want to force this woman to wait on her, but there seemed no other choice. Eastra washed her face, then took the towel. As she did so, she saw the ugly marking of a brand on the woman's arm. Eastra's former owner had not believed in branding his house slaves, but she knew of the barbaric practice. A wave of bitter resentment went through her. She would not treat this woman like a servant, a piece of property. "What is your name?" she asked the slave.

"Skena."

"And where do your people come from?" Eastra toweled dry her face and hands.

"From the north, a place called Cit Coit Caledon."

"Were you captured? Is that how you came to be here?"

Wariness lit Skena's dark eyes. "Aye, my lady." She gestured to a stool by the bed. "Please sit so I can undo your braids."

Eastra did as she was bid. A Pict, this woman must be. One of the Painted People. She thought she had glimpsed blue markings on the woman's hand, faintly visible beneath the dusky tan of her skin. The Picts were a fierce warlike tribe in the north who had never been conquered by the Romans. Cerdic and some of the other chieftains had once talked of joining forces with the Picts, but they were wary of the northern peoples. It was said they were headhunters who decorated their dwellings with the rotting skulls of their enemies. Barbarians, Old Agulwulf had called them. Eastra's mouth twitched at the irony.

"How long have you been in Londinium?" she asked Skena.

"I don't know. Several years, I think."

"Have you memories of your other life, before you were taken into slavery?"

Skena did not answer for a time. Eastra wondered if she had understood the question, or if perhaps she had probed too deep and upset the other woman. "I used to be a slave," she said encouragingly.

Skena's small hands stilled in the act of combing out Eastra's hair. "You were? How did you escape?"

Eastra hesitated. Dare she tell this woman her true background? It might give her hope, and hope was so important to a slave, as she well knew. "I was rescued by my people," she said. "They burned the villa where I was a slave, and I was taken to live in my uncle's household."

"Your uncle must be a powerful man," Skena said. "Tell me, if he rescued you, why did he let you fall into the hands of his enemies? Why did he allow one of them to make you his bedslave?"

Eastra searched her mind for an explanation of her circumstances. "I am not really a bedslave. In fact, I am with the tall warrior by choice."

Skena raised her dark brows. "And your uncle allows this?"

"It's complicated." She took a breath. "The fact is, I am a hostage. Nay, do not look like that. I suggested the arrangement to my uncle. I wanted to be with the tall warrior and this was the only way."

"You wanted to be with him—even though he is your enemy?"

Eastra shook her head. "He is not my enemy. His people and mine might be in conflict these past years, but I seek to change that."

Skena looked at her, dark eyes narrowed. "You are very bold for a woman and a former slave. What makes you think you have any say in this war between the Saxon and the British kind?"

"My uncle is an important man. If I can find a way to get him and the British warlord Arthur to trust each other, it would go a long way toward bringing peace."

"Who is your uncle?"

Skena's question surprised her, but Eastra reasoned she had told so much of the story already, it did not matter if the slave heard the rest. She did not seem likely to betray the tale to Aurelius or his family. Few slaves had any love for their masters, certainly not slaves who had been branded.

"My uncle is Cerdic, son of Hengist. He is overlord of the South Folke and part of the South Seax." Seeing the slave's confusion, she added. "Those are lands along the coast north and south of here. Lands even Arthur has ceded to my people."

"So you are a princess?" Skena's expression changed subtly. Eastra wondered if there was not a hint of hostility in her black eyes.

88 *Mary Gillgannon*

She nodded. "But no one must know of it. Here in Londinium, everyone must think I am Rhun ap Maelgwn's leman."

Skena spoke no more but began to help Eastra into the Roman-style garment. She wrapped it around Eastra's waist and carefully arranged the folds, then fastened it with a silver pin at the shoulder.

"You are very skilled," Eastra said. "Do you normally wait upon Aurelius's wife and daughters?"

"The daughters, aye. Lady Vesperia has her own bodyservant."

"It does not seem like such a harsh duty," Eastra said. "At least you do not have to work in the kitchens or in the stables."

"I think I would prefer that to waiting upon those mewling, whiny girls." Skena made a face.

Eastra did not know what to say. Skena obviously despised her life. And who could blame her? Vividly, she could recall her own unhappiness as a slave. "I'm sorry," she said. "I would aid you if I could."

"Of course you would," Skena said harshly. "After you have brought peace between the Saxons and the Britons, you will then free all the slaves."

"You think I am a fool, don't you?"

"A fool to think that because you share a man's bed, you have some power over him."

"But it's not that I share Rhun's bed—which I don't, yet. It is because I . . . I have some hope that he loves me, or will at least come to do so."

"Love?" Skena's brows shot up. "Verily, you are a bigger fool than I thought."

There did not seem to be anything to say after that. Eastra sat silent while Skena arranged her hair in coils on top of her head, securing them with bronze pins. When she had finished the task, the slave asked formally, "Will there be anything else?"

Eastra shook her head, and Skena left the room.

* * *

A brazier had been brought to drive the chill from the room, and the sweet smell of burning applewood filled the air. Rhun and Bridei stood near the brazier, sipping spiced wine. They had excused themselves briefly to wash off the dust of the road and change into wool tunics, but they declined to don the Roman attire Aurelius's servant offered. Now their host, reclining on his couch, turned probing eyes on them. "Before the women return, tell me why you have come to Londinium."

Rhun waited for Bridei to answer, since he was officially Arthur's messenger. His brother cleared his throat. "Arthur wishes to know what news you have of the eastern shores. He has made a truce with Cerdic, son of Hengist, and he wants to know what hope there is of the Saxons keeping it. Have you heard any word from Saxony or Jutland of ships gathering there, either to bring warriors or settlers to our shores?"

"The seas are quiet," Aurelius said. "If the seawolves are planning more invasions, I have not gotten wind of it."

"And what of other matters of Britain? Plots? Treachery? Anything Arthur should be aware of?"

Aurelius pursed his lips. "I know Arthur's son loves him not."

Rhun and Bridei looked at each other. Rhun said, "Arthur has given Mordred to Cerdic as a hostage. I worry what trouble he will stir up in the enemy's camp. And yet I think he is better off there than roaming around Britain spreading discontent."

Aurelius nodded thoughtfully. "Perhaps, although I don't understand why Arthur has not dealt with Mordred long before this. It seems to me the high king has the means to eliminate such threats to his power."

"You think he should have Mordred killed?" Rhun asked in shock.

Aurelius shrugged. "It seems logical to me."

"Nay, Arthur would not do such a thing," Rhun said. "He would not besmirch his honor and all he stands for by doing murder, and certainly not of his own son."

"There are those who say Arthur's honor will be his downfall." Aurelius's eyes narrowed and Rhun could sense warning in his watery blue gaze.

"Arthur believes how a man defeats his enemies is important. That there can be no true victory without honor."

Aurelius grunted.

Bridei broke the uneasy silence that followed. "Other than Mordred, can you think of anything else Arthur should beware of?"

"I'm not privy to the plans of the Saxons," Aurelius said. "But I think the peace will hold for a time, at least until something tips the balance of the scales to their side. What that will be, I cannot say. And yet I think the greatest dangers might come from within our borders, rather than from without."

Rhun's vague unease increased. What was Aurelius hinting about? Did the man even know himself what it was he feared?

They discussed other matters of interest—such as the crops that could be expected this year and the recent weather, which had hampered Aurelius in getting his ships back and forth from Less Britain. Then servants came in bearing more of the finely made couches. "We'll dine as Romans this night," their host said. Something must have showed in Rhun's expression, for Aurelius laughed suddenly. "Or would you rather squat down around the brazier and take your meal that way?"

"Verily I would," Rhun answered. "I can't quite get used to the idea of lying down while I eat."

"I keep to the Roman ways because it pleases my wife," Aurelius said. "Surely you can understand the importance of that." He motioned with his head toward the doorway. "Your lady—is she a Saxon?"

Rhun nodded.

"Odd to find one of Arthur's Companions keeping company with a woman of the enemy, although she is certainly beautiful."

Bridei said in a light voice, "She is more to my brother than a bed partner. The arrows of the Roman god Eros have struck him a mortal blow."

"Ah." Aurelius smiled broadly. "There are worse things, Rhun ap Maelgwn, than succumbing to a woman. I wish you well in the matter. Perhaps if this truce holds, you could even think of wedding her."

If Aurelius only knew, Rhun thought, that Eastra was the very means of making certain the truce did hold.

Abruptly, Aurelius turned toward the door and clapped his hands. "The women are here. Time to forget politics and enjoy ourselves."

The women filed in. Rhun found himself staring at Eastra. She was attired in a Roman stola, the flowing garment arranged in complex folds around her torso and baring one creamy-skinned shoulder. Her hair was piled on top of her head, and the silvery curls formed a glowing nimbus around her face. She looked like the statue of a Roman goddess come to life.

Aurelius cast a thoughtful glance in her direction, then hurried to escort his wife to her couch. The younger women took their places, and the servants began to carry in platters of food.

Never had she tasted such delicious food, Eastra thought as she nibbled the spiced meat filling in a rolled-up grape leaf. But it was difficult to concentrate on the exquisite flavors when she was so acutely aware of the slaves who served them. The two young men carrying the platters could only be Saxons. Their hair was near as bright as hers, their eyes as vivid blue. She knew Rhun was watching her, aware of how closely she followed the movements of the two Saxons. Did he guess how her heart ached for them?

But he was a prince, and used to being waited upon by underlings. They must have slaves in his father's household in Gwynedd. A deep resentment swept through her. Rhun thought himself as kindhearted and generous, but he easily accepted this kind of injustice. No doubt he believed conquered people were meant to serve their conquerors, that it was the natural way of things. But, in truth, it was ugly and corrupt. A man or woman did not become an unfeeling animal simply because their people had been defeated in battle. These vacant-faced youths knew anguish and despair and longing the same as anyone else.

She took another bite, thinking she must not allow her anger to be obvious.

She is not content, Rhun thought. Despite the comfortable and beautiful surroundings, the delicious food they dined upon, Eastra looked unhappy. Was it because everyone assumed she was his leman? Did the shame of that spoil her mood?

He watched her eyes following the two Saxon servants. Did she know them, or merely pity them because she had once served as they did now? If it came to that, would she choose the cause of her own people over anything she felt for him?

He pushed the thought from his mind. She owed him nothing. Why should she not feel a kinship with other Saxons, especially those who had been forced into slavery, as she had been? He should not have expected otherwise. Always, he was forgetting what she was: a hostage and Cerdic's niece.

The servants brought course after course, and the enameled cups were constantly refilled with rich, sweet wine. At last, groaning, Rhun put up his hand. "Enough! I'm on the verge of bursting!"

"And I also," Bridei said. He gave a laugh. "If I did not know Arthur counted you as one of his most valued friends, I would suspect you of trying to kill us with a surfeit of rich food!"

Aurelius waved dismissingly. "Life is meant to be enjoyed. I know you have been hard on the campaign trail these last years. You deserve a fine meal as payment for what you are doing for Britain."

"If only the other merchants in Londinium thought as you do," Rhun said. "But I fear they hardly appreciate what would happen to our homeland if not for Arthur."

"His reputation keeps the raiders at bay. He cannot win, but he slows down the tide so it comes in gently instead of inundating us and sweeping everything away."

"You don't think we can prevail?" Rhun asked.

Aurelius paused in eating a honey cake. "Look around while you are in Londinium. Everywhere, you will see Saxons—merchants, craftsmen and their families. They are here, building their houses alongside ours, raising their children. And those children will grow up and claim this place as their home."

"But if Arthur had not fought the Saxons these past thirty-some years, there would be many thousands more of them." Rhun indicated their luxurious surroundings. "They likely would have taken all this away from you, and Londinium would now be called by some harsh, gutteral Saxon name."

"True. Quite true." Aurelius smiled. "That is what I meant by Arthur slowing the tide."

Rhun sat back. He did not like to be told their cause was futile. But perhaps that was not what Aurelius was saying. He might mean only that Arthur and his Companions had served their purpose, that this truce was a beginning of what the future would be—a merging of Saxon and British, rather than a continual struggle between them.

Then he remembered Eastra. What would she make of his comments? Her face was expressionless, but he could sense her turmoil. Regret stabbed through him. He should not speak so coldly of her people in front of her.

Suddenly, Calida giggled. Rhun looked around and saw Bridei lean away from the young woman, trying to look innocent. But Calida's face was flushed and glowing, and it was obvious Bridei had been saying teasing, flirtatious things to her. Aurelius cleared his throat. "I think it is time for the ladies to retire." He looked to his wife, Vesperia. She rose and motioned to her daughters. Eastra also rose. She gave Rhun an uncertain look, then followed the other women out.

Aurelius gave a guffaw. "Bridei ap Maelgwn, you sly, cunning-faced rogue! Keep away from my daughter!"

Bridei grinned. "Merely some harmless flirting. It might put a little flush in her cheeks and help inspire some wealthy merchant to ask for her hand."

Aurelius laughed loudly, and Rhun heaved a sigh of relief.

Eastra sat down on the bed and began to pull the pins out of her hair. A knock sounded at the door. She called out, "come in." Expecting Skena, she was surprised to see Calida slip through the doorway.

The young woman stood there, her faced flushed and her eyes bright. "I'm sorry to disturb you this late, but I wanted to speak to you alone." Eastra regarded her with curiosity. Calida took a deep breath. "I wanted to ask about the dark-haired man, Bridei. He is not your patron, is he?"

"Patron?" Eastra stared blankly, then finally figured out what the young woman meant. "Oh, no."

Calida smiled, then came to sit on the bed beside her. "Then tell me about him. Does he have a lady or a wife back in his homeland?"

"I don't think so."

"And he stands high in favor with Britain's *Dux Bellorum?*"

Again, Eastra was at a loss. Finally, she grasped the term. "Oh, you mean Arthur. Aye, Arthur appears to regard him well. Otherwise he would not have trusted him with guarding a hos . . ." Eastra wanted to clap her hand over her mouth. The fact that she was a hostage was obviously a sensitive matter, and she did not want to betray Rhun's trust. "That is, Arthur must think highly of Bridei if he sends him to visit your father."

Calida nodded eagerly. "That is what I mean. My father must approve of Bridei—if he is Arthur's man."

Eastra wondered what she was getting at. "Why does it matter if your father approves of Bridei?"

Calida rose abruptly and began to pace. "Because if Bridei asked for my hand, my father would not refuse him."

"If Bridei . . ." Eastra stared. "But you've barely met him!"

"Yet he cares for me, I can tell." Calida gave a soft sigh.

She did not know whether to be alarmed or amused. The foolish young woman obviously thought Bridei's casual flirting meant much more. She gave Calida a stern look. "Now, look here, you don't even know Bridei. Although I don't know him well either, I am acquainted with his kind. That sort of man bestows his smiles and fond glances on nearly every comely woman he meets. It means nothing, merely that he finds you attractive. It certainly does not mean he is going to offer for you. Indeed, I doubt very much Bridei is looking for a wife."

"How would you know?" Calida said pettishly. "You are with his brother anyway, and a whore. How would you know what he thinks?"

Eastra gritted her teeth, wanting to tell this young woman she was not a whore but a princess, and that as such she did not have to waste her time giving advice to spoiled Roman brats! But remembering Rhun and his worries, she answered sweetly, "Well, since you have no regard for my opinion, perhaps you should seek out your own bedchamber like a virtuous and dutiful daughter."

Calida's face flushed and she flounced out of the room. Eastra sighed. As long as she was around men, playing the role of Rhun's leman would not bother her, but with women it was another matter. But why should she care what Calida thought? The girl was naive and foolish.

She turned her attention back to unsnarling her hair with

a fine-toothed bronze comb that had the design of a sort of half-naked woman on the handle.

"What were you thinking?" Rhun demanded as he and Bridei followed a servant through the outdoor peristyle to the sleeping quarters. "Flirting with the daughter of our ally—sometimes I think you have sawdust where your brains should be!"

"There was no harm done. She'll forget me in a few days anyway."

"That's not the point! You should be thinking of Arthur's business here in Londinium, not making eyes at young women!"

"I see no reason I cannot do both things," Bridei said stubbornly. "Do you think Aurelius took offense? Nay, he did not. He probably wishes I could be around the next time he invites an appropriate suitor to his house so I could tease his whey-faced daughter and make her flush as prettily as she did tonight. Women blossom with a little attention, and that maid is about to wither on the vine."

The servant stopped in front of a door and nodded to Rhun. "This is your lady's bedchamber."

Rhun looked at the closed door and said, "I'm not quite ready to retire yet. I think I will join my brother for a time."

"As you wish." The servant led them farther down the covered outdoor corridor to another bedchamber. There, he offered to fetch them some wine. Rhun declined the offer, and the man bowed and left them.

"Eastra's supposed to be your leman," Bridei said smirkingly as they entered the room. "Everyone will think it odd if you don't share her bed."

"No one will know except the servants." Rhun regarded the one narrow bed. "I'll take the floor. It should be warm enough in this place. Jesu, did you ever see such a waste of fuel? And it's summer, even. Aurelius must be as wealthy as Croesus to afford to keep lamps and braziers lit in every room!"

Bridei crossed to where their saddle packs lay on the tiled floor. "You've endured the life of a rough army camp so long, you've forgotten how civilized people live. I must say I admire Aurelius's way of life. I could easily get used to it." He dug into his pack and pulled out a dark blue cloak. "But you won't have cause to sleep on the floor anyway, brother. I'm going out." He wrapped the garment around himself.

"Where?"

"I have some business to attend to."

"More spying for Arthur?"

"Hardly. I've done my duty for tonight." Bridei grinned broadly. "My next assignation will be all for pleasure."

"A woman—you're going to meet a woman!"

"Precisely."

Rhun had a disturbing thought. "Not Calida. Surely you're not that foolish."

"Nay, not Calida. I've never favored simpering young maids. You should know I prefer my women experienced. They're more interesting that way. I get bored with bedplay soon enough. I want someone I can talk to."

"And you know someone here in Londinium?"

Bridei raised his dark brows. "I know several."

Rhun shook his head.

After his brother left, Rhun began to undress. He'd taken off his tunic when there was a knock at the door. Thinking that it was a servant, he quickly crossed the chamber and opened the door.

Eastra stood there. She had taken down her hair, but she still wore the stola. Her gaze took in his face, then traveled down his body. Rhun didn't speak. He couldn't. There was something in the way she looked at him. Worshipful. Adoring. He'd never had a woman regard him quite like that before, and he was acutely conscious of his naked torso. Indeed, it was almost as if she had run her fingers down his chest, the way her gaze affected him, raising goose bumps on his skin and making his nipples tighten.

She jerked her gaze back to his face and blushed. "Oh," she said. "I didn't mean to bother you if you were preparing to bed." He didn't answer, merely shook his head. She glanced at him expectantly. "May I . . . come in?"

He moved aside so she could enter. He half wanted to grab his tunic from the bed and cover himself. But then he realized such an action might embarrass her, make her think he had been offended by her staring. Besides, it was ridiculous to worry about his lack of clothing. She'd undoubtedly seen naked men before, living in Cerdic's household. Instead, in a breathless voice, he said, "I don't have anything to offer you. Would you like me to send for some wine?"

She shook her head. "I came here to tell you . . ." Her voice trailed off. She took a deep breath, turned, and paced across the room.

He could sense her turmoil, a kind of fear. "What's wrong?" He approached her. "Has something happened?"

She turned around and nodded, then hesitated again.

"What is it?" She was obviously upset. He wanted to comfort her. The urge to reach out for her and pull her into his arms, to cradle her against his chest as he had years ago, was nearly impossible to resist. He almost gave in to the urge.

Then she spoke. "Calida, Aurelius's daughter, she came to my room, asking questions about Bridei. She seems to think he might ask to wed with her."

He frowned. This was not what he had expected. It did not exactly explain the look of fear he'd seen in her eyes, her hesitation. Was she worried Aurelius would be angered that Bridei had charmed his daughter, perhaps led her to believe his intentions were different than they were?

"I spoke with Bridei on the matter myself," he answered. "I don't think there will be trouble. Aurelius chided Bridei about flirting with Calida, but he seemed good-natured and reasonable about it. And if Bridei does not take the matter any further—which he's assured me he will not do—then outside of Calida's disappointment, I don't think there's been any harm done."

"I'm glad to hear that." But she did not seem relieved. He could sense the tension in her body. Some instinct told him the matter of Calida and Bridei was not the reason she had come.

He moved closer. "What is it? What's wrong?" She gave him a helpless look. That was all it took. He went to her and gathered her in his arms. "All is well," he murmured, "I will not let anything happen. No one harm you." Despite the warnings in his head, his hand crept up to smooth her hair, feeling the delightful softness.

She melted into his arms. He gave a gasp at the feel of her slim body against his bare chest. With effort, he struggled to think of things to say to reassure her. He was vaguely aware he should find out what was wrong, why she was afraid. But it was hard to think. His being was flooded with such wondrous sensations. Such urgent sensations.

He moved his fingers to her face, cupping her delicate chin, then stroking the impossibly smooth, soft skin of her cheek. She shifted in his arms, moving so she could raise her head to look at him. The small change meant her breasts were pressed against his chest. He looked down at her, at her beautiful face, her moist, pink, tempting lips. He bent his head . . .

A sudden sound outside the door froze him inches away from her lips. He went still, listening. Footsteps. Light. Careful. They paused right outside the door.

He straightened and they both waited, breathless. A servant would surely knock. But the person seemed to simply be standing there, waiting. Rhun's mind shifted through the possibilities. An assassin, listening to see if he were asleep. Bridei, returning early and not certain if he should burst in, what he might interrupt. At the thought, he released Eastra and moved away from her.

Then, as quietly and surreptitiously as they had approached, the footsteps retreated. Rhun exhaled the breath he had been holding. "They're gone," he said.

Eastra nodded. "Maybe it was Calida," she said, "come to see Bridei. Then she lost her nerve."

"Aye," he said. He took another step back. What if it had been an assassin rather than a lovesick maid? What if the killer had come a few moments later, when they were kissing, when he was too lost to be aware of anything but Eastra? The thought chilled him, reminded him of the dangers they faced—and the power of this woman to so enrapture him that he was oblivious to everything else.

"I'll take you back to your bedchamber," he said. "Then lock the door behind you. I'll keep watch outside the door."

Her eyes widened. "You think someone would try to harm me? Us?"

He shook his head. "I don't know. But I promise to stand guard and make certain you are safe."

"But . . ." Her eyes were pleading. "Could you not keep watch in my room?" She looked around. "Or I could stay here until Bridei returns."

"Nay. You're too great a distraction. If I'm going to protect you, I must keep my wits about me." He smiled at her, trying to soften the refusal.

She gave him a desperate look. "I'm sure it was Calida we heard. I even think I smelled her perfume."

"Maybe," he said. "But we can't take that chance."

Six

Rhun woke to see Bridei standing by the bed. Although he had waited outside Eastra's door for a time the night before, he had finally made certain that her door was securely barred, then returned to his own bedchamber and gone to sleep. Seeing his brother's rumpled clothing and bloodshot eyes, he asked, "Rough night?"

Bridei grunted as he pulled off his tunic. "Not so bad. Just didn't get much sleep."

Rhun sat up and sniffed. "Jesu, what's that smell? Wine and something else." He sniffed again, trying to discern the source of the exotic odor.

"Regina does get a bit carried away with the perfume. Says in her business it's essential. A lot of her patrons aren't very fragrant in their persons."

"Ah, so Regina is her name."

Bridei shook his head. "Nay, she's just a friend. We didn't even go to bed, just sat up talking all night."

"Talking? About what?"

"About Arthur and the Saxons . . . and the Jutes and the Irish and everyone else who seems to want a piece of Britain these days. Learned quite a bit, I might say. Rather more than Aurelius had to tell us."

"So?"

"She thinks the Saxons may be planning to join up with the Picts in the north, and maybe the Irish as well—that

Cerdic is using this truce as an opportunity to make alliances so when he comes at us again, he will be even stronger."

"By the Light! That could be disastrous!" Rhun got out of bed and began to dress. "Why does she think this? Did she hear it from one of her customers?"

"Perhaps. She will not divulge her sources."

"But you trust her?" Rhun demanded.

"Aye, I do. The women who work for her are often former slaves. Having either escaped or been freed somehow, they seek to be their own mistresses and to earn their own bread. They make the most formidable group of spies a man could ask for. They listen to the patrons when they are in their cups, and they overhear a great deal."

Rhun sat on the bed and jerked on one of his boots. "I can't believe Cerdic would plan something so treacherous." He leaned back thoughtfully as he put on his other boot. "I wonder if Eastra knows any of this."

"Probably not. Indeed, I suspect only Cerdic's closest advisers are aware of his plans."

"But if he betrays Arthur, then Eastra will be . . ."

"Useless as a hostage," Bridei finished for him. "Arthur is not a brutal, vindictive man. Even if Cerdic breaks the truce, Arthur would not order Eastra's death. Now, if something happened to Mordred, that would be a different matter. But I believe Cerdic is too clever for that. He is using this truce and the exchange of hostages to buy time, time to sort out this alliance before he goes out on the war trail once again."

Rhun nodded. "Will you take this information to Arthur?"

"I'll send a message."

"Would it not be better to go yourself and explain things to Arthur?"

Bridei cocked his head. "Are you trying to get rid of me, brother?" He smiled. "That would be convenient, wouldn't it? You would be alone with Eastra, with no one to see when your fine resolve weakens and you—"

"That's not what I meant!" Rhun exclaimed. "I merely thought you should take this information to Arthur yourself. After all, it's a touchy business. What if someone intercepts your message?"

"It will mean nothing to them. I'll send it in code."

Rhun shook his head. "Arthur charged you with this mission to Londinium. I think it's irresponsible of you not to carry your news to him directly."

"He also charged me with helping guard our hostage on the journey to Gwynedd."

"But that was before he knew Eastra spoke Briton," Rhun argued. "Since we don't need you to translate, there's no real purpose in your accompanying us."

"Ah, but I have a fancy to go home to Gwynedd to see my mother anyway, and this journey gives me an excuse."

Rhun clenched his jaw. If he tried to argue any more, his brother would only grow more convinced than ever he wanted to be alone with Eastra. And, in truth, he did *not* want that. The more people around them, the better. He thought about the night before, how close he had come to kissing Eastra . . . and more, so much more. Fortunately, the sound of footsteps had interrupted them.

"All right," he said brusquely, "I accept your decision to accompany us. When do you think we can leave Londinium? Today?"

Bridei sat down on the bed and began to remove his boots. "Today I'm going to sleep. By tomorrow, after I've talked to a few more people, perhaps we can set off. In the meantime, why don't you take Eastra to the market and see the sights."

"This is not a pleasure trip."

"But we did tell Eastra our reason for coming to Londinium was to purchase goods to take back to Gwynedd. So unless you want her to think we lied to her, you'd best go out and buy a few things. If you think wine is too difficult to transport, then at least purchase some cloth goods for Rhiannon." Bridei fetched his saddle pack and dug out a leather pouch. "Here," he said, throwing the pouch to Rhun. "There's plenty of gold in there, enough to buy a bauble or two for Eastra as well as some silks and linens for Rhiannon."

"What do I know of cloth goods?" Rhun grumbled.

Bridei shrugged. "Nothing. You'll have to ask Eastra's aid, I guess." He stretched out on the bed and closed his eyes. "Unless you can think of something else to buy to make our story plausible."

Rhun glared at his brother. Bridei was always spinning tales and getting *him* tangled up in them. But it was true they had to give Eastra some story. Although he mostly trusted her, it was probably best if she did not know they were in Londinium to get news of her uncle's plans.

He took a deep breath, again remembering the night before. From now on, he'd have to be more on his guard. Last night he'd been convinced Eastra desired him, that she wanted him as much as he'd wanted her. But did her eagerness represent her true feelings for him, or was it an attempt to seduce him so she could learn his secrets?

Nay, he would not believe that of her. She was sweet and guileless, and her warm feelings for him were based on the fact he had saved her life all those years ago. She was not a treacherous spy, but a naive young woman who did not really understand the effect she had on men. Although she'd seemed to want him to kiss her, she likely had the same silly daydreams about him Calida had for Bridei. By the Saints, he was fortunate the footsteps in the hall had broken the spell and kept him from doing something dishonorable! He took a deep breath. And today he would be subject to the same temptations—damn Bridei!

He glanced at his reflection in the polished bronze mirror on the wall and stroked his jaw, trying to decide whether it was necessary to shave. At least he was not a black-bearded man like Bridei. He decided the gold stubble was tolerable. Besides, having a scratchy jaw was good reason not to let Eastra get too close. After last night, he realized he needed all the incentive possible to make certain he kept his distance.

A servant came to tidy the room. Rhun pointed to Bridei's prone form on the bed and told the woman to come back later. Then he asked the servant where he might find his host and was told Aurelius had gone down to the docks to see about unloading a ship that had just come in from Less Britain. Rhun decided to fetch Eastra and leave immediately for the market.

He knocked on Eastra's door, and she came to meet him in a Saxon-style gown of buttery yellow. She bid him enter, then looked down at herself. "Do I look all right? I'm not comfortable in the Roman stola, yet I fear Lady Aurelius will think ill of me if I wear my plain traveling gunna."

"You look glorious." He smiled at her. "Like a golden iris in a mountain meadow. No man in the market will be able to tear his gaze away from you."

"Is that where we're going—the market?"

Rhun nodded. "I told you we must buy some supplies for my father's household. I'm going to fetch our escort from the stables or wherever they found to sleep. You can wait in the garden while we saddle the horses."

Rhun left her while he went to get the other men. Eastra walked down the garden pathways, admiring the flowers and herbs, the splash of water in a manmade stone pool with a bronze statue of a plump, naked little boy standing in the center. Closing her eyes, she inhaled deeply. As the sweet scents of lavender and rose filled her senses, memories of the night before rushed over her. Rhun, his hair gilded gold in the torchlight, his strong neck and broad, well-muscled chest making him look like a warrior out of one of the legends.

At the sight of him, she'd forgotten that she'd come to tell him about her conversation with Skena. All words had fled from her mouth and she could only mumble and stare. And then when she did speak, she'd told him about Calida instead of Skena. Somehow she could not bear the thought of making him angry, as she was afraid he would be if he knew she had revealed their identity to a slave.

She shook her head, remembering. It made her ache to think of how he had looked. And the expression in his dark blue eyes—a beguiling mixture of hunger and tenderness . . .

"Dreaming of your lover?" a scornful voice said behind her. Eastra whirled around to see Skena. The slave girl cocked a dark brow. "I know he did not share your bedchamber last night. Does that mean you quarreled?"

"Nay, we did not quarrel," Eastra protested.

"Huh. You will."

"This a beautiful place," Eastra said, changing the subject.

"A foolish waste of time. There isn't a single thing growing here man or beast could eat."

"There are a few herbs," Eastra pointed out. "Some plants that can be used for seasoning food, or for healing— chamomile, basil, sage."

"Luxuries," said Skena contemptuously. "The Britons are soft and weak. I don't see why your people have not wiped them out by now."

"Few Britons live like this," Eastra answered. "I think Aurelius is more Roman than British anyway."

"You would defend your people's enemies?"

Eastra shook her head. "I don't share your hatred of the Britons. In fact, my goal is to have my people and theirs live alongside each other."

"That's not possible," Skena said in a cold voice. "The Saxons and Britons are different races. They will never be able to forget their hatred of each other and live in peace."

Eastra approached the herb patch and bent down to pluck a sprig of mint. She crushed the leaves in her fingers and breathed the fresh, pungent scent. Most of her people, the men at least, believed the same as Skena. But that did not mean they were right. What if Saxon and Briton intermarried and had children that were neither one race nor the other, but both? "I refuse to give up," she said loudly. "I will not be defeated, no matter what anyone says."

"Will not be defeated? What do you mean?"

At the sound of Rhun's voice, Eastra whirled. "Oh, I didn't know you were there." She looked around for Skena, wondering how long ago the slave girl had left. Had Rhun seen them talking? His eyes still gazed at her questioningly, and she knew she must answer him. She glanced around, searching desperately for some explanation for her words. "I . . . I was thinking about the weeds in the garden in my uncle's fortress. It's a kitchen garden, nothing like this. But I've always struggled to get rid of the pesky weeds."

It was a stupid lie. She could see by the expression on his face he did not believe her. She started to talk rapidly. "It seems somehow wasteful to grow things simply for their beauty. Except for that small plot over there, I vow there's nothing here that man or beast can eat."

Rhun raised his brows. "I'm surprised you're such a practical woman. I would have thought you would be admiring the splendor of the flowers and all the lovely scents."

She looked at him, feeling embarrassed. She did not want him to think she was an embittered shrew who despised flowers. "I'm not against cultivating plants for their beauty. I merely meant it seemed wasteful for them not to grow any vegetables here. Where do they get their food, anyway?"

"They probably buy it in the market," Rhun answered. "Which is where we must be off to if we mean to catch the best bargains. Come. Our horses should be saddled and ready by now."

He led her down the peristyle, then out a gate into the street. Their escort was waiting for them, fully armed and mounted. Looking at the troop of soldiers, Eastra knew a sinking feeling. She had hoped to have some time alone with Rhun, to encourage him to resume the amorous mood of the night before. Daringly, she said, "Do all those men have to go with us? We'll make a spectacle in the market. Everyone will take note of the fact that I'm a Saxon accompanied by a guard of Britons."

He gazed at her thoughtfully. "There's something in what you say. We would attract less notice by ourselves. But we do need to have some sort of protection. Perhaps they could accompany us to the market. Then we could leave our horses with them while we explore the shops and stalls on foot."

Rhun helped her mount and they set out, the horses' hooves echoing on the crumbling pavement. As they rode along, Rhun pointed out the remains of the Roman part of the city—streets and temples, the sprawling complex of the baths, its once vast pools now filled in with dirt and rubbish, a huge stone archway where swallows nested. Much of the masonry of the old buildings was crumbling away, while other parts had obviously been deliberately knocked down and the stonework taken away to be used in other structures. Here and there among the tumbled stones were newer timber buildings, with signs outside them indicating their purpose—cookshops and cobblers and taverns.

At last they reached the open-air market. Rhun called a halt and dismounted, then engaged in conversation with the dark-eyed, silent man who was the leader of their guard. The man cast a careful glance at Eastra, then nodded. Rhun came to help her dismount and they left their horses with the group of warriors.

Eastra felt a lightening of her mood as they left their guard behind and began to walk among the stalls of the market. This was what she wanted, to be alone with Rhun with no mocking Bridei to spoil his mood, no soldiers to remind him she was his hostage. The market itself was a delight. She gazed in wonder at the dozens of stalls full of luxury goods. Lush furs spilled over a counter, spotted, striped, gray, white, and tawny. Rhun saw her glance at them and took her arm to guide her nearer. "It gets cool in Gwynedd at night. Would you like a fur cloak to warm you?"

Eastra examined a pelt from some sort of spotted cat, admiring the soft, plush texture and the glowing gold and cream and rich brown of the pattern. "In truth, I think fur looks better on the animal than it does on any man or woman. And I own a cloak lined with red squirrel already."

She moved away from the booth and went to the next one, where colored glassware winked and glimmered in the sunlight. "Beautiful, isn't it?" she said to Rhun. "But hardly practical for taking on a journey."

"I can pack it in straw in a stout box," said the man behind the stall counter. "That's how these things were safely carried here from Byzantium."

"Where's that?" Eastra asked.

"Far to the east, on the other side of Rome." Rhun spoke behind her. "It's a vast distance to travel, especially for something so delicate and fragile."

Examining the man's fair hair and blue eyes, Eastra wondered if he were a Saxon. "Are you from Byzantium?" she asked.

"Nay, I'm from Mickelgard. Traders come to the market there from all over the north."

"The world is huge and wide, isn't it?" she mused as she and Rhun moved away.

"Aye, it is," he said. "And yet we fight over the small island of Preton when it is only a tiny, insignificant piece of the world."

"Preton?" she asked.

"That's what my people used to call Britain. The Romans changed the word to Britain."

"You speak of the Romans almost as if they were still your enemies, but many of your people have adopted Roman ways and even Roman speech."

Rhun nodded. "Roman influence is everywhere, but I don't think most of us ever stopped thinking of ourselves as Britons. Men like Aurelius are the exception. They live in cities where trade goods are plentiful, along with the coin to buy them. But most Britons live in the countryside and have gone back to the old ways. They dwell in round timber houses rather than square structures of plaster and stone, and they follow pathways that twist and turn rather than running in straight lines. The Romans adored wealth and luxury and put their faith in laws and rulers. My people care less for the tangible things that a man can touch and hold and more for things of the heart and the spirit."

Eastra frowned, trying to decide what Cerdic cared for. It was not wealth or luxury like the Romans, but neither was it quite the same as what Rhun held dear. Power was not something that could be touched or held in the hand, but it was the thing her uncle coveted above all else.

"Ah, look, there are the drapers' stalls. I must get some cloth goods for my stepmother." Rhun smiled at her. "Would you assist me? I vow, I know nothing about fabric."

"Of course," she said. "Although I'm not skilled at clothmaking myself."

"Is it because you are a princess that you were not required to learn such women's work?"

Eastra shook her head. "Most Saxon women of good family spend much of their time weaving and sewing. But I had learned only a little when I became a slave, and my duties in Gaius's household did not include such things." The familiar shame afflicted her. Would Rhun think less of her because she was not skillful at women's work?

"My stepmother has a passion for sewing and weaving," Rhun said. "As a harpist makes beautiful songs, Rhiannon creates garments that sing with color and life. But in our homeland only flax and wool are available, so I hope to purchase finer materials here. Help me pick out something special for her."

They stopped at a booth where Eastra carefully examined the rolls of fabric. She found most of them to be loosely woven and the colors flat and muddy. She started to move on, but the merchant called out to her, "Wait! I keep the finer goods in the back."

Eastra paused and looked at Rhun. He shrugged, and they waited for the stallkeeper to reappear. "The sunlight damages fabric," the man explained as he came back with several rolls of cloth under his arms. "I keep these hidden away." He spread out the cloth on the counter. "The finest silk from Byzantium." He gestured gracefully to a roll of shimmering green. "Cottons from Alexandria." He motioned to a deep red and rich saffron, then bent to retrieve something from under the counter. "And thread of spun gold to embellish it."

Eastra smoothed the fabric with her fingers, then looked at Rhun. "It's all exquisite. The colors deep and true. I'm certain your stepmother would be pleased."

Rhun nodded and pointed to a piece of pale blue that was half-hidden beneath the red and yellow. "And this, you must have this for yourself. It exactly matches your eyes."

"I told you, I have no skill at needlework."

"No need for that. Rhiannon will be happy to sew a gown for you."

"But she does not even know me. And when I am in her household, I will be a hostage, not a guest."

"She will not care. If I ask her, she will be pleased to make you something."

Eastra touched the blue fabric longingly. It was a beautiful color, much clearer and more pure a shade than the usual blue obtained by dying in woad. "All right," she said. "But I will find a means of repaying you—both of you."

Rhun smiled, making her heart turn over. She thought again how handsome he was. Dazzling as the sun. Strong and powerful as a spear in flight. But beneath the exterior of an assured, virile warrior, he was also gentle and kindhearted.

Rhun paid the merchant and explained to him they would have someone come to pick up their purchase later. As the man wrapped up the fabric in coarse sacking, they moved away from the stall. Eastra said, "Your stepmother must care for you a great deal. Is that not unusual when she has her own son to think of?"

"*Sons,* in fact. I have three other brothers besides Bridei—Gwydion, Mabon, and Beli are their names. And two sisters as well, Elen and Annwyl. But despite her own family, Rhiannon has always had time for me. I went to live with her and my father soon after they were married. My own mother died two years later, so Rhiannon has been like a mother to me since."

"Your mother was not wed to your father?"

"Nay. You might say I was sort of a mistake. But it worked out anyway."

"I don't understand."

Rhun smiled at her. "It's a complicated tale."

"I would like to hear it," she responded, her curiosity piqued.

He nodded. "This is my mother's version of it. My father might have a different one. My mother, Morganna, was wed to one of Maelgwn's captains, and when he was killed in battle, Maelgwn felt sorry for her, plus he was sad himself, because the man was his friend. So he started to go to see her, just to talk. Then one thing led to another and they went to bed. By the time my mother knew she was expecting a babe, Maelgwn was wed to a Roman British princess named Aurora. Morganna thought of telling him she was pregnant, but she didn't want to cause trouble. Then news came that Aurora was expecting as well, and my mother decided to go away and have her babe elsewhere.

"Soon after I was born, word came that Aurora had been delivered early and both she and the babe had died. My mother thought of going to Maelgwn then, but he was beside himself with grief. He loved Aurora dearly and her death nearly destroyed him. He even renounced his kingdom and lived in a priory for several years. In the meantime, my mother raised me and loved me. And finally, when she heard my father was back in the world of the living and fighting to reclaim his lands, she decided to take me to him."

"Why then? Why not before that, when he was grieving for Aurora?"

"I guess she was afraid he would hate me for being alive when his beloved Aurora was dead. The bards still sing tales of the two of them and how passionately he loved her."

"But finally he got over his grief and wed Rhiannon?"

Rhun smiled again. "Not exactly. He married Rhiannon because he needed the dowry of warriors she brought with her. He did not come to love her until later."

"You're right," Eastra said. "It's a strange tale."

"But with a happy ending. My father adores Rhiannon, although perhaps in a different way than he loved his first wife. And she—she knows how to keep him happy and content, which is not easy with a man like my father. They do not call him the 'dragon of the island' without reason. When he is wroth, he is very much like a fire-breathing beast!"

"And yet you grin when you speak of his temper," Eastra pointed out.

Rhun shrugged. "I've learned how to deal with him. And he is never as hard on me as he is on Bridei."

The easy way he spoke about his family aroused an ache in Eastra's chest, the nagging sense of aloneness that had haunted her ever since her mother and brother were killed. Rhun appeared to sense her distress, for he put his hand on her arm and said, "Come, let us explore the rest of the market. The goldsmiths' stalls are over there."

At the first shop, she pointed at a bracelet and necklace set depicting colorful beasts entwined and offset by strips of gold. "These are lovely."

"Irish enamelwork," Rhun said. "They're the best at it that I've ever seen. Even in Rome and Byzantium they do not fashion such remarkable work as this. See how bright the colors are? How lifelike and vivid the dragons and lions and birds appear?"

"Exquisite," Eastra agreed.

"But not for you, are they?"

She shook her head. "I possess too much gold already, and it always seems heavy and clunky to me."

They moved on to another booth, this one featuring ornaments of gold and bronze set with precious stones—emeralds, garnets, pearls, and jet. Eastra examined the pieces on the counter and shook her head. Then, as they were about to leave, something caught her eye. She reached up to touch a necklace hanging on a pole above the counter. It had a delicate copper chain and strung on the chain were glittering blue beads, as pale and transparent as water. "What are they?" Eastra reached up to finger one of the beads.

"Blue faience from Egypt," the merchant replied. He shrugged. "A mere trifle for a fine lady like you. Now these"—he pointed to a neckpiece set with deep red stones arranged on the crimson cloth covering the counter—"these are more worthy of your beauty."

Eastra nodded at the gaudy necklace. Then her gaze returned to the chain of glass beads.

"She will take that one," Rhun said decisively, pointing to the hanging necklace.

"But, sir," the merchant argued, "I sell necklaces like that to the whores of the city. Your lady deserves much better. Perhaps the garnet bracelet?"

Rhun shook his head. "She likes this one and she will have it. How much?" The small, swarthy merchant fixed Rhun with eyes as dark and glittering as the jet beads in one of his necklaces. "And don't think to cheat me," Rhun warned. "You've already said you sell them to the working women of Londinium. They cannot be too dear."

"Only two sestres," the man replied. "But since it is so little, why not also consider purchasing something else?" He gave Eastra a resentful look. "Perhaps your mother or sister would appreciate one of these other pieces."

"My stepmother cares little for jewels, and my sisters have a whole chest of them already." Rhun dropped two coins on the counter and gave the merchant an impatient look.

Sighing, the man undid the necklace from the pole and brought it down to hand to Eastra.

"Here, let me," Rhun said. He moved behind her and deftly fastened the clasp. Then he grasped her shoulders and turned her around. "Perfect," he said. He was looking not at the necklace, but at her face.

Gazing at his radiant smile, Eastra felt her insides turn liquid. He was so close. He was touching her, his big, strong fingers on her upper arms, the burning warmth of them seeping through the fabric of her gunna. His eyes were so deep and blue, like gentians, and the sunlight made the stubble on his jaw glint golden. He looked so male and beautiful and alive. She wanted to dissolve into him.

She heard him take a deep breath. He stepped back and his hands fell away from her arms. "Come," he said huskily. "There are many more shops to see."

The next stall carried weapons—enamel-handled daggers, war axes, lances, and swords. Rhun bought two knives, one with an enameled hilt and one decorated with silver wire. "For my little brothers," he said. He drew Eastra past the stall selling farm implements and tools, but stopped at one filled with baskets and other items woven of reeds. "I should get some of these for Rhiannon. They are light enough to carry easily and the workmanship appears excellent." He picked out several baskets and trays and paid the merchant, telling him as he had the others that a man would be by to fetch their purchases.

At the cobbler's booth, he bought two pairs of dainty shoes. "For my sisters," he said. "They're both small like Rhiannon. I will give Annwyl the red pair, to match her hair. Elen, the blue. She is dark like Bridei."

"And your brothers—what do they look like?" she asked.

"Beli has red hair like Rhiannon. Mabon and Gwydion look rather like Bridei, although I think they will be taller."

He grinned. "But don't mention that to Bridei. He can be sensitive about his height."

"But he's not small. He's taller than I, and I'm considered tall for a woman. For that matter, I know many warriors shorter than he."

"Ah, but they do not have a father and a brother who are considered giants," Rhun answered. "I think Bridei feels he has always lived in my shadow, and it does not help that I stand a handspan higher than he does."

"For all your bickering, you and Bridei still seem to care for each other."

"He is my brother," Rhun answered. "Whatever I think of his actions, he is still my blood kin."

Eastra nodded, thinking of Cerdic. She owed her uncle a great deal, and she certainly did not want to see him defeated. But she did want all this warring to cease. And she wanted Rhun. The more she was around him, the more she knew she loved him—and would do nearly anything to make him love her back.

They visited a few more shops, then started toward the end of the market area. A crowd was gathered there, and Eastra approached with curiosity. When she had gone a few steps, Rhun grabbed her arm. "Nay, I don't think you should see this."

"What? What is it?"

Rhun grimaced. "The slavers."

A chill went through Eastra, but she lifted her chin. "I *want* to see. I'm not afraid."

Rhun regarded her dubiously. "It's ugly and crude, not a sight for a woman."

"I don't care." She began to push her way through the crowd. If he had asked, she would not have been able to explain why observing the slave market was so important to her. Perhaps she wanted to know what horrors she had escaped, or see the plight of those who were not so fortunate.

A group of red-haired men were crowded onto a platform. They were shackled together, their shoulders slumped and their heads down. The slavemaster cracked his whip and one of the men glanced up. His blue-green eyes gleamed with a hatred so intense Eastra could feel it from where she stood, twenty paces away.

"They're Irish, by the looks of it," Rhun said behind her.

Eastra took a deep, choking breath. "And does it not grieve you to see them like this?"

"Aye, it does, but there is naught I can do."

"You could purchase them and set them free!"

"Aye, and then they would probably return someday to slit the throat of one of my countrymen. These men are prisoners of war. Selling them into slavery is the only way to keep them from joining back up with their own people and returning to harass our coasts in the future."

"But it's so cruel! I think death would be better."

"I agree with you. That's why when my father captures prisoners, he now gives them a choice—death or slavery."

Eastra shook her head and moved away from the Irishmen. She was looking down, deep in thought, when she felt Rhun pulling on her arm. She looked up in time to see a group of women gathered on another platform. Their breasts were bare; the rest of their attire so skimpy as to be indecent. She sucked in her breath.

"Come." There was a note of desperation in Rhun's voice. "This is not something you should see."

Eastra set her feet. "Why are they half naked?" she asked grimly.

Rhun let out his breath in a sigh. "They are being sold as bedslaves. Come away. Surely you do not want to see these women shamed."

She observed them carefully. None of them looked like Saxons. Several of them had bronze-colored skin and black eyes. One was near as dark as the Nubian they had seen the day before. In the front was a woman with reddish brown hair and speckled skin like a plover's egg. Compared to the rest of her exposed skin, her breasts looked very

white and full, and as Eastra watched, she saw milk trick-
ling from her nipples.

The slaver stepped forward and grasped the woman's
arm. "And here we have a fine young wet nurse." He
pushed her toward the crowd, then reached to squeeze her
breast. Bluish pale milk squirted out.

Someone laughed. "Yea, she is ripe and ready to give
suck."

Another man guffawed. "I would not mind a taste of
that myself. Why waste it all on a squalling brat?"

The man squeezed the woman's breast again to express
another gleaming stream. Eastra saw the woman wince, but
whether from pain or humiliation she could not tell. Eastra
closed her eyes, feeling sick. The slaver was handling the
woman as if she were a piece of livestock. The queasy
feeling built inside her.

She felt Rhun grasp her arm firmly. "Come away from
here," he murmured. "It's not seemly."

As he hustled her away from the slave market, Eastra
felt her dismay turn to anger. Why did Rhun want so badly
to get her away from there? Was he trying to protect her—
or himself? Was he ashamed of the way his people treated
that unfortunate woman? Or did the way the woman was
being treated remind him too vividly that Eastra herself
had once been a slave?

When they reached the edge of the market, Eastra jerked
out of his grasp and faced him. She was nearly hysterical
with impotent fury and remembered shame. All she could
think of was the way Cerdic's house carls had looked at
her when they found out she had been a slave. There was
distaste in their expressions, but also a lewd interest, as if
they were imagining her as a helpless captive at the whim
of her master.

"Aye, your father is right to offer his captives the choice
of death rather than slavery." She spit the words at him.
"For ever after, a slave is marked. A thing to be pitied and
held in contempt."

"Eastra, I'm sorry." Rhun's eyes were anguished. "I

didn't want you to see that. That's why I begged you to come away."

"Ah, but if I had not been there, would you not have gone to see? Would you not have enjoyed watching the women, naked and helpless?"

"Nay, nay," he whispered. "I think it's an abomination."

"Yet your people have slaves!" she cried. "You're no different than any of them!" She was sobbing now, her face streaked with tears. Her throat so convulsed with pain she could scarce get the words out.

He grabbed her suddenly and held her close. Her face was crushed against his chest; his big, strong arms gripped her tightly. "Oh, Eastra, I'm sorry, so sorry you had to suffer such torment and degradation. I have thought sometimes that it might have been better if I had not saved you, if you had perished in the flames, forever innocent and pure."

She could not hold back now. His words had touched the raw wound inside her. Shoving him away with all her might, she shouted at him. "Aye, then I would not be soiled in your eyes—a contemptible slave girl! Although I have told you otherwise, I know you think my master bedded me, that I am a whore in truth! That's why you shy away from me and avoid my gaze! You're like all the others!"

He looked at her as if she had struck him. She swallowed, wondering if she had gone too far, if he would erupt with anger to match her own. But his voice when he spoke was tense and sorrowful. "Forgive me. I didn't mean to hurt you. I want nothing more than for you to be safe. From me and from every man." He took a ravaged breath, then reached out. His big fingers grasped one of her braids and stroked it, softly, lovingly. "I see the pain inside you and it troubles me. But it does not diminish . . . what I feel for you. If only you were not my hostage and kin of my enemy, I would love you in a heartbeat. I would make you mine . . . forever."

Gazing at his intent, rapt face, she felt her anger dissolve and fall away. This man *was* different than the others. When he looked at her, he did not see a slave; he saw into her soul. She gave a little cry and reached out for him. He gathered her into his arms; his mouth came down on hers. It was far beyond tenderness. It was exquisite shimmering need. Liquid fire. Their bodies and souls as one. Rapture.

His fingers were tangled in her hair. His mouth bonded to hers. He offered her everything—his warmth, his strength, his potent masculinity. She was drowning in it, her senses awash with wonder. She had always known it would be like this . . . always known . . .

He threw her away from him so rapidly she fell. Dizzy, confused, she struggled to her feet. By then, the men were upon them, writhing shadows. The flash of a sword. Rhun, a whirling mass of fury and power. She saw him cut one man down. Then another. Still they came at him—slowly, warily, trying to avoid the lightning strike of his blade.

But he was invincible. The last man gave a cry and fled. Someone lying on the ground gave a rattling groan. Rhun grabbed her. He half carried her, his sword in his other hand.

He dragged her back to the market and the crowd closed around them. She heard him panting and the rapid thud of her own pulse in her ears. Confused, disoriented, she finally looked at him. A stranger—a berserker warrior from the old legends, his blue eyes bright as flames, his dark gold hair wild around his face, his jaw clenched in a grim, vicious mask.

"Sweet Jesu," he breathed. "That was close." He shook as head, as if shaking off a terrifying dream. Then his grip relaxed and he looked around. "Walk ahead of me," he said. "I don't think anyone would attack us here, but I can't be sure."

Seven

They retraced their steps through the market. It was very crowded and few people took note of them. Those who did quickly backed away at seeing a grim-faced warrior with his bloodied sword. As Rhun gently but firmly guided her along, his left hand on her waist, Eastra's mind whirled. In the space of a few heartbeats, she'd seen two very different sides of this man—the tender lover who had made her half swoon, and the ferocious warrior who had fought off six men by himself. It was hard for her to reconcile the two beings into one.

But as her shock faded, it was replaced by a kind of elation. For a brief moment, she'd experienced his desire and longing. He did care for her, she was certain. She licked her lips, remembering the taste of him. And if they had not been interrupted, there would have been more. Much more. She could imagine him touching her body, those callused warrior's hands moving over her skin with keen finesse. Her nipples peaked at the thought. She'd never wanted a man like this, with her whole, throbbing being. But now he was tense with caution. She wondered when she would ever have a chance to be alone with him again, to experience that magic when they had looked into each other's eyes and everything else vanished. She suppressed a sigh.

Eastra walked ahead of him, her pale hair like a beacon.

Rhun glanced around for the dozenth time, wondering if they were being watched. Someone had seen them leave the market to snatch a moment alone. In that moment, they had struck.

He took a deep breath. The attack had been well thought out. They had converged on them when he was most vulnerable, his every sense and faculty consumed by the woman in his arms. It was terrifying to consider what might have happened if they had waited a few moments longer to attack. In another second his hands would have been cupping Eastra's breasts, and he would not have been able to move so quickly. In another second the throbbing heat in his loins would have erased all rational thought from his mind. But his enemy had been impatient, and so he had survived. He had caught a glimpse of movement from the corner of his eye, and instinct had taken over from there.

He wondered what they would have done if he had not pulled himself together in time. Would they have killed him where he stood and then grabbed Eastra? She had not been touched, but that might be because he had pushed her behind him and they would have had to kill him to get to her. If they had succeeded, would she have been killed also, or captured? Was it possible she was the reason for the attack?

The questions gnawed at him. He needed to know what enemy he faced. Had Saxon spies discovered Eastra was in Londinium and sought to rescue her? Or did some other unknown enemy seek to kill him? Was Eastra merely a hapless bystander, or the goal of the attack?

They reached their escort. The men were sprawled out over a grassy open area playing knucklebones, the horses nearby, still saddled and bridled, their tails swishing at flies. The men got to their feet as they saw him, and Amlawdd saluted. Abruptly, his gaze went to Rhun's drawn sword. "Trouble?" he asked.

Rhun nodded. "We were attacked on the other side of

the market. I fought them off, but I have no desire to linger here."

Amlawdd nodded, then gestured toward the market. "Didn't you buy anything?"

"Oh, I near forgot," Rhun said. "Send Bryn and Merddin to fetch our purchases. Tell them to go to the second draper's stall. Also to the cobbler's on the far end, and to the man selling basketwork nearby. Have them take a pack-horse."

Amlawdd nodded. He gave the two men their orders, while the others fetched the other horses. Rhun wiped his sword on the grass and sheathed it. He motioned to his stallion, Cadal, now stamping and pacing. "You will ride with me, Eastra. If we are bothered further, I will be better able to protect you that way." As he grasped her slender waist to help her up, a lingering wave of regret swept through him. Although part of him shuddered at the thought of what would have happened if they had been left alone a few moments longer, another part of him still throbbed with yearning at the loss of that instant when they were entwined in each other's arms. If a man had to die, why not in the midst of the most enthralling embrace he had ever experienced?

They rode quickly through the city streets. When they reached Aurelius's house, Rhun slid off Cadal and quickly helped Eastra down. "I'm going to take you to the bed-chamber where you slept last night. I want you to gather up your things quickly. We're leaving Londinium to-night."

Her eyes were wide. "Do you expect another attack?"

"I don't know, but I'm not going stay here. Once we are on the road with our escort arrayed around us, I'll feel much more comfortable."

He spoke to the porter at the gate. The man let them in; then Rhun led Eastra through the garden toward the guest wing. When they reached the door of her bedchamber, he paused. "I'm sorry the day ended like this. I cautioned

Bridei before we even arrived in Londinium that this was not a pleasure trip. Then I forgot my own warning."

She smiled suddenly. "But for a while it was wonderful, was it not?"

His breath caught in his throat. He wanted to kiss her, to hold her in his arms once again. But he dared not. If he gave in to that intense, agonizing urge, they would be inside the room and sprawled on the bed in no time. He must remember his duty. And he must remember he had very nearly been killed a short while ago. "I must go," he answered thickly. He opened the door for her. She nodded and went in.

Rhun immediately went to the bedchamber where he had spent the night. If he had expected to find Bridei still sleeping it off, he was disappointed. There was no sign of his brother. Rhun quickly packed up his things in his saddle pack, then did the same with Bridei's belongings. Dumping the packs outside the door, he set out to find his brother.

"There you are."

Bridei looked up as Rhun entered Aurelius's atrium. He raised his dark brows. "What do you need me for, brother? I thought you would be content with Eastra's company for the rest of the day."

"She and I were just attacked," Rhun said bluntly. "Outside the market. Six men. I barely fought them off."

"By the Light!" Aurelius exclaimed, sitting up rapidly. "Where was your escort?"

"Not with them at the time, apparently." A hint of a smile curled Bridei's mouth.

Rhun glared at him. "We could hardly go tramping through the market with a full complement of warriors."

"Were the attackers Saxon or Briton?" Aurelius asked.

"Briton. But that does not mean anything here in Londinium, where everyone's loyalties are uncertain." Rhun grimaced. "They might well be working for the Saxons. They looked like the sort of base wretches who would hire themselves out to anyone who paid them well."

Aurelius frowned. "It seems like a lot of trouble to go to in order to kill one of Arthur's spies."

Rhun nodded. He thought the same thing, but he could hardly discuss his concern that the attackers were trying to abduct Eastra. Aurelius thought she was nothing more than his concubine. "Whatever their purpose," Rhun said, "I want to leave the city tonight."

"Now? But I have not visited my other contacts," Bridei responded.

"Well, you certainly had time enough—if you were not so busy flirting with the women and enjoying your wine." He motioned with his head toward the jeweled cup in Bridei's hand. "I doubt you'll learn anything more anyway, and I'm eager to leave this place before something else happens. Londinium makes me uneasy. With Saxon and Briton living side by side, it makes it difficult to know who is your enemy and who is not."

Aurelius rose. "I think your brother is right," he said to Bridei. "Someone obviously knows of your mission here. It might be dangerous to stay longer."

Bridei rose and set his wine cup on the table near the couch. "All right. Let me go pack my things."

"Already done," Rhun said. "And I met a servant in the hall and asked him to take our packs out to the stables. Now all I need to do is fetch Eastra and we can go."

Aurelius bowed to them. "Give my greetings to Artorius. And tell him that I'm sorry that his envoy met with trouble while visiting me. Assure him that I and many of the merchants of Londinium are cheering on his attempts to rout the Saxon seawolves from this land."

Rhun bowed back. "Thank you for your hospitality, Aurelius. I will give your regards to our commander."

Bridei also said his farewells. Then the two men left the atrium. "So what do you really think?" Bridei asked as soon as they were alone. "Do you think those men who attacked you were trying to free Eastra, or possibly take her for a hostage themselves to use as a bargaining tool against Arthur?"

"I don't know what to think," Rhun said. "Did you not feel that perhaps Aurelius was a little eager to get us out of his house?"

"Probably. The man wants no trouble intruding on his comfortable life, and once you told him your tale, it was clear we represented exactly the sort of complication he wishes to avoid."

"Do you think he could have sent the attackers?" Rhun asked.

Bridei shrugged. "If he meant to be rid of us, why not have us murdered in our beds? Or feed us poisoned wine as we supped with him?"

"Because that sort of thing would gain him dangerous attention. Having me attacked when I am far away from his house and in a public area is much more subtle and clever."

"But if you were killed, he would still have to be rid of me, or else I would go and make my report to Arthur anyway. For that matter, if he had wanted to kill *me,* he had plenty of opportunities last night. I went out with no escort into the darkened streets and to a part of the city that is not very savory. No, I think Eastra is the key. I think if you had not been with her, you would not have been troubled."

"You think Cerdic seeks to free her so he will have the advantage over Arthur?"

"It might not be that simple. Cerdic's niece presents a tempting target for any number of reasons. If nothing else, she could be ransomed for a great deal of wealth."

"But no one here in Londinium knows who she is," Rhun pointed out. Then he turned to face his brother. "Unless *you* have been too loose with your tongue!"

Bridei met his gaze easily. "Or unless the woman herself has given away her identity. You seem to think Eastra sees things the same way you do. But she is still a Saxon, for all that she clearly cares for you."

"That's just it!" Rhun exclaimed. "Whatever else she might do, I don't believe Eastra would plot to have me killed. Today I held her in my arms, and I know no woman could pretend what passed between us!"

"Did you now?" Bridei's mouth quirked, and Rhun wished desperately he had held his tongue. "I don't believe Eastra would plot your murder, either," Bridei continued. "But she might not have realized it would mean that. She might have accidently let slip to someone who she was—no treachery intended—and the information found its way to one of our enemies."

Rhun thought about Eastra talking to the slave girl in the garden. He had not overheard what they were speaking of, but it was possible Eastra had revealed her identity. And although the slave was not a Saxon, that did not mean she did not have connections with the enemy.

Rhun took a deep breath. He had to avoid being alone with Eastra. Not because he thought she would betray him, but because her mere presence was enough to addle his wits and throw him off his guard.

They left Londinium from the same direction they had entered. As they passed the towering ruins of the city gate, Eastra experienced a pang of bitterness. She'd had her chance to be alone with Rhun, but the moment had been destroyed by violence. Cursed, wretched war! Would she ever be free of its malignant poison? This conflict between Briton and Saxon had cost her everything she held dear. Would it also cost her a chance with Rhun? But he had assured her the journey to his father's fortress in Gwynedd would take some days. Surely during that time they would be alone again. And then, maybe, that potent fire would leap between them once more, and he would not be able to deny he cared for her.

They followed the Roman road west. As the sky turned the deep blue of summer twilight, Rhun and Bridei pulled to a halt. They spoke briefly. Then Rhun turned in the saddle and motioned to a distant stand of trees. "We'll camp there tonight. If we set a guard, we should be safe enough."

When they reached the grove of oaks, the men set about making preparations for the night. Eastra watched with interest. Rhun and the others were obviously experienced at living on the land. They set up tents, built a fire, and brought out provisions. Sitting around the now crackling fire, they passed around the food—dried meat, rolled-up chewy bannocks, and earthenware cups of a brewed drink much tangier than the ale Eastra was used to.

"It's made from heather," Bridei told her when she commented on it. "You have to acquire a taste for it, but believe me, where we are from, there is much more heather than barley."

He was sitting to her right; Rhun to her left. Rhun had spoken few words since giving the order to camp for the night. Now he ate silently and stared broodingly into the fire. She wondered what he was thinking about. The attack, most likely. It still made her skin prickle to think of the danger they had been in. "Who do you think sent those men?" she asked as she wiped the crumbs of the bannock from her hands.

Rhun turned to look at her, his face harshly illuminated in the firelight. "I don't know. Do *you* have any ideas?"

Surprised by the wary tone of his voice, she said, "You made it clear Arthur has enemies in Londinium. I assumed someone had recognized you as his man."

"But I'm not really Arthur's spy. Bridei is. And *he* was not attacked."

"What are you saying?"

It was Bridei who answered. "He's saying you were the reason for attack, that the men were trying to get to you."

"But why?" Eastra asked. "What use am I to anyone?"

"You could be ransomed," Rhun said. "I think Cerdic would pay a great deal to have his niece returned to him safely. Not to mention that for you to be abducted while you are our hostage would make us look like utter fools."

"But no one in Londinium knew I am Cerdic's niece," Eastra said, baffled. "You told everyone, even your friend Aurelius, that I was your concubine."

"That's true," Bridei said matter-of-factly. "She's likely right, brother. It very well could have been one of Arthur's enemies. As for why they attacked you and left me alone—I make an effort to cultivate the image of a man engaged in careless debauchery. Few men take me seriously, as a spy or otherwise."

Rhun gave a noncommittal grunt. Eastra sensed he did not believe his brother's explanation and still thought she had been the reason for the attack. She opened her mouth to argue against this reasoning, but even as she did so, she suddenly remembered Skena. She had told the slavegirl she was Cerdic's niece. It had been done in innocence, as a means of giving Skena hope that her own circumstances might someday improve. But what if Skena had shared the information with someone, someone who was an enemy of Arthur's?

Eastra's body went rigid. It was possible she had nearly cost Rhun his life. One slip of the tongue, and she had set his enemies upon him like flies on a carcass. If he were not such a superb warrior, if he had reacted an instant slower . . . her blood went cold at the thought.

She looked at him, wanting to tell him what she had done, but fearing that if she did so he would never trust her again. And he *had* survived the attack unscathed. No real harm had been done. She swallowed the incriminating words. No point revealing her foolish mistake if she did not have to. He was already wary of her because she was a Saxon. If she was to have any hope of making him fall in love with her, she must win his trust, not make him even more suspicious of her motives.

She smiled at Rhun. "No matter what the reason for the attack, I'm just very glad it did not succeed. You were magnificent, Rhun. You struck them down like Teutones himself, my people's god of thunder and lightning."

Their gazes met and held. As always, she could feel the magic move between them. That sense of closeness, of two spirits seeking out each other as if they were halves of a whole.

Beside her, Bridei cleared his throat. "I think I will take the first watch, since I slept most of the day anyway." He rose and walked off.

Rhun stared into the darkness, trying to forget the woman sitting nearby. She was so beautiful. And when she looked at him like that, it made him weak with need. He wanted to reach out for her and press her to his chest and hold her so close they could not be any closer but to be joined.

He indulged the fantasy briefly, then thrust it away. He was not a callow boy entranced by exquisitely lovely face and an enticing female form. He was a warrior, hardened and tempered by near fifteen years of fighting and hardship. No matter her allure or the stunning, worshipful way she gazed at him, he could not forget his duty. With effort, he forced himself to his feet. "I need to speak to my brother," he said. "The tent nearest the fire is yours."

He walked away quickly, a part of himself resisting every step. It was as if there was another person inside of him trying to force him to go back to her. But years of discipline would not be denied, and he was able to make himself do what duty and reason demanded.

Bridei turned to greet him as he reached the edge of the patch of forest. "Still playing the saintly martyr?"

"Not saintly, but sensible," Rhun said. "There can be nothing gained by further complicating things between Eastra and myself. I do this as much for her benefit as for my own."

"Of course." Bridei's voice was sardonic. "Always the noble one. And sensible, for certain. She might be a Saxon spy, after all."

"You don't really believe that, do you?"

"I don't know. I didn't have a clear look at her face when we discussed the attack. But you, you were watching her closely. Do you think she knows something she's not telling?"

"I would swear she is innocent. But there is still the fact she might be a tool used by others."

"Of course," said Bridei. "You never know who you can trust these days."

Rhun nodded glumly. He was fortunate to be alive, yet he could not feel triumphant or content. All he could think of was what might have been.

Eastra rose restlessly and started toward the tent. Half-way there, she paused, overcome with frustration. Rhun was drawing away from her. They'd had this brief chance to be alone—an opportunity to talk, if not to kiss or embrace—but instead of seizing the moment as she'd longed to do, he had walked off. The attack in Londinium had made him see her as his enemy.

She took a few steps in the direction he had gone, then paused. The moon was high and bright, and if she strained her eyes, she could make out Rhun's tall silhouette in the distance as he stood talking to Bridei. Somehow she would have to change his mind and convince him to trust her. But how could she do it if he would not even talk to her?

The next day dawned hot and bright. They returned to the Roman road and followed it west. Rhun and Bridei

rode at the front of the troop, with Eastra behind them
and the rest of the escort to her rear. She'd had a chance
to wash her face and hands in a stream they passed early
that morning, and she felt somewhat refreshed, although
she could see that this kind of travel, camping out every
night and riding for long stretches, would soon grow tire-
some.

They passed a few farmsteads, mostly deserted. Observing the rich land around them, Eastra was puzzled.
She wanted to ask Rhun why this part of Britain seemed
so sparsely inhabited. But something about the set of his
shoulders, the careful distance he put between them,
warned her he would not welcome any questions from
her.

A grim mood overtook her. For the first time on the
journey, she began to feel like a hostage. There were
armed men all around her, and although she knew they
were there primarily for her protection, given her changed
circumstances with Rhun, it gave her the sense of being
a prisoner. Had she made a terrible mistake in offering
to serve as hostage? Would she end up alone and miserable, locked away in a foreign king's fortress in
Gwynedd? She had not been happy in Cerdic's household,
but at least there she was treated with respect and deference. At least on some level she belonged there, with
her own people.

Now she was among strangers. The Britons looked and
dressed and behaved differently than Saxons. If Rhun was
at her side, it would not have mattered, but now he was
not, she was acutely aware of the imposing, silent warriors gathered around her, of the vivid colors of their
cloaks, the leather tunics and trousers they wore, their
dark or ruddy hair, even the different way their eyes
seemed to be set in their faces and the sharpness of their
features.

Although the day was as brilliant as ever, she shivered.
What had she done? Rhun, the light of her existence for

so many years—the very stuff of her dreams—had drawn away from her, and she was alone . . . and afraid.

"You should go back and ride with her," Bridei spoke quietly, then gave a half glance backward. "Exchange a few pleasantries with our guest."

"She's not our guest," Rhun responded. "She's a hostage." Even as he spoke the harsh words, something inside him winced. In truth, he did not feel that way about her, but it was dangerous to behave otherwise.

"All the same, she's a young woman, far from her home and family. In the interest of simple courtesy and kindness, you should make some effort to put her at ease."

Rhun gritted his teeth. "If it matters so much to you, my gallant brother, then *you* go back and speak to her."

"All right, I will. But don't ever say I tried to steal your sweetheart away from you."

Rhun stared grimly ahead. In another moment, he heard Eastra laugh. He cursed himself—for ever agreeing to serve as Eastra's escort, for stopping in Londinium on the way, and for ever being such a fool as to rescue a beautiful Saxon child all those years ago.

"It's good to hear you laugh," Bridei said. "I'd feared your experience in Londinium might have frightened you so much you would ride the rest of the way in silence, like a terrified coney."

"I don't scare *that* easily," Eastra answered.

"Good." Bridei smiled at her. "So tell me, what do you think of this part of Britain?" He gestured expansively to the landscape around them.

"It's very green and pretty. Fertile, too, I imagine. Which is why I have to ask—why do so many of the farmsteads around here appear abandoned?"

"Do you really want to know?"

She nodded.

"Saxons." He nodded. "I'm afraid it's true. These farms were burned out and ravaged years ago, back when your people came to destroy and plunder rather than to settle. They took what they could carry and moved on—to the next farmstead or the next holy house or whatever else they could find to ravage."

"Didn't the people fight back?" Eastra asked. "Didn't they try to defend themselves?"

"I'm certain they did. But you have to understand, there was no organized army back then. The legions had left a generation before, and the farmers and merchants who were left behind had never learned how to fight. Now, those of us who lived on the western coasts, we have been fighting and waging war the whole time. But the eastern and southern Britons had grown complacent under the eagle standard of Rome. They never realized they were going to have to face such a terrifying threat from the sea.

"And so the Saxons came and burned and murdered and stole whatever wealth they could find in their pathway. They penetrated deep into Britain, until they realized perhaps that they were too far from their boats and their bases on the coast. Then they left, carrying their booty. But by the time they came back, the pickings weren't so easy. They had Ambrosius to face."

"Who's he?" Eastra was intrigued by his tale; she'd never heard any of these things from her own people.

"Arthur's grandsire."

Eastra stared and Bridei nodded. "Aye, his father, Uther, was also Roman, or mostly Roman. His mother was a Briton, though. Through her he's related to my tribe, the Cymry."

"Arthur is your kinsman?"

Bridei nodded. "But that's not why Rhun and I joined his army. Among my people, blood ties don't always make for strong alliances. In fact, interestingly enough, although I have Irish blood in me, I still consider them my deadly enemies." Eastra gaped at him, and he nodded once more. "It's little talked about, but when I was in the north visiting my mother's people, I discovered that my great-great grandsire, Cunedag, was Irish. In fact, Rome brought him in to subdue the Decanglia and the Silurians, the two tribes that once controlled Gwynedd."

"How strange to be related to your enemies."

"Not so strange for us Britons," Bridei said, grinning. "I think sometimes we fight more bitterly among ourselves than we ever do against our enemies from the outside."

"Rhun said something like that." Eastra glanced to the front of the troop, wondering what he was thinking. "He said part of the reason he fought for Arthur's cause was because he admired Arthur's goal of uniting all of Britain."

Bridei shook his head. "A worthy goal, but it will never happen. It's the curse of my race to squabble and fight each other endlessly. It's the reason we will never be successful at ruling Britain the way the Romans were. I'm a bard," Bridei added. "And most of the songs and stories that are passed down from generation to generation tell of kings fighting kings and never is there peace. If it has always been that way, why should Arthur be able to change it?"

"But his grandsire Ambrosius apparently succeeded in gathering the people to fight the Saxons. So why don't you think Arthur will succeed now?"

"Because already the Saxon threat has changed and become less frightening and potent. Men like your uncle are willing to negotiate and make treaties. They seek farmland and security and peace for their families. They are no longer terrifying marauders who destroy everything in their path. And because the danger is no longer so obvious, men begin to whisper among themselves, wondering at Arthur's right to lead them, wondering if they would not have more to gain from staying home and guarding their own territory against their neighbors."

"The thought that Arthur will fail does not seem to distress you very much," Eastra pointed out.

Bridei smiled. "I'm not like Rhun. He believes in dreams and quests, and in fighting for something because it 'should' be. I'm a practical man. I can see the world has been this way for a long time, and no man, no matter how dedicated and noble he is, is going to change it."

A pang went through Eastra. Although Bridei's words made sense, she did not want to believe them. She preferred to hope, as Rhun did, that things *could* change for the better. Was that not what this journey was all about? She had offered to be hostage not only because she wanted to be with Rhun, but because she believed that by forming a bond with one of the "enemy," she might be able to help bring peace between Saxon and Briton.

She stared wistfully ahead at Rhun's tall form. Although she was pleased Bridei took the time to talk to her and explain things, she would much rather spend time with his brother.

He could not hear what they were saying, but Rhun was aware Eastra and Bridei were engaged in an intense conversation. The sound of their voices—Bridei's, low and musical, and Eastra's, light and feminine—made his stomach clench. His brother would charm her, as he did every woman, and she would forget all about him.

No matter that he told himself that it was better that way, the idea aroused a harsh ache inside him. He'd never felt for a woman what he felt for Eastra. The very sight of her made his heart swell in his chest, an exquisitely sweet longing rush through his body. It was not merely the hunger to touch her, to press flesh to flesh, but a craving for her spirit, her very essence.

But it was not meant to be. He'd known that from the very moment when he said farewell to her in the forest all those years ago—urging her to run to freedom, away from him, away from her deadly enemies. Their blood cursed them, made any future impossible. For a time he'd forgotten that, but it was time he remembered the bitter truth. And Bridei, curse his glib, handsome face, was exactly the man to remind him.

Eight

Eight

They paused near midday to eat a meal, then resumed riding. The direction they took was toward where the sun would set and a little north. Rhun was in the lead, with Bridei and Eastra behind, riding side by side. The rest of the warriors were arrayed around them, speaking seldom, their eyes always watchful and wary, as if they were wild beasts passing through a predator's territory.

During the break for the meal, Eastra had thought a lot about what Bridei had told her of the old Saxon threat, of Ambrosius and of Arthur, and how they had organized the Britons to fight their enemies. While she found it fascinating to learn the history of this conflict, she longed to speak of other things. Rhun's name seemed always on her lips. She wanted to know more about this man who had so beguiled her.

Finally, she let her horse drop back a little farther from Rhun's silvery gray mount, then faced Bridei and asked casually, "You've told me a great deal about Arthur and his cause, but tell me, how did you and your brother get involved in all of this?"

"Rhun hasn't told you?" Bridei asked.

"Some," Eastra hedged, casting a careful glance at Rhun. "But not how it all started out. He must have been very young when he went off to fight with Arthur."

"He was," Bridei agreed. "When he was about sixteen,

a holy man came to Deganwy. He ranted on and on about how all noble Christian warriors must join Arthur's cause and fight to fling the barbarian hordes back into the sea. Rhun was quite taken with the idea of saving Britain and fighting for the one true God." He grinned suddenly. "And then our father forbid him to go. Of course, he went."

"And Arthur took him into his army, despite Maelgwn's objections?"

Bridei nodded. "Among our people, sixteen is counted pretty much a man. Besides, Arthur was not one to let a promising warrior slip through his fingers. But it has rankled with our father ever since. I sometimes think Rhun's decision back then is what, more than anything, keeps Maelgwn from aiding Arthur's cause."

"So Rhun joined Arthur's army and ended up rising high in his favor?"

"Well, it took him some years. Even my miraculous brother did not impress Arthur's hardened commanders right away. He had to get a few battles under his belt. At first, he simply avoided being killed. Then he gradually learned how to defeat and kill other men. I don't think it's been easy for him. It's not his nature to be bloodthirsty. He's had to learn that it's a matter of kill or be killed. Now it's all instinct with him."

Eastra nodded. "I saw that. Before those men were even upon us, he had drawn his sword and attacked them. But he didn't seem to take satisfaction in it."

"That's his only flaw. He does not like to kill."

"You believe that's a flaw?"

Bridei shrugged. "Some will argue that it is in a warrior. Your uncle Cerdic might think so, for example."

What would Cerdid think of Rhun? Eastra wondered. If she wed with him, would Cerdic vow vengeance again Rhun, or would he accept the match? Rhun was certainly high born enough, a prince among his people. And if ever they were to live in peace together, Saxon and Briton must begin mingling their blood at some point.

But she was far ahead of herself. At this moment, it did

not seem likely Rhun would ever speak with her again, let alone want to make her his wife. She repressed a sigh. The more she learned about Rhun, the more she admired him and thought he saw things very much the way she did, despite being a man and a warrior.

To distract herself from the flash of pain that idea brought her, she glanced at Bridei once again. "And what of you? How did you end up in Arthur's army?"

There was a flicker of emotion in Bridei's dark blue eyes. Then he answered, "My journey was much more complicated than my brother's. I didn't run off to fight the noble, Christian cause. Indeed, I was banished by my father."

"Why?"

Bridei's mouth quirked. "I got into a bit of trouble, and my father lost his temper and said he was sending me north to live with my mother's people—to see if they could make a decent man of me. I didn't take kindly to the idea of being banished, so I ran away instead."

"But whether you are banished or ran away, it amounted to the same thing," Eastra suggested.

His mouth quirked again. "That's true. But I didn't see it like that back then. I was very young, even younger than Rhun. Only fourteen and looked it. I wasn't a precocious giant like my brother." There was a sharpness in his voice, and Eastra recalled Rhun mentioning that his brother was sensitive about his height. "I caught a ship for Less Britain and then from there wandered east."

"But you were so young. How did you survive?"

"I was not a formidable soldier like my brother, but I had a skill that served me even better than a fast and furious sword arm." He gestured to his saddle pack, where the curved end piece of a harp poked out. "I learned to play and sing when I was a small boy from my father's ancient bard, Aneurin. He said I had the gift of words, and that was more powerful than the mightiest weapon. Certainly it helped me to survive those early years. I wandered to markets and public areas and sat down and played my tunes.

Sooner or later someone would come up and ask me if I knew this song or that. I seldom did, but I would do my best to sing something that would please them.

"I was so young that I was no threat to anyone, and as a bard, I was welcome everywhere. I had to learn a bit of this tongue and of that in order to manage, and I found out I was good at it. By the time I sailed back across the sea, I had picked up a smattering of Saxon, as well as the Frankish tongue and a dozen other variations of Latin."

"And so you returned home and joined Arthur's retinue as an interpreter?"

"Not exactly. I was not so sure of myself as that. No, instead I went north, to my mother's people, to the place I was originally supposed to go to serve out my sentence of banishment."

"And what happened there?"

Bridei laughed. "Why are you so certain anything happened? I might have lived quietly and uneventfully there for several years."

Eastra regarded him dubiously.

"All right." He gave another rumbling laugh. Despite his lean, graceful build, he had the deep, rich voice of a larger, more robust man. "I got into trouble there as well. That's when I decided to seek out my brother. I figured he would not refuse to help me. Besides being a tenderhearted soul compelled to rescue the hapless—as you well know—he's always felt a kind of responsibility for me, poor bastard."

"And he took you in and suggested Arthur make you his interpreter?"

"No, that came after. All Rhun promised was that I would entertain the men and inspire them with tales of the old heroes. But then Arthur found out I knew Saxon and urged me to cultivate the skill. I used to drive the slaves in his camp to near distraction by pestering them to speak with me." Abruptly, Bridei paused and, eyebrows lifted, said, "Sorry. I forgot you were once a slave yourself."

Eastra stiffened, waiting for the familiar distress to grip

her. To her surprise, it didn't come. Knowing Rhun accepted her for what she was and did not care about her years as a slave made all the difference. "It doesn't matter," she said, meaning it. "Although I feel sorrow for those who still must suffer the humiliation of slavery, I don't want to dwell on that part of life, but instead look forward to the future."

"And now you are hostage," Bridei said. "Is that a better sort of captivity?"

Despite herself, Eastra could not help casting a glance at Rhun, riding a half dozen paces ahead of them. "Aye, it is better," she agreed. "For if I am not mistress of my fate, I am at least treated as someone of worth." *And I am near the man I love,* she added in her thoughts. *For all the good it has done me.*

Rhun forced himself to scan the densely forested hills surrounding them, searching for any hint of soldiers—the flash of a shield boss, the furtive movement of an archer, the restless movement of horses. He must be on his guard. Be ever vigilant and alert. But, curse it, it was damned difficult when a part of him was constantly distracted by the awareness of Eastra and Bridei riding behind him, talking companionably.

He could not hear a word of what they said, but once in a while he would catch the inflection of their voices or even their soft laughter. Whatever they spoke of, it was not unpleasant, or at least Bridei was telling it in a way that was amusing.

Harsh, grinding jealousy made Rhun's muscles go taut. He should entertain Eastra and make her laugh, not Bridei! But then he told himself he was being a selfish, arrogant fool to think such thoughts. He had decided he must stay away from her, and yet it was only simple decency to provide their royal hostage with companionship and put her at her ease. If he could not do it himself, at least his brother could try to relieve her loneliness and the hardship of travel.

If only Bridei were not so good at it, so skilled at beguiling people, especially women. And so remarkably handsome. While Rhun had never had reason to doubt his own attractiveness to women, he knew he could not compare to his brother. The maids fair swooned over Bridei, murmuring about his "raven tresses" and his "eyes like wood violets," cooing over him as if he were a girl. Rhun knew his own physique, however impressive, was marred by battle scars, his hands battered and gashed from years of wielding a weapon, his skin weathered from spending so much time outside. He looked very much the nine years older he was than Bridei.

And then there was Bridei's skill with words. He knew how to coax and cajole, how to tease and flatter. When he sang, men said he could charm the very stars out of the heavens with his voice. It was a voice to bring tears to the eyes, to wring emotion from the depths of the soul. Between Bridei's voice and his looks, Rhun had always thought there was a kind of magic about his brother, some sort of enchantment he had from Rhiannon, who more than a few people believed was a sorceress.

But *he* had no magic, although fortune had smiled upon him in many ways. He knew he was a skilled warrior, and Arthur valued his judgment and his ability to read people and make decisions. To be among the high king's inner circle was no mean accomplishment. And yet with women . . . many had approached him, but always he knew they did not really care for him, but sought him out because he was a prince, heir to Gwynedd, and one of Arthur's Companions.

Somehow it seemed a better thing to be like Bridei and have women love you for your face and your voice. At least those things were part of the man, while status and power were not real. They could be lost. And once they were lost, what happened then? Did the women drift away, although they'd once spoken words of devotion and love? He wanted a woman who cared for him because of *himself,* his very essence, the secret, hidden part of him no man really knew. *Eastra,* his mind told him. She could love him and know him that way.

But then he reminded himself of all the complications between them. It was dangerous to get close to her—if nothing else, because he could not think clearly when she was near. And this was a treacherous journey they embarked on. He could feel it the farther they rode west. The landscape was changing from farmland to pastureland. The way became more rugged, the trees denser. Soon they would be traveling much of the time in forest, and they would have to be alert every moment. The incident in Londinium had made it clear they had enemies watching them. Watching and waiting.

And there were other reasons not to yield to his urge to be near Eastra. Even if they made this journey safely, what then? She was still a hostage, and a woman of the enemy. If war broke out again, it would be cruel to have grown too close to her. For how could she endure it, to be torn between what she felt for him and what she felt for her own people? To face the day when he rode out to kill her kin?

The thought was chilling, and Rhun told himself he must keep it ever present in his mind. Eastra was innocent and naive. If she had yielded to the moment in that hidden alleyway and kissed him willingly and eagerly, it was because she had not thought far into the future, had not considered the pain and grief that could come about from their falling in love.

A sharp pang went through him. What splendor had been in that moment. He had never known he could feel such things with a woman—as if her very being was made of light and music, filling him until he was bursting. It seemed they had floated above the ground, away from the squalid alley where they stood, and glided into the heavens.

He took a deep breath, then guiltily looked around. For a moment, he had relaxed his guard and been caught up in his own thoughts. In that moment, danger could have struck. At least they had an escort. If they had to depend upon him to spot all the hazards ahead of them, he feared they would be lost!

But wary and cunning as were the warriors accompanying them, it was *his* duty, his responsibility to see them safely to Gwynedd. And he could not do that if he were riding beside Eastra and gazing on her beautiful face. Aggravating as the current situation was, he could not change it. Bridei would have to remain her companion, and he her protector.

"Still mooning over my brother, are you?" Bridei's sly words startled Eastra. She gazed at him openmouthed, then said, "Am I so obvious?"

"Just a bit. Let's say if he were a fat fowl and you were a fox, you'd have leaped upon him and devoured him by now, every feather and scrap of gristle."

Eastra sighed. "I'm sorry. I can't help it."

"Obviously not."

When Bridei did not speak further, Eastra asked, "Do my feelings for your brother offend you?"

"No. In fact"—he grinned—"they amuse me quite a bit. Not very kind of me to say when I know you're suffering, but I've never seen my brother like this before. Gone is the cool, calm, unruffled commander, the keen, dangerous warrior. He seems almost human these days."

"No, that's not very kind," Eastra agreed. "And furthermore, we were speaking of my feelings, not his."

"Oh, but his are the same, I assure you. He's eaten up with it, absolutely devastated by the knowledge that he wants you, almost more than he wants to be a good and dutiful soldier."

"Almost?"

Bridei shrugged. "He hasn't given in yet. Oh, I know he kissed you—and likely a little more—just before you were attacked in Londinium. But that's just a taste that's whetted his appetite. Right now, he's trying to be good, trying to stay away from you. And I'm actually helping him, can you believe that? If I were ignoring you, he would feel even more guilty, and maybe he would weaken sooner. But I'm bored, I'll admit it, and you are an intelligent and interesting woman. Why shouldn't I flirt with you a little? It makes the time pass by, at least."

Eastra was nonplussed. Bridei talked so openly about things she had some inkling of, but felt she must hide in the name of discretion and good manners. Finally, she said, "That's all it is, isn't it? You're talking to me to be kind, and also to make the time pass?"

"Actually, I don't usually do things to be kind." Bridei's grin was wicked. "But your second assumption is true. Also, it's entertaining to see my brother squirm and writhe with jealousy. It's a perfectly normal emotion, but he probably hates himself for feeling it. He's remarkably virtuous and boring about that kind of thing."

Eastra frowned at him. "Some of the things you say— sometimes I wonder at your character."

"Oh, don't bother wondering," he answered blithely. "I'm as bad as you think. It's Rhun's calling in life to be good. I'm the evil one."

Eastra was startled. "I . . . I don't think that's true. Otherwise you wouldn't talk about it like that. You must have some conscience and kindness inside you or you would not . . ." She paused, struggling to understand what she meant to say.

"Or I would not be charming and pleasant—is that what you think? But evil is not always dark and repulsive. Sometimes it's just the opposite."

"No, I was thinking that if you were truly evil, Rhun would not spend time in your company."

"Why not? He's my brother. He feels a sense of responsibility to me. Maybe he even thinks some of his goodness will rub off."

Eastra shook her head. She could not put her finger on

it, but something inside her told her Bridei was not truly wicked, that he was more like his brother than he knew.

"Still don't believe me?" Bridei flashed her another grin. "What if I told you that the reason my father banished me when I was fourteen is because I raped a woman?"

Eastra stared at him. "Why would you . . ." She shook her head. "From what I can see, any number of women would lie with you willingly. Why would you need to force one?"

"Would you lie with me?" His dark blue eyes were piercing. Eastra's mouth was suddenly too dry to answer. "No?" he said slowly. "Well, that's sort of the way it was. And, in my defense, I didn't hurt her. In fact, I rather think she liked it. But someone told my father and he was outraged." Bridei's smile had faded, and he looked bitter and angry. "He would not even listen to my side of the story. Shouted at me, told me I was a monster and I had inherited the tainted blood of his line. I guess both his sister and his mother were real pieces of work, and I look a lot like them. So he banished me."

While what Bridei said shocked her, Eastra was still not convinced he was as bad as he said. "But if you regret what you did . . ." she began cautiously.

"But do I?" Bridei raised his dark brows. "At least I discovered what my father truly thinks of me. And now I'm free. I'm not bound by duty and honor like Rhun is. I can do what I want, whatever pleases me."

Eastra was unsettled. Bridei's outlook on life disturbed her. If everyone thought like that, there would be no tribes, no duty and law, no sense of order and structure in life. "What about your mother?" she said. "Don't you care what she thinks? Rhun says she is kindhearted and loving and good. Even if your father has turned from you, don't you want to make *her* proud of you?"

Bridei shrugged. "My mother will love me no matter what. She doesn't judge people or close her ears to them because of something they've done. She's not so obsessed with right and wrong and good and evil. She believes people must follow their own path in life."

Eastra found herself even more intrigued than she had been previously by this woman called Rhiannon. But her son—the way Bridei talked about things made her feel as if the ground had shifted between her feet.

"I've said things that trouble you, haven't I?" Bridei spoke softly. "I do the same thing to my brother. He dislikes how I make things seem complicated, until they twist and turn around like the twining knotwork on a piece of Irish jewelry. He prefers the old Roman way, with everything organized and logical. Or the Christian one, with the world divided neatly between good and evil."

Eastra nodded at Bridei's insights into his brother. She could see Rhun was like that, and it appealed to her a great deal. It seemed somehow solid and secure, the way his arms felt when they were around her.

"Unfortunately, the way Rhun thinks allows little room for entanglements like beautiful Saxon princesses." Bridei's grin was back. "For him, you're a problem . . . and a delicious temptation."

Eastra blushed. It was clear Bridei understood all too well what had occurred between her and Rhun back in Londinium.

They rode in silence a way. Then Bridei said, "Now, here's a proposition for you. If I could contrive a way to make Rhun pay attention to you once again, to make him fall hopelessly in love with you—would you go along with it?"

Eastra regarded him cautiously. "Are you suggesting something dishonest or deceitful? Because if you are, then I will tell you that I won't do it. I value my own honor more than that. I will not betray my own people, and neither will I betray Rhun."

"It's not dishonest, although it could, perhaps, be dangerous."

"Dangerous to whom?"

Bridei shrugged. "To both of you. Once you are caught

up in the throes of passion, you will be vulnerable. I will do my best to see no harm comes to either of you, but I am not Rhun, the mighty warrior who can slay six men by himself."

"So," she said slowly, "the danger you speak of would come from Rhun's enemies?"

"Where else?"

Eastra chewed her lip. Bridei had just told her he was untrustworthy. Now he offered to help her win Rhun's heart. "Why are you doing this?" she asked. "You've made it clear you think primarily of yourself and your own interests. What have you to gain by bringing Rhun and me together?"

"Perhaps I care for my brother's happiness." Bridei's voice was bland. "It's clear having to stay away from you is eating him up inside. Besides, I will benefit as well. While Rhun fancies himself more alert and better able to look after you if he does not spend time in your company, I think otherwise. I believe if he were not so agonized over the conflict between what he sees as his duty and what is in his heart, he would actually be better equipped to get us all to Gwynedd safely."

Something about Bridei's explanation did not sound right. Eastra decided he was probably up to some mischief—in fact, she was certain a lot of his interest in helping her was based on a childish urge to stir up trouble. But even knowing that, some part of her could not help responding to his offer. Rhun *did* need to forget his sense of duty for a time. It would be good for him to cast aside his worries and sense of responsibility and enjoy a few moments of pleasure. Their breathless, thrilling embrace in Londinium had ended all too quickly. Her heart was in her throat as she said, very softly, "Tell me, what is your plan?"

He could not bear it! Rhun shifted away from the campfire, his whole body taut. There was something so intimate, almost conspiratorial, in the way that Eastra and Bridei were behaving this night. They sat next to each other, eating pieces of the roasted hare that Dewi had brought down with his sling and cooked over the fire. They did not talk much, but what they did say was exchanged in a murmur, as if they wished no one else to overhear.

Soon after they had stopped for the night, Bridei had offered to take Eastra down to a nearby stream so she could wash. As they walked off together, Rhun had felt a wave of fury rise up inside him. It should be *he* who guided Eastra among the cool forest glades and pointed out the pale dewdrops and purple bog orchid growing in among the fern and bracken, *he* who showed her how to creep quietly through the woods so they might spy a fawn and its mother come down to drink at the water or catch a glimpse of a bright lapwing or blue tit flitting among the trees. *He* was the one who should share these wild pleasures with Eastra, not jaded Bridei, who was familiar with the fleshpots and markets of Narbonne and Londinium, but knew little of woods lore.

A little while later, Bridei and Eastra had reappeared and joined the rest of the company around the fire. While the fact they sat next to each other galled Rhun, it reassured him to think that at least they were in his sight. The meal passed slowly. Afterward, Bridei rose to his feet. Rhun exhaled a sigh of relief. Perhaps now they would all seek out their beds and he would have a moment's peace from the raging jealousy that was eating him alive. But then he saw Bridei head to his saddle pack, piled with the others, and get out his harp. Rhun closed his eyes, fighting off frustration. He wanted to throw Bridei into the nearest tree, then smash his harp into pieces on the ground. Anything to keep Bridei from playing for Eastra.

Bridei sat down crosslegged a short distance from Eastra, and the strings of the harp shimmered in the firelight. He set his hand to the instrument and played a ripple of notes. Like a cascade of water, they danced through the air. In his rich, deep voice, Bridei began the tale of Kiernan and Olwen. He sang how fair Olwen was with her white brow and her shining hair like a river of gold. Of the bold and heroic Kiernan, and of the tender love they shared for each other. And he sang of all the trials Kiernan had endured to win his beloved.

Then he sang another song, this one of a battle. His voice swelled and rose to the treetops as he described the clash of weapons and the fierce combat, then softened to a throbbing whisper as he told of the deaths of Cadwallon and Achlen, of their bravery and valor, how the women wept for them and the linnets and nightingales in the treetops added their voices to the fallen heroes' lament.

Glancing over at Eastra, Rhun felt something inside himself snap. He jerked to his feet and walked off into the trees. There he stood in the darkness, taking deep breaths, trying to calm the turmoil inside him. It was almost as if he hated his brother. He wondered what kind of person he was to feel such rage at his own kin. After all, he did not really believe Bridei would try to seduce Eastra—even his amoral brother had more honor than that. But Bridei was obviously winning her over, charming her, making her forget all about *him* and the special moments they had shared in Londinium. He told himself it was for the best, that Eastra could never be his anyway. But his heart roared and raged over the loss like an animal in pain.

At last, in the distance, the silvery voice of the harp grew still, and he could hear nothing but the vague rustlings of the birds in the trees as they roosted for the night and the soft whisper of a night breeze in the boughs overhead. He took a deep breath, knowing he should go back and seek his bed so he would be fresh in the morning, yet well aware he would never be able to sleep. As soon as he closed his eyes, he would be tormented by the image of Eastra's rapt expression as she watched Bridei.

Instead, he sought out Dewi, who was guarding the periphery of the camp, and told the warrior he would take first watch again. Although Dewi said nothing, Rhun could feel him observing him with a speculative look, and he had

the awful realization that every man in the troop was aware
of his bitter jealousy. He was flooded with humiliation, and
in his rage all he could think of was going back to camp
and thrashing Bridei senseless.

But then he would be doubly a fool, he told himself.
Such a childish display of temper would change nothing
and might even make Eastra favor Bridei all the more. He
did not need to remind her he was a harsh, ruthless warrior
when it was already clear how much she preferred Bridei,
with his graceful tongue, his charm and sophisticated allure.

Staring miserably into the darkness, he wondered how
things could have come to this sorry pass—that he should
be reduced to this level of self-pity and despair. His whole
purpose in life had been to wield a sword and to fight for
his people, his country, and his God, but Eastra had robbed
him of his rock solid belief in that cause. For how could
she—beautiful, fine, and intelligent as she was—be his enemy? His faith in all the things he thought he believed in
was suddenly in doubt. He felt lost and helpless.

No wonder the bards sang tales of lovely maidens and
their power to bring down mighty warriors. It was true.
Eastra, with her sweet smile and her glowing beauty, had
done what no warrior could. She had brought him to his
knees.

He grimaced, fighting for control. He would not give up
yet. Somehow, he would find the will to survive this journey. He would drive them all ruthlessly, that they might
reach Gwynedd as soon as possible. Once there, he would
deliver Eastra to his father's fortress and then ride away as
fast as Cadal would take him.

The next morning, Eastra and Bridei rode along silently.
This day it seemed he had no stories to share. Instead, he
was waiting, wondering what she would do, if she would
follow his advice. She had not decided yet.

Rhun's behavior this morning had been just short of rude, and she began to wonder if she had misread him. Maybe he didn't care for her after all. Those few moments they had spent in each other's arms in Londinium might mean nothing to him. Or perhaps he blamed her for the attack that came after. He might see her as a danger to himself and want to be rid of her as soon as possible. Certainly his brusque treatment this morning implied he felt that way.

But in her heart she did not believe that. Rhun was behaving like a man seething with frustration and jealousy. Jealousy—aye, that was it. As short-tempered as he was with her, Rhun was positively hostile to Bridei, as if looking for any excuse to leave him behind. And Rhun would only be jealous if he felt something for her.

She decided he did care for her. All he needed was some encouragement, the right circumstances to make him confront his feelings. She could bring about those circumstances, if only she had the courage to do so. Chewing on her lower lip, Eastra considered what she had to lose. If Rhun truly did not desire her, her plan would anger him all the more. Even then, his sense of honor would not allow him to be too unkind to her. Her heart would be broken, but at least she would know for certain her dream was futile.

But if, on the other hand, her instincts about Rhun were true, then oh, what delights, what magic they might enjoy together! To be alone with Rhun, to feel his strong arms around her, to smell his enticing male smell, to press her mouth to his and taste him . . .

Her breathing quickened at the thought. There were risks in her plan, but there were always risks in gaining something worth having. They were barely out of the glade where they had camped when Eastra looked at Bridei and nodded. This day she would risk her heart.

* * *

Rhun glanced up at the sullen, gray sky. It was going to rain before the day was over. Although he did not like the prospect of traveling in the rain, he'd done it many times before. They could all don the oiled leather capes they kept in their packs and keep on riding. But with Eastra in their company, that did not seem like such a desirable course of action. It might be better to find a sheltered spot and make camp for the night. But that would delay their journey all the more, and he could see them all huddled in a makeshift lean-to, Bridei and Eastra beside each other, and he forced to watch them. No, better to press on.

The forest was growing denser and it was slow going. There were places they had to travel single file. That gave him a respite for a time, to know Bridei and Eastra could not easily talk as they rode. But the thick cover made him uneasy in another way. If anyone planned to attack them, this would be a good opportunity, with all the warriors strung out in a line and unable to fight off an ambush.

Were they in danger? It seemed unlikely they had been followed all the way from Londinium. And yet something inside him, some instinct, would not allow him to relax. He felt tense and jumpy, like an animal being hunted.

"Rhun." He turned as he heard Bridei call softly from behind him. "Can we not stop for a time?" he asked. "Just a brief respite to stretch our legs and have a drink?" Bridei motioned with his head toward Eastra, suggesting she was the reason for his request.

Rhun frowned. This was not the best place to call a halt, and it was scarce past midday. He glanced back again, and Bridei raised his brows. In his expression was a clear message saying, "What sort of barbarian are you that you would consider denying a woman these few comforts?"

Rhun's grimace deepened. How did Bridei always manage to put him the wrong, especially when it came to Eastra? He went a little further until they reached a small clearing. Then he turned and shouted back to the other men, letting them know they were going to stop for a time. Rhun dismounted and, out of the corner of his eye, saw

Bridei helping Eastra off her horse. He took a deep breath, fighting for control, then watched as Eastra walked off quickly into the underbrush.

Rhun approached his brother. "Is she ill?"

Bridei shrugged. "I don't know. She merely asked me to ask you if we could stop for a time. You *have* driven her pretty hard on this journey."

Rhun gritted his teeth at Bridei's scolding tone. But his brother was probably right. He had given little concern to Eastra's comfort. And she was not only a woman, but a princess, and no doubt used to having someone wait upon her. He was suddenly struck by what a bumbling oaf he was. While they were in Londinium, he should have insisted they find some young woman to serve as her maid. But who could they have found? He was quite certain Eastra would reject the idea of having a slave, but by what other means would they have been able to procure a female bodyservant to make this journey?

It did not matter now, he told himself. It was too late to find a female companion for her. He was simply going to have to be more considerate and try to make her as comfortable as possible on the rest of the journey.

After a few moments, he glanced up at the leaden sky. The threat of rain increased by the moment. Where had Eastra gone off to? He hoped she hadn't strayed too far from the path. It was easy to get lost in woods like these. He felt a twinge of anxiety, thinking he should have insisted one of the men accompany her. Or gone with her himself. He was responsible for her. If anything happened . . .

He took a deep breath, then went to his pack and dug out his oilskin cape. "I'm going after her," he told Bridei.

Nine

A fat drop of rain struck Eastra on the nose. She brushed the wetness away and gave the sky an uneasy glance. Bridei's plan did not include rain, and she had not thought to bring her cloak. While finding cover under some trees would provide a little protection, if she did that, how would Rhun ever find her?

Doubts crowded her mind. Bridei had told her to wait until they reached more forested country. Then she was to act as if she needed to relieve herself and go off a distance from the others. Rhun would come to look for her—Bridei assured her of this—and then she would pretend to have sprained her ankle. While Rhun examined her ankle and decided what to do, she would have some time alone with him, an opportunity to reawaken the burning hunger they had experienced in the alley in Londinium.

A simple plan, and only a little deceitful. But she had not figured on the weather turning bad. As the wind whipped her traveling gown and tore at her braids, she considered forgetting the whole scheme. There would be other opportunities to entice Rhun. She could implement her plan tomorrow as easily as today.

She started back. After going some distance, she stopped. She'd thought that clump of hazel bushes back there was the one she'd passed soon after leaving the others. But if that were the case, she should be near the horses and the rest of the traveling party by now. She turned around, trying to remember what landmarks she'd passed. Suddenly, all the trees and bushes seemed to look alike. More raindrops splattered on her face, increasing her sense of urgency.

She thought she recognized a hawthorn bush and a stand of oaks further on, but then things grew unfamiliar again. The rain was increasing, making her shiver as it dampened her thin gown. Concerns about Rhun finding her were suddenly replaced by the need to seek shelter. She spied a sort of draw and headed in that direction. At least there she would be out of the wind.

When she reached the hollow, she heard the sound of water running and realized she was near a small stream. Instinct warned her to climb to higher ground, in case the rain was heavy and the stream flooded. She crossed the stream and made her way up a ridge. The rain pelted her harder and she gave a gasp of cold and exasperation. Spying a huge oak, she headed toward it. She sank down into the blanket of mast and dead leaves beneath the tree. This was as good a place as any to wait out the storm. But that did not change the fact that she was hopelessly lost.

Where was she? Had she run away? But where would she run to? And to whom? Dark thoughts filled Rhun's mind as he hurried through the woods. What if Eastra had planned to escape all along? What if some of her countrymen had been following them, waiting for an opportunity to steal back their princess?

But that made no sense. Why would the Saxons pursue her so deep into British territory? Why not rescue her nearer to Londinium, if that was their scheme?

Or what if she been abducted by some other of his enemies? Some chieftain who was in league with the Saxons might have come up with a plan to kidnap Eastra and throw the truce into jeopardy. Stealing Arthur's hostage would be

a good way to embarrass him and discredit his cause. But
the way Eastra had insisted they stop, then gone off alone—
it suggested she was part of the plot. He could scarcely
believe she would betray him like that.

Maybe there was some other explanation. In this sort of
broken woodland, it would be easy for someone unfamiliar
with the area to lose their way. What if she had simply
gone off to find some privacy and been unable to find her
way back?

Anxiety stabbed him. He reminded himself it was unlikely anything would happen to her. Wolves did not usually
attack people unless they were starving, and this time of
year there was plenty of prey. She could easily find water
to drink and a few berries to eat if she became hungry.
She could not have gone far. He would find her eventually.

He glanced back the way he had come, wondering if he
should alert the others that Eastra was missing. Then he
felt a drop of rain, and he decided that although Eastra
might not be in danger, she could end up miserably wet
and cold. He would not waste precious time by going back.
Better to search for her right away, while she must still be
close by.

The rain began to drizzle down upon him in a steady,
cold shower. Rhun hardly felt it. He was too caught up in
finding Eastra. He'd been searching for what seemed like
a long time. It was as if she had vanished.

He sighed in frustration. The thought came to him that
she might have made her way back to the others and be
waiting there. But if that was the case, why hadn't Bridei
or the other men sounded the horn as a signal, or even
called out for him? Now that the wind had died down, he
would surely hear their shouts.

For that matter, why had he not thought to call out for
Eastra? If she were in the area and wanted to be found,
she would surely answer. But if he were wrong and she
had been abducted, shouting would alert his enemies as to
his whereabouts. Alone, he would be an easy target. He
thought of the apprehensive mood he'd been in all day, the

nagging conviction they were being followed. He decided
to go back and get some help. The men could divide up
into groups, then systematically search for her, calling out
her name.

He had scarce gone a few paces when he saw her. She
was huddled up under a large, spreading oak, her pale hair
the only thing that made her visible in the gloom.

"Eastra!" he called out.

When he approached her, she raised her head and gave
him a frightened, anguished look. "Oh, Rhun!" she cried,
"I'm so glad to see you." To his surprise she did not stand
up, but remained huddled down. "I've twisted my ankle,"
she said as he drew near. "I was not able to walk back and
find you. And then it started to rain." She gave a shiver.

He quickly pulled off his oiled leather cape, then sank
down beside her and arranged the waterproof material to
cover her. He could feel her trembling, and he gathered her
onto his lap and put his arms around her. Her gown was
wet through, and her hands when he touched them were
icy cold. He rubbed them between his fingers. Tremors
swept through her. He clutched her tighter, feeling her body
warm.

"I got lost," she mumbled.

A deep sense of relief went through him. She had not
been abducted, nor had she betrayed him. The anguished
doubts left him and he began to relax. He continued to
hold her, feeling her body warm. Then, gradually, he was
aware of her in a different way. Of how lithe and soft her
body felt in his arms. Of her smell, like a mist surrounding
him, warm and sensual and female. His shaft grew hard,
and he had to shift her weight slightly so he was not so
uncomfortable.

He looked at her and saw the color was coming back
into her face. Her eyes appeared dark and wild, her lips
rosy, plump, and tempting. It was so strange, he thought.
One moment he was full of concern and worry for her. The
next, he was on fire with lust. He knew he should release
her. He should examine her ankle to see how bad the injury

was. But he did neither of those things. Instead, he bent
his head and kissed her.

She tasted of rain and forest, but beneath those things
he discovered the even sweeter nectar of her mouth. She
made a small noise, a sigh of contentment. He tightened
his arms around her and deepened the kiss. She opened
her mouth, inviting him to explore, and suddenly he was
falling, falling, down into a world ancient and full of mystery.

Warm skin, the throb of the heartbeat in her throat. The
feel of her breast, so soft and perfect in his hand. The
tender peak tightening beneath his fingers. Her breathing,
fast and rhythmic as he shifted her off of him. He spread
the oilskin cape on the ground, then helped her lie down
on it. Shoving aside the damp fabric of her gown, he nibbled and mouthed his way down her neck to one swollen
nipple. He suckled her, feeling her body stiffen and his
own answering response. Cupping her other breast in
greedy fingers, he laved and licked the silken skin until
she arched her back and moaned.

And then, mindless, he was pushing her skirts up, finding the linen loincloth and tearing it away as if it were a
frail husk guarding some ripe succulent fruit. A glimpse
of creamy thighs and the delicate, dark gold thatch between
them. He touched the soft, hidden folds and her body quiv-
ered as if he were a harpist striking a stirring chord. He
could feel the echo of the note throbbing inside him, and
there was nothing he could do but answer it with his own
harsh, male melody.

He kissed her long and hard, his fingers on her, readying
her, easing her. With each kiss, she yielded more to him,
both her openings wet and slippery and hungry. Her slim
form trembled with need. He fumbled with his clothing,
too urgent and desperate to do more than free his shaft.
For a second he stared at her, memorizing the vision of
milky, feminine beauty, the exquisite perfection of her face.
Then, taking a deep breath and closing his eyes, he pressed
himself against her wetness.

THE DRAGON PRINCE 161

Eastra felt him against her, big and hot and alive, and she urged him nearer, on fire with her own raging, violent need. With splayed thighs and upthrust hips, she welcomed him. Then came sharp stabbing pain and her eagerness faded. She felt him go still, aware of her discomfort.

"I'm sorry," he whispered. "But the worst is over. Will you let me . . . finish?" His voice was choked, harsh, and she was aware only the slimmest thread of control held him back.

She nodded. "Finish, then next time it will be better."

A storm unleashed, or the waves of the sea, pounding her. Her insides seemed split, stretched, shattered. But beneath the dull ache, another sensation. A hint of pleasure, of swelling need and a reawakening of that sharp, urgent craving. She moved her hips, searching for the something that eluded her.

Then, suddenly, he gave a great cry and went still, his weight upon her. The waves of pain and pleasure receded and she felt sore and squashed and uncomfortable. Rhun shifted to lie beside her, and suddenly she was cold. She sat up and adjusted her clothing to cover herself. He pulled her down next to him, then raised up on his elbow and leaned over to kiss her. "Eastra," he murmured.

His eyes were dazed, unfocused, his whole face so soft and relaxed that he reminded her of a little boy. He smiled at her, a wondering, wide-eyed smile. "What you do to me . . . I vow I feel as if I have fallen through one of the fairy mounds and awakened in another world. But . . ." He glanced around them and said ruefully, "I see I am really still in this one after all." After a moment, he asked, "Are you all right? I mean, did I hurt you?"

She shook her head.

"And what about your ankle? I swear, I didn't even think of it. Does it pain you greatly?"

Eastra hesitated, then said, "It still throbs, I guess, although I forgot it while we were . . ." Abruptly, she was embarrassed. She could hardly believe they'd done what they'd done. It was what she had wanted, but . . . there was so much unfinished business between them. What did he truly feel for her, besides desire? Did he love her, or was what they shared merely lust? It had not felt like that. It had been awe inspiring and magical for her. What about for him?

"By the Light!" He sat up, shaking his head. She could see he was also discomfited. "I never meant to . . ." He looked around them. "Anyone could have come upon us. I can't believe I was so foolish, so inconsiderate . . ." He looked at her, and there was a kind of despair in his eyes.

As she moved to sit beside him, warm liquid dripped down her thighs. His seed. They might well have made a babe. The thought shocked her, but even so, she knew she must put aside her own unease and reassure him. After all, she was the one who had enticed him, deliberately schemed to get him alone, to arouse his sympathy and concern and, ultimately, his passion. "Don't worry," she said. "It was . . . wonderful." She could feel herself blushing.

"But to take you like this . . . in this place . . ." He looked around again, as if disbelieving what he had done, deflowering a woman under an oak tree in the middle of a rainstorm.

But it was not raining now. Indeed, from what she could see of the sky through the tree branches, it was clearing rapidly. "It's all right," she told him. "The truth is, I wanted it as much as you did. And this is not such a bad place. The Saxons believe trees, especially great oaks like this one, are full of power. Perhaps we were both touched by some sort of magic, the hand of the gods."

She could see that didn't reassure him. He frowned. A twinge of warning sounded through her. What if he regretted what they had done so much he never wanted to do it again? What if she had tricked him into something that would cause him grief, the memory of it make him miserable?

"You liked it, didn't you?" she asked anxiously. "I was not a disappointment to you, was I?"

He took a deep breath and stared at her, his blue-gray

eyes deep and intent. "It was miraculous. Astounding. Have no doubt of that."

"But . . ." She held her breath waiting.

He shook his head. "Where do we go from here? By rights, I should wed you, but that cannot happen because of who you are. Don't you see? We're trapped. Things are hopeless between us, and yet now we know how extraordinary it might have been." He touched her face gently, and his eyes were sorrowful.

She wanted to shout at him, to demand to know why it was so hopeless, exactly *why* they could not wed. But that seemed too forward, too presumptuous. Maybe he really did not want to wed her. As much as he desired her, he might still want his heirs to be British, not half-Saxon mongrels. Taking pleasure in lying with a woman was much different than wanting to make her his wife. She thought of her uncle and the several concubines he had kept since she came back to his household. He would never marry any of them. They were not of high enough status to make appropriate consorts for a powerful chieftain. Rhun might well feel the same about her. She had contrived to obtain her heart's desire, and now she found it was not enough.

Rhun's heart twisted in his chest. She looked so sad, so forlorn. How could he have done this, become so caught up in his body's needs that he completely lost his head? But it had not felt crude and carnal. It had been sublime, even spiritual, as if their souls had been joined as well as their bodies.

He took a deep breath. There was no going back, no unmaking this thing. He must figure out what to do next. For one thing, he must get her back so she could change into some dry garments. He motioned. "Let me look at your ankle."

She nodded and pulled up her skirts so her legs were exposed. Ridiculously, he felt awkward. He had just made love to this woman, but somehow there was still something terribly intimate about examining her bare ankle. He touched the cool, smooth skin gingerly. "It does not seem swollen. Can you put weight on it?"

She looked at him, distress evident in her pale, expressive eyes. "Nay, I don't think so."

He repressed a sigh, dreading the continued closeness her injury forced upon them.

"I'm sorry," she said. "I didn't mean to cause you trouble."

"It's no trouble." He managed a smile. "I'll carry you." He put on the oilskin cape, then picked her up.

She adjusted herself so her arm was around his neck, her head against his shoulder. "I hope I'm not too heavy," she breathed.

"Of course not. I've carried roe deer that were a good three stones heavier than you."

She was light enough, her body fine-boned and delicate, but with such delicious soft contours. He thought of the liquid weight of her breast in his hand, the plush curve of her buttocks. She felt precious and delightful in his arms, as if there was something so *right,* so perfect in the way their bodies fit together.

A wave of anguish swept over him as he strode forward. He wanted to forget all about Bridei and the others, forget about Arthur and the war with the Saxons, carry her away and never go back. He remembered another moment like this, over ten years ago. He'd felt much the same then, wanting to stay with the wide-eyed Saxon child he'd rescued, to protect her and see her to safety. Now the urge was even fiercer and more compelling. This was a woman he held in his arms, a woman he'd just loved with the fullness and depth of his being. She affected him, drew him, in ways no child could.

But his dilemma had not changed. Duty called to him, his responsibilities as one of Arthur's captains, his oath to his liege lord and to their cause. How could he forsake that oath? It was a part of him. How could he defy everything that he was—a warrior, a soldier? Turn his back on his whole existence? And yet in the deep, secret part of himself, he wanted to do exactly that. To be a different man, a man like Bridei, who thought of nothing but his own needs and urges.

The thought of his brother decided him, and he paused, getting his bearings. The way Bridei lived his life was sad and futile. It could lead only to self-loathing and contempt and ultimately to despair. Rhun put one foot in front of the other, walking steadily. And with every step, the pain in his heart grew sharper and more unbearable.

She'd been wrong, Eastra thought. She closed her eyes, not wanting to see the grim, determined look on his face, not wanting to accept that their idyll was over and nothing had changed. Nothing. She'd believed once he'd made love to her, Rhun would finally see they were meant to be together. But, obviously, that hadn't happened. He intended to continue on their journey, to take her to his father's fortress and fulfill his duty to Arthur. He'd spoken no words of love, and his refusal to marry her was a clear enough indication of his feelings. She'd gambled and lost.

A lump swelled in her throat, but she fought it back. She wouldn't cry and let him see her humiliation. No one else must know of it, either. She would tell Bridei that by the time Rhun found her, they were both too wet and cold to worry about anything except getting back. She only hoped he believed her; Rhun's brother was too clever by half.

She felt a sudden hitch in Rhun's stride. Then he came to a halt. She opened her eyes and glanced at his face, hoping for one brief second he had changed his mind and wanted to be alone with her a little longer. His expression dashed all her hopes and aroused her dread. She jerked her head around to see what had caused him to appear so stricken. Through the trees, she saw a mass of armed warriors, Britons by the looks of them. She heard Rhun suck in his breath, then slowly, carefully, turn around and begin to walk back the way he had come. "Don't make a sound," he whispered.

The hair on the back of her neck stood on end as she

realized what had happened. Bridei and the other men had been captured. If they did not get away quickly, they would also fall into the hands of the enemy soldiers.

There was a hissing sound near her ear. Then an arrow struck a tree ahead of them, lodging in the bark, quivering menacingly. Rhun went instantly still. She felt his body tense. They'd been spotted.

Rhun turned around slowly. A heavily bearded, dark-haired man stood on the ridge above them. "That's a wise fellow," the warrior said derisively. "It would be all too easy for that arrow to have struck a little further to the left."

"Take me." Rhun spoke in a clear, strong voice. "And let the others go. I'm the one you want."

"Are you?" The man cocked his head. "We'll have to ask Urien about that."

"Urien? Doesn't the king of Rheged have anything better to do than molest travelers passing through his lands?"

"Apparently not." The man spoke in dry, ironic tones. Then he motioned with his head to indicate Rhun should approach.

"If you see an opening, make a run for it," Rhun whispered as he started toward their captor. Then, with a hiss of exasperation, he added, "Damn, I forgot about your ankle. Well, forget that notion. We'll have to throw them off the trail some other way. Keep to the story that you're my concubine, a Saxon slave I purchased in Londinium. They may know who you are anyway, but it's worth a try."

Eastra nodded. She felt so bad for him. Because of her, he was in this predicament. If she had not wandered off and then enticed him, they would have been with the others and he would have remained on his guard. He might have spotted the enemy troop before they could be captured. She repressed a sigh. If she'd brought danger to him, she'd never forgive herself.

They reached the others. There were about twenty foreign warriors gathered around them. Their captors were dressed similarly to the other Britons, although some wore feathers and animal skins as a kind of badge or personal symbol. Their swords were drawn as they surrounded Rhun's men. Eastra looked around for Bridei. He was standing off to the side, appearing utterly calm and unruffled.

The man who had spoken earlier said, "These two." He gestured to Rhun and Bridei. "They'll be going with us to Caer Louarn. And the woman. As for the rest of them, take their horses."

The warriors sprang into action, herding Rhun's men into a group, then gathering up the horses and tying their leads to their own mounts.

"Will we be allowed to ride?" Rhun asked. He was glowering. A muscle twitched in his jaw.

"Aye," the enemy leader answered. "The woman can travel with you."

"Why not leave her here?" Rhun said. "I can't think Urien would be interested in a Saxon slave girl I purchased in Londinium."

The man regarded Eastra carefully. Her face grew hot as his eyes roved over her. "Oh, he might well be interested in her." He grinned.

"And what of Morguese?" Rhun demanded. "I can't think she would tolerate her husband keeping a foreign concubine in her household."

The man shrugged. "That is for the two of them to decide. If nothing else, the Saxon would fetch a good price as a bedslave."

"She's not for sale!" Rhun spoke sharply. He took a step toward the man.

The man laughed. "I wasn't proposing to purchase her. She's Urien's captive, just as you are." His smile widened. "I wonder how much your father, the great Dragon, would be willing to pay to ransom his sons?"

"Not much." Bridei stepped forward. "I'm sure he believes he is well rid of us. He has never reconciled himself to the fact that my brother went off to fight for Arthur's cause. As for me . . ." He shrugged. "He sent me away from his fortress some years ago. I rather think he'd just as soon not have us back."

"We shall see," was all the man said. "It's up to Urien to decide anyway."

Rhun and Bridei were ordered to mount up, although not on the horses they usually rode. Rhun helped Eastra into the saddle of a roan mare, then slid in place behind her. They started off. The enemy leader—whom Eastra had heard one man refer to as "Caw"—rode in front. Then came another warrior, then she and Rhun, and then several more warriors. Some distance back, Bridei was accompanied by the rest of the force.

"Who's Urien?' Eastra whispered after they'd gone a short distance.

"A typical British chieftain," Rhun said. It sounded as if he were gritting his teeth. "Answers to no man and claims total authority over his own domain."

"Is he Arthur's enemy?"

"I don't know. I'm not certain what he wants with us. Perhaps only to gloat over the fact he captured us so easily." He swore.

"I'm sorry," she murmured. "If I had not gotten lost, none of this would have happened."

"It would have changed nothing. They simply would have waited for another opportunity to come upon us unawares. They have been following us since yesterday."

"How do you know?"

Rhun shook his head. "I felt them. But I could not see them, so I could not act on my fears."

"But why did they follow us? What do they want?"

He shook his head grimly. "I think we will have to wait until we arrive at Urien's fortress to find that out."

She sighed and shifted on the horse. Her crotch felt damp and sore, and without the loincloth to protect her privates, every step the horse took seemed to aggravate her discomfort. If her experience with Rhun was near to perfect bliss, this was the very opposite.

The forest grew denser, more impenetrable, the trail narrower. They finally had to ride single file. The air was thick and heavy, filled with moisture from all the growing things. Eastra thought of the tales of the forest in her people's homeland across the sea. Stories of people lost in the woods forever, eaten by wolves or dragged underground by malevolent spirits. She shivered. This place seemed gloomy and uninhabitable. What did the people who lived here do for food? There was no cleared land to grow crops. Did they survive by hunting deer and boar and gathering berries and nuts in season?

Then, abruptly, the forest thinned, and she could see animals had been grazing under the trees, keeping the brush down. The trees grew sparser still, and they were in a region of mixed forest and grassland. She saw black and brown cattle grazing and some pigs rooting at the edges of the pasture. They reached cleared land, planted with strips of rye and barley, but no wheat. Further on were outbuildings and small, round wooden dwellings. At last, they came in sight of the fortress. It was built on a hilltop and protected by a ditch and a high palisade that was partly timber and partly stone.

"Urien's fortress?" she asked.

Rhun nodded. Eastra felt another wave of foreboding. The place looked well-defended and secure; it would not be easy for them to escape.

They followed a trackway up the hill, and the leader of the captors, Caw, shouted up something to the man in the tower guarding the gate. The big timber gate creaked open, and they rode in.

In the muddy yard, which seemed crammed to bursting with people, dogs, and livestock, Caw's men began to dismount and hand their horses off to servants. As Rhun climbed down and reached up to help her off their horse, Eastra saw Caw approach. He motioned curtly. "Come with me."

He led them toward a huge round timber structure. Thinking of her disheveled appearance, Eastra quickly ran her hands over her hair and tried to smooth her gunna.

Rhun glanced back at her. "Remember," he whispered, "you're supposed to be a slave." Eastra jerked her hands away from her hair. She must do her best to uphold Rhun's story, not merely for her own safety, but to please him. She still felt guilty they had been captured because of her selfish actions.

The structure they entered seemed to consist of one huge room with a hearth in the center. Furs and bright weavings hung from the walls, and the several supporting columns had been ornately carved and then painted with the images of strange faces and wild beasts. Around the hearth, several stools and low tables were arranged, and at the far end sat a man in a tall wooden chair. Numerous fox pelts, the heads still attached, hung from the chair. The man had long dark hair and a full beard growing gray, and his face was craggy and weathered.

Observing this impressive chieftain and the barbaric splendor of his dwelling, Eastra's spirits sank. Urien reminded her of Cerdic. The same shrewd, ruthless aura of power surrounded both men.

"Rhun ap Maelgwn!" The man's voice rumbled through the room. "I have not seen you since you were but a stripling. You've grown up fine and tall like your father. And Bridei." The man's dark eyes fixed on Rhun's brother with fierce cunning. "I was surprised to hear you had joined the great Arthur's cause." His lip curled in contempt. "I thought you had more sense than that."

Eastra had almost forgotten about Bridei, so focused she was on Rhun and what had happened between them. She watched Rhun's brother smile one of his dazzlingly ingratiating smiles as he answered, "I had nothing better to do, King Urien. And as you remember, I like being in the middle of things."

"Ah," Urien said, "so I do. Well, Morguese will be pleased to see you. She was off in the forest when word came of your arrival. She'll be here soon."

"By then we intend to be on our way!" Rhun's voice rang out, as harsh and commanding as Urien's. "You have no right to hold us prisoner. We've interfered in no way with your authority or your lands!"

Urien drew back his massive fur- and leather-clad frame and his eyes narrowed. "You crossed my lands without my permission. I consider *that* interfering with my authority."

She heard Rhun exhale in exasperation. "And how were we to get that permission without crossing those lands to speak to you? You know very well I and many others have often taken this route on our journey to Gwynedd."

"But you had no intention of stopping, did you? Although my wife is kin of yours, you did not think to visit her, nor to afford me—the chieftain of these lands—the courtesy of offering you the hospitality of a meal. Instead, you ride across my domain like a pack of sneaking cattle thieves."

Eastra felt Rhun's tension increase, as if he wanted to spring on Urien and throttle him. She held her breath, terrified that if Rhun made such a move, Urien's guards would injure or kill him.

Then Bridei spoke, his voice cool and mellifluous after Rhun's aggressive tones. "I urged him to stop. But my brother is an impatient man, eager to be home and bring his stepmother the gifts we bought her in Londinium. He knew if we stopped at your dun, courtesy would demand we share a meal with you. Then Morguese would beg us to stay and entertain her with news of the world outside Rheged. Our visit might well drag on several days. Meanwhile, Rhun is anxious to pay his respects to his family and return to Arthur's camp. There is peace between Arthur and the Saxons for now, but . . ." Bridei shrugged expressively. "You well know how the Saxon kind are. In a day or a week, they might well decide they don't yet have enough land and break the truce."

Urien cocked his head, as if considering Bridei's explanation. Then he looked directly at Eastra. "You speak disparagingly of the Saxons, yet you travel with one of their kind in your company."

"A new maidservant for my lady mother, Rhiannon,"

Bridei answered. "We purchased her in Londinium. Her
needlework is said to be superb. I thought my mother would
be delighted to learn Saxon sewing techniques. Eastra is
of noble family. All of her kin were killed years ago in a
raid. She has been a slave ever since."

Urien grunted, appearing unconvinced. "Hard to imagine she is not a bedslave, with a face like that." He smirked
at her.

Eastra felt Rhun go rigid next to her, but Bridei answered, "Believe it or not, her skill in needlework makes
her worth more than any pleasure she could give a man in
bed. There are many beautiful Saxon women, but few of
them are skilled seamstresses. And, as I said, she is a gift
for my mother, not my father."

"Not that your father would even look at her," Urien
said. "He is bewitched by his red-haired spouse, just as I
am by my own lovely Morguese." He smiled as he looked
toward the door. Before she turned to see the woman who
must be Morguese, Eastra noted Urien's smile was faintly
mocking.

Eastra had never seen a woman like Morguese of
Rheged. Once she had undoubtedly been spectacularly
beautiful, with dark red hair that hung to her knees, pale,
creamy skin and eyes there were neither green nor gray but
a touch of both, like the glistening foam on a storm-tossed
sea. But time had made inroads into her beauty. There were
strands of white in her thick hair and faint lines marring
her haughty features. Even so, time had not altered the aura
of power that surrounded her. Eastra could not put her finger on what made this woman such a jolt to the senses.
Although she was not much taller than Eastra, somehow
she seemed to fill the room, dwarfing even Urien's feral
menace.

"Bridei, my darling cousin." Morguese came forward
and kissed Bridei full on the lips. Then Morgeuse approached Rhun. "Rhun, what a delight to see you again
after all these years." Eastra watched in shock as Morguese
planted a very uncousinlike kiss on *his* lips. Rhun all but

squirmed until Morgeuse moved away, trailing some exotic, heady scent in her wake. She faced her husband. "What brings my darling kin to Caer Louarn?"

"They came to visit you on their way to Gwynedd," Urien answered with an innocent smile.

For a moment, Eastra thought that Urien was lying to cover up the fact that he had really kidnapped Morgeuses's "darling kin." Then she saw the faint, knowing look on Morgeuse's face and realized Urien's wife was well aware of what he was about. "How delightful," Morgeuse said, her face catlike with contentment. "We must insist they enjoy our hospitality a good long while."

Ten

"Damn Urien! He's playing some sort of game with us!" Rhun paced across the bedchamber where he and Bridei had been taken by a servant and told to dress for the welcoming feast. "You know he isn't simply detaining us here so his wife can enjoy the pleasure of our company! I vow he has some more sinister scheme in mind!"

Bridei shrugged nonchalantly into an embroidered tunic. "So he's lying through his teeth. So what? There's nothing we can do about it. We'll just have to wait and see if we can either escape or convince Urien to free us."

"And you!" Rhun resisted the familiar urge to grab his brother and shake him. "You appear utterly unperturbed by all of this. Why is that, I wonder? Did you know all along this was going to happen?"

"How would I know? I've been with you every moment since we left Londinium."

"That's just the point." Rhun decided to give voice to his vague suspicions. "In Londinium, you went off to do your spying, and ever since then, disturbing things have kept happening."

"You were attacked in Londinium and now we are being detained by one of Arthur's enemies—and you think me to blame for both things?" Bridei shook his head. "You're grasping, brother. You knew this mission had its dangers.

It's pretty harsh to blame me for every misfortune that befalls us. After all, we're on the same side."

"Allegedly," Rhun grumbled. But deep down, he knew Bridei was right. He was lashing out blindly, desperate to find someone to blame for their predicament. Everything Bridei said was true. They'd known many of the British chieftains thought Arthur was gaining too much power. It was no surprise a man like Urien might harass them, knowing they were on a mission for Arthur. "Do you think Urien knows who Eastra is? Do you think he is keeping us here because of her?" A spasm of fear went through Rhun. What if Eastra were in danger?

"I don't know, but I will try to find out," Bridei answered.

"How?"

Bridei's mouth quirked. "Morgeuse."

"Ah, I'd forgotten the two of you have a special relationship." Rhun could not keep the bitterness from his voice. "And while you are at it, see that she does nothing to Eastra."

"What do you think she would do to Eastra?"

Rhun snorted. "There's no telling what sort of wicked spell she might work on an innocent like Eastra."

"You speak as if you believe the stories that Morgeuse is a sorceress."

"Well, isn't she?"

"Perhaps. But her power's not much different than the kind of power Rhiannon has, and you're not afraid of her."

"I *know* Rhiannon would never hurt anyone, while I'm not so certain of Morgeuse. All I know is when Urien ordered Eastra to go with Morguese, this sense of dread came over me."

"Maybe you're afraid Morguese will teach Eastra how to bewitch you." Bridei grinned.

"Huh." *Too late for that,* Rhun thought to himself as he began to change his own clothing. He was *already* bewitched. Nay, that was misstating it. He was in love. What else could this feeling inside him be, this desperate longing to be near Eastra, to hold her and keep her safe forever? Merely being away from her this short while made him frantic. And when he thought about the future and their inevitable parting, he felt such deep anguish he was not certain he could go on.

He ran his fingers through his hair, then splashed his face with water a servant had brought them. "What do you think Urien intends to do with us?" he asked as he toweled dry.

"If I had to guess, I'd say he's simply going to detain us here for a good while."

Rhun jerked around. "How long?"

Bridei shrugged. "If I knew that, I might unravel the rest of his plan. Relax. If Urien had meant any of us harm, we would not be here. We would be back in the forest, already carrion for the wolves and ravens."

Rhun sighed as he exchanged his leather riding trousers for some of soft wool. Why had he agreed to this ridiculous journey? It would have been much simpler to take Eastra to some other stronghold, Tinegal perhaps. It was far from the Saxon lands and Arthur's headquarters at Camlann, but could be reached by crossing lands that were ruled by the high king's allies. This journey to Gwynedd—it was madness. Yet he had agreed to it, reasoning in some part of his mind hidden even to himself that it would give him an opportunity to be with Eastra that much longer. Now his obsession with this woman might have cost his commander dearly and could yet endanger them all.

He recalled his coupling with Eastra, the blinding speed with which he had thrown aside all restraint and rationality. Merely to touch this woman was to turn into a lust-raddled fool.

A servant came to lead them to the feast hall. With a grim look at Bridei, Rhun fell in step behind their escort. He had to stop thinking about Eastra. It was more important than ever that he keep his wits about him.

* * *

"That you're a slave does not mean you have to dress in rags," Morguese purred. "I'm certain we can find some clothing that will enhance your charms."

Eastra felt her body go rigid. She was in a sumptuous bedchamber, ostensibly for the purpose of helping Morguese prepare for the feast. But a tiny red-haired woman had assumed the responsibility of helping Morguese dress and was now combing out her thick auburn hair. Eastra had waited, anticipating that some task would be required of her. Now, it appeared Morguese had more devious plans in mind.

"Come here, sweeting," Morguese coaxed. "Let me look at you more closely."

Repressing a shiver of dread, Eastra approached Morguese, who was sitting on a stool near the hearth. "Such a lovely creature." Morguese reached out long, elegant, be-ringed fingers to examine one of Eastra's braids. "And exquisite hair. I've never seen any that shade before. I'm certain Rhun must have paid a very high price for you. In Londinium." She smiled smugly and her strange eyes glinted green, like marshlights. She nodded to Eastra. "Turn around."

Eastra obeyed, although she knew her face was hot with color. She might as well be in the slave market, the way this woman inspected her.

"Mmmm. I've heard tales of such things," Morguese murmured. "Of princesses, even queens, who fell into the hands of their enemies and ended up as scullery maids. How sad, very sad. To go from having such power to having naught."

Eastra whirled around, wanting to see her adversary's face, to gauge whether she knew the truth or was simply guessing. But Morguese's jewellike eyes revealed nothing—except a kind of terrifying power, a startling energy that made Eastra look away. Anxiety shivered down her body. What if this woman ensorceled her and made her reveal all her secrets?

"You're trembling, child." Morgeuse stood, the movement light and quick. "Fear does not become you. It demeans your beauty, makes you look pale and insipid. But perhaps that is how you've had to appear in order to fool your captors into believing you have accepted your lot as a slave. But I know better. You are defiant and proud and not meek at all. You intend to have it back some day, all the power and esteem that was once yours."

Eastra went rigid. It was as if this woman could read her thoughts!

Morgeuse responded with a satisfied smile. "They do not call me the witch of the north without good reason. No doubt you have been raised to believe power is a thing that belongs to men. But that is far from true. In fact, women control everything that is important. Urien fancies himself a great man, guiding the future of Britain. He is no different than my kin, Arthur. But it is not up to them. I have looked into the scrying bowl and *seen*. It is my power, my magic that will endure!"

Eastra stood frozen, mesmerized by this woman who was like no other she had ever met. Morgeuse of Rheged dared to challenge even the warriors of her race.

"About your attire for the feast tonight . . ." Morgeuse tapped a finger on her chin. Abruptly, she was a woman once more, no longer a seer prophesizing the future. "I think something subtle would be best. A fabric pale and shimmering, so that you glow like a flame in the dimness of the hall.

"Nevyn." Morgeuse snapped her fingers. "Bring me the pale green gown I wore for the Beltaine celebration three years ago, the one that faded so badly when you washed it. Shoddy workmanship, I say. A good dye should not fade. Or perhaps I was not meant to wear it after that. What if that is a sign that I should not wear the gowns I use for the ceremonies more than once? The Goddess might feel cheated, after all." Morguese frowned, and Eastra heaved a sigh. It was a relief to be in the presence of a mortal woman once again, haughty queen though she might be.

The gown was finely made and elegant, not the provocative garment Eastra had worried it would be. She and Morgeuse were the same height, so although the Rheged queen was more generously built, the gown fit tolerably well. Nevyn combed Eastra's hair and loosely braided the front; then Eastra was deemed ready by Morgeuse. They proceeded to the feasting hall. Once they reached it, Morgeuse surprised Eastra by telling her to follow Nevyn to the kitchen area. "You're supposed to be a slave," she said with a faint smile. "Let's see you behave like one."

Eastra soon found herself moving around the feast hall with a pitcher of mead, filling cups. She really did not mind her role of servant this night, if it gave her an opportunity to get close to Rhun. Gradually working her way around the other warriors gathered by the hearth, she reached Rhun and, trying not to tremble, filled his cup. He glanced up, his eyes full of anger and frustration, but then she smiled at him and his expression changed to one of yearning. Eastra's heart soared. He could not deny what was between them. It showed too clearly on his face.

She moved away, hoping he had the sense to drink his mead quickly so she could return to serve him once more.

To Rhun's right, Urien said something, and Rhun struggled to listen. He had to remain wary and alert, to remember the danger they were in. But it was very difficult with Eastra so near, moving like a flame of light in the pale green gown, her milky skin and silvery gold hair completing the luminous effect. He wanted to reach out for her, to take her in his arms.

But he could not. It would be terribly dangerous to let his enemy guess she was more to him than a gift for his stepmother. If Urien knew who she was and how Rhun felt about her . . . his stomach clenched at the thought.

"The slave girl . . ." Urien was saying. "It appears she has been trained to serve food as well as to do needlework. She has not spilled a drop, and she moves among the men with remarkable grace." He looked at Rhun, an ironic grin twitching his mouth. "Perhaps after the meal, we could have her dance for us."

Rhun went rigid. The idea of having the whole hall of men looking at Eastra, enjoying her beauty, made him almost physically ill. "Just because she can serve mead gracefully does not mean she can dance," he retorted. "As far as I know, the Saxons do not indulge in such activities. Although they set some store by their heralds and poets and are expert craftsmen, I don't think music matters much to them."

"Still," Urien said, "it might be interesting to see if she has a natural gift for it. After Morgeuse dances, of course."

Rhun's mind raced. He had to save Eastra from performing for these crude warriors. He could not subject her to such embarrassment and degradation. Bridei, he thought, shooting a glance at his brother. He might be able to think of a plan to spare Eastra. But how to talk to him? Bridei was seated on the other side of Morgeuse, some distance away.

Eastra carried in a platter of bannocks, offering the steaming cakes to the warriors to use in sopping up the juices from the chunks of meat they cut off from the roast boar carcass set up on a plank near the hearth. Rhun watched her, observing her agile movements. Demure but queenly, she was the epitome of refined womanhood. An intense longing built up inside him. If only there was some way, after this war was over, that he could make her his wife. But that was a vain hope. The war with the Saxons had gone on since a hundred years before he was born.

She came near, offering him a bannock. Again, she smiled at him, her teeth white and even, her blue eyes as soft and tranquil as the summer sky. He lost himself in her gaze, remembering her skin, her softness, her delicate female scent . . .

"I think your plan is witless, Rhun ap Maelgwn," Urien said beside him. "You should take her for a concubine. I'm certain you can find your stepmother some aged crone to aid her in her sewing. There is no need to waste such beauty."

Rhun looked sharply at Urien. The old chieftain laughed, his still sound teeth glinting pale yellow in his gray-streaked beard. Rhun jerked his gaze away. Everything was going awry. He'd made a fool of himself in front of his enemy. Curtly, he nodded to Eastra, indicating that she should move on. As she did so, Urien laughed again.

The feast dragged on. Rhun had no appetite. He wondered if Urien were serious about having Eastra dance. The idea gnawed at him.

The wooden platters and the remains of the feast were cleared away by Eastra and the other servants. She disappeared for a time, and Rhun prayed she would remain in the kitchen. But all too soon she returned with another platter, this one filled with honey cakes. From the edge of the room, Rhun heard the soft thump of a drum, then a sparkling cascade of notes from a harp. A second harpist joined the first, the two instruments blending to make a richer tone. The lilting tones of a shepherd's pipe were the last to join the melody.

The drumbeats quickened in tempo and the music grew more stirring. Morgeuse rose like a lazy cat from her cushion between Urien and Bridei. She ran her fingers through her thick mane, then moved languidly into the open space where the roasted carcass had been. Some of the warriors edged back to afford her more room.

She motioned to a small flame-haired servant, and the girl came forward carrying a cloth bag. Morgeuse drew out the contents and with the girl's help, began to tie the small bronze bells to her wrists with leather thongs. As Morgeuse drew up her gown so the girl could tie bells to her ankles, Rhun saw his hostess was barefoot.

Slowly, as if testing each movement for the sound it made, Morgeuse began to dance. The bells rippled and chimed, blending with the rest of the instruments into a rich tapestry, thrilling and wild. Rhun felt his heartbeat quicken. Morgeuse's lush form, clad in crimson, undulated like bright liquid spilling across the room. Her feet tapped rapidly against the hard-packed earthen floor of the hall, making the bells shimmer and sing. The melody was irresistible. It surged and subsided, like the waves of a sea lapping against the senses. Rhun exhaled a deep breath. He felt the music enter him, reaching down into his soul. It seemed to draw out all the aching turmoil inside him and concentrate it until it was a fine, golden thread pulling his thoughts out into infinity.

He closed his eyes. His body was a husk blown in the wind, swirling and dancing in the mindless breeze. He soared above the land, like a kestrel gliding on the air, high above the mountains of Gwynedd. He saw the land spread out below him, heartbreakingly beautiful. Beyond Gwynedd stretched the rich blue green of the rest of Britain. Wild, deep-hearted forests. Rolling, jewel-green hills banded with the hammered filigree of silver and bronze rivers. And the sea beyond, vast and untamed.

Gradually the tempo slowed; then in a glistening, sad cascade of notes, it ended. Rhun felt himself floating back to earth. He opened his eyes and looked around, wondering if anyone else had been affected as he had. The rest of the warriors sat silent and spellbound. Morguese shook her head, as if dispersing the last remnants of her magic.

The musicians began another song. It was light and festive and gay, altogether different from the earlier melody. Rhun released a sigh. He had expected Morgeuse's dance to be sexual and provocative, but it had another sort of power. It drew a man's spirit into the music, made him feel lost and helpless before forces much greater than he was. He struggled against the new melody, not wanting to be affected. But why fight something so cheerful and benign? This tune reminded him of being a boy, the bright weightlessness of his body, the untainted wonder of being alive.

Morgeuse's dance was playful, energetic. He was impressed that she could move so quickly. Her face was flushed, her eyes bright, and her hair flowed over her body like spilled wine. As the pace of the dance quickened, the warriors began to pound their fists on the small tables in front of them. They shouted and whooped, urging Morgeuse on. She was a flame swirling in the breeze, a ray of some bright sunset casting them all into her glory.

When she finally whirled to a breathless stop, the men cheered loudly. Rhun wanted to join them, but an uneasy thought held him back. Urien had spoken of having Eastra dance. Would he make good on his threat?

Eastra stood at the side of the room, her gaze riveted on Morgeuse. Never before had she seen a woman hold the attention of a whole group of men, making them feel her power. It was exhilarating, fascinating. No Saxon woman, even the wife of the most powerful king, would ever dare such a thing. Among Eastra's people, women were honored and valued. They could own property and enter into legal contracts. But they always deferred to men. They were not bold and proud; they did not flaunt themselves in front of a crowded hall.

Eastra struggled to decide what it was about Morgeuse that was so compelling. Was it the graceful, expressive way that she moved, interpreting the music, making it come to life? Was it her beauty, the sheer animal vitality of her voluptuous body? Or was it some sort of magic, a power that could not be seen, only felt? Eastra wished she knew her secret, and the thought came to her that maybe if she asked Morgeuse, the woman might teach her a bit of her skill. Urien's wife did not seem hostile. Indeed, there had been a vague sort of warmth in the way she dealt with Eastra earlier.

A planned formed in Eastra's mind. She wanted to learn a little of Morgeuse's technique for making men pay attention to her—just a subtle hint of it so she would not always be so overlooked and unimportant. Even Rhun had a tendency to ignore her. He never asked her what she wished to do but told her what he thought was best. He treated her like a child—a dear and precious child but, nonetheless, someone incompetent to make decisions about her own life.

She was puzzling on how to approach Morgeuse when

she heard someone call her name. Gazing across the smoky room, she saw Urien motioning to her. A wave of apprehension instantly made her muscles tighten. She walked slowly toward him. Had she neglected to keep his cup filled? The look on his face suggested something more important than that. He was watching her intently, clearly seeing her as a woman rather than a nameless servant.

Her mouth went dry, and she glanced at Rhun. The alarmed expression on his face did not reassure her. Had Urien tired of this cat-and-mouse game he played with them? Was he now going to reveal he knew her identity? Then what would happen? Would he imprison her? Or kill her and send word to Cerdic so the bitter war would resume?

A vague smile played across Urien's face as she drew near. He looked relaxed and a little drunk. "Eastra." He said her name slowly, slurring it a little. "Beautiful lass that you are, would you dance for us?"

Eastra stared, too startled to respond.

Hearing Urien's words and seeing the stricken expression on Eastra's face, Rhun felt something inside him snap. He got to his feet, his fists clenched at his sides. "Nay." He made his voice firm, although he tried not to raise it. "You have no right to ask such a thing of her."

Urien still smiled, but his response was low and controlled, taut. "I addressed my question to the woman. Let her answer."

The coil of fury tightened inside Rhun. Urien had her trapped and he knew it! Eastra was trembling. Rhun could see the fear in her lovely eyes. She started to speak . . .

"Nay! I will not permit it!" The words rushed out of his mouth, outraged and violent.

Urien stared up at him, quirking a bushy brow. "You're a guest here, Rhun ap Maelgwn. *You* do not issue commands."

Rhun thought frantically, trying to find an argument that Urien would listen to. "She's my slave! I should be the one to order her to dance, not you!"

"Then order her to dance."

Rhun could sense the threat behind his words. The warriors seated around the hearth shifted subtly, preparing to leap to their leader's defense. Then everyone went silent and still, waiting. Rhun looked at Eastra. Her expression was desperate. Once before, she had implored him with her eyes, begging him to save her. He had not. Instead, he had walked away and left her to be enslaved and degraded.

"Nay." He spoke precisely as he drew his eating knife from its sheath on his belt. "I will not. She is my slave, to do with as I see fit. *You* will not give her orders."

He heard Eastra gasp. Then, with a sudden flurry of movement, there were Rheged warriors all around him. "Seize him," Urien said calmly. "Prince Rhun has apparently forgotten what it is like to be a guest in a noble household. Perhaps a few days of quiet contemplation will remind him of the courtesy his position requires."

They were taking him away! As if he were a prisoner, a conquered enemy! Eastra wanted to cry out, but she was too shocked to make her mouth work. She stared dumbly as Rhun was led from the hall. Then Urien turned his gaze on her once more. She thought he was going to ask her to dance again. She meant to refuse, to show them she could also be brave and defiant. Instead, Urien smiled. "I've changed my mind. The time for dancing has passed." He snapped his fingers. "You may return to your task of clearing away the remains of the feast."

Eastra began to move numbly around the room, gathering up platters and cups. She felt a sense of horror over what had happened to Rhun. Once again, she had complicated his life and caused him difficulty. The sick guilt built inside her.

As she carried her burden of dirty dishes to the kitchen shed, tears stung her eyes. She had to do something to help him. But what? If only she could speak to Bridei.

She returned to the hall carrying a ewer of mead. When she neared Bridei, she caught his gaze, then made a subtle movement to indicate she wanted to speak to him outside.

A short time later, she saw him say something to Urien, then get to his feet. She held her breath. Would they let him leave the hall, or was he also a prisoner?

Bridei walked casually to the door and went out. Eastra waited until he had been gone a few moments, then set down the ewer and followed.

It was dark outside the feast hall. Only a few smoky torches illuminated the pathway to the kitchen. Their flickering light cast wavy, shifting shadows. She moved away from the torchlight, struggling to adjust her eyes and figure out where Bridei had gone.

"Eastra."

The quiet voice sounded next to her and she jumped. "By Freya!" she breathed.

"Sorry." It sounded like he was grinning.

"Can you not be serious for once!" she hissed. "Rhun is a prisoner! Who knows what they will do to him?"

"They won't do anything to him. Unless he dies of sheer fury and aggravation, he'll be well enough."

"But the way they are treating him—like some common captive!"

"Maybe it will be good for him. Force him to calm down and think rationally. For once."

"That's not fair!" She wanted to strike Bridei. "It's *my* fault he is in this predicament. I should have said something, made it clear to Urien I would not dance for him." The guilty thought crossed her mind that she had not meant to refuse. In fact, she had been on the verge of trying to emulate Morgeuse's skillful performance.

"And what would that have accomplished? Urien would have stood his ground, and Rhun would still have acted like a hotheaded fool. Don't you see? Urien planned this whole thing. He provoked Rhun deliberately. He wanted some excuse to claim offense. Now Rhun has given him one."

Eastra saw the trap their host had sprung. It angered her, but hardly eased her guilt. "It's still my fault," she said glumly. "If I had not enticed Rhun . . ." She stopped, re-calling suddenly who she was talking to.

Bridei laughed. "It's a bit late to worry about that, isn't it? My brother's obviously smitten, and smitten badly. He'd take on Urien's whole army to fight for your honor. Or for that matter, Cerdic's army. Aye, *you* make him vulnerable to his enemies, but it's hardly your fault. He fell in love with you long ago. Whatever you did back there during the storm does not make that much difference."

"We did nothing! Nothing at all!" Eastra drew in a sharp breath. She could not let Bridei guess what had happened under the great oak. He would think her a wanton. And given that Rhun had said he would not wed her, it was true.

"Oh, aye. Nothing." Bridei laughed again.

"Stop it!" She struck out and hit something solid, Bridei's chest. "Stop laughing! We must do something. Rescue Rhun, then escape somehow!"

"Escape? From this stout fortress, guarded by two score of fierce warriors? Unless you know a way to sprout wings and fly, I don't think there's much chance of that."

"But we have to do something. We have to try . . ." Eastra took a deep breath. Bridei implied it was hopeless, but she could not accept that.

"Why do we have to try to escape?" Bridei's voice cut into her thoughts. "We are none of us in any danger here. Urien knows my father would wreak terrible vengeance upon him if he harmed Rhun or me in any way. And as for you, even if Urien knows who you are, you are worth more to him alive than dead. In the meantime, we are safe, well fed, comfortable . . ."

"You're certain Rhun is comfortable? That they do not have him in some dark, rank hole?"

"Urien would not mistreat him. I've told you that. As for the comfort of his thoughts, I don't doubt Rhun is suf-fering the tortures of the damned in that regard. But it has ever been like that for him. You are merely the latest means he's found to make himself miserable."

That much was true. Ever since she had found him again, she had made Rhun unhappy. "So you are saying we wait here and do nothing? But what about the truce? What about Arthur? If your leader learns we have not arrived in Gwynedd, he will think something has happened. He might blame Cerdic and go to war against him. Perhaps that is even what Urien plans to happen!"

"Perhaps." Bridei said. "But there is nothing we can do about it, is there?"

Eastra heaved a sigh. Bridei was worse than no help at all.

"Don't be so discouraged," Bridei said. "I'll tell you what I will do. I will try to find out Urien's plans from Morgeuse. Then we'll know how urgent the need is to get away."

"How will you find out anything from Morgeuse?" Eastra asked. "She does not seem like someone who could be tricked into giving up information."

"Ah, but there is every likelihood that Morgeuse has different things in mind than her husband does. She might even be willing to help us."

Eastra considered Morgeuse's scornful comments about Urien and Arthur. Perhaps they had an ally there. "I will talk to her also. If I can get up the courage for it, that is. Did you see how all the men watched her dance? And there was not lust in their eyes, but a kind of adoration. I have never known a woman who had that sort of power."

"Ah, Morgeuse, she is a witch, have no doubt of it. Even Arthur is afraid of her."

"And you?" Eastra asked. "Are you afraid of her?"

Although she could not see him, she could well imagine Bridei's smug expression as he answered. "She may be a witch, but she is yet a woman. And I have not yet met the woman who can ensorcel *me*."

Eleven

As Eastra returned to the hall, she met Morgeuse coming out. "There you are. I had wondered where our little Saxon had gone. My husband says I must not let you out of my sight, for fear you will steal the wits of the other men as you have Prince Rhun." A flash of guilt afflicted Eastra. Morgeuse smiled. "Oh, don't worry, your lover has not been harmed."

"He's not my lover," Eastra said quickly.

"A pity," Morgeuse said. "Although Rhun always appears so stiff-necked and dutiful, I don't doubt he is a lusty man beneath that serious façade. It will merely require the right woman to lure him away from his noble ideals."

Eastra almost squirmed. It was unsettling to have this woman guess her less than honorable thoughts. She *had* plotted to distract Rhun from his obligations to his king, to make him care more for her than for the cause he fought for. Thinking about it, she felt devious and heartless.

"Come. I tire of these men with their loud drunkenness. Let's go to my chamber where we can talk."

Eastra followed Morgeuse among the twisting shadows. After the darkness of the fortress yard, the queen's chamber seemed to glow with warmth and light. Although she had been in the room before the feast, Eastra had been too anxious then to take note of the furnishings and to sense the heady private world Morgeuse had created.

The walls were hung with rich tapestries, the floor covered with mats and furs and cushions. The two bronze lamps that lit the room were fashioned in the shape of elegant beasts—one a sort of deer, the other a bird with arched, delicate wings. The motif of animals appeared everywhere. The carved wooden table had claw-like feet. Proud dragons' heads rose from each corner of the bed.

The other impression was of color—rich gold, scarlet, deep blues and greens, pale saffron, rose, and lavender. Compared to the spare, open rooms of Roman houses, or even the crowded interior of a Saxon hall, this place appeared crammed to bursting. Chests and baskets were piled around, masses of clothing hung from a pole, small jars, bowls, and boxes covered every surface. And emanating from this mass of luxury was a multitude of exotic odors— spices and crushed herbs and other less identifiable scents. It was a feast for the senses, a dizzying swirl of color, shape, and fragrance—confusing, beguiling, and somehow disturbing. Eastra could feel Morgeuse's power here.

The queen seated herself on a cushion on the floor, smoothing her skirts around her. She pointed to a cushion nearby. "Sit. I will have Nevyn bring us some wine."

Eastra saw that the small red-haired girl had followed them. She was like a shadow, moving so silently and stealthily it was unnerving. Eastra observed Nevyn more closely as she fetched a ewer and some cups from some hidden corner of the room. The young woman had speckled skin like the wet-nurse slave in Londinium, and her eyes were pale and almost colorless. She poured a cup of wine each for Morgeuse and Eastra, then one for herself. Then, with the delicate grace of a cat, she took a seat on a cushion nearby.

"Ah," Morguese said. "Now there are three of us. A much more fortuitous number than two." Eastra realized they were seated in a kind of circle, almost exactly the same distance apart. Morgeuse nodded to the girl. "Nevyn is my apprentice. I wanted to pass on my knowledge to someone and since, alas, I have no daughters, I had to find a likely young woman to train. Nevyn is from Ireland. She was shipwrecked on the coast of Powys, the only survivor. No one wanted her for a slave, but I saw immediately she had some natural aptitude." Morgeuse turned her attention to Eastra. "And now I have you as well."

A shiver afflicted Eastra. She had wanted to learn some of Morguese's magic, but now, realizing it was actually going to happen, she was frightened. What sort of strange business was she getting involved in? What would Rhun think if he knew? Somehow, she did not think he would approve.

"Most men abhor women of power," Morguese said, as if reading Eastra's thoughts. "Even my husband only tolerates my abilities. He sees me as a kind of weapon he can use against his enemies, but he must be careful the blade does not cut him, too." She smiled faintly.

Eastra felt a sudden panic. Morgeuse's words alarmed her, and the small, crowded chamber seemed to grow close. She wanted to run away, to escape. But if she showed her fear, Morguese might be offended. And she needed Morgeuse's help to free Rhun and escape.

"Don't worry," Morguese said. "You need only journey as far as you want to—for tonight, at least. Now, close your eyes. Nay, before you do that, take off your sandals and unloosen the girdle around your waist. It is best to be naked, but I doubt you are ready for that."

Eastra did as she was told. As she resumed her seat on the cushion, Morgeuse added, "Remove your earrings and necklace. Metal is a thing fashioned by men and does not please the Lady."

As she removed her earrings, the sense of unease built inside Eastra. Without jewelry she felt naked. Cerdic had taught her she must always wear some sort of ornament as a mark of her status. Even while posing as a slave, she had continued to wear the necklace Rhun had purchased for her in Londinium under her gown and small bronze earbobs in her ears. "I will take off the earrings, but I would rather not remove the necklace. It was a gift and is made of glass more than metal."

Morgeuse shook her head. "Glass is also made by men, a mimicry of the jewels that grow naturally in the depths of the Mother."

Reluctantly, Eastra removed the necklace. It was as if all the ties that bound her to her past had been severed. All she wore now was the gown Morgeuse had given her.

"Aye, you must leave the past behind to go into the future." Morgeuse smiled faintly. "Now, close your eyes. Place your hands on your knees and listen to your heartbeat."

Eastra obeyed.

Morgeuse continued speaking, her voice low and vibrant. "Feel the blood pulsing through you, flowing along your veins. It is warm and full of life. Salty and sweet like the rivers and oceans of the Mother's body. Feel how the blood warms your flesh and makes it alive. Feel your bones beneath the flesh. They are the last part of a babe to be formed, to grow hard and rigid. They will be the last part of you to decay into the earth, to turn to dust and return to the Mother.

"Breathe. Feel the air enter your lungs and give you life. When a babe takes the first breath at birth, it cries in pain as its spirit enters its body. And someday your spirit will leave your body with one last sighing breath."

Eastra felt strange. Morgeuse's voice seemed to have entered her, making her aware of her body in a way she had never been before. It was startling and yet intriguing.

"If you were a man," Morgeuse continued, "that would be the end of the mystery. But you are woman, so there is more. Deep within your body is your womb. It grows and recedes in rhythm to the moon's light. In the blood of your womb is power—that is why men abhor it. You have the ability to create life, a great gift. In that way, you are as powerful as the Goddess. But to make a babe, you must open yourself to a man, take his seed and nurture it inside you. Be careful how you choose, what man you lie with, for if you make a babe with him, the tie between you can never truly be severed."

Eastra thought of Rhun inside her, under the great oak, loving her. She was glad she had opened herself to him. She hoped Morgeuse's words were true, that the bond she felt between them was forever. Except they had not conceived a babe—at least not that she knew. A shiver went through her at the thought a babe might be growing inside her.

"Now, feel your breasts. Feel their heaviness. Feel them fill with milk to feed your babe. Pale, glistening milk, as magical as any of the Mother's gifts."

Her breasts did feel heavy, swollen, the nipples distended and pricking against the smooth fabric of her gown. But that was impossible. Even if she were with child, it was too soon for there to be any signs. Not one full day had passed since Rhun and she had lain together. But there also seemed to be a weight in her belly, a kind of movement . . .

Disturbed by the sensations she felt, Eastra opened her eyes.

"Frightened?" Morgeuse asked.

She nodded.

"That means you were very close to 'seeing.' The trick is to get beyond the fear, to allow yourself to go where the Goddess leads."

"No," Eastra said. Her vague unease had become a kind of dread.

Morgeuse shrugged. "So you are not ready. It does not matter. The Goddess is patient. Many people ignore Her all their lives, and She still does not turn from them." She rose gracefully.

Eastra worried that despite her words, Morgeuse was angry. What if Morgeuse refused to help her?

The queen went to the table and poured water on some herbs burning in a bowl. Their soothing scent was replaced by a damp, earthy smell. Estra got to her feet. "Wait. Please."

Morgeuse cocked her head and looked at her, her green eyes opaque and unfathomable.

"I came here because I thought . . . I thought you might help me."

"Help you?"

Eastra nodded. "Somehow I must see that Prince Rhun is freed. It's my fault he lost his temper and drew his knife."

"What else?"

"Then . . . we must leave this place. What your husband is doing is wrong. He has no right to hold us prisoner!" Eastra grew bolder as her indignation caught fire. If Urien kept them here and by his meddling caused the truce to be broken, there would be more bloodshed and suffering. "You said yourself he was trying to control things he should not, that you have seen what the future holds."

Morgeuse's face was still neutral, unreadable. "So you believe I should go against my husband's orders and set you free?"

Eastra nodded. "You said your power was greater than his. If you do not fear him, then do what is right!"

Morgeuse laughed. "What an innocent you are. Right and wrong are terms men have made up to justify their actions. What must be, *will* be. That is the Goddess's way."

"You won't help us?" Eastra felt the anger drain out of her. She felt tired and defeated.

"I didn't say that, only that it isn't time yet. There is a purpose to your being here. Until I know what it is, I will not aid you."

At least there was some hope Morgeuse would help them escape eventually. Perhaps it was just as well to wait. Eastra realized she did not really have the energy to rescue Rhun and ride off this very night. A few days more should not matter. "Thank you," she told Morgeuse. "If you will at least consider helping us, I would be most grateful."

Morgeuse smiled. "I hope you feel that way when the time comes. Things have a way of turning out much differently than we expect."

Eastra was too tired to argue. All at once she felt dead on her feet.

"Nevyn," Morgeuse spoke briskly. "Show Eastra where she will sleep. It's not luxurious, but then, a slave can hardly complain."

Morgeuse well knew she was not a slave, Eastra thought as she followed Nevyn to a small adjoining chamber. Why she kept up the pretense, Eastra did not know. Nor did she care at this moment, she thought, as Nevyn pointed to a straw-filled pallet on the floor. All she wanted to do was close her eyes and forget everything.

Nevyn brought her a blanket, and Eastra curled up and went to sleep.

Rhun paced across the tiny chamber, then back again, the straw on the floor making a swishing sound against his boots.

Clean straw. For all its smallness, his prison was reasonably furnished. There was a chamber pot in one corner, a faded blanket in the other. His host had even seen fit to provide him with a jar of water and a leather pouch full of bread and cheese. He would not starve nor be too uncomfortable.

But he might go mad from sheer aggravation, he thought as he paced. How could he have let Urien goad him into such outrageous behavior? He'd never before acted like such a rash, hot-tempered fool!

It boggled his mind to think of it. All these years he'd prided himself on being able to keep his head, to deal with his opponents skillfully and cunningly. And now, when it was more important than ever, he'd made a complete dolt of himself.

What would it have mattered if Urien had forced Eastra to dance? It would not have killed her, even if it did cause her embarrassment and upset. He had to put things into perspective. He was responsible for keeping their hostage physically safe, not protecting her from every distress imaginable.

But the thing was, he wanted to protect Eastra from everything. Lock her away in a safe, comfortable chamber and make certain she never suffered or wanted for a thing the rest of her life. He wanted to make it all up to her, the degradation of being a slave, the loss of her family, every hurt that had ever been inflicted on her.

But he could not. Nor should he try.

He sighed heavily. Somehow, he had to overcome his obsession with Eastra and concentrate on escaping. Once he was out of Caer Louarn, he must find Arthur and tell him what had happened, warn him that Urien, and perhaps other chieftains, were working against him.

But Eastra—how could he leave her? He had to. She would be safe enough. If Urien were going to harm her, he would have done so already. Besides, Bridei would still be here. Despite his doubts about his brother, Rhun did not believe Bridei would allow any ill to befall their hostage.

He sighed again, then turned his attentions to plans for escape.

Over the next few days, Eastra followed Morgeuse and Nevyn everywhere, assisting the younger woman when necessary, but mostly watching as Morgeuse ordered the day-to-day activities of the fortress—overseeing food preparation and storage; the weaving, dying, and sewing of cloth; the cleaning and refurbishing of the hall. Morgeuse also took Eastra and Nevyn into the forest several times, ostensibly for the purpose of gathering herbs. Morgeuse pointed out numerous plants and explained some of their uses, and they filled their gathering baskets heaping full. But Eastra sensed Morgeuse had another purpose in leaving the fortress. She seemed to be searching for something. Her manner was quiet and contemplative, absorbed in her own thoughts.

Eastra tried to talk to Nevyn, but the other woman kept her distance, her pale eyes giving away nothing. Finally, Eastra gave up wondering what Morgeuse was up to. It was clear if she wished for the Rheged queen's help, she would have to be patient.

Eastra often saw Bridei around the fortress. He appeared to be enjoying himself, playing draughts with the other warriors during the day, strumming on his harp and drinking with them in the evenings. He even went out on a hunting expedition with Urien's men and returned flushed and jubilant over the great stag they'd killed.

On the fourth night they were there, she caught Bridei on his way to the privy and asked him if he had thought of a plan for their escape. He shrugged and said he had not come up with anything yet, but he was still thinking on it.

Eastra returned to the hall, seething with frustration. It seemed they would remain Urien's prisoners until the end of the sun season. She worried about what was happening in the world outside the dense forests of Rheged, whether the truce had held or if Cerdic and Arthur had resumed fighting. She wondered if anyone guessed they were being held prisoner. Or if anyone cared.

This night she was called upon to serve while the warriors feasted on fresh venison. She did her duty, but her mind was elsewhere. Only when she saw Morgeuse near the entrance of the hall, motioning to her, did she snap to alertness. When she reached Morgeuse, the queen made a movement to indicate Eastra should follow her and be quick about it.

They went out, leaving the noisy, drunken atmosphere of the hall. A bright full moon lit the yard of the fortress. Morgeuse led her into a shadowed place behind a building and said, "Would you like to see your lover? If you are quick and quiet, there is time for you to be alone before any of the men notice."

This time Eastra did not protest that Rhun was not her lover, but nodded rapidly.

"Come," Morgeuse said.

Eastra had not been certain where Rhun was being held. She was startled when Morgeuse led her to the outer edge of the fortress and indicated a passageway leading into the ground. "He's down there. I'll stay outside and keep watch."

Eastra studied the narrow opening. Morgeuse said, "This is not the time for escape. Although you could get him out of his prison and to the gate, you will get no further. Urien is no fool. When the mead flows freely, he makes certain only his most trusted men stand guard. Enjoy your time together, and know when the moon is dark again, your lover will have a chance to seek his freedom."

With these words, Morgeuse gave Eastra a gentle shove toward the opening. Struggling against the dread that choked her throat, Eastra stepped into the pitch-black passageway. There were stairs leading downward. They led to another passageway, which led to a door. She called softly. "Rhun. Rhun, are you there?"

"Eastra?" His voice whispered out of the darkness and curled around her body, igniting a fierce ache of longing.

"Aye," she answered. She fumbled with the leather latch on the door, her fingers nerveless and clumsy.

And then she was inside. She wished she had brought a torch. Only a tiny opening in the ground above let in a sliver of moonlight. She could not see him, but she knew he was there. "Oh, Rhun." She reached out for him, seeking his familiar warmth, his smell. His body felt big and solid and wonderfully comforting. They clutched each other like drowning souls dragged from the violent surf.

"Eastra, Eastra, you smell wonderful. Like sunshine and flowers. Like my dreams." Gently, he pulled her arms from around his neck. "How did you get here? Is there anyone standing guard outside?" He turned toward the door.

"Aye. There is. Bridei bribed one of the men to let me see you, but there is no chance of escape." The lie came from her lips as if beyond her control. Somehow she knew she could not tell him that Morgeuse stood guard. If he knew there was only an unarmed woman between him and freedom, he would make a dash for the gate.

"Damn!" He released his breath in a sigh. Eastra felt a stab of guilt. What if Morgeuse were wrong? What if there was a chance they could get by the guard? After all, most of the men were in the hall, drunk on mead and sluggish from gorging themselves on venison.

"I have to get out of here," Rhun said. She felt his body tense with distress. "I have to go to Arthur and warn him."

A twinge of irritation rose up inside her. All he could think about was escaping. What about *her?* Was he not pleased to see her? "I'm trying to find a way out of here," she said. "But it is difficult. The fortress is well guarded."

"Of course it is. Oh, Eastra, my dear sweet Eastra." His mood had shifted again. He held her close and nuzzled her hair. Breathlessly, she realized she must find a way to keep his attention. She pressed against him and put her arms around his neck. Then she kissed him.

He met the kiss with hungry eagerness. He moaned and she felt his arms tighten around her. She let herself go limp. Her breasts were pressed against his chest, her belly against his groin. She opened her mouth, yielding to him, letting him know she was his to do with as he wished. His tongue was in her mouth, tentative at first; then, when she accepted him, caressing and exploring. His hands moved down to cup her buttocks. He pressed her tighter against him and she felt his shaft, hard and demanding, straining against his trousers. She squirmed, partly on fire from his kisses, partly in a calculated attempt to arouse him further.

He gave another groan and pulled away. She waited, panting. There was a battle raging inside him. Which would win? Duty? Or desire?

"Oh, Eastra, I should not, but I cannot help myself." His voice was ravaged.

"Rhun, please. I want this. I want *you.*"

He made a harsh, almost animal-like sound, then crushed her to him. Dragging up her skirts, he found bare skin. Stroking, kneading. She clutched him tightly, barely able to stand. Then he found the aching apex of her thighs, and she let his callused, exquisitely tender fingers support her weight. Tremors of fierce pleasure raked her body. She moaned. Ah, to have him touch her like this . . . sublime . . . perfect.

But there was more. To be joined. To feel his shaft stroke her womb as his fingers were stroking the swollen, wet opening between her thighs. He was kissing her neck now, driving her to madness. "Please, Rhun," she murmured.

He released her, and she thought she would go mad with impatience. But then she saw he was arranging a blanket on the straw, directly beneath the hole in the ceiling that let in the small sliver of moonlight. Boldly, she pulled her gunna over her head, then slipped off her sandals. She wanted to be naked with him.

She went and lay down on the blanket. She felt him standing over her. He could not see much of her, she knew. But it was enough. "By the Light," he muttered. "You are so beautiful."

She reached her arms up to him, urging him near. In a part of her mind, she felt amazement at what she was doing, her daring, wanton behavior. Some sort of madness had entered her. All she could think of was being joined with him, flesh to flesh, with nothing in between. She heard him removing his own clothing. Then he was kneeling over her, kissing her neck, her breasts. She arched her back, offering herself. She wanted everything, every pleasure he could give her.

The roughness of his unshaven jaw rasped against her skin, contrasting with the smooth warmth of his lips and the fluttering softness of his long hair. Her nipples tightened and throbbed, and the deep inner center of her pulsed with urgency. Then his hands were on her hips. Her thighs. She felt him opening her, spreading her. Cool air against heated flesh. Then his mouth touched her, warm wetness, glorious pressure against sentient, helpless need. Lips and tongue and teeth. He played upon her, striking sparks inside her. They whirled and caught, raging in violent splendor.

Colors and light. She was caught in a wild spiral. And then, gasping, she floated back to earth.

He was leaning over her, his face near hers. She could smell the musky scent of herself mingling with his maleness. "I've wanted to love you like that since I first saw you in Cerdic's household." he whispered. "A woman. A radiant bloom that has fulfilled every promise of that lovely child I rescued."

"But there is more," she reminded him. Her voice was breathless, desperate. "I want you inside me." She reached out, feeling for the raw proof of his desire. Her fingers closed around the warm, rigid rod of flesh. So big. It amazed her to think of such an impressive, substantial thing inside her. Yet it had fit before, and now she was even more ready.

She wondered if he breathed, he remained so still as she caressed him. She feared to be clumsy. How was she supposed to touch him? She let her fingers do what they willed. Explore. Squeeze. Fondle the amazingly soft, tender tip—he gasped. Then glide along the long, stiff length to reach the coarse hair, the heavy, rounded shapes beneath. His ballocks. Full of his seed. Seed he would put inside her, deep into her womb.

Suddenly, she could not wait. "Please," she whispered, knowing he would understand, knowing he waited only for a sign from her.

She helped guide him to her opening. He thrust in. Deep. More than she expected . . . she was not prepared. She fought for control, to catch her breath. Harsh, solid flesh stretching her, impaling her. He shifted position, stroking slowly, as if he meant to get her used to him. Her body relaxed and yielded. And then she was caught up in the maelstrom, the raging storm inside her, the strong, even tempo of his thrusts.

She felt her womb contract like a frenzied beast. She arched her hips. Spread her legs wider, offering him access. Offering him everything.

His body jerked. He groaned. And it was over.

She wanted to weep. She did not know why. A gasping sob escaped her.

"Eastra, my love." His arms were around her. Tender. Protective. He kissed her cheek, reassuring her. "My sweetness. My darling." She fought back tears, wondering what was wrong with her. "I'm sorry. Did I hurt you?" He sounded anxious, upset. She shook her head. What he had done to her body was one thing. What he had done to her soul was another.

"Oh, love. You are so innocent. I should not have let you push me so close to the edge. For a moment there, I lost control. I should have been more careful."

"It was what I wished," she choked out. "It was exactly what I wanted." That was true. She had wanted him to lose control. To spill his seed inside her, a great gush of life. Or maybe the Goddess had driven her to do this thing.

A strange feeling afflicted her as she slid from his arms and sat up. Did Morgeuse still wait at the entrance of the prison, a few feet above their heads, bathed in the soft light of the moon? Did she know what they did? Had she even planned it?

She turned to look at her lover, sprawled naked on the blanket. The spot of moonlight illuminated the coarse gold hair on his chest, but she could not see his face. She leaned over him, finding his mouth and kissing him. "I love you, Rhun ap Maelgwn."

He exhaled a sigh. "And I love you . . . but that does not mean . . ."

"Hush." She pressed her hand to his mouth. "Don't say it. I can't bear to hear those words."

He sighed again. She lay her head down on his chest. Tears squeezed from under her closed eyelids. She waited a moment, then sat up again. "I must get back," she said. "I might be missed."

"Of course." His voice was toneless, sad. As she dressed, she wondered what she had done to both of them.

She went out the door of the chamber and closed it behind her. It latched with a dull thud. She heard him try it from the inside and knew it was locked. Climbing the stairs, she pushed through the entrance at the top and climbed out into the moonlit night. Morgeuse was nowhere to be seen.

Twelve

He was going mad, Rhun thought as he lay naked on the blanket-covered straw. It was as if some other man had invaded his body and now controlled his actions. A man like Bridei, who gave no thought to duty and responsibility but only to the pleasure he could seize in the moment. Why else had he just done what he'd done—wasted his only opportunity to escape making love to Eastra? Even now, he felt drugged, his senses so suffused with the bliss of their coupling that he could not think clearly.

Sweet heaven, it had been good! Better than he'd imagined sex could be. The woman he desired most in the world, willing and eager, hungry for everything he could offer. She bewitched him, disordered his senses. He'd heard of the technique of kissing a woman's most intimate parts, but never tried it. Yet at the time, it had seemed the most natural thing in the world. He'd known she would taste sweet and delectable. Known she would reach her peak. And once she'd peaked, she'd be able to take all of him. He would not have to hold back, to worry about hurting her.

But the other—her touching him—that had been a revelation. Those delicate fingers teasing and caressing, displaying a boldness he had not dreamed she possessed. What had happened to the demure maid in Cerdic's longhouse, her eyes downcast, her manner so discreet and shy? With her rare coloring, Eastra had always seemed untouchable, pure and chaste. But she was not. She was almost lusty in her appetites. Not the child he had rescued all those years ago, but a woman in her prime, rich and earthy, and remarkably satisfying.

Rhun's mind reeled as he stood and began to dress. Every day, his life grew more complicated, his feelings more tangled and difficult to sort out. The thought of leaving Eastra, even for a short while, aroused a gnawing ache inside him. Yet he knew he had no choice. Duty called to him. His oath to Arthur allowed no room for love, no matter how transcendent his feelings. And love with a Saxon princess was even more forbidden and hopeless.

He thought of her telling him not to speak of the future. Surely she knew things between them were doomed. Those fleeting glimpses of ecstasy were all they would ever have. Perhaps that was why she'd offered herself so blatantly, because she'd known the impossibility of their circumstances. He'd felt tears on her face afterward, as she grieved for the brevity of their time together. Now he wanted to weep as well, to lie down on the straw floor of his prison and sob like a child. But he was a man, a man with responsibilities, people who depended upon him, men who might end up dying if he failed them.

A sobering thought, and one that weighed heavily against the magic of what he'd just experienced. He had a duty not only to Arthur but to all the Companions and all the other men who followed Arthur, believing in his dream.

He went to the door of his prison and again tried the lock. It was as secure as ever. He gave a groan. For a bare candlehour in heaven, he'd failed himself and his cause. But it would not happen again.

Eastra hurried among the outbuildings of the fortress. She needed to find Morgeuse and speak to her. The wetness of Rhun's seed trickled down her thighs as she ran. It was uncomfortable, but also made her feel exhilarated. Such a tangible reminder of what they had shared.

When she reached the corridor leading to Morgeuse's chamber, she saw someone leaving the queen's apartments. She pressed herself back against the wall and waited for him to pass by, drawing in her breath in surprise when she saw it was Bridei. "What do you here?" she whispered.

Bridei did not answer, but pressed a finger to his lips and shook his head. The glimmer of a smile lit his handsome features. He moved past Eastra and out into the night. She stared after him, then continued on to Morgeuse's room. Knocking on the door, she waited. There was no answer. She tried again. When there was no response, she considered going in and seeing if Morgeuse was asleep. But then she realized how rude that would be.

She went down the hall to her own chamber. There was no sign of Nevyn. After washing her hands and face and reluctantly wiping away the stickiness between her thighs, Eastra lay down on her pallet. She went over the events of the night in her mind. Why would Morgeuse promise to stand guard, then disappear? Why would she say she was going to help and then insist that Rhun could not leave his prison? And most of all, Eastra wondered, why had she listened to Morgeuse? Why hadn't she freed Rhun and tried to escape? But she had not. Instead, she had enticed him to make love to her, to couple wildly on the straw-covered floor of his prison.

It was almost as if Morgeuse had put a spell upon her, Eastra thought. A shiver ran down her spine. What if Morgeuse never meant to help free Rhun? What if the queen had some other sort of plan in mind? And Bridei—what part did he play in all this? The way he'd looked when she met him the hallway, like a man leaving his lover. But who was his lover?

Her thoughts seemed to tumble over and over and she could not sleep. Even when she finally put her doubts about Morgeuse aside, the heated memories of what she had shared with Rhun kept her awake. Had she truly done those things? Touched him so daringly? Allowed him, nay urged him, to kiss her so boldly?

The memory was vivid and clear. Her body felt odd, both relaxed and intensely alive at the same time. It was a dream, a wonderful dream, and yet it was real. She smiled into the darkness. She and Rhun were bound together now. He would not be able to forget her.

She got up and poured herself a drink of water. Where was Nevyn? she wondered, glancing at the empty pallet in the corner. Never before had Morgeuse's apprentice been gone all night.

There was one tiny window in the room, very high up. Eastra climbed up on the chest beneath it and tried to see out. All that was visible was the full moon. Morgeuse had said when the moon was near dark, she would help Rhun escape.

Eastra awoke to the rustle of clothing and the soft sounds of someone washing. Nevyn was leaning over the bronze bowl, splashing water on her face. As Nevyn toweled herself dry, Eastra examined her critically. Had she just returned to the room? If so, where had she been all night? With Bridei? Nevyn did not seem like the sort of woman who would appeal to him, but then, from what Rhun had said, his brother was not very picky about his bed partners.

Nevyn's freckled face was inscrutable, as always. Eastra, dressing, asked her, "Do you know what Morgeuse has planned for us today?"

Nevyn shook her head. "The queen is still sleeping. If you are wise, you will not disturb her, but make yourself useful in the weaving shed."

Despite her surprise—Morgeuse never slept this late—Eastra dutifully went to the weaving shed. About midday, Morgeuse came to find her. Eastra followed her out. "The time has come to make preparations for Rhun's escape," Morgeuse said when they were alone. "I have told my husband I have visited the prisoner and he is growing weak and sickly due to lack of sunlight. I will insist that from now on, he must be brought out into the yard for fresh air and exercise each day. On the day when the Mead Moon has half waned, I will arrange for the door to his prison to be left open."

"And the men at the gate?" Eastra asked. "How will we get past them?"

"I will make certain they are otherwise occupied."

Eastra nodded. She could not wait. In only a few days, they would be free. "What about Bridei?" she asked. "Will he be coming with us?"

Morgeuse shook her head. "His job will be to distract my husband's warriors with songs and stories. He will stay in the hall and keep them content."

She was not disappointed to learn Bridei would not be going, Eastra thought as she returned to the piece of fabric she was weaving. Oh, to be alone with Rhun! She did not care about any of the hardships that might be ahead of them—finding food, having to travel on foot, the dangers of the forest. All she cared was that she and her beloved would be together.

The next few days passed tediously. Although she caught glimpses of Rhun when he was allowed out in the yard, Eastra knew she dared not let on she was aware of his presence. She must be patient, she told herself.

At last, the day of the half moon arrived. Eastra could scarce concentrate on the tasks Morgeuse had assigned to her. She moved through her duties with a growing restlessness. That night, there was another feast—one of the hunting parties had brought back a young boar. The men drank heavily and gorged themselves. As usual, Eastra helped serve.

After the meal, Urien announced that Bridei ap Maelgwn, the great King Arthur's bard—there was derision in his voice as he spoke the title—would entertain them. Bridei went to sit in the place of honor beside Urien. He drew his hand across the strings of his harp and a ripple of silvery notes brought quiet to the hall. Eastra stood in the corner of the room, watching with the other servants. Her body felt taut with anticipation. At any moment, Morgeuse would rise from where she sat on the other side of Urien, discreetly cross the hall, and whisper in Eastra's ear that it was time to meet Rhun.

But nothing happened. Bridei sang a long song about a battle, then a more cheerful song about a boy and his falcon. As he began a playful, rather obscene ditty about a pair of lovers, Eastra edged toward the door. Perhaps she was mistaken, and Morgeuse was not going to signal to her it was time to go. The queen might be worried Urien would observe her actions and grow suspicious.

Eastra went out into the darkness. Nothing seemed amiss. She heard a dog bark in the distance. Then she began to run toward Rhun's underground prison. When she reached it, she looked around. As quickly as possible, she jerked open the wooden door and let herself down into the passageway.

"Rhun?" she called softly. She paused to listen. All she heard was the rhythmic thud of her own heart pounding in her ears. She continued down into the passageway. As she reached the door to the prison chamber, she called out again.

Going to the door, she pulled on the latch. The door opened with a creaking sound. "Rhun?" Still hearing no response, she grew uneasy. What was wrong? Why didn't he answer?

She entered the chamber. The little patch of moonlight revealed only piled up straw. She searched the rest of the chamber, dreading to find Rhun lying there, injured or otherwise incapacitated. She found nothing but a chamber pot. Even the blanket they had coupled on was gone.

She straightened, knowing she was too late. But if she had been supposed to meet him near the gate, why hadn't

Morgeuse told her? She scrambled out of the passageway and began to run, then hurried back after remembering she had forgotten to replace the door over the passageway. Let Urien's men think all was well until they came to get Rhun and bring him up for his daily exercise. By then, they would be far away. Or would they? As she started to run toward the gate, the sick, sinking feeling inside her grew.

She prowled the area around the gate, searching for Rhun's tall form hidden in the shadows. Above her in the watchtower, she heard two men talking. She froze. Perhaps their plan had failed and Rhun had been recaptured already. But where had they taken him?

She heard the sound of someone climbing down the ladder and pressed herself flat against the wooden palisade wall. A man walked past her and continued on. Eastra sighed. There seemed to be nothing for her to do but return to the hall and see if Morgeuse knew what had happened.

Bridei was still strumming his harp and singing when she entered. Morguese sat next to Urien, looking as content and unruffled as ever. Eastra tried to catch the queen's eye, but Morgeuse's attention, like everyone else's, was focused on Bridei. At last, Eastra saw Nevyn heading toward the door. She followed her out. As soon as they had reached the yard, she grabbed the maidservant's arm. "Nevyn, what's happened? Tell me!"

Nevyn stared, her pale eyes expressionless.

"Where's Rhun?" Eastra demanded once again. "Did they recapture him?"

Nevyn still said nothing.

Eastra fought the urge to shake her. "What went wrong? Where are they holding him?"

"Rhun is gone," Nevyn answered slowly, "although no one must know until morning."

"Gone? You mean his escape was successful? But where am I supposed to meet him? Should I bring anything, or has Morgeuse taken care of our supplies?"

"By now he should be quite far away. He left at dusk."

Eastra felt as if she had been struck in the stomach. He

had left without her. She told herself something had happened, some circumstance had made it impossible for him to wait for her. But a dark fear overruled all her frantic reasoning. What if he'd never intended to take her with him? What if their coupling had been his way of saying good-bye?

She returned to the hall. It seemed very bright and warm, overwhelming. Near the door, one of Urien's warriors—Grimlyn, who was forever teasing her—called out, "What's wrong, little bird? You don't look well."

"It was . . . something I ate," she mumbled. The misery broke over her; she did indeed feel ill. She half staggered over to one of the benches and sank down. Somehow she had to pull herself together, to act as if nothing was amiss, as if she had not been duped and betrayed by the man she loved. And by Morguese. Eastra realized suddenly the queen must have known she was to be left behind. Did she pity Eastra for being such a fool?

By Freya, she could not bear it! Morgeuse had promised to help her, had known how she felt about Rhun, and still she had been part of it, pretending to share Rhun's plan with her, and yet all the while knowing only he would be leaving Caer Louarn.

She stood and walked across the hall to where Morguese sat. She must have looked very grim and determined, for even Urien gave her a startled look. "Morguese," she said. "If I might have a word with you."

Morguese nodded and rose, her face a serene mask. They left the hall. Eastra strode briskly toward the queen's apartments. She wanted privacy for this confrontation. When they reached Morgeuse's chamber, they went inside. Eastra turned to face the older woman. "You lied to me. You let me believe that when you helped Rhun escape, I would go with him."

Morgeuse shrugged. "There was no lie. I merely did not tell you everything."

Eastra exhaled in a gasp of fury. "How could you? Why tell me *anything*, then? Why get my hopes up, let me believe he cared for me . . ." She took a deep breath, too overcome to continue.

"He does care for you," Morguese said. "But he cares more for his duty to Arthur." She shrugged again. "It's the way of men to put matters of politics and war before the desperate yearnings of their own hearts. It does not mean he does not love you. It does not mean he will not eventually realize his folly and come back for you. You must be patient."

"Patient! I have waited half my life for this man! I can't bear to wait any longer!"

"It's a woman's burden to wait. For the seasons to turn, for her belly to ripen with a child, then all the long years as the child grows. You *will* learn patience, for, verily, you have no choice."

Eastra collapsed on a stool among the clutter. She wanted to weep, but she could not. There was too much anger mingled with her pain. "I loved him, believing he loved me back. That with every kiss and caress, I was binding him to me, making him love me."

"And you *have*. He fled Caer Louarn like a man running for his life. But it is not Urien he fears, or even the dark, enclosing walls of his prison. It's his feelings for you that terrify him."

Eastra buried her face in her hands. Morguese's words did not console her. The ache inside her did not ease. Finally, she raised her head. "You have spells and potions for so many things. Have you anything to mend a broken heart?"

"I cannot mend it, but I can make you forget for a time. Wait here. I'll have Nevyn fix you something that will help you sleep." Morgeuse started to leave.

"Nevyn," Eastra said bitterly. "Does she know what has happened? That I have given myself to a man who cares more for his war commander than for me?"

"Nevyn, I promise, does not scorn you for falling in love. She has her own troubles."

"Bridei?" Eastra asked.

Morguese nodded.

Eastra released her breath in a sigh. "When I saw him hurrying out of here, I thought perhaps he had been to see you."

Morguese laughed. "Bridei has not been my lover for many a year."

Eastra was startled. "Then you mean . . . that once . . . you and he . . . But what about Urien?"

"My husband is a most unusual man. I told you he wields me like a weapon. He believes if I lie with other men, I will learn their secrets and he will gain power over them."

"But is it true?"

"Sometimes." Morguese smiled sweetly.

"And you are content with this? To let your husband use you against his enemies?"

"I said he *thinks* it gives him power. In fact, I know very well what I'm doing. I obey no man, only the Lady."

After Morgeuse had left, Eastra sat on the stool, thinking hard. What would it be like to live her life like Morgeuse did—afraid of nothing, secure in her own authority, answering to no man?

The draught Nevyn brought did help Eastra sleep. And in the morning, when she awoke, she did not feel quite as hopeless, nor experience Rhun's betrayal so harshly. She washed, then went to the kitchen shed. She felt rather queasy, but she had eaten almost nothing the night before. The plump, cheerful cook offered her a piece of barley bread spread with butter and honey and told her to sit and eat. Eastra obeyed willingly.

While she was eating, Bridei came into the kitchen. He grinned at her, then gave the giggling cook a kiss on the cheek. Old Glynis produced another piece of bread for Bridei. As he started to leave, Eastra followed him out. "Bridei," she called.

He turned to face her, his mouth full. She took his arm and led him away from the main pathway, behind the kitchen shed. She averted her face, not wanting him to see her pain. "Do you know what Rhun's plans are? Where he is headed?"

"He will go to Arthur's stronghold at Camlann."

"And then what? Will he come back and rescue us?"

Bridei shrugged. "Perhaps, if he has the time. But if Cerdic has broken the truce, it is likely Rhun will march to war with Arthur and his men."

The lump in her throat grew bigger. If Rhun had gone to fetch them help, that would have been easier to endure. "Does Urien know Rhun is gone?"

Bridei nodded. "He had the man who last guarded Rhun taken out and flogged."

Eastra felt a surge of pity for the unsuspecting man. Morgeuse was the one who should be flogged, not him. No, she did not really mean that. She was angry at the queen, but she did not want to see anyone suffer. She was so tired of intrigue and treachery. "What do you think Urien will do to us? Will he lock us away?"

"I doubt that. If he did, his men would miss my music in the hall and my company on their hunts." Bridei grinned broadly. "And everyone would miss being served by lovely Eastra the Saxon."

Ignoring his silly compliment, she said, "So what do we do? Wait here for the war to be over?"

"You must be patient," Bridei said, echoing Morgeuse. "Once I have earned Urien's trust, it will be easy to plot our escape."

And what would she do then? Eastra wondered. Where would she go? Back to Cerdic's household? If his thanes thought her defiled because she had once been a slave in a Roman British household, they would think her even more despoiled now. The pain welled up inside her. If Rhun did not care for her, she was not certain if it mattered what happened, if she lived or died. She closed her eyes against the tears that threatened, then she felt Bridei touch her arm.

"Rhun will not forget you," he said. "Someday, when he has fulfilled his duty, he will return to you."

A frail hope. Yet she grasped for it greedily. What else could she do?

"Eastra, come quickly! Urien is asking for you!" Anna, one of the serving maids who had become a friend to Eastra, pulled impatiently on her sleeve.

Eastra rose from the bench where she sat sorting peas, and started out of the kitchen lean-to after Anna. Urien was asking for her? What did that mean?

As they hurried along the path toward the feast hall, Estra wracked her brain for some possible explanation for the king's request. Nothing came to mind. Since using her as a means to incite Rhun, Urien had ignored her. But then she saw the large group of warriors in the yard near the gate. Foreign warriors, with a distinctive style of dress and a large banner in their midst. The banner immediately reminded Eastra of Rhun's device, except it was not a red dragon on a field of white, but a gold dragon on a field of crimson.

She could make out Urien talking to another man in the middle of the gathering. A very tall man. Then the other man turned, and Eastra knew instantly she was staring into the face of Maelgwn the Great. He looked to be even taller than Rhun, the tallest man she had ever seen. He had dark hair and a beard, both streaked liberally with white. The stamp of his features reminded her more of Bridei than of Rhun, but his vivid blue eyes were startlingly familiar.

All her life, she'd been around formidable men, but this warrior embodied the very essence of power. It radiated from him, making everyone around him appear inconsequential. She was reminded of Morgeuse dancing, the force of animal energy radiating from her voluptuous form. But that was female energy, and this man's power was very different. Very male. Danger and cunning, a predator poised to pounce. As Eastra approached him, her throat went dry and her knees wobbled.

Before she reached him, he bowed his head in a gesture of courtesy. "Eastra the Saxon," he said in a deep, rumbling voice. "Your beauty is every bit as exceptional as I had heard." He stepped toward her and clasped her hand in both of his huge callused palms. "My wife is anxious for you to come and show her the needlework skills of your people."

He turned toward Urien as he said this. Urien smiled like the shrewd fox he was, and responded, "My wife has been enjoying Eastra's company and was loathe to part with such a dutiful servant. But of course she will allow her to accompany you to Gwynedd to meet her rightful mistress."

"What about my son Bridei?" Maelgwn asked.

"Bridei is free to go as well." Urien shrugged.

"And what of Rhun, my older son?" Maelgwn's voice grew silky and dark. "Where is he?"

"Gone." Urien waved his hand. "Left some days ago. Apparently, he had business with Arthur he thought was more important than visiting his father and stepmother."

"Arthur. Of course," Maelgwn said. "Tell me, what do you know of Arthur's situation? Last I had heard, he had entered into a truce with Cerdic, one of the Saxon leaders. But we both know truces are often broken."

"I've heard nothing. Up here in the north, we don't concern ourselves with the war with the Saxons."

"Of course not," Maelgwn said. "Why would you?"

Although the two men appeared to talk freely, Eastra could sense the tension between them, as if they were two stags pawing the ground and shaking their massive antlered heads at each other before they engaged. Urien was very wary of Maelgwn, perhaps even afraid of him. That was why he lied. She wondered if Maelgwn believed his lies, or if he was merely pretending to accept them.

"Come in to the hall and be welcome," Urien said.

"Perhaps, for a time. But we will not linger here overnight," Maelgwn answered. "As I said, my wife is anxious to meet her new Saxon servant, a gift from her son and stepson." He looked at Eastra as he said this, and the intensity of his gaze made the breath seem to leave her body.

The two men went into the hall, followed by their warriors. Eastra started toward the kitchen shed, but someone caught her arm. When she looked around, there was Morgeuse. "Come with me," the queen said.

"Should I not be serving our guests?"

"We've servants aplenty. Besides, you will be leaving soon."

Eastra wondered what that meant. Did Morgeuse want to say good-bye to her? Or was she afraid Maelgwn would be displeased if he saw his wife's servant being treated like a common kitchen wench?

She followed Morgeuse to her bedchamber, feeling more unsettled than ever. She was leaving, but the prospect failed to offer any relief from her inner turmoil. For all that he reminded her of Rhun, Maelgwn the Great was a frightening man. She wondered what would happen when his wife found out she really had only average skill at weaving and sewing—unless Maelgwn knew she was Arthur's hostage and was simply playing games with Urien. That seemed very plausible, and it would explain the taut way the two men spoke to each other.

When they reached the sumptuous chamber, Morgeuse turned and looked at Eastra, cocking her head in a thoughtful gesture. "What's wrong? You do not seemed pleased with the path that has opened up ahead of you."

Eastra hesitated, then said, "I'm not certain I want to leave here and go to Maelgwn the Great's household."

"Why not?"

"I . . . I don't know," she answered truthfully. "Rhun will not be there, and it will seem strange to be in the household of his family without him."

"Maelgwn is no ogre, despite his impressive demeanor. In fact, he has a reputation for being unfailingly kind and courteous to women. And his wife . . ." Morgeuse smiled faintly. "She will not eat you either, I promise."

Eastra could not get rid of the uneasy feeling in the pit

of her stomach. Although she had been a prisoner at Caer Louarn, the fact she had come there with Rhun had made her feel safe.

Morgeuse was still looking at her. "Would you like to try the 'seeing' again? Perhaps if you knew what the future held, you would be more at ease."

Eastra nodded. Morgeuse's magic continued to intrigue her. Perhaps this time she would learn something useful, something that would help her get Rhun back.

Morgeuse knelt down near the small table that held the pottery bowl of herbs. She added several handfuls of herbs from the several jars on the table, then a small pinch of some sort of powder. Lighting a candle from the lamp burning by the door, she set the herbs to burning. They crackled and sparked, filling the air with a dense, sweet smoke.

"Everything is ready," Morgeuse said, "Sit down and let us begin."

"Do we not need Nevyn to make the circle?" Eastra asked.

"Nevyn is busy and there is not much time. Now, close your eyes and let your mind wander free. If the Goddess wills it, the visions will come."

Eastra did as she was bid. The smoke seemed to tickle her nose, then make her sleepy. She shifted restlessly. Nothing was happening. Last time, Morguese had guided her, told her what to feel. She tried to recall the things that Morgeuse had said, urging her to feel her body, the blood flowing through her veins, the air moving in and out of her lungs as she breathed.

Her limbs grew heavy, but at the same time, a strange lightness came over her. She was moving, floating down a corridor. She saw Rhun. He was wearing a mail shirt and sitting on his horse, as if going into battle. He looked beautiful, so strong and proud and golden, and yet his eyes were full of pain. She wanted to call out to him, to reassure him, but she could not. Her voice caught in her throat and strangled there.

He did not see her, but looked past her. What he saw

seemed to make his face contort with anguish, as if he could not endure it. Again, she tried to call his name. This time there was sound, but still he could not hear her. He was locked in some sort of terrible struggle with the thing he saw in the distance. She tried to move toward him, to find some way to make him see her, to drag his attention away from the terrible vision.

And then she was sucked back down into darkness, swirling, dizzying darkness.

When she opened her eyes, she was sweating, her body tense and rigid. Morgeuse gripped her hand tightly. "Are you all right?" she asked. Eastra nodded, although she was not at all certain it was true. She felt nauseated and weak.

"Blessed Mother, you have dark dreams," Morguese murmured.

"It was Rhun." She met Morguese's gaze. "I saw him, and there was this terrible expression on his face . . . of grief. Of horror . . ." She shuddered. It had been so awful to see his pain and not be able to help him.

"Very often things are darkest and most troubling right before your path straightens and the way becomes clear. That you saw something that distresses you does not mean there is no happiness in your future."

Eastra gave a shaky sigh. A plan was forming in her mind. She would speak to Maelgwn the Great, despite her fear. She would tell him what she had seen and ask him to take her to Rhun instead of back of Gwynedd. Surely if she explained his son was in danger, he would listen to her.

Morgeuse lifted her up and embraced her. "Don't look so sad, my dear. I have seen glimpses of your future as well, and things are not nearly as hopeless as they appear. Now, let us pack your things, such as they are."

Maelgwn the Great was as good as his word. He and his men did no more than have a drink in Urien's hall. Then they all gathered at the gate. Eastra went to join them, carrying her bag of possessions, including numerous gifts from Morguese. As she reached the throng of men and horses, she saw Bridei out of the corner of her eye. She turned to look at him and, as she did so, she saw a sort of shadow disengage from him and disappear among the crowd. Nevyn, she thought, saying good-bye.

Bridei's face wore a grim expression. Was he that distressed about leaving Nevyn? Eastra wondered. Then he came toward her and said fiercely, "I'm not going. My father did not come to rescue *me,* but his beloved Rhun. I'll not go back to Gwynedd like this, as if I were one of his possessions he has come to claim!"

Eastra was shocked by the vehemence of his reaction. "What will you do?" she asked. "Ride off as soon as we leave the fortress?"

"I doubt he will let me," Bridei said. "But as soon as possible, I intend to get away."

"Where will you go?"

Bridei's mouth twisted. "Back to Arthur, I suppose. At least he has some respect for my abilities as a translator and spy."

"Take me with you!" she pleaded.

Bridei looked at her. "My father is not a complete fool. I may be able to slip away, because he won't expect it, but there's no way for you to leave unnoticed. My father will see it as his responsibility to guard you well. Besides, it would be much too dangerous for the two of us to travel alone, especially when it's clear to anyone who sees you that you are a Saxon."

Eastra heaved a sigh. It seemed she'd exchanged one prison for another. "What about your father? If I asked *him* to take me to Rhun, would he do it?"

"Doubtful. He knows you are Arthur's hostage, even if he pretends not to. He also knows you were bound for Gwynedd when we were captured. He'll worry that it would be unsafe to take you to Arthur's camp. And he's probably right." Bridei gave her a thoughtful look. "There are those among Arthur's Companions who would like to see the truce fail. What better way to ensure that than for an 'accident' to befall his hostage?"

A chill ran down Eastra's body. Without Rhun to protect her, she suddenly felt acutely vulnerable. But then she remembered her "seeing." She feared Rhun was not safe either. "Bridei, please find Rhun and warn him to be careful."

"Careful of what?"

"Tell him . . ." She struggled for words. How could she make Bridei understand? "Tell him I'm afraid something's going to happen. Something awful."

"Why do you think this?"

"I had a 'seeing,' as Morgcuse calls it. I saw Rhun, dressed up for battle, and the expression on his face . . ." she shook her head. "It made my heart go cold. It was as if he had suffered some unendurable shock, or experienced something that caused him enormous pain and suffering. Not the physical kind of pain, but as if something had devastated his spirit, his very soul."

"Morguese has taught you to look into the future? I'm surprised. I didn't think she would share her secrets with someone like you."

"Why?" Eastra asked defensively. "Because I am a Saxon?"

"Because you are . . ." Bridei squinted, as if seeing her for the first time, then shook his head. "I should have guessed, I suppose. But, like most men, I was distracted by your beauty and your youth. I didn't see there was more to you."

Eastra exhaled in consternation. "You speak in riddles! Don't you understand? I'm terrified something is going to happen to Rhun! Will you help me? Will you go to him and beg him to—" She hesitated. She wanted to ask Rhun to come back to her, to leave Arthur's army and ride to Gwynedd so she could see him and hold him and touch him and assure herself he was safe. But she could not do that. "Please tell him to take care of himself, to be wary . . ." Her voice trailed off. How could she warn him against that which she did not understand?

Bridei nodded. "I will tell him. I will let him know you have seen him in your dreams and you fear for him."

Someone called her name, and Eastra turned. The kitchen servants and weaving women had gathered to say good-bye to her.

Thirteen

They rode out of the gates of Caer Louarn with Maelgwn at the head of the troop and Eastra in the center, surrounded by warriors. Bridei was somewhere to the rear. She wondered how long he would wait before he slipped free of his father's army. The men around Eastra talked quietly as they rode, and she was aware of a certain cadence to their speech she had not noticed in Rhun or Bridei's. Perhaps they had been away from their homeland for so many years they had lost that distinctive way of speaking.

Since they had left Caer Louarn late in the day, they did not travel very far before it grew dark. When they reached a clearing, Maelgwn called a halt. As his men dismounted and began to make camp, Eastra slid off her horse and waited, wondering if someone would come and tell her where she would sleep. To her surprise, Maelgwn himself came to speak to her. He was accompanied by a gangly red-haired youth whom she presumed was his armor bearer. "This is Beli," Maelgwn announced. "He will see to your needs and get you settled for the night."

Maelgwn left, and young Beli faced her, as stiff and alert as a soldier on guard. "My lady, can I bring you something to eat or drink?"

"Do you think there is a stream nearby where I can wash?" she asked.

"I will fetch you water, my lady."

Beli dashed off. Eastra was bemused. After playing a slave these past weeks, it was very agreeable to have someone wait upon *her*.

Beli returned carrying a earthenware jar and a bronze bowl. A cloth was draped over his arm. "My lady." He gestured to a tent another man had just set up nearby. "If you would like to go in and refresh yourself, I'll wait outside."

He put the washing things down on the leather floor of the tent, then left again. Eastra washed her face and hands. Beli returned with an armful of goods. He carefully arranged a bedroll in a corner of the tent, then lit an oil lamp.

"Now I will fetch your supper, my lady," he said, bowing.

Eastra felt overwhelmed. Beli was treating her like a queen. When he came back with a platter of food, a wineskin, and a stool tucked under his free arm, she smiled at him and said, "Thank you for your kindness, but now please go and feed yourself. You have been busy every moment since we arrived, and I'm certain you're hungry."

He bowed again. "Thank you, my lady. I will return quickly, to see if you need anything else before you retire."

He bent down to leave the tent. "Wait," she called.

He turned. For a moment, his blue eyes regarded her with frank admiration. Then he lowered his gaze. "Yes, my lady. Will there be something else?"

"I was wondering . . . what have you been told about me?"

"My lady?"

"Maelgwn—what did he say to you when he ordered you to wait on me?"

"My father said you were a Saxon princess and our honored guest."

"Maelgwn is your father?"

"Aye. I don't much look like him, do I?" His expression was rueful.

Eastra searched the young man's features for any resemblance to Rhun. She could not really see any, but his coloring—dark red hair and light blue eyes—was so different, it was hard to see past it.

"I favor my mother." He shrugged. "Not that it is such a bad thing, mind you, but I do hope that someday I am tall like my father."

"How old are you?"

"Fourteen."

"Then there is plenty of time for you to grow. My brother was near your height at your age and I'm certain he would have been fairly good-sized."

"Would have been?"

"He was killed in a British raid."

"I'm sorry." He gave her a sympathetic look, then said apologetically, "My family—except for Rhun—have never supported the British cause. We are Cymry, not British."

"I don't hold anyone to blame for what happened to my family. My father and uncle raided their share of British farmsteads in their day. I hate *all* war, all fighting. I want there to be peace."

He smiled at her. "You sound like my mother. Yet even she is reconciled to the fact that it is the way of men, to fight and kill each other."

She decided that when Beli smiled, he did look a little like Rhun. A pang went through her. Where was Rhun? Was he safe? The urge to see him and assure herself nothing terrible had happened to him nearly overwhelmed her. She scrutinized the young man. How much did Beli care for his half brother? If she told him Rhun might be in danger, would he be willing to help her go to him? She said, "Rhun told me your mother, Rhiannon, has the sight—do you believe this?"

He nodded. "I know sometimes she 'sees' things or has dreams about things and then they come to pass."

"Well, I have had a seeing or a dream about your brother Rhun. And in my dream I sensed he was in terrible danger. Because of that, I want to go to him, to warn him. Will you aid me?"

Beli frowned. "You should tell these things to my father, not to me."

Eastra made her voice pleading. "Bridei says Maelgwn will not allow me to go to Rhun."

"Why not?"

"Because . . ." Eastra hesitated. What could she say to this young man to convince him he should help her? She moved nearer to Beli. "Because I am Arthur's hostage, and your father means to keep me a prisoner at his fortress."

Beli's troubled expression deepened. "A prisoner?"

Eastra nodded. "Think about it. Although he told you to treat me with every courtesy, if you look around, you will also see I am guarded every moment."

Beli glanced toward the tent entrance, then back to her. "Perhaps it is true, but even so, I can't ignore my father's wishes."

"Even if your brother's life hangs in the balance?"

Beli shook his head sadly. "Nay, not even for that. Rhun chose his path years ago. He is a grown man and formidable warrior. Besides, if what you saw was a true 'seeing,' it's doubtful you can do anything to change what will come to pass."

"But if he knew about the danger, perhaps he could somehow turn it aside."

"Perhaps." Beli nodded. "But it does not have to be you who tells him of your dream. My father could send a messenger to Rhun and warn him that way."

Eastra exhaled in frustration. Beli's solution was no better than Bridei's. "But the thing is . . ." She hesitated. How could she make him understand? "The thing is, I *love* Rhun. I *need* to see him and talk to him myself. Until I do, I will be in torment!"

Beli looked at her, and a half dozen emotions crossed his youthful face—regret, sympathy, and a kind of tenderness. But there was also resolve and duty there. He shook his head. "I'm sorry. I can't defy my father over a matter such as this. As my mother always says, if it is meant to be, then it will be."

Eastra turned away. She felt very tired and disappointed.

Beli left, and she sat down on the stool. She closed her eyes and tried to clear her mind and let her thoughts wander so she would have a seeing. But she could not seem to relax. All she could think about was her last vision of Rhun. She struggled for a while longer, then opened her eyes and sighed. It did not seem she had learned any of Morguese's magic after all. Or maybe the burning herbs with their fragrant odor had something to do with being able to see the future. Giving up, she went to bed.

In the morning, Beli came to her and told her Bridei had left in the night.

"Is your father angry?" she asked.

Beli shook his head. "I think he expected it."

They set off soon after. The forest gradually thinned into open country, a hilly, rocky landscape dotted with small patches of scrubby pine, yew, and rowan trees. Goshawks and kestrels circled overhead, and the air grew damp and clammy despite the fact it was summer. In the distance, Eastra could see the mountains Rhun had told her about, their brooding dark shapes like thunderclouds on the horizon.

They rode through deep valleys where the pastureland was brilliant green and bright with poppies, daisies, purple clover, and other flowers Eastra did not recognize. They climbed rocky desolate hills and crossed a myriad of streams, some with waterfalls tumbling over the rocks to form small pools surrounded by green moss. Finally, they came into a broad valley where on either side of a gleaming river grazed beautiful horses. Then they followed a trackway along the river, passing several farmsteads, where hedges of thorn enclosed several round, thatched-roof structures.

Beli, coming back to bring her some food about midday, asked her what she thought of Gwynedd. "It's beautiful," she said. But a part of her remained uneasy. This place seemed cut off from the rest of the world, a strange, somehow daunting realm full of rocks and sky and mist. It was so unlike the part of Britain she had grown up in, and she thought this brooding, wild world must shape the people who lived here. Was that why Rhun was so different from any warrior she had ever known? She shivered at the thought, sensing for the first time she did not really know the man she had fallen in love with.

But it did not matter. Her fate was inextricably bound up with Rhun's. She had felt it that day when they made love under the great oak. It had been more than a joining of their bodies; it seemed a merging of their very souls.

Late in the day, Eastra took a deep breath and suddenly knew that distinctive, tangy odor for what it was. "We're near the sea, aren't we?" she commented to Beli.

He nodded. "My father's main fortress, Deganwy, is very near the coast. We'll be there soon."

Leaving the river, they climbed a ridge. When they reached the top, a sprawling hilltop fortress was visible in the distance. Sensing home, the horses seemed to quicken their pace.

Dusk was falling as they reached the gates of Deganwy. There was the familiar confusion as everyone dismounted and servants came to lead away the horses and deal with the baggage. Eastra saw Beli talking to a small, plump woman with reddish fair hair going gray. Although she did not look as Eastra had expected, she decided the woman must be Rhiannon, Maelgwn's queen. The woman gave Eastra a critical look, then spoke to Beli.

Beli came over to her. "Come, my lady. I'll show you where you will sleep."

He took her to a small sleeping chamber, comfortably but not extravagantly furnished. "A servant will be here soon to tend you," he told her. "Gwenaseth thought you might want to eat in your room and wait until tomorrow to meet everyone."

"Gwenaseth?"

"She's the woman I was speaking to. She runs Deganwy." Beli grinned. "I'm not exaggerating. Even my father defers to her."

"But what about . . ."

"My mother? She does not generally involve herself in the day-to-day activities of the fortress. The twins are still young, and she has her sewing and her pottery. Gwenaseth thrives on being in charge, so it's a happy arrangement for everyone."

Beli left. A young woman with curly dark hair and blue eyes came and helped Eastra undress and bathe. Her bag of possessions had been brought to the room. Thinking she would not see anyone this night, Eastra put on only a linen shift. Then she sat on a stool while the servant, Melangel, combed out her damp hair. They were almost finished smoothing out the tangles when there was a knock at the door. Eastra stood up quickly, suddenly aware of her immodest attire.

But it was not Beli bringing her food, but a small, delicately made woman. Between Melangel's deference and the woman's red hair, Eastra guessed this must be the lady Rhiannon, Rhun's stepmother. She smiled warmly at Eastra and held out a basket. "I've brought you some fresh bread and apricots for your supper. Also a jar of milk. I've heard the Saxons enjoy drinking it even after they are grown. And it seems like a healthier beverage than wine or ale."

"Thank you," Eastra said. "I do like milk, and I have not had any for months." She took the basket, thinking Lady Rhiannon was not at all what she had expected. Despite her vivid hair—threaded here and there with strands of pure white—this queen had none of Morgeuse's fiery sensuality. She was cool and still, her beauty ethereal. With her milk-white skin, heather blue eyes, and dainty, almost childlike features, she seemed like some sort of lovely vision conjured out of the mists that drifted over the hillsides of Gwynedd.

Rhiannon's smile deepened. "Were you expecting someone different? Someone more impressive, perhaps?"

"Of course not," Eastra answered quickly. "You are every bit as beautiful as both Rhun and Bridei said you were."

"That is kind of you to say, but after bearing five children, I'm certain I have lost some of my allure. Yet that is a small price to pay for the joys of motherhood."

Eastra could not help glancing at Rhiannon's slender form. It was amazing to think this tiny woman had borne six children.

Rhiannon observed the direction of her gaze. "Despite what people think, broad hips do not always mean a safe delivery," she said. "Other factors are more important—whether a woman's womb opens easily, that the babes are positioned properly, and the afterbirth be expelled completely. The ability to give birth safely is often inherited," Rhiannon continued. "Tell me, Eastra, did your mother or your aunts have difficulties in childbed?"

"Nay, not that I know of."

"Good." Rhiannon nodded as if satisfied.

Eastra thought that this was a very odd thing for them to be discussing, unless Rhiannon could see the future and knew one day Eastra would be Rhun's wife and, hence, kin of sorts to Rhiannon. The idea thrilled Eastra. But she could obviously not ask such a thing. Instead, she said, "I have heard you can see the future. Is that true?"

Rhiannon smiled. "Sometimes I see things and then they come to pass, but that does not mean I know what's going to happen before it does. I get tiny glimpses only, and even then I do not always know what they mean, how the pattern fits together."

Eastra said shyly, "I have had a kind of seeing myself. It felt like a dream, but I was awake. I saw your stepson, Rhun, and he seemed terribly distressed, as if he had seen something horrifying. I worry that he is in danger." She raised her gaze to Rhiannon's. "Do you think it might be a true seeing? Do *you* sense he is in danger?"

Rhiannon did not answer at first. Then she said, "There are many kinds of danger." There was something hesitant and wary in her expression, and Eastra experienced a twinge of fear. Rhiannon turned to leave. Eastra wanted to stop her, to insist that she elaborate on her words. But while she was struggling how to phrase her request, Rhiannon murmured "good night" and slipped out the door.

Eastra gazed after her in consternation. Then, with a sigh, she went to fetch the basket of food. She was very hungry.

The night was warm and brightly lit by moonlight. Rhun stood in a clearing beyond the stout timber walls of Camlann. He was bare to the waist and panting heavily. A faint breeze riffled his hair and cooled the sweat on his torso. Taking a deep breath, he raised the heavy broadsword in salute to his imaginary opponent, then thrust it forward. In his mind, his opponent met his blow. He twisted, pulling away, then drew back the weapon once again. It sang through the air, the thin tempered blade hissing as it barely missed the phantom warrior. Rhun whirled and brought the sword down in a slashing movement.

He pulled back again, breathing heavily. Wiping his sweaty hands on his trousers, he prepared to continue the battle. His arms and shoulders ached and perspiration beaded on his face and body, but he did not intend to stop until he was so utterly weary he could scarce walk.

Once more the sword hummed through the air, alive, invincible. Rhun felt the trance come over him. No thought, only instinct. His body moving of its own accord, his mind blank. Blessed oblivion. A kind of release.

"Still play this foolish game, do you?" The voice came out of the darkness behind him. In Rhun's mind, no words registered, only sound. He whirled and, still in his battle daze, prepared to kill his opponent. He drew back the sword, then went limp with sudden awareness. "Bridei, you fool! Don't you know better than to surprise me like that?"

"Were you going to kill me?" Bridei stepped into the moonlight, his smile lazy.

Rhun let out his breath and shook his head. "Luckily

for you, I usually look before I strike. But, damn you, it was close! I wasn't even thinking, just reacting."

Bridei nodded to the broadsword in Rhun's hand. "I didn't know you still played at battle games. I thought you'd outgrown such things. Or is it that you don't get enough fighting these days and it makes you restless?"

"It's not the lack of fighting that makes me restless, and you know it. Now, tell me, what are you doing here? What's happened? Did you get away from Urien? And what about Eastra? Where is she?"

"One question at a time. First of all, Eastra is safe and well cared for. By now, she's at Deganwy, being fussed over by Gwenaseth and Rhiannon."

"But how? Did Urien finally agree to let you leave?"

"Having received word that we were being held by Urien, our dear father decided to rescue us." Bridei's voice was harsh with sarcasm. "He showed up outside Caer Louarn with a large troop of warriors. Urien is no fool; he does not want war with the Dragon. So he acted as if we were free to leave all the while."

"And Maelgwn took Eastra back to Deganwy?"

Bridei nodded. "And assigned Beli to wait upon her as if she were royalty. Which she is, of course."

"And you. Why didn't you go to Deganwy with them?"

"You mean, why didn't I go to my childhood home, to be welcomed into the bosom of my loving family?" He gave a snort of disgust. "I mislike heartfelt, tearful reunions. Besides, Eastra wanted me to find you."

"So you could let me know that she is well?"

"Nay, so I could warn you."

Rhun frowned. "Warn me about what?"

"Well, apparently your little Saxon princess has been dabbling in the magical arts. She claims to have had a 'seeing,' a premonition of what the future holds for you."

Rhun suddenly felt cold. He had feared Morgeuse's influence on the innocent Eastra. It appeared he had been right to worry. His jaw tightened in fury. "What has Mor-

geuse been up to?" he demanded. "What sort of unchancy
business has she involved Eastra in?"

"I don't know. Only that Eastra claims she had a seeing
or a dream or something where she saw you, and you appeared to be in great turmoil and distress. She was not
more specific than that. I told her you were a big boy and
could take care of yourself, but that didn't satisfy her. I
think if she thought she could get away, she would come
running to your aid herself."

"Jesu, that would be madness! She must be protected
and guarded at all times. And for her to come here now,
when tensions are so high . . ." Rhun shook his head.
There were constant rumors at Camlann about Cerdic and
how he was gathering his war host in the east and having
secret meetings with the Picts in the north. Arthur's men's
resentment and mistrust of Cerdic might well affect how
they treated Eastra. "Arthur even refused to let me go back
for her. He said as long as I was certain Urien wouldn't
harm her, it served no purpose for me to leave Camlann
when we might be marching to war any day. I think even
he believes the truce is doomed."

"Ah, so that is why you're out here, wearing yourself
down in mock combat with an invisible enemy. You feel
guilty about Eastra, so you take it out on yourself."

Rhun sighed. "It's complicated. I want to go to Eastra
more than anything. But I know it serves no purpose. As
long as she is safe, it's better that we do not meet."

"Why? Are you afraid if you saw her, all your noble
resolve would crumble away? That you care enough for her
that you might betray your sworn oath, your *duty,* in order
to be with her?"

There was a mocking amusement in Bridei's tone that
infuriated Rhun. His hand tightened reflexively on his
sword hilt. But then he took a deep breath. There was no
point being angry at his brother for stating the truth. That
was *exactly* what he feared. It was as if a battle was going
on inside him—a battle between his feelings for Eastra and
the very essence of his responsibilities as a soldier. "I never

thought I could feel this way about a woman." He sighed again.

"Well, it was bound to happen," Bridei said cynically. "The same idealistic nature that drove you to join Arthur's cause at sixteen has now turned you into a lovesick wretch. In contrast, I know how to keep my wits about me, to look out for myself. I'm not going to commit myself to any man's cause, nor fall in love with any woman."

"I think your attitude makes for a lonely, empty existence," Rhun said.

"Oh, really? Then why is it I'm going into the fortress to find a warm, willing woman to cuddle up with for the night, while you are out here trying to exhaust yourself enough so you can go back to your lonely bed and eventually get a few fitful hours of sleep?"

A few fitful hours of sleep. Glumly, Rhun realized that he would be lucky to enjoy even that much rest. Every time he lay down and closed his eyes, he was tormented by memories of making love to Eastra, of running his fingers through the silk of her hair and tasting the warm, fragrant softness of her skin. Hours later, he would still be tossing and turning, the bedclothes wrapped around him, chilly with his own sweat, his insides aching with a sense of loss that gnawed at him until he felt like he was being eaten alive.

And now, hearing about Eastra, his yearning for her was even more intense. She had dreamed of him. She feared for him. How could he not go to her, to reassure her?

He set his jaw, realizing he could not deny his feelings any longer. He must see Arthur and somehow convince him to let him go to Deganwy. But how? He dared not reveal how he felt about Eastra. It might make Arthur question his loyalty. But there must be some excuse, some explanation he could give.

Bridei had already started off toward the fortress. Rhun called him back. "I need your help," he said to his brother.

* * *

The windows in Arthur's council room had been unshut-
tered and a cool breeze blew through, making the lamplight
waver. Arthur sat in his big carved chair. Next to him
hunched his scribe, Flavius, squinting over a parchment.
Arthur looked up and smiled as Rhun entered. The sick
feeling in Rhun's stomach grew more intense. Never before
had he lied to his commander. "Sire," he began. "I would
like to ask a favor. My brother, Bridei, has just returned
from Gwynedd."

Arthur nodded. "Aye, he made his report to me a while
ago. I was pleased to learn our hostage was safe at your
father's fortress. Although Maelgwn and I have not always
seen eye to eye on things these past years, I trust him in
this matter. I believe he will guard Princess Eastra most
diligently." Arthur's hawk-like gaze pierced Rhun. "Now,
what is your favor?"

"My stepmother, Maelgwn's wife, has been ill since this
spring. I would like to go and see her. I thought I would
have a chance to visit her when we took Princess Eastra
there, but Urien altered my plans."

"Maelgwn's wife is ill? I didn't know this."

Rhun's stomach lurched. What if Arthur had spies at
Deganwy? "It may not be a serious illness," he said
quickly. "But she is such a delicate woman, it worries me
to learn of her ailing. Besides, as you said yourself, if the
truce is broken, there will be a battle for Britain to end all
battles. I would like to see the woman who has been like
a mother to me one more time."

He could see Arthur weighing the matter in his mind.
He had asked few favors of his commander in well over
ten years of service. And Arthur, who had never known his
birth father or mother and had lost his foster parents early
on, honored the bond between parent and child more than
most men. "Deganwy is what—two days' ride from here?"
Arthur asked.

"Aye, and while I am in the north, I could send out the word to the chieftains there, to give them one last chance to join our cause."

Arthur snorted. "If they have not joined me yet, they will not do so for this next battle. I think they are all hoping I will be killed and Britain will go back to what is was, a disordered rabble of petty chieftains, squabbling endlessly with their neighbors. They are too stupid to see the Saxon threat will change their lives forever, and my desire to lead them has nothing to do with seizing power and everything to do with trying to make certain there is a Britain left for *any* of us to govern."

As always, Arthur's impassioned words evoked an intense response in Rhun. They *did* have right and goodness on their side. Unlike so many men, Arthur fought not for his own personal glory, but for a dream—a dream that would mean a more prosperous and safer existence for their children and their children's children.

Arthur put up his hand. "Go, then. I will not deny you this, not when all of us could be dead in a fortnight. Visit your stepmother and, if you can, try one last time to convince your father it is time to fight for Britain. I know he doesn't begrudge me the high kingship, that he sincerely believes it's foolish to make war with the Saxons. But urge him to consider the matter one more time, to think long and hard on whether he wishes to have his grandchildren grow up speaking coarse Saxon or the wild music of the Cymry tongue."

"I will speak to him," Rhun said. It was the least he could do, he thought as he left the council room, now that he had betrayed his ideals, and all for the sake of a Saxon.

Bridei met him at the soldiers' barracks. "What did he say?"

"He let me go. I think he believes I might be able to persuade our father to join his cause."

"And the lie about Rhiannon?"

Rhun grimaced. "I used it, though the words burnt like bile in my mouth."

Bridei shrugged. "The lie hurts no one. The course of history will not be changed because you sought out your ladylove."

Rhun regarded his brother dubiously. Something inside him told him that with this lie, the pattern of his life—and perhaps the lives of everyone around him—had been irrevocably altered.

Fourteen

"Have you ever seen the ocean before?" Rhiannon asked as she and Eastra walked down the sloping trackway from the stronghold.

"Aye, when I was a child. I remember how it smelled. I also remember my brother warning me not to venture into the fens, the marshland bordering the beach. He said there were places there where the spirits of the dead lived, and they would grab my legs and pull me down into the muck and I would never be seen again." Eastra gave a rueful laugh. "I believed him, and so the whole time, even when we were on the open beach, I kept my eyes on the ground, worrying I would be swallowed up at any moment."

"It was cruel of him to tease you," Rhiannon said.

"Not really cruel. There are very dangerous spots in the fens, places where even a man can get caught and not be able to get free but slowly sink to his death. My brother was trying to protect me." A wave of sadness afflicted her. She'd never had a chance to see her brother grow up, to find out what sort of man he would have been.

"You miss him, don't you?"

Eastra nodded. "Silly, isn't it? He's been dead over ten years now, but still I think of him."

"Of course. You love him, and love does not end with death." Rhiannon reached out and touched her arm. "But perhaps if you would consider this, you would be comforted. I think when we love someone a great deal, even after they die, their spirit stays with us. I think your brother is with you now, watching over you."

A strange sensation came over Eastra. There were times when she had felt that way, as if Cynebeold had spoken to her. She stopped and looked at Rhiannon. "What makes you say something like that? Do *you* feel him? Do *you* believe he is with me?"

Rhiannon only smiled.

Eastra began walking again. Even though Rhiannon's words were comforting, the way she talked about things reminded her of Morgeuse. She recalled how Morgeuse had coaxed her into being part of her rituals, had taught her to "see" things. But in the end, Morgeuse had betrayed her.

She glanced at Rhiannon. In the three days she had been at Deganwy, the queen had been very solicitous and kind. Like Morguese, Rhiannon was reputed to be a powerful sorceress. Morgeuse had used her, made her part of some twisted scheme to thwart her husband. What did this woman want? Did she also mean to ensnare Eastra in her web of magic, to use her as Morgeuse had? She stopped walking once again. "Why are you taking me to see the ocean? I am a hostage and a Saxon. What is your purpose in being friendly to me?"

"Purpose?" Rhiannon's face was expressionless. "Do you think I need a purpose to be kind to another woman, especially one who is young and troubled, who has had a life of hardship and loss?" She shook her head sadly. "You do not have to trust me. I would not expect you to. But, please, give me a chance to help you. I was once very like you. I had been abused and hurt. I did not know where to turn, how to find my way in life. Another woman helped me, enabled me to see things more clearly. That is the only purpose I have."

Eastra was still not satisfied. "I beg your pardon for seeming suspicious and ungrateful, but you see, Lady Morgeuse said much the same thing to me and I later discov-

ered her words were false. She did not care for me, but
only for how she might manipulate me in a way that fur-
thered her goals."

"Morgeuse." Rhiannon smiled. "In a way, I admire her.
She is so fearless, so strong. But she is also misguided.
She thinks the power of the Goddess can defeat the male
force, that she can meddle in the realm of men and make
things 'better,' as she sees it."

"You don't believe that?"

Rhiannon shook her head. "The female realm is separate
from the world of men. I fear Morgeuse's clever schemes
will turn on her and she will suffer greatly."

"But her power is real. I've seen it. Felt it."

"Aye, it is real. But it's not meant to be used as she is
using it."

"Why not? Why shouldn't a woman try to control things
and change the course of events? I think we would make
less of a mess of it than men have made!" Eastra felt herself
becoming angry. She could not help resenting the stupidity
of men, their passion for war and power.

"But once you involve yourself in the world of men,
you are subject to the rules of that world," Rhiannon said.
"And those rules are against all the Goddess stands for.
She represents patience and timelessness, harmony and balance. Men's goals are always petty and small compared to
the vast, eternal earth. She is beyond them. She represents
the things that last." She motioned. "Come. Let us go down
to the sea and I will show you what I mean."

They followed the pathway along the river to where it
turned into a great, wide estuary teeming with birds. Everywhere Eastra looked there were waterfowl—waders and
dippers, herons, swans, fulmars, and gulls. They covered
the shoreline like huge pale flowers; then, when startled,
rose to the air in soaring clouds. The smell of the mudflats
was strong, of rotting things washed up from the sea. Eastra
wrinkled her nose, and Rhiannon said, "It's the smell of
death, but also of life. There is much to eat here. The tidal
pools teem with fishes and shellfish. Many birds raise their

young here, in nests on the cliffs and in the sea holly and marsh grass among the dunes."

They walked along the shoreline, veering east until they reached a broad, sandy beach. Rhiannon bent down and took off her sandals. Eastra did the same.

The sand was wet and cold beneath her feet as they walked down to the waves. When they had almost reached the water, Rhiannon spoke. "The surf rolls in, over and over, endlessly. The tide comes in and goes out. It's like the heartbeat of the earth, an eternal rhythm. The ocean and the rivers and streams flow through the Mother's body, like the blood through our veins. The water feeds her flesh as the blood does ours. And yet the sea is also like her womb, pouring out life onto the land. Did you know that everything comes from the sea? That even we once dwelt there? We were much different then, not human yet. But we have memories of it. And that is echoed in the long months when we swim inside our mothers' wombs."

She turned to Eastra and spread her arms wide. "Do you see the pattern, how it's all connected? This is the female realm. Compared to it, the shallow concerns of men are no more significant than a small pool left when the tide recedes. It will soon evaporate and leave nothing behind but a stinking puddle of dying creatures who will either be eaten or dry up and blow away on the wind. But the sea—it will endure, as the Goddess and her power will endure. Men may fight and kill, seeking power, seeking land. But their quest is futile. They can never possess what they long for. The magic, the pattern, eludes them because they never look beyond their own realm."

Eastra sighed. "The world of men might appear insignificant to you, but it has caused me much pain. *Men* killed my family and enslaved me. Their greed and ambition near ruined my life." The world of men also threatened everything she shared with Rhun, but she did not say this.

Rhiannon nodded. "I, too, have suffered because of the blind cruelty of men. When I was very young, one of them hurt me very badly. But the Goddess healed me. She opened my eyes. And even though I am wed to a warrior, a man whose very existence is caught up in the male realm, I must remember never to lose sight of the true pattern beneath."

"Aye, how do you do that?" Eastra asked. "With all your knowledge and power, how do you endure being wed to a king? Your husband's very title bespeaks a world of ambition, war, and power."

Rhiannon smiled. "My husband is older, and I like to think he has learned some wisdom over the years. Yet we do not always agree. He still thinks like a man, for all the Goddess has taught him. It's a dilemma, but I take comfort in the fact he is what he is meant to be. The Goddess does not wish to deny male energy. It's part of the magic of life. All females in season need the male to plant the seed that will grow inside them. And for our kind, males are also protectors, hunters who bring us food, warriors who defend us from other warriors."

"But if they did not always fight each other, we would not need protection," Eastra said in frustration.

"But it is the way of males to fight, to compete against each other. Stag fights stag during the rut. Dog foxes, birds, even the soft, timid hare fights for the chance to mate with a female. That's how the Goddess ensures only the strongest and healthiest have offspring. And all life is a battle to survive. That is also part of the pattern."

Eastra could not help sighing. Rhiannon's words made sense, but did nothing to ease the turmoil inside her. She feared Rhun had chosen the male realm—his responsibilities as a warrior—over her and the deep, dark magic that had connected them when their bodies were joined.

"I'm sorry to see you so distressed," Rhiannon said softly. "I would ease your suffering, if I could. The first step is to try to let go of your anger. You cannot change the past, so you must accept it. If you don't, it will fester inside you and poison the rest of your life. You cannot want that, especially now you are carrying a new life inside you."

A new life inside you—it took a moment for Rhiannon's words to sink in. "What?" Eastra gasped. "What did you say?"

Rhiannon smiled. "I wasn't sure I should speak of it, but then I decided the knowledge you are carrying a child might help you. It's a great gift, the greatest magic of all."

Eastra felt stunned. A child? Rhun's child? What did this mean for them? Would a child bind him to her? "I . . . I didn't know," she said woodenly. "I mean, I had not thought about it. I've lost track of time these past weeks. I don't even remember the last time I bled." Then she looked at Rhiannon. "How do you know? How can you be certain I'm with child when I myself have no certain knowledge of it?"

Rhiannon appeared thoughtful. "Perhaps I should not tell you this, given that you seem so angry at Morgeuse, but . . ." She shook her head. "There is no other way to say it. I had a seeing . . . before you even came to Deganwy."

"What did you see?" Eastra demanded.

"I saw you with your belly swollen. I do not know yet if the babe is a boy or girl. But it will be born next spring, sometime after the Seed Moon."

She wanted to ask Rhiannon if she knew the child was Rhun's, but she could not quite get the words out. What if Rhun didn't want the child? What if he thought she had tricked him into coupling with her so she would conceive? She remembered one of her uncle's house carls speaking contemptuously of women who deliberately got pregnant in order to entrap a man.

Then she thought of something else. Why had Rhiannon mentioned Morgeuse? What did the Rheged queen have to do with her pregnancy? A prickling sense built along her spine and suddenly she knew why Morgeuse had sent her to Rhun that night. "Did Morgeuse . . . did she . . ." She felt vaguely sick. She'd known Morgeuse had used her; she had not guessed how hopelessly ensnared she had been.

Rhiannon nodded. "I believe she used some sort of spell,

a kind of enchantment. But don't be alarmed. It was meant to be. Perhaps Morgeuse helped things along, but her motives were not cruel nor selfish. I think she believed it was important that the child be conceived at that time, on that particular night."

Eastra recalled how aroused she had been, how desperate to have Rhun make love to her. She had been so wanton and eager, holding nothing back. She shivered. Morgeuse's magic had worked very well. She touched her stomach. Could there really be a child growing inside her? She didn't feel any different. So far, she had experienced only the vaguest fatigue, and she had thought that was because she wasn't sleeping well because she was so worried about Rhun.

She glanced sharply at Rhiannon. "Does anyone else know? Maelgwn? Beli?"

Rhiannon shook her head.

"Good. I don't want anyone to know."

Rhiannon quirked a brow. "In time, it will be obvious enough."

What was she to do? If Rhun found out about the babe before she could talk to him, he would think she had been trying to trap him, to force him to wed her, or least bind him to her so he could not escape. He would be disgusted by her manipulations. But if she could speak to him and explain about Morgeuse's spell, then maybe he wouldn't blame her so much.

But when would she see him? What if he went off to war without her ever having a chance to talk to him? She remembered her seeing and the agonized expression on his face. Did *that* have something to do with the babe?

Rhiannon reached out and stroked her shoulder. "I understand. You don't want anyone to know until you tell the father. Well, you won't have too long to wait. He's on his way here."

Eastra stared at the woman beside her. Rhiannon's violet blue eyes had a distant, misty look, and her mouth was curled into a tender smile.

* * *

"Damned mist," Rhun muttered. He jerked his horse to a halt, then reached up with his free hand and pulled up the hood on his heavy woolen mantle.

Bridei drew up beside him. "We'll have to wait it out. This mountain country is treacherous enough when a man can see where he's going. It would be suicide to try to ride in this stuff."

"I *know* we'll have to stop," Rhun grumbled. "I'm trying to find some sort of shelter so the waiting isn't so miserable." He dismounted, then squinted into the mist, waiting for the heavy white mass to shift. When it did, he spied a tumble of rocks about knee high. It would afford them a dry place to sit, at least. "There's some rocks about ten paces to your right," he said. "Won't keep us dry, but it's better than nothing."

In seconds, the mist was on them again, but they managed to stagger blindly over to the rocks. No need to tether the horses, Rhun thought as he let loose of the reins. The beasts knew better than to wander off. He crouched down, feeling for the rocks, then sat down when he found one flat enough to sit on. He could just barely make out Bridei no more than two paces away, finding his own resting spot.

"Llud, that was fast," Bridei said. "One minute it was clear; the next we were swallowed up in the dragon's breath."

"I hardly think it's any sort of enchantment. Just the cursed weather up here in the hills."

"Well, it was your idea to go this way instead of keeping to the coast road—so sure you were it would be faster."

Rhun adjusted his cloak more tightly around his body. The mist chilled his face, but at least it was summer. They would not freeze to death.

Frustration churned inside him. Whatever had possessed him to decide to go this way? Bridei was right. The old Roman roadway, overgrown and crumbling as it was, would still have been faster. And now, with the mist, they might lose a whole day. There was the distinct possibility it would keep them penned in until nightfall. What an uncomfortable, godforsaken place this would be to spend the night!

As if having the same thoughts, Bridei said, "Do you think we should get out our gear before the horses wander too far?"

"I suppose so. Stay here and keep talking. If I get turned around, the only way I'll be able to find this spot is to head toward the sound of your voice."

"Right, brother. If there's one thing I can do, it's keep talking. Or maybe I should sing." With that, Bridei broke into song. It was some sort of lament, Rhun noted as he inched his way forward with his hands out, feeling for warm, solid horseflesh among the shifting whiteness. Cadal nickered when he found him. Rhun spoke soothingly to the stallion as he groped in the saddlebag. Behind him, he heard Bridei, his rich, well-trained voice sounding so clear and close, he might have been standing next to Rhun. Although he tried to concentrate on what they would need for the night, Rhun found himself responding to poignant sadness of the melody. "By the saints! Can't you sing something more cheerful?" he exclaimed.

Bridei stopped and said, "It's an old, old song about a beautiful maiden who gets stolen by the fairies and taken to the underworld. She dwells there for three lifetimes, then finally convinces them to release her. When she returns to the mortal realm, her earthly lover is long gone, dead and buried. So she roams the hills looking for a fair-faced, handsome youth to be her new paramour."

Having found food, blankets, and his leather pouch with flintstone and tinder, Rhun made his way back to Bridei. Fortunately, the mist thinned momentarily and he could almost see where he was going. "I hate those ancient, traditional songs," he said, as he dumped their provisions among the rocks. "They're always so gloomy and mournful."

"But appropriate. Who knows but that we will wake in

the morning to find the mist cleared, but also that three lifetimes have passed?"

Rhun sighed heavily. He'd been so anxious to see Eastra, he'd tried to take the shortest route. Now it appeared they would be delayed for nearly a full day.

Bridei said, "You know, I'm having a hard time understanding this. You left Urien's stronghold over a fortnight ago. Plenty of time to make your report to Arthur, then return and rescue Eastra. But instead you moped around Camlann for days, then suddenly decided the night before last that you *had* to see her. What's changed? Have you made some sort of decision regarding our lovely Saxon hostage? Are you finally going to admit you're in love with her and ask her to be your wife?"

Rhun felt the familiar weight descend upon him. "Don't you see—I can't marry her! She's a Saxon, and our hostage. It's impossible!"

"Then what are you going to say to her? She's going to want some sort of commitment from you, some assurance that if she gets with child, you aren't going to abandon her."

Rhun sucked in his breath. "I had not thought about a babe." What would he do if Eastra were carrying his child?

"Well, you should, foolish brother of mine. It only takes one time, and I know you've been intimate with her more than once."

"And *how* do you know that?"

"Losing their maidenhood changes a woman, makes them bolder. I saw every sign of that soon after we were taken captive by Urien. And then, one night before you left Caer Louarn, Morgeuse worked a spell. If Eastra did not let you love her *that* night, Morgeuse is not the sorceress I think she is."

With a rush of feeling, Rhun remembered making love to Eastra in his underground prison. The experience had been so intense, so overwhelming. He'd thought that was love, but what if it was merely one of Morgeuse's charms, binding him to Eastra against his will? "Damn that meddling witch," he muttered. "Why couldn't she leave well enough alone?"

"I don't know, but she was adamant about it being that night. She said the spell wouldn't work the same any other time."

Rhun turned to face his brother, although he could not see him in the mist. *"You* were a part of it? *You* helped her?"

"By the Light," Bridei said angrily, "I thought it was what you wanted! It was certainly what Eastra wanted! I didn't see the point in arguing with Morgeuse. I figured she was giving you both your heart's desire!"

Rhun reached out and grabbed his brother's arm. He was furious. He'd known Morguese was trouble, but he'd never guessed *he* would be the target of her loathsome magic. "What does Morguese want from us? From *me?* Does she have some sort of scheme in mind? Or was she just amusing herself at my expense?"

"I tell you, I don't know! Morguese doesn't trust men. She'd never tell me what she was up to. The only reason I knew anything about the spell was that I was part of it."

Rhun clutched his brother tighter, fingers digging into flesh. "What the hell does that mean?"

"Relax, brother. I didn't have to drink your blood or anything too gruesome. All she asked me to do was make love to her little apprentice, Nevyn. I guess she put a spell on us, too, so that our ardor and passion transferred to you and Eastra. It was simple enough. Nevyn was half mad for it anyway. Hard to imagine such a tiny, quiet wench could be so passionate. I vow I still have the scars on my back from her fingernails."

"That's appalling!" Rhun shouted. "She's barely more than a girl!"

Bridei pulled away. "She was a maid, aye, but not *too* young. Most men wed off their daughters at that age, and as I've told you, she was more than eager."

"But to use her in some repulsive rite!"

"I didn't use her; Morgeuse did. And I have every reason

to believe Nevyn knew exactly what she was about. 'Sex magic' she called it. The woman I bedded was no quivering, blushing maiden, but an acolyte of the Great Mother herself."

Rhun tried to calm his breathing, to overcome the helpless rage Bridei's revelation had aroused. Although he despised Morguese's manipulations, he had to get past his anger and discover her motivations. What did Morgeuse want with him and Eastra?

"I don't see why that changes anything," Bridei said. "You've been infatuated with Eastra since you set eyes on her in Cerdic's hall, and she with you. Maybe all Morguese wanted to do was get you together and force you to admit your feelings for each other."

Rhun snorted. "I hardly see Morgeuse as a matchmaker. Nay, you can be certain she had some devious purpose in mind. But what is it?"

"Maybe Eastra knows, or at least can shed some light on the matter. The two of you need to talk, that's for certain."

Rhun sat down heavily. Eastra. How had things gotten so confused and muddled between the two of them? As if their situation wasn't bad enough, now Morguese had complicated things even more. How could he be certain what he felt for Eastra was real and not some sort of enchantment?

Oh, it was real, he decided. And Bridei was right. He had been in love with Eastra since that day in the longhouse. Or maybe even since the day when he defied his commander and saved her life. But all this aching longing inside him did not change the fact she was a Saxon princess. Because of that, he could offer her nothing but passion and dreams and, in the end, heartbreak.

"Oh, God," he groaned. "Why am I even doing this? I should leave her alone, never see her again, like I'd planned."

"So you don't think you can wed her," Bridei said thoughtfully. "You're probably right. Arthur wouldn't allow it. That doesn't mean you shouldn't see her. At least while she's a hostage, you might as well enjoy her company. Grab what moments of happiness you can. That's what *I* would do, brother, if I were ever dense-witted enough to fall in love. And maybe somehow it will work out. If Cerdic breaks the truce and you go to war and Arthur wins, as the victor you could petition Cerdic for the right to marry his niece. For that matter, if Cerdic were dead, there would be no obstacle to the marriage. If I were you, I would be thinking of ways to be rid of Cerdic"

"You want me to commit murder? What noble plans you have for me! If I did something like that I would not be *worthy* of Eastra, nor any other woman!"

"Not murder. But you are involved in a war with Eastra's kin. I'm merely saying it might be to your benefit if Cerdic broke the truce. Then you could kill him on the battlefield and have no compunction about it."

"If Cerdic breaks this truce and we go to war, I will probably end up dead myself," Rhun said flatly.

"Arthur thinks things are that hopeless?"

"Aye. The word is that the Picts have joined forces with Cerdic, and maybe some of the Irish as well. We can't fight on three fronts—not when half of our countrymen refuse to join our cause."

"Can you blame them, under the circumstances? Why should they sacrifice their lives for Arthur? Why should *you?*"

"For a dream, a dream of a united Britain. And because if they do not fight now, they end up fighting for the rest of their lives anyway. The ravens are circling, brother. The barbarians mean to crush us between them."

"But the Picts are not much different than the Cymry. And even the Irish—father has told you the tale of our great-grandfather Cunedog, hasn't he? He was Irish, but he settled the wild lands of Gwynedd and Manua Gotodin and became as 'Prydan' as the rest of them. And the Romans, they supposedly conquered Britain. For centuries they dwelled here, but do you see any sign of them now? All that's left is a bunch of ruined buildings and fools like Aurelius."

"But the Romans changed Britain, made it something different. Taught us to fight wars with strategy and skill. They improved trade, introduced us to many civilized comforts, brought a kind of peace and order to the land it has not seen before nor since."

"And the Saxons will change Britain, too, but it might not be all bad, either. From what I've seen, they are not so different than us, except they are better farmers." Bridei thought a moment. "And deep down I believe they are less warlike, less hotheaded and impulsive. That might be good for Britain. In fact, it might accomplish exactly what you wish for. Arthur—or any British chieftain—will never unite the people of this island, but the Saxons might be able to."

"But they will never win over the Picts," Rhun said. "Nor the Cymry, either. Neither of them will ever join forces with the Saxons. They are too stubborn, too fierce and independent, like our father." He grimaced.

"Our father." Bridei's voice dripped scorn. "He's from another time, another world. A time when, to hear him tell, warriors were much more valiant than they are now, their deeds greater and more heroic. He lives in the glorious past, the realm of the bards, where everything is brighter and more vivid than the present. I dabble in that world, too, so I suppose I cannot blame him for being seduced by it. The imagination always colors things the way you wish it had been. I remember when I was a boy and he would be talking to me, but his gaze looked past me, seeing another time, all the memories crowding his thoughts. I wonder how my mother endures it—to know a part of him dwells forever in the past with his beloved Aurora."

For all the sarcasm in Bridei's voice, there was a kind of wistfulness there as well. Rhun understood that. The tale of Maelgwn and his first wife was touching enough to inspire a dozen laments. To think that out of grief over losing Aurora in childbirth, his father had actually given up his kingdom for over five years and dwelt in a priory. Knowing how impatient and contemptuous Maelgwn was of the clergy, it seemed even more remarkable. But if Eastra died, Rhun knew he would feel the same, as if a part of his soul had been cut out. That was why he was going to see her, against all his better sense and reason.

He grabbed up his saddle pack and began to rummage in it for something to eat. As soon as the fog lifted, they would set out. They were not far, just a few valleys over from a long vale that led down to Deganwy. At the thought, his body tightened with expectation and yearning. Eastra would haunt his dreams for the rest of his life. He wondered if the same were true for her. If he died, would she mourn for him for years? He did not want that; it grieved him to think of her being unhappy. Another reason to be careful what he said to her. He could make no promises. If war came, he might be dead in a fortnight.

He sighed. It seemed cruel to bind her to him even more closely, to make her hope for a future that could never be. But he knew he would not be able to help himself. His feelings for her were too intense, too overwhelming. And if he were really going to die, why should he not know some happiness in the brief time left to him? He had cursed himself for becoming like Bridei, for forgetting his duty and seizing pleasure and satisfaction in the moment at hand, but right now it seemed like the only thing to do.

He wondered if some of Morgeuse's love spell still clung to him. Or maybe it was this place, this ancient, haunted land of mountains and mist. Time did not seem to matter here, and the goals and dreams of one man's lifetime seemed as inconsequential as one small stone skittering down the hillside.

"Hand me the wineskin," Bridei said. "And I'll sing you a song to cheer you up."

Rhun nodded. For once, he was willing to listen to his brother's advice and drown his sorrows in wine and music.

Fifteen

"Let me carry the basket!" Mabon cried.

"Let me! Let me!" echoed Gwydion. "I'm the eldest."

"By a few heartbeats only," Mabon returned. "We're the same age in truth. Mama said so!"

"Come now, don't squabble," Elen, their older sister, said with a laugh. "If you're going to walk with us, you have to behave. What do you say we let one of you carry the basket there, and the other the way back?"

"It will be full on the way back," Mabon said. "I'm the strongest, so I'll carry it then."

"Nay, *I'm* the strongest."

"Are not!"

"Hush, children," Rhiannon said softly. "If you are too noisy, I won't show you the fox den on the way to the berry patch. You'll have to be quiet if you want to see the kits playing."

The twins went silent. Eastra glanced at Rhiannon, amused by her ploy to distract her youngest children from their fighting. She had not raised her voice or threatened them with any sort of discipline, but the quarrelsome, rambunctious five-year-olds obeyed their mother instantly. Rhiannon had a gift, Eastra thought, of bringing calm and peace whereever she went. But then, for someone with such lively children, such a skill was probably necessary for survival.

As Eastra followed Rhiannon and the children along the worn pathway to the forest, she could not help musing on the different natures of Rhun's half siblings. The dark-haired twins seemed to take after Maelgwn and were quick and passionate as fire. They had the sort of competitive natures that made it easy to imagine them as warriors someday. Sixteen-year-old Elen also had near black hair, but appeared as cool and ethereal as the mist, very much like her mother. Her younger sister Annwyl had red tresses and a fiery temperament to match her coloring. And then there were Beli and Bridei—one red-haired, one dark; one dutiful and sweet, the other rebellious and cynical.

Eastra decided Rhun must have taken after his mother, Morganna. Not only was his coloring much different than the rest of his family, but he was not hot-tempered and excitable like Maelgwn, but more like the earth, solid, real, dependable. A fierce ache shot through her at the thought. How she needed him, his big, strong arms around her, the tender glow in his beautiful blue eyes warming her, his smell, so alive and male and intoxicating. She thought of his babe growing inside her. When would she have a chance to tell Rhun about the baby? When would she ever see him again? Rhiannon said he was on his way, but days had passed and there was no sign of him. Sighing, Eastra turned to glance back toward the fortress.

Rhiannon gave her a sympathetic look. "I thought if you went berrying with us, it would lift your spirits."

"I'm sorry. I don't mean to be in such a melancholy temper."

"Of course not. But if you are unhappy, perhaps it would be best if you returned to the fortress."

Eastra nodded. She did not really want to leave, but neither did she want her mood to ruin things for the others.

"Why don't you take the path along the river?" Rhiannon suggested. "The blue meadow cranesbill and harebells are specially pretty right now. And you might find some early raspberries there if you decide to do some berrying after all."

Repressing another sigh, Eastra turned and took the path to where the trackway ran along the river. She could feel her despondency increasing, like a terrible weight inside her. Rhun was not coming. Now she was safe at Gwynedd, he had no interest in her. She'd never meant anything to him. A few hours of pleasure, that was all she had been to him.

Even as she wallowed in her bitter thoughts, a voice inside her screamed "no!" She could not believe he did not care for her. It was only that his sense of duty was stronger than his feelings for her. That must be why he did not come. Arthur needed him. Another wave of anxiety swept over her. Did that mean the truce had not held? Would there be war again, the endless fighting that had destroyed everything she ever cared about?

Tears filled her eyes. Tears for herself, for the loneliness she felt even surrounded by Rhun's family. Tears for the babe she carried, that it might never know its father. Tears for her own dead kin, for the child she had been, that playful, innocent girl whose life had been altered forever. And tears for Rhun, the man she loved more than her own life. She would give up everything if only he would be safe.

As she neared the river, the way grew slippery. Eastra swiped away her tears so she could focus on where she walked. When she finally glanced up, her heart did a sudden lurch. She could see two figures leading horses, approaching Deganwy from downriver. Jerking to a halt, she stared. They looked so familiar, so . . . She gasped. It was Rhun and Bridei!

She wanted to run to him and throw herself into his arms. Instead, she forced herself to walk toward him at a steady, sedate pace. Rhun saw her and handed the reins of his mount to Bridei. He started toward her. When he had almost reached her, he stopped. Eastra also came to a halt and faced him uncertainly. He stared at her. "I'd forgotten," he said. "Forgotten how beautiful you were."

Eastra closed the distance between them. Then she was in his arms, eyes closed, reveling in the feel of him, the wild, earthy, male scent she remembered so well. He stroked her face with his fingers. "Eastra, my darling. Everything was worth it for this. Everything."

His voice, the rumbling, warm sound of it, filled her soul until she thought she would burst. His arms tightened around her and she felt him rub his stubbled jaw against her hair. Then he began to kiss her. He kissed the side of her head, then released her so he could move his lips to her face. Tender kisses, although his whiskers were rough against her skin.

Their mouths mated, merged. Their bodies entwined, desperate to be close. Their essences combined. The magic rose between them, warm and alive, swirling around them like a glowing light. The rest of the world fell away, and there were only the two of them. Finally, Rhun pulled away. He looked at her, his expression so tender, his face so beautiful. *Now,* she thought, now is the time to tell him about the baby.

"Sorry to interrupt, but as soon as I'm gone you'll have the whole place to yourselves." Bridei spoke from behind them. "I left your horse over there, Rhun, tied to that thornbush. Give my regards to my mother."

Rhun slowly disengaged himself and turned to face his brother. Eastra could feel the magic that had surrounded them fading away like mist in the sun. "You're leaving?" Rhun said. "You'd come this far and then run off without seeing anyone?"

Bridei shrugged. "I would have liked to have seen my sisters. And the twins. They were barely born when I left."

"They're in the woods." Eastra pointed. "At the berry patch. Even if you won't go into the fortress, at least see your mother and your brothers and sisters."

Bridei hesitated. Eastra could see the longing in his face. For once he did not look cynical and distant. Then his mouth quirked into a grim smile. "Like as not, I'll be dead in a month. Or so my brother predicts. Under the circumstances, it would be kinder of me not to see them. They'll mourn me less if I'm but a vague memory."

Dead in a month. She turned to Rhun. "What does he mean? What's happened?"

"Nothing's happened yet. But . . ." He shook his head. "Cerdic is said to have allied himself with the Picts, and possibly even the Irish."

Eastra felt ill. He was coming to say good-bye before he went off to war. She could sense it. She turned away, unable to face the expression on her lover's face. A part of her wanted to rage at him, to strike him with her fists, to demand to know how he could leave her, how he could leave his child growing inside her. She thought briefly of telling him about the babe, wondering if it would make a difference.

A wave of hopelessness gripped her. She knew Rhun, and he would do his duty no matter what. A child could not hold him back from fighting for his people, any more than she could. If she told him now, it would change things. And she wanted whatever little time they had together to be shared only between the two of them, without worrying about the complication of the babe.

"You think Cerdic will break the truce?" she asked.

Rhun nodded. "I don't think he ever meant to honor it. It was merely an excuse, a distraction, so he would have time to seek allies among Arthur's enemies."

"What about me?"

Bridei spoke. "Arthur will take no action against you while his own hostage is safe. And it serves no purpose for Cerdic to harm Mordred."

"But there will still be war?"

Rhun nodded solemnly. Eastra turned away again. She did not know if she could bear to lose Rhun all over again, to have him leave her, knowing she might never see him again.

"Well." Bridei cleared his throat. "I'll set off. I'll see you, brother, on the battlefield, if not before. Princess Eastra, fare you well."

She faced Bridei. He had protected her and kept her company through many trying times. She could not let him leave without saying good-bye. Embracing him fiercely, she whispered, "Fare *you* well." She drew away. The lump in her throat was agony. But she would not let herself cry. If she started weeping, she feared she would never stop.

She watched Bridei leave, thinking what a waste it was. He was so handsome, so witty, with a voice that could charm the very stars from the heavens. And all that might well be destroyed by one swift swordblow, that silver tongue silenced, the sparkle in his dazzling blue eyes be quenched forever.

She inhaled sharply, blinking back tears. Then she faced Rhun resolutely. "You've come to say good-bye, haven't you?"

He nodded, looking almost as miserable as she felt.

"How long? How much time can you spare away from the high king?" She spat out the last words. Her anger was rising once again. It was better to be angry than to weep.

"Only a day or two. I want you to know I . . . I lied to Arthur. I told him Rhiannon was ailing and that was why I must come here."

"You lied to your commander? I'm amazed. I must stand very high in your favor to cause you to go against your noble principles of duty and honor."

"I had to see you." Rhun's voice was an anguished whisper. She wanted to close her ears to it. "I have been able to think of nothing else for weeks. I'm half mad with loving you."

She moaned, feeling all her bitterness dissolve away. She could not be angry with him. He was too dear to her, too precious. Her gaze drank in his compelling, handsome face. How she loved him, this magnificent, golden warrior, this man who had haunted her dreams since she could remember. "Show me," she said. "Show me how you love me."

She heard his sharp intake of breath. Then he nodded. "I will show you. I know the very place—a hidden glen where no one will disturb us. An enchanted place, where nothing else will matter but you and me." He reached for her hand. "Come. It will be faster to take my horse, and I have all the things we need in my saddle pack."

He led her to his stallion, then lifted her up on the animal's broad back. He didn't climb up behind her, but instead untied the reins and began to lead the horse. He guided the stallion back toward the forest. After following the edge of the woods for some distance, he drew the horse into the trees. The sweet scent of growing things enveloped them, and the sound of water running filled their ears. The ground was mossy and damp, and hazel and rowan bushes crowded the pathway. Delicate fronds of fern and bracken were crushed beneath the horse's hooves, giving up a scent of earth and shadow. Eastra saw a little runnel off to their left, at first no more than a little ribbon of glistening water tumbling over the rocks, then getting bigger and bigger until it was a good-sized stream. The air grew more moist, dense and thick, the foliage an even brighter, more vivid green.

Rhun stopped, then came back to help her off the horse. "I can't take Cadal any further." He tethered the horse and dragged down his bulging saddle pack. Turning to her, he said, "It's only a little way now."

She followed as he pushed his way through the dense underbrush. The gnarled branches of hazel curled around them like beckoning hands and the ground sloped downward, slippery with moisture. Eastra quickly grew tired of trying to maintain her footing. Sweating and panting, she wondered if this arduous journey would be worth it.

The sound of running water grew louder. They climbed down into a small ravine. After catching her breath, Eastra gave a cry of delight. They were in a kind of hollow in the heavily wooded hills. On one side was a small waterfall, tumbling down the rocky slope to form a foaming pool. On the other side, a pile of rocks had dammed up the stream and there was a little sheltered space nearby, a mossy nook edged with white dewdrops and tiny purple orchids. Rhun went to the mossy patch and, opening the pack, began to arrange things. Eastra watched him spread out his oiled leather cape, then a blanket. He gestured for her to join him.

When she reached him, she expected him to kiss her, but instead, he began to undress. She watched as each fascinating detail of his body was revealed. His broad shoulders, the sleek expanse of his chest with its soft swirls of dark gold hair and deep pink nipples. His flat, narrow belly. He sat on a rock as he took off his boots, then turned slightly sideways as he drew down his trousers. Eastra suppressed a gasp. His erection jutted out, massive from this angle. As he bent over to pull his trousers the rest of the way off, she admired the erotic, muscular shape of his buttocks. He turned to face her, grinning. "Enjoy it now," he said, nodding to his upthrust shaft. "For even my passion for you cannot maintain it through this."

Tossing his trousers aside, he made his way to the edge of the pool and began to gingerly lower himself in. When the water reached waist high, he turned to look at her. "Cold," he said.

He splashed himself, then rapidly ducked his head under water. In another second, he was out and shaking himself like a wet dog. "Jesu, that's freezing." He stumbled over to the blanket and, grabbing another blanket from the pack, rapidly dried himself. Then he knelt beside her and pulled her into his arms. She squealed at the coldness of his body. "Warm me up," he whispered. "Fill me with fire."

She kissed him in answer, feeling his flesh heat even as they embraced. Her fingers stroked the smooth skin of his back, up to his neck and his still wet hair. The heat radiated out from where their lips were joined, hot, wet mouth against hot, wet mouth. She pressed herself against him, feeling his shaft grow hard against her. The provocative sensation made her wriggle her hips in longing. Her breasts were aching, her nipples hard. Fire danced along her body.

She drew back, breathless, wanting to be naked herself. He leaned back on the blanket, his proud, deep pink erection gleaming between his thighs. She began to undress for him. Slipping off her sandals, she untied the girdle around her waist, then drew up her skirts and pulled her gunna over her head. With her fingers grasping the hem of her shift, she hesitated. She'd never been fully naked in front of him before, not in daylight. But the heat building inside her body made her feel reckless and wanton. It was such a wild, primitive place. She wanted everything between them to be just as raw and primal and pure.

She dragged the shift over her head and stood before him, intensely aware of her own body, soft and curved and female, her breasts heavy and abundant, like flowers blooming. The swollen pink of her areolas. The rounded shape of her hips. Her maidenhair, like golden moss curling near the hidden, mysterious pool of her womanhood.

She watched him looking at her with an expression of almost worship. He made her feel like a goddess, as powerful and richly beautiful as the earth mother herself. She felt free and weightless and alive.

"Your braids." He gestured, and she realized she wasn't as unencumbered and free as she could be. She undid her plaits and raked her fingers through her hair, feeling it soft and light against her body.

"Your hair is like sunlight," he said. "Or moonlight. I want to hold it in my hands and feel the cool silkiness of it against my body. Come to me." He motioned. "Come to me, my queen of light."

She shook her head. There was one more thing she wanted to do. She went to the edge of the rocks and lowered herself into the pool. The deep, dark chill of the water seemed to suck the life from her. She stayed in only a few gasping seconds, then climbed out shivering. Rhun opened his arms to her. "Why did you do that?" he asked, laughing. "Didn't you believe me when I told you how cold it was?"

She snuggled against him. "I wanted to be clean for you," she said.

He stopped rubbing her arms as he had been doing. "Why?" His voice was a husky murmur. "Do you want me to taste you everywhere like I did last time?"

She nodded, suddenly too aroused to speak.

"Ah, that is my dream as well." He released her so she could lay back on the blanket. She closed her eyes, embarrassed to think of her boldness. Once before she had urged him to do this, but then she had been bewitched, caught up in Morgeuse's spell. Now nothing but her own pure desire made her stretch out her body, offering it to her lover like a banquet.

She felt his warmth as he leaned over her, then the soft pressure of his lips against her neck. He nuzzled her, then licked his way up her neck and made her moan with the soft, wet warmth of his tongue inside the whorl of her ear. She shivered at the deliciousness of the sensation, melting as he kissed his way down to one of her nipples. He sucked it deep into his mouth and she moaned again. Her breasts were more sensitive than ever, primed to be suckled by a babe. But this was a man, teasing, mouthing, using his teeth to graze the exquisitely tender skin of her nipple. She arched her hips, wondering if she could bear any more. An urgent need filled her insides, making her want their joining with a fierceness that took her breath away.

She cried out as he mouthed her other breast. Then he kissed a pathway down her belly. She spread her thighs for him, no longer caring if she appeared too eager, no longer thinking of anything but the hunger building inside her, the need that blotted out everything else.

His mouth caressed her most intimate parts. Sublime pressure. The tantalizing roughness of his whiskers rasping exquisitely against wet, sensitive flesh. The world twisted and bucked. Her body shimmered and writhed with pleasure.

He was drowning, surrounded by a fabulous mist of femininity. Intoxicated, bewitched, overwhelmed. She tasted so good, scented with the rarest essence. Her body was silky, liquid perfection, lush and bountiful. He wanted to merge himself with her. To fill her softness with his hardness.

He felt her peak. Tasted the hot river of her release. Felt

the shuddering rapture grip her body. But there was more. So much more he could give her.

He raised himself, still stroking her tenderly with his fingers, then fitted himself against her throbbing wet opening and thrust in deep. He heard a low, harsh moan that he realized only vaguely had come from his own throat. How perfectly he fit inside her, as if they had been made for each other. Open and welcoming, her body embraced his. As he began to move, he felt her own answering rhythm. A kind of dance, their bodies moving as one. Together they were divine, magical, a thing of fire. The flames rose higher, raging, consuming both of them. He gasped and lunged, stroking deep, feeling her womb, feeling her body convulse around him, tight and desperate as she peaked again. She forced him to the edge. Another deep stroke and they plunged over the precipice together.

Intense and rapid, his senses overwhelmed. And the aftermath was heaven. The woman in his arms, as soft and yielding as a dream. He lay upon her, hoping he was not crushing her. But he did not want to lose this delicious closeness, this sense of peace. He wanted to carry this moment with him forever, a talisman against any darkness, any suffering.

He opened his eyes, marveling again how beautiful she was, his queen of light. Her mere existence gave his life meaning, filled him with hope, made him dream dreams. For so long now, there had been a shadow over his heart, a sense things were not as they should be. But with her, all felt right and good and true.

He brushed a strand of hair away from her face, marveling that flesh could be fashioned into a form so exquisite. He adored her mouth, her nose, the curve of her cheek, the way the lashes of her closed eyes made perfect dark crescents. He ran his fingers through her hair, so fine and soft and as pale as the sun glowing through the mist. She opened her eyes—a fine, light blue like the fairest of summer skies—and smiled at him.

"This is a beautiful place," she said. "Since I have come

to your land, I have not been easy here. Everything seems
so sad and wild, all dark stones, somber hills and gloomy
skies. But in this place, I feel a kind of peacefulness. If
the land is a goddess, then the goddess of your people is
very fierce and demanding. But here I can sense her warm,
tender heart."

Rhun laughed. "Aye, I can see that. Perhaps that's why
I used to come here when I was young, to puzzle things
out and fashion my dreams of the future."

"And what did you dream when you were a boy?"

He turned away, feeling the outside world pressing
against their circle of happiness. "I wanted to be a great
warrior, like my father. I wanted to do great things."

"And you have," she whispered.

He shook his head. She wanted to comfort him as a
mother comforts her small son, speaking soothing words
and stroking his forehead to make him sleep, to forget the
trials and disappointments of the day. But he was a man,
and he knew her words for what they were. Tenderness.
Love. But not the truth.

"I accomplished so little. Held back the tide for only so
many years. And at what a cost? Not merely the men I've
killed, but the Companions who have fallen beside me. It
is because of them I keep fighting. I don't want their deaths
to be in vain."

He sighed and Eastra's heart twisted in her chest. If only
there were something she could do to help him, to make
him feel better about his life. She thought about the babe.
If he knew he had sired a child to live after him, would
that comfort him? Or make him more despairing?

But again, she hesitated to tell him. She wanted him to
love her again, to arouse that mindless heated passion, con-
jure the heaving, untrammeled ecstasy that would cling to
them and leave them both with shining, pure memories of
what they had known together. She reached up and pulled
his face down to hers, kissing him with slow tenderness
that soon turned to gasping, urgent need. And then they
were lost again, tumbling wildly in a strong, fierce current

of passion, frantic and helpless, as the flood carried them out to the wide, endless sea.

"I suppose we must go back," Rhun said. "Rhiannon and the children will have returned from berrying by now. They will worry if they don't find you at the fortress."

Eastra said, "I think Rhiannon knows I am with you."

Rhun looked at her and nodded. "She probably does. When I was younger, she often unnerved me by knowing exactly what I was thinking, or where I had been. Which is why I probably should ride back with you."

"What? You were thinking of running off like Bridei did, without even stopping to see your family?"

"Aye. And for the same reason. That they might mourn me less if I am but a distant memory to them. But if Rhiannon knows I am here, it's only right that I go to the fortress and let them fuss over me." He grimaced.

"Don't you want to see them?"

"Of course I do. But it will not make it any easier to leave when I have to."

"How long?" She whispered the words, dreading to hear his answer. "How long can you stay?"

"A day or two at most. It took longer to get here than I had hoped. I was delayed a whole night in the mountains when a mist came up and trapped us there."

They reclined on the blanket for a while longer, not speaking. Both of them dreaded leaving the glen. It was a refuge, a timeless, magical place where neither the future nor the past mattered. But finally, with another sigh, he rose and began to dress. She did the same, taking time to wash herself again in the freezing water, then donning her shift and gunna and sandals.

They walked back to Rhun's horse. Cadal was trying to graze on the hawthorn bush he was tied to. "Don't worry," Rhun reassured the beast. "When we get to Deganwy, you shall have a mound of fresh, sweet hay to eat."

They walked back to the fortress, Rhun leading the horse. On the way there, they talked about inconsequential things. Eastra told him about the children, how they had grown, what pretty young women his sisters were, and that so far Maelgwn had refused to entertain any offers for them.

"He's going to have to let them go sometime," Rhun said as they neared the gate. "He can't keep them locked away at Deganwy forever."

"He says he wants them to marry for love, to be able to choose the man they will marry. But whenever any young warriors come to visit, he has his bards make up songs ridiculing them. Humiliated, the young men flee Deganwy and your sisters remain unwed."

"Poor Papa," Rhun laughed. "Most men can scarcely wait until their daughters reach marriageable age and they can bargain them off to seal alliances. He's just the opposite. I don't think he will ever think any man is good enough for either Elen or Annwyl."

"No, your poor *sisters,* you mean. Are they to die unwed and childless because he cannot bear to part with them?"

"I will speak with my father," Rhun said. "Maybe I can convince him to give them more freedom. Why, they must be near sixteen and seventeen years old by now. Jesu, where has the time gone? I remember when they were just little mites and I would carry them on my back and feel like the great, strong older brother."

They reached the gates of the fortress and were instantly surrounded by wellwishers. Even the guards came down from the watchtower to greet Rhun. Other warriors, their women, servants and craftsmen and children and dogs, all crowded into the yard to welcome him.

"I swear." Gwenaseth was both laughing and crying as she embraced him. "Rhiannon said we were to have visitors, but I never thought it would be you. It's been so long, Rhun. I've missed scolding you and trying to keep you out of trouble. Missed it sorely."

"And I've missed you and your sharp tongue," Rhun answered, hugging the tiny woman.

And then the crowd parted to let Maelgwn through. He nodded solemnly to his son, then grabbed him for a crushing bear hug. Eastra saw the two men were nearly of a size, although Rhun was leaner and not so massive as his sire.

Maelgwn drew back and said, "Where's Bridei? I thought he would come with you."

Rhun looked uncomfortable. As Rhiannon came and hugged him, his discomfort became even more obvious. Eastra could tell he dreaded telling them Bridei would not be arriving. "Bridei felt Arthur might need him," Rhun said. "Cerdic is hosting on the eastern shores. The order to march could come at any time."

Maelgwn swore at this, and Eastra thought even Rhiannon looked distressed. Her own stomach clenched with dread. Despite what she had shared with Rhun, nothing could change the fact he was leaving her again and might never come back.

"We need to talk about the war with the Saxons," Rhun said.

Maelgwn nodded. Rhiannon took Eastra's arm. "Come with me. I'll help you dress for the evening meal."

Eastra followed Rhiannon to the bedchamber she shared with Maelgwn. "I've been wanting to give you something," Rhiannon said as they entered. The spacious bedchamber was simply furnished and dominated by a huge bed. Unlike Morgeuse and her piles of clutter, Rhiannon kept few trinkets or decorative objects. The room bore the mark of a man more than a woman, with heavy wooden chests for storage arranged around the room and weaponry hanging from the walls. Eastra thought it interesting that Morgeuse appeared to shun the symbols of male power, while Rhiannon was perfectly comfortable with them.

Rhiannon went to one of the chests and, after digging through it for a time, pulled out a wooden box. She sat on a stool to open it, then searched through the mass of glittering jewelry inside until she found what she was looking for. Raising her gaze to Eastra, she held out a necklace. "Sapphires from the far east," she said. "They're perfect for you; they match your eyes."

Eastra started to shake her head, but Rhiannon spoke firmly. "I want you to have them, and the earbobs to match. They've been gathering dust in here for who knows how many years. This is the treasure hoard of Cunedog, Maelgwn's great-grandsire. Likely no woman has ever worn these pieces since he plundered them from some unfortunate merchant ship."

Eastra held out her hands to take the necklace. It was fashioned of gold squares set with stones as blue and clear as the quiet pool they had bathed in that afternoon.

"Wear it with the blue gown I made for you," Rhiannon said. "Tonight you will look like a princess of your people."

"You're too generous," Eastra said, still feeling stunned. The gold in the necklace alone made it as valuable as anything she had ever possessed. "You should save this for one of your daughters. They both have blue eyes."

Rhiannon shook her head. "It doesn't suit them. And I have plenty of other finery to give them when the time comes for them to leave here and marry."

"Do you think Maelgwn will ever allow that to happen?" Eastra asked, remembering her earlier conversation with Rhun.

"He will have no choice. It's the way of life. The female in season chooses her mate and goes off with him to create the next generation." She stood up and approached Eastra. "Let me fasten the clasp for you." Rhiannon helped Eastra put on the necklace, then stepped back. There was something so satisfied and yet enigmatic in her expression, Eastra could not help asking, "What is it? What do you see?"

"I see you. You will be a queen, Eastra. A powerful queen."

"No." She shook her head. "That's not what I want. I

don't want power or wealth. I only want there to be peace, for this babe I carry to not have to grow up afraid."

"Did you tell Rhun about the babe?"

Eastra shook her head. She did not know how to explain her decision in a way that did not sound foolish or selfish. "If you can see the future, Rhiannon," she said. "Then tell me what the future holds for Rhun. Will he . . ." She took a ravaged breath. "In the battle that he says must come, will he . . ." She could not say the word. To speak it seemed too unchancy, as if she were prophesying his death.

Rhiannon shook her head. "I don't know what the future holds for my stepson. It seems that the closer the person is to me, the less is revealed to me about their fate. There is a kind of protection in that. If something tragic is going to happen, I don't have to suffer twice."

"But you knew Rhun was coming today. You even told Gwenaseth to prepare a lavish meal."

"But that had something to do with you, I think. I can see things regarding you."

"Then tell me if I will be happy in the future, for that will tell me everything!" Eastra could hear her voice trembling with emotion, feel the tension stealing over her body.

"I can't tell you that. My visions are vague and fleeting."

"Can't tell me? Or won't?"

Rhiannon put her hand on Eastra's arm. "Life is difficult, but there is always a purpose for everything. Now go and dress. Make yourself beautiful for Rhun, so he will have that memory of you. Hurry now. The food will be served soon. I will send Melangel to help you."

Clutching the priceless necklace in her fingers, Eastra left the queen's apartments.

Sixteen

By the time Eastra reached the hall, most people were seated. She looked around for Rhun and finally spied him surrounded by eager siblings. Gwydion and Mabon both sat on his lap, squirming as each tried to dislodge the other. Elen and Annwyl sat on either side of Rhun, while Beli stood nearby. Eastra hesitated, wondering if she should find a seat elsewhere, but then Beli spied her and came to escort her to Rhun. "Eastra's our guest," he told Elen firmly when they reached the table. "She should sit next to Rhun."

"Nay, that's not necessary," Eastra began. But Elen was already rising. "Sit," she told Eastra. "I'm going to help Gwenaseth anyway."

As Eastra sat down on the bench next to Rhun, he gave her a brilliant smile. Then his gaze rested on the necklace. His expression turned amazed. "Rhiannon gave you that, didn't she?"

"Aye. I tried to refuse, but she insisted."

Rhun nodded. "She's right. It suits you perfectly." His eyes met hers, their expression so heated and intense that Eastra felt a blush creep up her neck. "You've never looked more beautiful." He leaned near and added, "Except when you are wearing nothing at all."

Now her face was flaming. But she looked around and realized the only ones who could have heard Rhun were Mabon and Gwydion, and they were too young to understand anyway. They were also too engrossed in getting Rhun's attention. Mabon grabbed at his older brother's hair, crying out, "Rhun, Rhun, listen to me. We saw a fox family today and one of the kits almost let me get close enough to touch it. Mama says I have a way with animals. I'm going to train horses when I grow up."

"But I'm the better fighter," Gwydion insisted, pawing at Rhun's other shoulder. "I'm going to be a great warrior someday. As great as Papa."

"Well, you'll never be as big as Papa if you don't eat," Rhun said. "And that means you must both go to your mother. I'm not going to have any young pups dribbling their pottage onto *my* lap."

"I'll take them," Annwyl said. "I'm sure you and Eastra have much to talk about." She rose and dragged her reluctant brothers away.

Eastra looked at Rhun, then took a bite of bread spread with butter and honey and thought about all that was left unspoken between them. Swallowing she said, "What did your father say when you asked him about sending warriors to fight for Arthur?"

Rhun's expression turned grim. "He said he would not waste good warriors on a cause that can't be won. He told me if Arthur were wise, he would sue for peace with both the Saxons and the Picts. Set up boundary lines and divide the island between us."

"What about that?" Eastra asked. "Why couldn't Arthur do that?"

"Because the agreement would never hold. Cerdic—or some other Saxon after him—would get greedy and want more land. And then the fighting would start all over again."

"But this way . . ." Eastra shook her head. "You yourself have suggested Arthur can't win, so why bother fighting? Why not accept the inevitable?"

"You sound like my father! 'Why not just give up?' he asked me. I'll tell you why—because even if we don't win this battle, with every month and season of resistance, we slow down the enemy's advance. And every year we hold them back, they absorb more of our ways, become more like us. Look at you, Eastra. You speak our tongue fluently, are familiar with our music and our tales, even dress like a British woman."

She touched the blue gown Rhiannon had made for her, fashioned in the Cymry style.

Rhun continued, "When you have children, I can't help thinking they will be raised not only to honor Saxon customs, but British as well."

His words cut through her. Did he think when all of this was over that she would go back to her own people and marry one of Cerdic's lesser thanes? That she would someday share her bed and bear children for a Saxon? Did he think she had so little love for him that she could ever forget him and bind herself to a man who had been his enemy? Her voice when she spoke was taut and cold. "I'll never wed a Saxon. *Never.* I could not."

He flushed, looking as if he had just realized what his words implied. "I was speaking hypothetically," he said. "Not about you, but other Saxon women like you."

"What other Saxon women are there like me?" she asked. "Do you know any? All the Saxon women I know who have had any contact with the British are either dead or enslaved!"

"We should not speak of these things," Rhun said. "I don't want to ruin what time we have left together."

A fine time to consider that, Eastra thought bitterly. The sense of intimacy, of being joined body and soul, had evaporated as quickly as the water from the chilly pool had dried on their bodies. The horrible conflict between their peoples had risen up once more, dividing them, destroying any hope for happiness they might have shared. Now Eastra was glad she had not told him about the babe. It was her secret, a living promise of their love. Something that could not be tainted nor damaged, ruined by the harsh words that had come between them.

She picked at her food. Rhun also appeared brooding

and morose. She wished his brothers and sisters would come back so she would not have to be alone with him. To sit beside him and feel his coldness was like a dagger in her breast.

The meal dragged on. A few people came to speak to Rhun, but they did not linger long. As the servants began to clear away some of the tables for music and dancing, Eastra wondered how she was going to endure the rest of the night.

Then there was a commotion near the doorway and she saw a mud-spattered warrior greet Maelgwn. The king's face grew grim. Then he gestured, pointing to where Rhun was sitting. Beside her, Rhun rose, and she could feel the tension in his body.

"Bedwyr." Rhun's voice sounded strange as he spoke to the man, a small, dark warrior with hard eyes. Eastra vaguely remembered him from the council meeting in Cerdic's longhouse.

"Prince Rhun." Bedwyr bowed. "I've come to tell you the truce is broken. Mordred is dead, and Arthur swears vengeance. He says to tell you to bring what men you can convince to join us and meet up with our forces on the march north."

"Where will the battle be fought?" Rhun asked in a strangled-sounding voice.

"Cerdic has taken over the old Roman fort of Eburacum. The Saxon seawolves have joined up there with the Pictish curs, and they will come down upon us like a ravening pack if we do not ride to stop them."

Eastra saw Rhun nod. Then he glanced her way, the briefest of looks. "And the hostage?" His voice was a thin whisper.

Bedwyr looked at her then, too, with eyes like a bird of prey. "You know your duty."

Rhun exhaled, and the life seemed to seep out of her at the same moment. Bedwyr had just ordered her death.

A part of her accepted it. If she could not have Rhun, did she really want to live? But then she thought about the babe and realized she could not sacrifice its life with her own. She would have to try to escape, to run away before Rhun could carry out his duty—killing her. Warily, she glanced around. Maelgwn did not answer to the high king. He was an ally, as were Rhiannon and the rest of the people of Deganwy.

As if in answer to her thought, Maelgwn approached and put his huge hand on her shoulder. "You have brought your message," he announced to Bedwyr. "If you make your way to the kitchen, I will see you are fed before you leave Deganwy. I'm certain you are in a hurry to return to your commander." Maelgwn nodded to his son. "There are things we must speak of ere you leave."

Rhun rose. He appeared pale, in shock. She could not help pitying him. She loved him too much not to care that he had been forced into an awful dilemma. No matter what he chose, he would be wracked with guilt the rest of his life.

Not that she intended to allow him to carry out his duty. Her death would serve no purpose. It would not bring peace. Indeed, it would inspire her uncle to fight even more fiercely. Though Cerdic might not care for her, she was a symbol of his power. He would not let her death go unavenged.

But Arthur must feel exactly the same way—that was why he had ordered *her* death. And Cerdic must know that, know she would die and the war escalate and become even more bitter and destructive. Why had he done it? she wondered. Killing a hostage to incite his enemy to war was not something she could envision her uncle doing. A strange sense went through her. Something was not right here.

She looked around for Rhiannon. If anyone could help her puzzle out this thing, it was the queen. She saw Beli nearby, looking perplexed. "Where's your mother?" Eastra asked.

"She went to put the twins to bed," Beli answered. As

she started to move past him, he grasped her arm. "What's wrong? What's happened? I couldn't hear what was said."

"There's going to be war, a terrible battle." She brushed by him and made her way out into the courtyard. Seeing Bedwyr coming back from the kitchen, she hurried the other direction. Twice she glanced behind her, wondering if he might not decide to pursue her and kill her himself.

But no one followed her. She continued running until she reached the wing where the children slept. She met Rhiannon coming out. "Something's wrong," she told the queen. "I don't understand why my uncle would kill Mordred. I think it's a trick. Someone wants Arthur to order my death. Then war will be inevitable."

Rhiannon nodded. "You may be right. I have sensed treachery surrounding you from the moment we met."

"I have to go to my uncle," Eastra said abruptly. "I must speak to Cerdic and find out the truth. Once he sees me alive, perhaps he will honor the fact that Arthur has shown me mercy. Then there might be a chance for them to meet and work this out. If Arthur and Cerdic could talk, just the two of them, I think they could come to agreement. It is their supporters—my uncle's thanes, Arthur's Companions—who make peace impossible. I think many of them *want* war. For without war there is no plunder, no glory, and that's what they live for."

Rhiannon looked thoughtful. "If war must come, it will come. But I do think it is time you went back to your own people. I will ask Maelgwn to provide an escort for you."

"And Rhun?" Eastra asked, then wished she hadn't spoken.

"Do you wish to say good-bye to him?"

She shook her head. It would be unbearable to face him now. To see the anguish in his eyes and know he was torn between his sense of duty to Arthur and his feelings for her. And also to know that if his sense of duty prevailed, her lover, the man who was the father of her unborn child, might be willing to sacrifice her life.

* * *

Rhun glanced absently around his father's council room, thinking how different it was from Arthur's. The high king's headquarters contained a huge round table for all the Companions to sit around and was decorated with luxurious furnishings. This chamber was stark and empty, as if it were hardly used. There was a layer of dust on the furniture, and the parchment maps and other documents were all neatly rolled and put away on shelves along one wall. Maelgwn—his lands guarded by the mountains and strong treaties made in his younger days—had been able to live in peace for over a score of years.

Once Rhun had despised his father for choosing to live a quiet life, content to rule his small corner of Britain and ignore the turmoil afflicting the rest of the country. But now he wondered if his sire's choice did not show wisdom after all. Maelgwn had given his people two decades of peace, an opportunity to raise their children in prosperity and safety. Meanwhile, Arthur had fought the Saxons and lost countless companions and friends and warriors. Now that Mordred was dead, Arthur had no heir to follow after him. When the Saxon tide finally swept over them, would anyone remember what Arthur had done?

Maelgwn was probably correct in thinking the Saxons would never penetrate this far, never conquer Cymry lands. Maelgwn's dynasty might well endure, while Arthur would be forgotten.

Rhun sighed heavily. It did not matter that he saw these things now. He had made his choice years ago, and there was no escaping it. He was Arthur's man.

The door opened with a creaking sound. The lamplights wavered as Maelgwn entered. He approached Rhun and said, "I'm sorry I kept you waiting."

The remark surprised Rhun. In his experience, his father never apologized.

"I suppose you'll be leaving now. You'll have to go with Bedwyr, off to fight the enemy."

Rhun nodded. Maelgwn moved nearer. He put his hand on Rhun's arm. In the flickering lamplight, an expression of weariness dragged down Maelgwn's features, revealing the over five decades he had lived. He said, "I may never see you again, and I don't want this parting to be one of bitterness. Even if we have quarreled and argued every time we've met as men, I don't want you to forget that I love you. You are my firstborn and you have grown up to be a fine, courageous man. I am proud of you, my son."

There were tears in Maelgwn's eyes. Rhun felt them start in his own. So much to say. So little time.

Rhun stood and Maelgwn embraced him, a fierce, spine-cracking hug that reminded Rhun his father was not quite yet in his dotage. Then he released him and turned away. "It's a brave, heroic thing to do your duty, even when it is onerous and painful. I honor you for your courage, even as I wish it did not have to be like this. But no matter what you have sworn to Arthur, there are oaths that take precedence over those given to men."

Maelgwn turned, his face composed and kingly once more. "Your stepmother and I raised you to honor and respect women, to acknowledge the sacred gift they possess of being able to create life. Despite your belief in the Christian god, we hope you will not turn away from the Goddess, the great mother herself. If Arthur calls upon you to offer up Princess Eastra's life in exchange for Mordred's, no matter your oath, you must refuse that duty. You are Arthur's man, but you are the Great Mother's own flesh."

Rhun felt a wan smile forming on his lips. No wonder Maelgwn was acting so tense and strange. He worried that he had to protect Eastra. "Do you really think I could do such a thing?" he asked. "Even if I could get past the thought that I am killing a woman and an innocent, there is the matter that I love Eastra more than my own life."

"You've decided then? You will refuse Arthur's order?"

Rhun nodded. "I have to. As you have said, to be a

dutiful, devoted soldier is a noble thing, but it's only part of what I am." He looked away. Now it was his turn to be overcome with emotion. "What I have shared with Eastra is beyond any oath I could have sworn to either man or goddess. I feel she is a part of me. Without her, I scarce want to live."

"Then why are you leaving her to go and fight a war you cannot win? Why not stay here and wed her and give her children? Why not allow both of you a chance for happiness?"

Rhun shook his head. "Because as much as I love her, I *am* still Arthur's man. I could not live with myself if I did not go to him now. Even what I share with Eastra would not be enough for me to overcome my guilt over breaking my oath."

Maelgwn exhaled sharply. "I tell myself I have not raised a fool, that you are simply young and rash and have not learned the real lessons of life. Rhiannon would advise me to hold my temper, to let what must be, be. But I will say it is near impossible for me to stand by and watch this"—he sputtered—"this pigheaded idiocy of yours!"

Rhun's mouth twisted into a bitter smile. This was the father he remembered. Tender and loving one moment, hot-tempered and domineering the next. There was a kind of comfort in Maelgwn's fury. It ignited his own stubborn will and made it possible for him to do what he had to do. "But in the end, you will listen to Rhiannon, father," he answered coolly. "You always do."

Maelgwn glared at him, then started for the door.

Rhun took a deep breath as his father left. He knew Bedwyr expected him to set out this very night, but there were some things he had to do first. He must say good-bye to Rhiannon and the children. Then he would go to the chapel and pray for strength—the strength to see Eastra. He would find her and, if she let him, he would love her one last time. Then, in the morning, he would leave.

* * *

The door to her bedchamber opened. Eastra looked up from packing. She had expected to see Rhiannon, and her heart did a little jump when she realized Maelgwn was standing there. As always, he intimidated her and made her uneasy. Maybe it was because he reminded her of Cerdic. The same sense of power, of implacable will, seemed to flow from him as it did from her uncle. She straightened. If she intended to face down her uncle and force him to listen to her, she might as well practice being brave with Maelgwn.

"I have come from talking to Rhun," he said. "I can assure you he has no intention of harming you. There is no reason for you to leave Deganwy."

Eastra cleared her throat and tried to make her voice sound strong and calm. "Did Rhiannon not tell you? I mean to go to see my uncle. To talk to him and try to convince him to honor the truce, or to at least give Arthur a chance to negotiate another one. I'm going to try to stop this final, awful battle from taking place."

Maelgwn shook his head. "Although I don't know your uncle, I know a little about the Saxons. I don't think Cerdic is the kind of man to listen to a woman, no matter if she speaks good sense. I think you are wasting your time." He walked across the room and, looking thoughtful, picked up the sapphire necklace from where she had laid it on a chest. As he examined it, Eastra wondered if he was angry Rhiannon had given it to her. Perhaps since it was really *his* property, he would not recognize his wife's right to offer it to someone else. She opened her mouth to say that she was not taking it with her, that she truly had no right to it. But then Maelgwn suddenly looked at her, and the intensity of his blue eyes—as vivid as the stones in the necklace—froze the words in her throat.

"I know you want to stop this war," he said. "I think

you are a brave and courageous woman to attempt such a thing. But I must plead with you not to leave here, but to stay and work your powers of persuasion on my son instead of your uncle. Convince *him* not to go and fight this war. I feel as if he is going to his death. A wasteful, stupid death, since Arthur cannot win. And even more wasteful because of what he leaves behind." His gaze grew almost tender. "He loves you, and your love can save him. I beg you to do this . . . for both of us."

She released the breath she had been holding in a shuddering sigh. If only she could do what Maelgwn asked. But she knew she could not, for no matter how she tried to bind Rhun to her, no matter what heart-stopping intimacy they shared, he would still choose to leave her. And having that knowledge, she was unwilling to do as Maelgwn asked, to try to make Rhun stay and then have her heart broken when she failed. "I'm sorry," she said. "Your faith in me is misplaced. Rhun loves me, but he loves his duty more. I will not fight a battle I can't win. I don't even plan to see Rhun before I leave."

She had to resist the urge to touch her stomach as she thought of the babe, the gift Rhun had given her that no one could take away. But she did not want Maelgwn to know she carried his grandchild. She feared if he knew of it, he would be more insistent than ever that she not leave Deganwy. Thank the Goddess Rhiannon understood her situation and was willing to help her. She invoked the queen's name as she said, "Rhiannon has promised you will provide an escort for me. I hope you have not changed your mind. You could keep me as a prisoner here, but I beg you not to."

Something in Maelgwn's face changed, and he looked suddenly thoughtful. "Of course I will provide an escort," he said. "You have never been our prisoner here, only an honored guest." He bowed. "Fare you well, Princess Eastra. I wish you the best in your journey and in your purpose. May the Goddess protect you and keep you."

She nodded back, embarrassed by his deference. He was

a king, while she was only a princess, the princess of a people who did not usually count women as very important. But somehow, she had to try to overcome that, to make a difference, despite her sex.

Rhun started out of the chapel. It seemed that he had been praying for hours. But none of it—the comforting ritual, the familiar surroundings of the chapel of his boyhood, the heartfelt quest for answers—none of it had afforded him any peace. He was exhausted, so weary in mind and spirit that he wondered if he could perform even if Eastra allowed him to make love to her. And yet he wanted to leave her with something, some breathtaking memory of what they shared, the magic of their coupling, something to sustain her even if he never saw her again. He told himself that as soon as he beheld her beauty, his body would stir to life. The anguish and grief would fall away and they would share one last night of ecstasy and contentment.

He approached the guest bedchamber where he knew she slept. As he was almost to the door, he sensed a shadow moving behind him. He turned and was startled to see Balyn and Elwyn, two of his father's oldest companions. There was a faint hiss as they drew their swords. His eyes widened as he realized what was happening. "Here, now, Rhun," Balyn said in the rumbling voice that matched his bulk, "we don't want to hurt you. But rather a few sword cuts than a Saxon war axe in the throat. We're here to escort you back to your old bedchamber."

"Damn him," Rhun swore. "I can't believe Rhiannon would let him do this."

Balyn took his arm in an iron-like grip. "The queen doesn't command us. We're the king's men. And *he* says you'll be staying at Deganwy."

Rhun sighed. He could try to fight, but what would that accomplish? Every man in the whole fortress answered to his father. If Maelgwn didn't want him to leave, he would not be going anywhere.

He let the guards quietly escort him to the doorway of the bedchamber, then turned and faced them. "If I'm going to be a prisoner, at least let me have some company. I would ask that Princess Eastra be brought to me." In the torchlight, he observed the odd looks on their faces and added quickly, "On my honor, I would not harm her. My father knows that. I'm sure if you ask him, he will agree to let me see the princess."

Balyn cleared his throat. "I'm sure he would, but that hardly matters. She left Deganwy a few hours ago."

"Left?" He had been resigned to his imprisonment, the fact his father had seen fit to physically prevent him from joining Arthur, but this new information aroused a kind of panic inside him. "How could my father allow her to leave? Doesn't he know Arthur has pronounced her death sentence? How could he do something so foolish?"

Rhun started to push past his guards, determined to somehow stop Eastra and get her safely back to Deganwy. They grabbed him. He struggled fiercely, screaming, "Eastra! Eastra!" A dozen men came out of the shadows. He fought them all, but it was no use. Finally, hoarse and aching from the ordeal, he was shoved into the bedchamber and the door locked behind him.

Panting, he rose to his feet. He considered beating on the door, seeing if he could get Rhiannon, his brothers or sisters, some of the servants who remembered him—any of them—to help him. He realized it was hopeless. There would be guards outside the door, and they would let no one enter except those who honored the king's will.

He went to the bed and slumped down upon it. Then there was a sound at the door, and he lunged up again. He started forward, half ready to resume his fight.

But it was Rhiannon who slipped through the door as it opened. She shut it carefully behind her and faced him with a tranquil expression.

"How can you let him do this?" Rhun demanded. "I'm

a man grown! He has no right to control my life! To dictate what I do!" He softened his tone. "Help me, Rhiannon. You know this is not right. You once hid from Maelgwn for months and let him think you were dead. You defied him because you resented the way he treated you like a possession. Well, now he is doing it to *me!* If I want to throw away my life in Arthur's cause—as he puts it—then it is my right to do so! It is *my* life to give, no matter how foolish he thinks the sacrifice!"

Rhiannon put her hand on his arm. "I cannot sway him in this. He's afraid. He feels he has lost Bridei. He cannot bear to lose you as well."

"But is that love? Or simply his selfish need to control me?"

"It is love. You have to understand. He has never really gotten over losing Aurora and the babe. That loss near broke him, and he does not want to endure such grief ever again."

Rhun shook his head. "I'll never forgive him for this. He'll find that he'll lose me anyway. I think Bridei was right to refuse to come here and have our father meddle in his life." A look of pain flashed across Rhiannon's face. "I'm sorry," Rhun said. "I did not mean to remind you. If it helps at all, know that Bridei wanted desperately to see you and his brothers and sisters. But his bitterness toward Maelgwn won out. And now . . ." He shook his head again. "Now I understand why."

Then abruptly, he thought of Eastra, and his sense of anxiety returned. "I don't see how he can keep me here and yet let Eastra leave. Doesn't he understand? Arthur has ordered her death. How can he let her go out into the war-torn countryside? Anything could happen to her!"

"She has an escort," Rhiannon said. "Two dozen warriors. Maelgwn believes she will be safe."

"But where is she going?" A terrifying thought came to him. "Surely she's not going to go to Arthur. She would not do something so witless, would she?" He had a sudden image of Eastra kneeling before Arthur, offering up her life if the high king would agree not to march off to war against the Saxons.

"Nay, she's not going to Arthur, but to Cerdic."

Rhun felt stunned. Eastra was going back to her people. Would she wait in Cerdic's camp until the battle was over and Arthur and his Companions destroyed? Although he knew she would be safe with Cerdic, it still felt like a betrayal.

"She's going to try to stop Cerdic from fighting," Rhiannon said. "She thinks once he knows Arthur has spared her, Cerdic may be willing to agree to another truce."

What an absurd, naive, little fool she was! Rhun shook his head. "Cerdic will never listen to her. Never."

"She feels she must try," Rhiannon said. "In her way, she is as stubborn as you are."

"All her efforts will be for naught. Cerdic is determined. Why else would he have killed Mordred? He could have broken the truce and brought about this battle without murdering a hostage."

Rhun could not help wondering about that. To kill Mordred seemed wasteful and cruel; he had not thought Cerdic was either of those things. He shook his head again. He didn't understand why all of this was happening. It was almost as if this final, terrible battle was part of some inevitable plan. He knew there were those, particularly among Arthur's Companions, who would say this was all God's will. But he could not believe that. Why would God want Arthur—his shining sword of truth—to die fighting a battle he could not win?

Rhiannon touched his arm again. "Rest now. You cannot change any of this. You must learn to accept it, and to have faith that the Goddess is with you, no matter how terrible things seem."

Rhun gave a snort of disgust. Although he admired Rhiannon's placid faith, he could not share it. The thought that either the Christian God or the Great Mother had a hand in things no longer reassured him. Why had he been in Cerdic's longhouse that day to once again behold Eastra's shining beauty and lose his heart if the result was going to be pain and suffering for both of them . . . and this absolute despair in the end?

Seventeen

Eastra glanced back in the darkness, back toward Deganwy. This was the most difficult thing she'd ever done, to leave Rhun, to tear herself away from the man she loved more than her own life. But she had to do it. The babe growing inside her represented the future, and she must try to influence that future for the better.

The pain inside her flared into life. She wished with her whole being that she had never laid eyes on Rhun, or that he had done his duty and killed her in the longhouse all those years ago. Then she would never have known this terrible grief, this suffering. But then, she would have also never known those ecstatic moments in the hidden glen above Deganwy. And she would not have conceived this child, this precious life growing in her body.

She touched her stomach. There was a tautness to her belly, a slight roundness to her lower abdomen, but no other sign of pregnancy. It was her secret. Hers and Rhiannon's. She wondered if she should tell Cerdic about the baby. Would it influence him to listen to her? Or give him another reason to make war against the Britons? She would have to wait and see, to gauge his mood when she saw him.

At the thought, she experienced a twinge of foreboding. It would not be easy to face down her massive, frightening uncle. But she'd done something similar with Maelgwn and survived. She took a deep breath. According to her escort, they had two days' journey ahead of them. Plenty of time to plan strategy. Or to lose her nerve.

They followed the coast, then turned north to enter Manua Gotodin, a heavily forested country. They met few people there, but when they did they had only to say the name Maelgwn the Great and they were allowed to pass by unmolested. Rhiannon was a princess of the Brigantes, the tribe that dwelt in this land, and her marriage to Maelgwn had formed a strong bond between the two peoples.

Eastra had been surprised to discover young Beli was part of her escort. He told her he had begged to go and his father had finally relented, muttering something about making different mistakes this time. Eastra decided this must have something to do with Bridei's estrangement from Maelgwn. At any rate, she was glad to have Beli for company, a familiar face among her grim, serious guards. But there could be a downside to traveling with Rhun's half brother. Sometimes the way Beli smiled or spoke reminded her of Rhun and made the familiar bubble of longing rise in her chest until she could scarcely bear it.

After crossing the heavily forested lands of the Brigantes, they traveled east toward the old Roman fort of Eburacum. Here Cerdic had massed his troops, joining forces with the Picts from the north.

A wave of horror swept over Eastra as they neared Eburacum and saw the huge warhost spread out over the hills around the fort. There must be ten thousand men, she thought. Cerdic and his thanes and house carls were inside the ruined walls of the old Roman settlement. To reach them, they would have to pass through this whole vast army camp.

They neared the perimeter of the most outlying camp and were confronted by a group of warriors, small, swarthy men, nearly naked except for leather loincloths and an abundance of ornaments fashioned of bronze, shells, and feathers. They all wore feathers in their long, straggly hair, the bluish gray feathers of the blue heron, and their faces were marked with blue lines and symbols. As Eastra drew closer, she realized these men must be Picts, the "painted people," as the Romans had called them.

The tallest man stepped forward and spoke to Owain, the leader of her escort. "Britons," he asked sharply. "What do you here among your enemies?"

"Not Britons," Owain answered, "but Cymry. We come in peace, as an escort for Lady Eastra, princess of the Saxons. She's here to see her uncle, Cerdic Hengistson, the Saxon war leader. Will you take us to him?"

The man's gaze darted to Eastra. He scrutinized her, then moved off and huddled together with his men. Eastra whispered to Beli, standing beside her, "Do you think they will agree?"

"I don't know. It depends upon Cerdic's relationship to their people."

Time seemed to drag on. Several of the men glanced back at Eastra, their expressions awed and uneasy. To break the tension, Eastra said to Beli, "How do they get those blue marks on their faces?"

"They make small holes in the flesh, then put dye into the holes. As the flesh heals, the color remains. The patterns they use are sacred signs, communicating with the Old Gods."

The Pictish leader returned. He made a kind of motion with his hand, a gesture of deference. "Princess Eastra, we will take you to your kinsman." He looked at Owain. "I give you my oath she will be safe."

"As we have given our oath to protect her," Owain said angrily. He shook his head. "She cannot go alone. We must accompany her."

The Pict's expression did not change. He looked at Eastra. "Princess, will you allow us to escort you?"

"Nay," Owain interjected. "*I* will not allow it."

Eastra stared at the strange, small warrior watching her. Despite his savage appearance, the Pictish leader had such dignity, such a proud, fearless way of carrying himself. She believed he would take any oath he gave very seriously.

"Do you believe in the Goddess?" she asked him. "The Great Mother?"

He nodded solemnly. "We call her Anu."

"Will you swear in Her name I will be safe?"

"I so swear," the man answered.

Eastra turned to Owain. "I'm satisfied," she said. "I believe I will be safe with these men."

"I can't let you go," Owain retorted. "Maelgwn commanded me to guard you with my life."

Beli stepped forward. "Then I release you from your duty to my father." He nodded to Eastra. "I believe this is what Maelgwn would have wanted."

Owain's gaze narrowed. "You're scarcely more than a boy. I would not even have agreed to take you along if the king hadn't insisted."

"Nay, I'm not just a boy!" Beli's blue eyes flashed defiance. "I'm a prince of the Cymry, and you will obey me in this!"

Owain drew back, looking startled, like a man bitten by a pet puppy. Then he looked at Eastra. She tried to return his gaze with the serene, patient expression Rhiannon used in getting her way.

After a moment, Owain said, "I suppose I have no choice. Maelgwn also told me to treat Princess Eastra as if she were my own queen. If you wish to entrust your life to these men, so be it."

A vague shiver of fear went through Eastra, although she tried to suppress it. That was exactly what she was doing—entrusting her life to these fierce, wild men. She took a step forward, and the Picts surrounded her, forming a wall of warriors bristling with spears. She turned to say farewell to Beli. "The Goddess be with you," she said.

He took down her traveling pack and handed it to one of the Picts to carry. "We will wait here for you," he said.

She shook her head. "I don't think I will be coming back. But . . . I will send word to you, some sign showing I am safe." She began to walk into the Pictish camp.

She tried to hold her head high, to appear calm and

unafraid. Everywhere, men left their gatherings around the cookfires and approached, staring. They came in groups, and Eastra noted each clan seemed to have a distinctive animal symbol they incorporated into their attire. One group wore bearskins around their shoulders despite the heat, and had bear claws strung on leather thongs around their necks. Other clans carried the wildcat's spotted fur as their symbol, wore hawk feathers in their hair or adorned themselves with boar tusks. One tribe had gone so far as to smear a light streak down the center of their dark hair so they looked like badgers, whose fur and striped tails hung from their waists.

Eastra thought of Rhun's symbol, the red dragon of Cymry. The dragon wasn't a real animal, but a fantastic creature out of legend. It seemed an appropriate symbol for him, a man who believed in dreams and bright, shining ideals. A lump formed in her throat. By now, Rhun would have rejoined Arthur's men and be preparing to march into battle. Would she ever see him again—her great golden warrior, her champion and hero?

The pain inside her grew so intense she could scarce walk. She reminded herself why she was here—to stop the war, to save Rhun's life and the lives of so many other men. If only she could convince Cerdic to talk to Arthur before they fought. Arthur could not win, not against this huge army. Perhaps he would think twice about sacrificing the lives of his men if he were given an opportunity.

She squared her shoulders, her resolve deepening. The babe inside her made her feel powerful. When she met with her uncle, she would pretend she was Morgeuse. She would call up the magic, the Goddess's energy. She would make him listen to her.

At last they reached the edge of the northern warriors' camp. Along the way, Eastra had noticed the Picts seemed poorly equipped. The weaponry she'd seen was mostly old and made of bronze rather than iron. It would not stand up against the superior weaponry of the Britons. But despite their lack of resources, she sensed the Picts had their own kind of strength. They were lean, hungry men, and they were fighting for the survival of their race, their offspring, their future.

The Saxons were also fighting for their future, but the mood in their camp was much different, Eastra realized as she crossed the invisible barrier and entered the territory of her people. Here there was a sense of expectancy and eagerness in the air. These were the tall, strong warriors she remembered from her childhood, with long golden hair and fierce blue eyes. Their weapons were terrifying, she knew— the *seaxe,* which could cleave a man in two; spiked balls attached to a club that was swung in a deadly arc, for the purpose of crushing the opponent's skull; maces and spears and huge broadswords that rivaled those of the Britons.

Her heart pounded at the thought. She could easily imagine one of her countrymen killing Rhun, see his blood running on the ground, see his beautiful face smashed by a blow from a Saxon warrior. Before he died, would he look into his opponent's pale blue eyes and remember her?

She shuddered, and some of her Pictish escort turned to look at her. They were uneasy as well. They did not like venturing into the realm of their so-called ally.

The Saxons they saw hardly took note of their party. Their attitude toward the Picts was clearly one of tolerance edged with a kind of contempt. Eastra wondered how the Picts could bear to fight beside men who had so little respect for them. But then she remembered the northern men's desperation. They felt they had no choice. If they were going to keep their lands, they had to ally themselves with the Saxons.

Perhaps their scheme would work, she decided. From what she'd heard, no Saxon would covet the Picts' homeland. It was too hilly and heavily forested to be farmed. It was good only for grazing, and even then it took a large territory to feed a herd.

Her people desired the rich southern lands. That's what they were fighting for. Her confidence in her purpose wavered. How could she convince Cerdic to be content with

the coastal lands and the areas of the south their people
had already settled when there was so much rich, desirable
land left to conquer? She would have to think of a plan,
and she would have to do so quickly.

They entered the arched stone gateway of Eburacum. On
either side were watchtowers, abandoned now to the swallows who built their nests in the crumbling stonework.
There was no need for sentries to watch for the enemy
here. She followed the Pictish leader down the half paved,
weed-ridden street to a large, square building in the center
of the fortress. The roof was half fallen in, but the walls
looked solid. Above the doorway was hung the embossed
bronze ceremonial shield of her uncle, decorated with two
white horsetails that drooped limply in the heat. Two of
Cerdic's house carls, standing guard, stepped forward.

The Pictish leader walked fearlessly to meet them. "We
bring you the Princess Eastra," he said loudly in Saxon
touched by the burred, lilting accent of his people.

Eastra faced the sentries, recognizing them as Beornwold and Aelfric. They stared at her. Then Aelfric, his eyes
cold as the western sea, stepped aside so she could enter.
She walked down a corridor lit with oil lamps and decorated with the badly scarred mosaic of a beast she knew
was called a panther.

At the end of the corridor was a large room, and there
sat Cerdic at a table, eating his midday meal. Two other
men were with him. Eastra recognized the large, fair-haired
man as Ossa, the leader of the Jutes. The other was a man
she did not know, although she sensed she had seen him
before. He was young and foreign-looking, with brown hair
and a slender build. The three men looked at her in surprise, then Cerdic spoke. "Eastra," he said. "How . . ." he
cleared his throat so he could speak in normal tones. "How
do you come to be here?"

"Did you think I would be dead? That Arthur would
have me killed?" She spoke coldly, seizing her advantage.
He had willingly sacrificed her life when he murdered
Mordred.

Something shifted in Cerdic's gaze, and his voice when he spoke was slow and careful. "Why should Arthur have you killed?"

The question surprised Eastra, but she tried not to show it, to maintain a hold on her anger. "Because I am the hostage you gave in exchange for Arthur's son, Mordred. Since you have killed Mordred, it seems reasonable Arthur would have me put to death. As I understand it, that is the purpose of hostages. Each side holds something of value of the other's, and that is the deterrent that keeps the peace. But obviously"—she faced her uncle challengingly—"I was not that much of value to you."

Cerdic did not speak, but wiped his mouth and pushed the platter in front of him to the other side of the table. Then he gestured to the young, dark-haired man beside him. "This is Mordred, and he looks very alive to me."

Eastra stared at the youth, and he stared back with green eyes like a cat. An eerie sense of recognition sent a chill down Eastra's spine. Mordred did look familiar, although the day of the hostage exchange she had scarcely paid any attention to him. Was there some other reason his appearance unsettled her?

"But . . ." It was her turn to hesitate. "A man came from Arthur's camp and said Mordred was dead."

Cerdic shrugged. "Obviously, he was misinformed."

Either that, Eastra thought, or he was trying to incite Arthur to make war. The implications of Bedwyr's message struck her. Had Bedwyr been lying? Or was he simply carrying on the message Arthur had received? Then the sudden thought came to her that if Mordred was alive, the truce might yet hold. There was no reason for Arthur to march against them.

"Uncle, you must send a message to Arthur with some proof his son is alive. He is planning to go to war against you. His troops are marching here even now. If he knows Mordred is alive, he will retreat and this battle can be avoided."

Cerdic gazed at her. "I'm pleased you are alive and well,

niece. You must believe me when I say I did not think Arthur would harm you, hostage or not. I have been told he is a man who honors women, a man whose conscience would not allow him to order the death of an innocent girl."

Eastra tensed at the term "girl." She was hardly a child. Indeed, she carried a babe in her belly, the ultimate proof of her womanhood.

"But as for making peace with Arthur," Cerdic continued. "I can't do that. War will come. It *must* come." He glanced at Ossa with an expression of satisfaction, then back at Eastra. "And knowing we will soon do battle, we must get you to safety." He motioned. "I will have Beornwold escort you out of camp."

She was being sent away, dismissed. A kind of fury rose inside her. "Nay," she said. "I will not go. I will stay here and speak and you will listen to me!"

Cerdic was clearly startled by her words. Then he grew angry. A hot flush spread up his face and his eyes glowed like blue flames. "I see that while you were a hostage, you learned the bad manners and the shameless boldness of a British woman. But now you are among your own kind, and such behavior will not be tolerated. What you have to say is of no consequence!"

"You must listen!" Eastra exclaimed. "As hostage, I risked my life for you. I might well have died at the hands of Arthur's men. For that sacrifice, I think I deserve to be heard!"

"Let her speak. It might be amusing." Mordred spoke, his expression coy and condescending. Abruptly, Eastra realized he was not acting like a hostage. His posture and tone of voice implied he was Cerdic's equal. What did that mean? Had Mordred betrayed his father? Did he conspire with his father's enemies to bring down the high king?

It took a second for the shock and dismay to sink in. If Cerdic and Mordred had planned this, deliberately spread the false report that Mordred was dead in order to incite Arthur to act . . . She felt sick. Sick and weak. To have come so far and confront complete failure. She searched her mind, struggling to find some line of reasoning that might sway Cerdic. "Arthur's army is huge," she lied. "And they are well-equipped, experienced soldiers." She glanced back toward the Pictish camp, her voice thick with scorn. "Not undersized savages with ancient daggers for weapons."

There was a flicker of interest in Cerdic's eyes. "Did Maelgwn the Great decide to join Arthur?"

Eastra hesitated. She wanted to answer that the king of Gwynedd meant to bring his full army north and that she had never seen such stalwart, fearless warriors as the Cymry. But something told her the lie would serve no purpose. Cerdic had scouts. He would find out soon enough that Maelgwn had chosen to remain out of the fray.

"Nay, but there are others."

"Name them," was Cerdic's response.

Miserably, Eastra shook her head. "I don't know their names. Only that their army is huge and, as I said, much better equipped and trained than *your* allies."

"The northern men may be small, but they are fierce," Cerdic said. "And they are the best archers I've ever seen. They will cut Arthur's front line to pieces before they even reach us."

She remembered many Picts had carried quivers of arrows on their backs. She also remembered Rhun discussing what fine archers the Cymry were, and how with them in his army, Arthur would finally have the advantage he needed to defeat the Saxons once and for all. The queasy feeling in her stomach intensified. She had lost this war of words. And because of her failure, Rhun might well die. She had a sudden, horrifying vision of him with a goose-fletched arrow in his throat.

"The lady doesn't look well," Mordred said. "Perhaps you should have someone take her to my mother's dwelling. I'm certain she'd be happy to make a tonic for the princess."

She did not like this young man. There was something

sneaky and sinister about him, and the lustful way he looked at her aroused her disgust. In some ways he was like Bridei—charming and handsome and flirtatious. But he lacked something, some innate quality that made Bridei's glib, cynical manner more amusing than repelling.

She considered that Mordred had not only betrayed his father, but that his betrayal might well bring about Arthur's death. A shudder of loathing went through her. Mordred was corrupt. There was no other word for it.

She was led to another building with a colonnade in front and a small, dirt-filled fountain near the doorway. Despite her inner turmoil, Eastra could hardly wait to meet Mordred's mother. She could not help being curious about the woman who had given life to this cruel, monstrous youth, the woman who had enticed Arthur, the high king of Britain. It must have taken place twenty-some years ago, judging by Mordred's age. Arthur had not been high king then, but he must still have been a powerful and important man, one whom Eastra would have thought too serious and high-minded for casual love affairs.

As she stepped into the entryway, she smelled something sweet, a heady mixture of herbs and flowers. Her first thought was that it must be from some wild blossoms in the tangled overgrowth outside the building, some remnant of the garden that a fine Roman dwelling such as this would certainly have had. But then she considered that the fortress had been abandoned nearly a hundred years before. It seemed unlikely any cultivated blooms would survive that long.

The scent grew more familiar, tickling a memory in her mind. She froze in place. Nay, it could not be true!

"Don't be afraid," the warrior escorting her said. "She's a witch, aye, but she won't hurt you. Indeed, she'll be pleased to have another woman in camp. She's been grumbling for days about the fact we Saxons don't allow wenches into our war camps. What utter foolishness." Beornwold shook his shaggy, golden head at the thought. Eastra's throat was so dry she could not answer him.

She remembered the first time she'd met Morgeuse and observed her brilliant green eyes and catlike demeanor, the first time Urien's queen had spoken of her contempt for Arthur and her hints of a plan to ruin him. A shudder went through Eastra as she took a step forward, dreading what she would find.

The main room of the dwelling was dim compared to the daylight outside and it took a moment for Eastra to be sure it really was Morgeuse, seated crosslegged on a fur on the stone floor, surrounded by jars and baskets, cushions and chests. In front of Morguese was a bowl of oil, glimmering faintly in the lamplight.

Morguese looked up. "Eastra!" She smiled. "So the Goddess has answered my prayers after all. I was hoping She would send me another woman—even a whore or the wife of one of the Picts would do. But here you are, my lovely Eastra, a Saxon princess carrying a British babe in her belly. How absolutely perfect."

"Hush!" Eastra implored. "No one must know about the babe! No one!"

"Of course." Morgeuse's smug smile did not falter. "I need you. I need to work a spell of protection for my son. You carry the blood of his enemy. With your energy added to mine, we will keep him safe."

"I won't do it!" Eastra cried. "Mordred is a traitor to his own people and a cruel, self-serving monster. If Arthur dies, it will be his fault. Patricide is considered a vile thing among my people. I'll have no part in this!"

Morguese raised an auburn brow. "Of course Arthur will die. I have seen it in the scrying bowl and in the flames. Mordred is going to kill him."

Eastra took a step back, aghast. "How can you even say such things? What sort of creature are you that you would plot against the man who once was your lover and use your son as the instrument of his death?"

Morgeuse's smile vanished and she suddenly looked bitter and angry. "It did not have to be like this. If only Arthur had accepted Mordred, loved him as a father is supposed to love his son." She shook her head. "Arthur never understood. He believed Mordred was conceived in sin. Because I used a spell to bring him to my bed, he thought that the act was tainted by magic and that the child would grow up to be some sort of demon. He told me to go away and have the baby in secret, then leave it out for the wolves."

Her smile returned. "Of course, I did not. And you have seen Mordred—is he not handsome and well made? Arthur's fears have come to naught. Although I have since decided it is not that Arthur feared Mordred would be deformed, but that he sensed his son was going to usurp him someday, and proud, arrogant Arthur could not bear that."

She does not understand the high king, Eastra thought. Having been in the man's presence several times and heard many accounts of him, Eastra did not believe Arthur was obsessed with power. Obsessed with his vision for Britain, aye, but not with personal glory. Still, that Arthur would tell a woman to kill her child, his own son, that was disturbing. It bespoke a kind of madness. Did Arthur despise Morgeuse that much? Did he also despise the Goddess from which her powers arose?

She had many new questions, although some of her old ones had been answered. Knowing Mordred was Morgeuse's son, she could guess a little at their scheme. By sending word that Mordred had been killed, they had forced Arthur into this battle. Mordred was obviously going to fight against his father and try to kill him.

She shook her head. "If Arthur dies, what purpose does it serve? Cerdic will never allow Mordred to be king. What has he to gain by killing his father?"

"Certainly Mordred will be king!" Morgeuse stood gracefully and smoothed her gown. "Cerdic has promised it!"

Eastra knew her uncle well enough to know he would never share his power with a man like Mordred. He would have only contempt for a man who betrayed his own people for the sake of his personal ambitions. Cerdic might be ruthless, but he was utterly loyal to his kin and countrymen. He would expect the same of his allies.

But Eastra did not say that. She knew Morgeuse would not believe her anyway. Instead, she took a deep breath, feeling as if the ground beneath her feet had suddenly shifted. She had more questions, many more. "And what is my part in all this?" she asked. "Why did you detain me at Caer Louarn? Was that part of your plan to break the truce? And why did you put a spell on Rhun and me so we would make love and conceive this child?"

"It was Urien's idea to capture you, not mine. He thought if you were killed, Cerdic would fall upon Arthur and destroy him. He also wants to see Arthur die, but not for the same reasons as I. Urien thinks Arthur has too much power. When Arthur claimed sovereignty over all the kings of Britain, that was too much for him."

How close she had come to death, Eastra thought with a shiver. "But nothing happened to me while I was at Caer Louarn," she pointed out.

"Urien is not as ruthless as I am. Once he saw you, he was loathe to order your death. He thought you were too lovely and sweet to kill. And then I told him the Goddess would not be pleased if you died, that She had plans for you."

"What plans?"

Morgeuse shrugged. "I don't know, but I have seen you in my visions, dressed like a queen. And the babe you carry"—she gestured to Eastra's midsection—"the Goddess was very clear to me that you and Rhun must couple and conceive a child, and that it must be done on a specific night. There is something special about this babe, although I don't know what. I have my own plans and ambitions, but if the Goddess asks for something, I do not question her. I obey."

It was all such a tangled web of deceit and treachery, Eastra thought, and she was at the very center of it.

"Come, my dear," Morgeuse held out her hand. "You

must sit down. A woman in your condition must be careful to conserve her strength."

Eastra allowed herself to be led over to the bearskin spread on the floor. She sank down and Morgeuse propped several cushions behind her. "How are you feeling?" Morgeuse asked. "Has the child quickened yet?"

Eastra shook her head, feeling dazed and almost light-headed. There were still so many questions left unanswered. "Did Urien plot my murder in Londinium?" She looked up at Morgeuse. "We were attacked outside the market by a half dozen warriors, but Rhun fought them off." She remembered how magnificent he had been, how awe inspiring. The familiar pain pierced her.

"Nay, Urien's power does not reach so far. But there are many other men in Britain who might have planned such a thing as a way to break the truce." Morgeuse moved to the other side of the chamber and began to fuss among the clutter there. "And it was not Rhun who protected you that day, but the Goddess."

Was this true? If a dozen chieftains wanted her dead, but she remained alive, was that not a miracle? Had the hand of the Goddess truly shielded her all this while? Yet Rhun's strong swordarm had struck down her enemies. Poor Rhun. He had not known what an enormous task he'd taken on when they set out on their journey. Nor had he known about the cunning, twisted plot against Arthur.

Eastra sat up straight. What if Rhun knew this battle was not a final, glorious stand for his dream, but a deadly trap? For that matter, what if *Arthur* knew Mordred was alive and plotting his death? She mentally shook herself, trying to get rid of the sense of helpless lethargy creeping over her. She had to leave this place, find her escort, and intercept Rhun and Arthur before they marched into battle. If she could speak to Arthur himself, tell him what Morgeuse and Mordred planned, she might be able to change the high king's fatal course.

Morgeuse approached her, smiling. In her hands was a

jeweled cup. "Drink this," she purred. "It will ease your distress and help you sleep."

Eastra took the cup and pretended to take a sip. She searched her mind frantically for some means of distracting Morgeuse. Finally, she said, "I'm very hungry. Would it be possible for me to have something to eat?"

"Of course you are hungry. Shame upon me for not thinking of that. I know I was famished all the while I carried my own children. Wait here a moment and I will fetch someone to bring you food. What would you like?"

Eastra pretended to ponder the question. "Perhaps some fruit—an apple or some apricots. And some milk." She knew these things would be difficult to procure in an army camp where the men mostly ate dried meat and rough bread, perhaps supplemented by raisins or figs. Fresh food was a luxury and not readily available outside established settlements and towns.

"Hmmm," Morgeuse said. "That may be difficult, but I will see what can be found."

As soon as Morgeuse had left the tent, Eastra poured the contents of the cup into the edge of the bearskin. Then she rose and hurried toward the door. She peeked out and saw Morgeuse talking to a young slave boy—Irish from the looks of him. His expression was one of dismay, and Eastra could tell Morgeuse was speaking to him harshly, perhaps threatening him if he did not obtain what she wished.

Eastra glanced around, wondering if she could escape while Morgeuse was talking to the slave boy. It did not seem probable. In only a moment or two, Morgeuse would return to the house and, finding Eastra gone, send men after her. In broad daylight, it would be impossible to make her way through the huge army camp and not be seen and intercepted.

She returned to her place on the bearskin and pretended to be sipping from the cup when Morgeuse entered. "It may take a while," Morgeuse said. "Perhaps you should sleep for a time, until the food arrives."

Eastra nodded agreeably. "I do feel sleepy," she said, guessing the drink was meant to have that effect.

Morguese made her a sort of bed on a pile of cushions and covered her with a brightly woven blanket. Then, while Eastra pretended to doze, Morgeuse went back to her place by the bowl of glistening oil. She chanted some words and began to burn some of the pungent herb in a copper bowl. Eastra realized Morgeuse was trying to see visions in the surface of the oil. She wondered if Morgeuse would see enough to know she planned to escape.

Time passed. Morgeuse began to sway and talk to herself. She seemed to be in a trance. Eastra sat up. When Morgeuse did not turn around or give any sign she was aware of her, she got to her feet. Morgeuse still did not move. Eastra picked up her pack of supplies from where Beornwold had put it on the floor and started slowly toward the door. Her body was tense and rigid, her underarms clammy with sweat. It did not seem possible she would be able to walk right past Morguese. But nothing happened as Eastra reached the door and hurried out. It was as if she were invisible.

Outside, the sky was deep twilight blue. There was still enough light to see by, but not enough that she could be easily seen. She took her mantle from her pack and put it on, covering her hair with the hood. Then she began to walk cautiously along the deserted, ruined streets of the fort. Here and there, groups of men were gathered around cookfires. No one seemed aware of her as she passed by. Eastra wondered if it were her cloak—woven in a soft pattern of blue and green that blended into the shadows—or if it were magic. Did the Goddess shield her from her enemies this night?

She made her way out the gate of the fort and looked around for the Picts who had escorted her there. Not seeing them, she decided she would have to try to find her way by herself.

She had walked some distance through the camp when she suddenly became aware of shadows to her right and left. Taking a deep breath, she threw back her hood so her light hair was visible, and said in a chilly voice, "I am Princess Eastra, Cerdic Hengistson's niece. If you are wise, you will let me pass safely."

"We know who you are, Princess," someone answered. One of the shadows took on the form of a man. She could not really see him in the darkness, only catch the gleam of his eyes in the fading light. But she recognized his voice as the Pict who had taken her to Cerdic.

"I seek the Cymry men who brought me here," she said.

"We will take you to them," the man answered.

Once again, she had an escort of small-statured warriors, bristling with weapons and adorned with the beautiful symbols of the wild beasts they honored. It was eerie to walk among these fierce, untamed men who struggled to survive in the harsh lands of the north. They lived close to the Mother's heart, she thought, and surely She would not let them perish. But then she remembered the coming battle. One of these warriors might be the one to kill Rhun, her beloved. Nay, she would not let that happen. If the Goddess were with her, she would use Her power to stop this abominable war!

When they reached the edge of the Picts' camp, she saw Beli. The moon had risen and by its light she could make out the expression on his face, see the questioning look in his eyes. She shook her head. "Cerdic would not listen to me. But I will not give up. Now I must go to Arthur. I have learned many things, things that may well alter the course of this war after all."

Eighteen

Beli tried to persuade Eastra to rest before setting out to find Arthur. While she agreed to eat first—she was in fact terribly hungry—she refused to wait until morning to begin their journey. "By then, Morgeuse will be searching for me," she told him. "She might also alert Cerdic, and although I doubt he cares what I do or whom I talk to, I'd rather not depend on his indifference."

After Eastra had a quick meal of the usual dried meat and bread, washed down with a little wine, the Cymry rode off in the night. Beli insisted she ride with him and, resting against his narrow but solid chest, she was able to doze fitfully. It always seemed as if she had slept only a few moments when she jerked awake, instantly aware they were on an urgent mission. But after several stretches of uneasy rest, she woke to find that it was growing light in the east. They had traveled all night and made good progress, following the old Roman road south.

As the sun rose, suffusing the sky with milky shades of rose and gold, they saw the British camp in the distance. It appeared to be a much smaller force than the combined warhost of Saxons and Picts. But the Britons had horses, Eastra reminded herself. And Rhun had told her many times that a cavalryman was worth ten warriors fighting on foot. Even now, they could see the warhorses being brought in from the picket lines. They were magnificent beasts, bred from Arabian stock bought in Narbonne across the eastern sea and the descendants of horses left behind by the Romans.

Before they reached the perimeter of the camp, Eastra, Beli, and Owain dismounted and discussed how to proceed. Owain wanted to find Arthur and bring him to Eastra, who would wait in the woods nearby. He worried that if Eastra should be recognized by Arthur's men, she might be taken prisoner or even killed.

Eastra argued that except for Arthur's Companions, few of the Britons had ever seen her, and if she wore her cloak over her light hair, she should be safe enough. Besides, she was not certain Arthur would agree to meet with her. Confronting him in his tent might be the only way she would have a chance to speak to him. Reluctantly, Owain agreed he and Beli would escort her through the camp.

The Britons were obviously preparing to march. Armor bearers and servants hurried to and fro, carrying weapons, leading horses, dismantling tents. In the midst of the confusion, Eastra wondered if they might not pass unnoticed all the way to the center of the camp where Arthur's purple pennant, adorned with a golden bear and white eagle, marked the headquarters of the high king. But they were finally stopped by a grizzled-looking sentry who demanded to know their business.

Owain replied they were on their way to speak to Arthur. When the sentry continued to glare at them suspiciously, Owain provided the additional information that he was one of Maelgwn the Great's captains. Once again the Cymry king's name opened the way for them. The sentry's dour expression brightened, and he immediately offered to take them to Arthur.

The sentry led them through the churned mud and scattered refuse of the departing army to the headquarters of the high king. There they were again questioned by guards. While Owain once more invoked Maelgwn's name, Eastra looked around, hoping desperately for a glimpse of Rhun. A part of her wanted to forget all about talking to Arthur and instead seek out her love and somehow convince him to leave with her.

But she could not do that, she told herself. More was at stake than Rhun's life. If the Britons marched into battle against the Saxons and the Picts, hundreds, perhaps thousands, of men might die. For the sake of those men and their families, she had to try to stop the impending battle.

The guards finally motioned Owain forward, but blocked the way when she and Beli tried to follow. "The lady is known to Arthur," Owain insisted. "I believe he would wish to see her." When the guards still balked, he drawled contemptuously, "Has the high king grown so cautious that he will not allow a young maid into his tent for fear she is a spy or an assassin?"

Owain's sarcasm had the desired effect. Eastra was waved forward.

They entered the tent. Arthur was seated on a stool by a small table, peering at a parchment map. It seemed to Eastra that he had aged since she last saw him. The lines bracketing his mouth and etching his forehead appeared deeper, and he'd lost flesh.

Owain bowed. "My lord, I am Owain ap Pharic of north Gwynedd." At the word "Gwynedd," Arthur seemed to straighten. Then Owain said, "And this woman is Princess Eastra of the Saxons." Although Arthur did not react to this, the youth seated on the floor of the tent polishing the high king's armor jerked his head up.

Owain nodded to Eastra. She pulled the hood back and squared her shoulders. Then she bowed, "Sire."

There was a long moment as Eastra caught her breath and gathered her thoughts. "No doubt you thought I was dead," she began. "But I am alive. And so is your son, Mordred. No matter what you have heard, be assured he still lives. I spoke with him only a day ago." Arthur did not respond, only waited, his gray eyes piercing her, as if he could, by force of will, see into the very marrow of her bones. "But all is not well. Mordred plots with my Uncle Cerdic to bring you down. They have joined forces with the Picts, and they intend to bring their combined army against you." She hesitated at the coldness of her next words. "Mordred has vowed to kill you himself. I heard him say so with my own ears." What did he feel, she wondered, this man who was like a god to so many, but so hated by his own flesh and blood?

Arthur let out his breath in a sound that was almost a sigh. The weariness she'd glimpsed when she first saw him seemed to weigh upon him even heavier. "Why do you come here?" he asked. "Why tell me these things? Did Cerdic send you?"

"Nay. If Cerdic had known my intentions, he never would have let me leave his camp. I come here on my own. I came because"—she struggled to sound convincing— "because I am tired of seeing men die, of seeing families ripped apart by grief, children torn from their parents. I want this fighting between our peoples to end. One of your captains, Rhun ap Maelgwn, has told me he does not believe you can win this war. If that is so, why not end it now, before more men die? If the Britons go back to their farmsteads and settlements and forts, Cerdic will leave you alone. Cede to him the east, and the north to the Picts, and you will still have half of all the south of the island for your own people."

"And Cerdic's sons and grandsons?" The glimmer of a bitter smile played upon Arthur's mouth. He shook his head. "Nay, they will not be satisfied with part of Britain. They will want it all, and then the fighting will begin all over again."

Eastra feared he was right, but that did not mean she intended to give up. "Aye, but until then, we might have peace for a generation. Or even longer. Time to raise our children, rebuild our settlements, to heal the damage that two score years of war have wrought."

"I believe you are sincere, Princess Eastra. And brave and noble as well. But you must understand, the die is cast. There is no turning back. I have lived my whole life, sacrificed near everything I hold dear, for the sake of this dream. I cannot abandon it now."

"No matter who suffers?" she asked angrily. "Are you not a compassionate man, a *Christian?* I have heard that your god told his followers to love their enemies. Yet you have unceasingly shed the blood of my countrymen, slaughtered women and children, burned and plundered and ravaged from one end of this land to the other!" She was almost shouting now. All her anger and grief came rushing in like the tide. She wanted to hurt him, to make him think about what, *exactly,* his noble dream had wrought. "Your son despises you, and who can blame him? You were willing to sacrifice even *him,* your own flesh and blood, for the sake of your ambition!"

Arthur's face changed. The weary, resigned expression was gone, and he stared at her with a stunned expression. "Who told you such a thing?"

Eastra hesitated. Mordred might be the very weapon she could use against him. If she could arouse the high king's regret for what he had done in the past, perhaps she could influence what he did in the future. "Morguese told me," she answered. "She told me what you said when you learned she was carrying your child."

Arthur glanced at Owain and at the servant polishing his armor. "Leave us," he said. It was the command of a man used to being obeyed.

"Eastra," Owain pleaded.

She shook her head. "Do as he asks."

When they were alone, Arthur took a step toward her. She could see his hands were clenched into fists. Fear swept over her. He took another step nearer and dread choked her throat. "What does Morguese want with me now?" he demanded. "Why did she send you here?"

Arthur's eyes looked cold and sinister. Eastra swallowed. What was she thinking, goading this powerful man when he was already beset on every side? She struggled for composure. Although Arthur might strike her in a rage, she did not think he would kill her. "Nay, Morgeuse did not send me," she responded. "But she did tell me you ordered her to leave Mordred out for the wolves when he was born. She said you wanted him to die because he might interfere with your dream of ruling all of Britain."

As quickly as it had appeared, Arthur's anger seemed to vanish. "That was not the way of it at all . . . but even so, I do owe penance for that, for telling her to kill him at birth." He sighed heavily. "But I was very young, and overwhelmed by what we had just done. She had tricked me, and I was angry, angry enough to compound the sin, to make it into the curse it has since become." He gave a kind of shiver, and then his eyes met Eastra's. "But wretched Mordred is not all my doing. She spoiled him, raised him to be ambitious and power-mad. By the time he came to me, he was already ruined. I tried to give him a chance, to offer him what love I could, but it was too late."

Eastra nodded. She believed him. There was something wrong with Mordred. She had felt it as soon as she met him.

Arthur sighed again. "Or maybe it was our sin that blackened his soul beyond redemption."

"Sin?" she asked, puzzled. This was the second time he had used that word. She knew it was something bad, something evil, but she was not certain exactly what Arthur meant. "Is it because she used a spell to entice you into her bed? Is that why you were angry? Is that why it was a sin?"

Arthur gave her a desperate look, as if he were pleading with her to understand. "You're not Christian, are you?"

Eastra shook her head.

"But your people do have taboos, things that they are not allowed to do, lest they lose the favor of their gods—is that not right?"

"Aye."

"Well, what Morgeuse and I did is considered . . . taboo. You see, we have the same father. She is Uther's bastard, just as I am. For us to share a bed is . . . well, for people who worship the old gods, it is considered unchancy and dangerous at the very least. But for a Christian, it's an abomination."

"Morguese is your half sister?" Eastra could only gape. "But then why does she hate you? Why does she plot your death?"

"If you were to ask Morgeuse that, she would say she is only obeying the Goddess, and that I must die because I have fought to make the Christian God more honored than the Great Mother. She will say she has seen my death, and hence it must come to pass. As for what glory she has *seen* for Mordred, who knows? Even if I die, few men will follow him."

That was true, Eastra thought. No Saxon would trust a man who killed his father. That thought led to another thought, and she seized upon it. "Mordred means to kill you," she said. "Knowing what he is, what he is capable of, do you truly think it wise to face him on the battlefield?"

Arthur's expression grew grim. "If he wants to kill me, he'll have to fight better than I have ever seen him fight. I'm old and slower than I used to be, but that has only made me more cunning and shrewd. But, nay, I will not shy from battle because I fear him, even though a secret part of me wonders if that is not his destiny, to kill me and finally cleanse me of my dread sin. For if I die by his hand, the debt will be paid, and maybe then God will see fit to answer my prayers and allow my people to triumph."

Eastra did not understand his reasoning. All this talk of sin and debts seemed very odd. If Arthur had been tricked into lying with Morgeuse, why did he feel he was to blame?

She would have to ask Rhun sometime to tell her more about this Christian God who seemed so rigid and harsh, so demanding of his followers. Rhun. That was the other reason she had come here. It was clear she had failed to dissuade Arthur from going to war against Cerdic. He seemed resigned to his fate, determined to follow his dream to its tragic, deadly end. But that did not mean Rhun had to die as well.

"There is a man I love," she said. "One of your Companions, Rhun ap Maelgwn. I am carrying his child, and I would not have it left fatherless ere it is even born." She touched her stomach. "If you would release him from his vow to you, his oath to fight for Britain, I would be most grateful."

What a hopeless, pathetic request it was. She had nothing to bargain with. There was no reason for Arthur to do as she wished, to give up one of his best warriors when he obviously needed every man he could inveigle, entice, or threaten into fighting for him.

Arthur moved back to the table in the center of the tent. He fingered one of the rolled-up parchments lying there. "As I have said, you are courageous and bold, Princess Eastra, a most remarkable woman. And so young and lovely it near breaks my heart to look at you. No doubt you have suffered. I hear the pain in your voice when you speak of your dead kin. For that I am sorry. I have never given my men orders to kill women or children. But war is brutal and harsh . . . as you well know." Her heart sank at the realization he was going to refuse her. "If I could grant your request, I would," he continued. "But . . . I have not seen Rhun for over a sennight. He went to Gwynedd to see his sick stepmother and hasn't returned."

She stared at him. "Hasn't returned? But . . ."

"I have kept hoping, thinking he must still be trying to persuade his father and some of the other chieftains to join us." He raised his gaze to hers. "But since I do not in truth know where he is, I can hardly release him from his vow."

It was Eastra's turn to be stunned. She had assumed Rhun had joined up with Arthur's army as soon as he left Deganwy. That was four days ago. Where was he? Was Arthur correct in thinking Rhun was still trying to secure allies for the coming battle?

For days she had been pushing herself, fighting through the exhaustion, forcing herself to go on. She had told herself if she could only speak to Cerdic and then to Arthur, she could halt this upcoming battle and save untold lives.

And beyond her quest to bring peace, her other hope had been to find Rhun and somehow find a way to keep him from danger. Now, all at once, the disappointment and futility of everything she had done caught up with her. She felt exhausted and weak, utterly despairing. With effort, she struggled to stay on her feet.

"Princess, are you well?" Arthur's voice came from a distance. She heard him calling out for help. In a second, strong arms gripped her shoulders on either side. Beli spoke, his voice tender and concerned. "Come, lady, you must lie down for a time. And eat something."

In moments, she was herself again and resisting Beli's attempts to take off her sandals. "Nay, I do not need to lie down, merely sit for a while. And I will eat something, I promise."

"It's amazing she has managed this journey," Arthur said. "She cannot be far along with the babe, and most women are tired and weak during the first few months."

"Babe! What babe?" Owain's voice rose in a roar. "You mean to tell me she is with child?"

"So she said," Arthur replied. "She told me that she was carrying Rhun ap Maelgwn's child."

Beli gave a smothered laugh. "I'm going to be an uncle!"

Owain swore. "Of all the foolishness! All these days of riding and eating camp food—she might well have miscarried!"

"Nay, not this babe." Eastra touched her stomach tenderly and smiled. "Morgeuse told me the Goddess has special plans for it."

Owain continued to grumble. Beli hugged her. Arthur said, "I would willingly offer you the use of my tent, princess. But the fact is, my army is already on the march, and I must take my leave of you."

"When will the battle take place?" Eastra asked. "This day, or the next?"

"It will take all of today to reach Eburacum and secure

our position. The war horns will not sound until early to-morrow morning."

The dull ache of despair threatened to weigh her down. Her worst fears were on the verge of being realized. Yet there was hope Rhun would escape the slaughter. If they rode south, they might be able to intercept him before he joined Arthur's army. She looked at Owain, wondering how she was ever going to be able to convince him to let her back on a horse.

It was a delightful dream. Eastra was kissing him, her mouth as light and caressing as the stroke of a butterfly's wing against his skin. She drew back and smiled, as beautiful and radiant as the most resplendent sunrise. He leaned nearer, hungry for another taste of her sweet, sweet lips. Something seemed to be in the way. He looked down. Her belly was swollen, round and firm as an unripened fruit. He touched it in awe, and beneath the taut skin there was a ripple of movement. He met her gaze and she leaned forward, their lips touching. Seeking to deepen the kiss, he reached out for her . . .

The glorious reverie vanished, and he found himself lying on the narrow bed in his childhood sleeping chamber, clutching the light summer blankets tightly in his arms. Disappointed and restless, he rolled off the bed and began to pace. He heard a cock crow in the distance and knew it was almost morning anyway. Not that he had anywhere to go or anything to do this day. He grimaced at the ironic thought. A prisoner in his own father's fortress. What an ignominious, irritating fate. How could Maelgwn do such a thing to him? And how could gentle Rhiannon allow it?

A moment after he had the thought, there was a knock at the door. As soon as he snarled the word "enter," his stepmother appeared carrying a tray of food. She looked at him and said, "You seem out of sorts this morning, Rhun. What's wrong?"

"I had a dream," he answered, surprising himself. Since waking and realizing the heady, sensual fantasy was not real, he had tried to put it out of his mind. But now, seeing Rhiannon, he could not help thinking about Eastra's swollen belly and the way it had felt beneath his fingers, magically alive. "I dreamed about Eastra," he said grudgingly. He paced across the small room. "She was with child."

"Maybe it's a true dream," Rhiannon said.

He turned to look at her, and a prickling sensation ran down his spine. His stepmother's expression was as serene as usual, but was there not a hint of amusement in her soft blue eyes? "What do you mean?"

She shrugged, smiling faintly. "It happens. You've been intimate with Eastra, and that's the purpose of coupling, after all." She raised a brow. "It's not all about pleasure, Rhun. There are other reasons for a man and a woman to be drawn to each other."

He took a step toward her. "Are you telling me . . ." He let his voice trail off. "But she said nothing to me . . . and I held her in my arms, saw her naked . . ."

"The signs are subtle in the beginning. Sometimes a woman does not even know herself."

He took a sharp breath. "Tell me true. Is Eastra with child?"

Rhiannon nodded.

"How long have you known?" His tone was accusatory, angry.

"Since she came to Deganwy. Nay, it was before that. I saw her in a dream, much as you did."

"And you said *nothing?*" He was outraged. Always before, he'd trusted Rhiannon, seen her as an ally against his father's uncertain temper. But now she had allowed him to be kept as prisoner, and had just revealed that she'd kept a momentous secret from him for weeks.

"Eastra asked me not to, and it really is her place to tell you."

"Why?" He felt as if a hole had opened up in the ground in front of him. If only he'd known, he would have done so many things differently.

"You would have to ask her that. Maybe she wanted to feel that when you finally told her you loved her, it was because of what you felt for *her*, not because of the babe."

"Of course I love her. How can she doubt that?"

"Ah, but you love your duty more, don't you? You were planning to leave her, to go off and fight Arthur's war, knowing you might be killed." Rhiannon shook her head. "That's hardly love, as I reckon it."

"But . . . I had no choice." His voice came out hoarse and agonized. How vividly the turmoil returned, the sense of being torn in two. "I swore an oath. I was Arthur's man long before I met Eastra."

"So you see the matter. But she saw it differently. Because she's a woman, not a warrior."

Rhun inhaled sharply. The urge to see Eastra, to hold her in his arms, was almost overwhelming. "If I'd known, I would have at least said a proper good-bye to her. Told her I loved her." He shook his head. "Made some preparations to see she was taken care of, that the babe was named my heir . . ." He looked at Rhiannon. "But now it's too late. She's gone back to her own people."

Her expression was tender. "As long as you both live, it's never too late."

"Aye." He looked around the room, trying to think what he needed to take with him. Again, he met Rhiannon's gaze. "The battle is probably already over, or soon will be. Can you convince my father to finally set me free?"

She nodded. "I think I can. He has wrestled with his conscience in this matter. He knows some guilt for imposing his will upon you, a man grown."

"He'd *better* feel guilty," Rhun muttered. Then he began to pack.

* * *

"We'll go no further," Owain said. He turned to look at Eastra, his face as stern and forbidding as she had ever seen even Cerdic look.

"But we can't see the whole battlefield from here," she protested. "What if Rhun arrives with reinforcements and I can't reach him before he joins the fray?"

Owain gave her another forbidding look. "Oh, and certainly if he does appear, I'm going to let you go riding across a battlefield to find him! You can forget that nonsense. You're going to stay on this hill if I have to tie you to one of those rocks!" He jerked his head toward a stony outcrop overgrown with heather.

Eastra looked at Beli, wondering if, when the time came, he would help her. But maybe she wouldn't have to face that circumstance. Maybe Rhun wouldn't come.

But why not? The question gnawed at her. He had been so determined, so insistent he must go to Arthur's aid. What had happened? Had he been hurt? Killed? Her already distressed stomach heaved at the thought.

She had wanted to ride south and try to intercept Rhun before he reached the battlefield, but Owain had dissuaded her. There was no way of knowing which direction Rhun might arrive from, the Cymry warrior insisted. It was better to ride along behind the British army train and hope they would see him. But they had not. And now the battle was about to begin and there was no sign of him.

She took a deep breath, steeling herself for the horror she was about to witness. The idea of watching two armies clash, of seeing men kill each other, repulsed her like nothing she'd ever faced before. Yet if there was a chance Rhun might be fighting this day, she could not forsake him. She would call upon the Goddess to send him strength, to guide his sword arm, to see him safely through this battle.

She wished fervently she'd learned enough magic from Morgeuse to know how to make a charm of protection. But another part of her mind wondered why there was any reason to think that the Goddess would intervene. Rhiannon had told her the Great Mother cared nothing for the petty concerns of men, their childish search for power, their passion for killing and death.

The battlefield was spread out below them, and they could see the two armies filling the valley. From this distance, they looked like a swarm of insects, or two snakes, the flash of warriors' helms and mail shirts like the scales of two huge serpents slithering into the vale from opposite directions. She could make out a banner here and there, a splash of color amid the grays and browns. "Do you see Arthur?" she asked the men.

"Nay," Owain answered. "But he's probably leading one of the cavalry wings. They won't move in until the infantry has engaged." He pointed. "See? Both sides have reinforcements hidden in the trees and massed along the river. It will be a long battle. It might last all day."

Eastra nodded, grimacing. If she could spot Arthur, then perhaps she would find Rhun.

The Britons' horns sounded, harsh and strident, the Saxons' answered, and she forgot everything else as her heart leaped into her throat and she gripped the sapphire necklace around her neck so tightly her fingers went numb. She could tell the Pictish archers had begun their work, for here and there along the British line, men began to fall. She turned away, sickened.

"Aye," Beli said. "It's best you don't watch. It might mark the babe."

Resolutely, Eastra faced forward once again. She had made a vow to see this thing through, and so she would.

The two armies seemed to seep together. She saw churning dust rise where they were joined. Now the valley was like a hive of maddened bees, roiling with movement. A dull roar rose up to the hilltop where they watched. The sound vibrated through her flesh, filling her with dread.

It seemed to go on for hours. Sweat dripped down Eastra's brow. Since she could judge so little about what was taking place below, her attention gradually shifted to other sights and sounds around them. She was aware of a curlew scolding from the grass nearby, warning that they were too close to its nest. She felt the soft breeze blowing past, sweet with pine and heather. And she saw flocks of large dark birds flying by.

"Ravens," Owain said, observing the direction of her gaze. "It's said they can hear the clash of arms from miles distant. They come to feast on the entrails of the fallen."

"Llud's silver hand!" Beli exclaimed. "That's no way to speak in front of a lady!"

"She should know what gruesome sights she might behold if she decides to ride down into the fray," Owain answered coldly.

Eastra shivered though the sun blazed down on them. Owain was right. Brave and determined though she might be, she knew she could not bear to go down into the valley and see the horrible slaughter taking place there. Men were falling faster; the ground was thick with bodies. She thought surely it would be over soon. But then there was the blare of more horns, and horsemen surged forward from the British side. She looked again for Arthur and glimpsed a flash of purple at the head of one cavalry wing. Did Rhun ride at his side? she wondered. Frantically, she searched for a glimpse of the familiar red and white banner. There was no sign of it.

The plan was obviously for the two groups of horsemen to surround and engulf the Saxon and Pictish footsoldiers, but Arthur and the other riders were hampered by narrowness of the valley, and there were so many of the enemy, wave upon wave of them, surging down from the hills beyond. Cerdic had chosen well, Eastra thought grimly. He had the advantage in numbers and the perfect terrain from which to launch his attack. And if they had to, his army could fall back to the ruins of the old Roman fort.

But retreat would not be necessary, Eastra could tell. There were too many Saxons and Picts for the Britons to overcome. No matter how many of the enemy they killed, there would always be more. She saw the British line sag and fall back. The cavalry surged in to fill the gap. Then they were surrounded. Her gaze scanned the hills behind

the Britons, wondering if they had more warriors hidden
there among the trees. Had Rhun come through with reinforcements?

There were no more charges by the Britons. Those men
left did not retreat, but fought steadily, yielding ground with
painful slowness. She looked again for Arthur and could
not see his banner anywhere. Had it been dragged down
into the morass of bodies littering the field? Had the high
king himself fallen?

"What's happening?" she demanded. Throughout the
battle, Beli and Owain and the other men had exchanged
only a few words, and then they spoke so quietly she could
not hear what they were saying.

"It's as we expected," Beli answered in a taut voice.
"Your uncle has prevailed."

"Aye," Owain added. "But what I don't understand is
why Arthur doesn't sound the retreat. If the Britons pulled
back now, it would not be a complete massacre."

"Perhaps Arthur can't sound the retreat," Eastra said.
"Perhaps he's already dead."

Both men looked at her. "What makes you think that?"
Beli asked. His expression made her realize he thought she
had experienced some premonition of the outcome of the
battle.

"I know no more than you," she assured him. "But I
heard Mordred vow to kill his father, and since Arthur's
banner is no longer visible, I fear the worst."

"Will you mourn him?" Beli asked. "He was your uncle's enemy, and I know that his hold upon Rhun cost you
dear."

Eastra nodded gravely. "I will mourn him. I've never
met another man like him." Perhaps there were no others,
she thought to herself. A king who fought for a dream,
rather than his own power. A warrior who fought for peace.

Only her beloved Rhun was as noble as Arthur, and she
could not admire his urge to self-sacrifice the way she
could admire Arthur's. His life belonged to *her* and to their

320   *Mary Gillgannon*

child, and in her mind he was not free to squander it for the sake of a dream.

"Oh, Rhun," she murmured. "Where are you?"

Nineteen

It was almost nightfall before Owain thought it safe to go down into the valley. Even then, the men rode on either side of Eastra, swords drawn. The only light to see by came from torches and the pale glow of a half moon rising over the hills. Most of the battlefield was dark, hiding the carnage Eastra knew must be there. The moans and screams of the wounded and dying echoed through the darkness, filling her with dread. Was Rhun among those poor souls? How would she ever find him?

Owain had decided it would be wisest for them to seek news of the battle from the Saxons, since they were the victors. They left their horses in a thorn grove, then walked cautiously toward the fort. Before they had gone far, Owain accosted an exhausted-looking Saxon and dragged him over to Eastra. "Speak to him in his own tongue," he told her. "That way he will know we are not the enemy."

She told the man she was Cerdic's niece and she had come for news.

Haltingly, he answered her questions. Aye, the Britons had been totally routed. Arthur was believed to be dead and, with him, all of the Companions. A few of the Britons had escaped, but so few Cerdic decided it was not worth the trouble to chase them down and kill them. The losses on the Saxon side had not been grievous, but the Picts had suffered heavy casualties. It was the way they fought, the warrior explained, throwing themselves into the fray like madmen.

At some point, the man seemed to snap out of his battle trance and question what she was doing there. He warned her it was not safe to remain so close to the battlefield. Looters roamed the area, unscrupulous wretches who stole from the corpses and finished off the wounded so they could steal from them as well. He also told her Cerdic had returned to the fortress, but it might be best if she waited until morning to search him out.

Eastra agreed with this advice. She had no desire to meet with her uncle this night. He was likely still angry at her for speaking to him so boldly and then leaving his camp. The man started to walk away, but then she called out as an afterthought, "And Mordred, Arthur's son and Cerdic's ally, where is he?"

"Dead," the man answered. "They say Arthur stabbed him in the throat even as his own life's blood was draining away. Cerdic ordered no burial or death ceremony for Mordred. His words were, 'That one can rot in the mud were he lays.' "

"Where did Mordred die?" Eastra asked. "Do you know the place?"

"Down by the river, near where it curves."

Eastra immediately began to consider where she could get a torch.

"What did he say?" Beli asked.

"He said Arthur and all his companions are dead. Mordred was also killed."

Eastra glanced around. Seeing a man with a torch, she approached him and smiled ingratiatingly. "I'm Cerdic's niece. I've come from the fortress where they are tending the wounded. We need more torches there. Would you let me have that one?"

The man gaped at her. "Cerdic's niece? And he has you tending the wounded?"

"I wanted to help." She lowered her eyes demurely.

"Here," the man thrust the torch at her. "I suppose the living have more urgent need of it than do the dead."

"Thank you," she murmured.

"Now what are you planning?" Owain asked, coming up beside her.

"We're going down to the river. We're going to look for Mordred."

They returned to their horses. Owain held the torch and led the way, grumbling. Their course took them through the woods where Arthur's cavalry had waited. They encountered few bodies. Those Britons left alive had made it their mission to collect their fallen comrades. All the corpses that remained, scattered among the trees, were Picts. Eastra felt a stab of grief each time Owain shone the torch on another of the small, fierce warriors.

Even to herself, she could not explain the urgency that drove her in this quest to find Mordred. She knew even if Arthur had fallen nearby, the high king's body would have been borne off hours ago.

But then there was a keening sound, a bone-chilling cry of grief and pain, and Eastra knew why she had come.

They hurried toward the river, down almost to the water's edge. The torch's light revealed the spectacle of a wailing woman standing knee-deep in the shallow water, struggling to drag something to shore. Her hair was unbound and wild, but Eastra recognized Morguese. "Help her," Eastra said to Beli and Owain, her voice shaking. Even though she knew Morgeuse had brought this tragedy on herself and her son, Eastra could not help pitying her. She thought about how she would feel if it were her child lying lifeless in the water, her own flesh and blood, cold and dead.

The two men and the hysterical woman managed to get Mordred onto the riverbank. Morgeuse immediately threw herself upon his prone form, weeping. She seemed oblivious to everyone and everything around her. They all stood there, listening to her moan and cry until Eastra could endure it no longer. She leaned over and touched Morguese's shoulder. "Come, get warm," she said. "You can do no more for him."

Morguese whimpered. She stroked her son's face tenderly. In death, Mordred looked very young, and much more innocent than he had been in life. The wound in his throat had bled out, so there was no sign of his violent death. His face looked peaceful and relaxed, as if he were sleeping.

"Come," Eastra said again. Morguese allowed herself to be helped up. She was haggard and wild-eyed, her hair tangled around her body in limp, muddy strands, her gown torn and filthy. Eastra could scarcely recognize this woman as the powerful priestess she remembered dancing with supreme, hypnotic confidence in Urien's hall.

She put her arms around Morgeuse. "Owain will build a fire." She nodded to him as she said this. "We'll wrap you up and get you warm." Morguese clung to her hand as they waited for the men to fetch the flintstone and other supplies from the horses' packs.

They camped there for the night, with Mordred's body lying a few feet away. Owain had covered it with his cloak. Strangely, Morguese dropped off to sleep almost immediately. It was Eastra who lay awake, staring up at the few stars visible through the trees. She felt numb and empty. Too much had happened this day. Death was all around her. Far in the distance, she could still hear men screaming in pain. And not a dozen paces away, Mordred dreamed the endless dream of the dead. She tried to imagine it in her mind, Arthur wounded and bleeding, but still strong and canny enough to manage a last swordthrust. With that one blow, he had sent his son to the otherworld to pay the debt he believed must be paid.

She shivered at the thought, wondering at the forces at work around her. Her faith in Morguese's power had been shattered. What did that mean for her and for the babe growing in her belly? She touched herself, wondering how many weeks it would be before the babe quickened and she experienced the first real stirrings of new life inside her.

Rhun's child. It might be all she had left of him. And yet she did not believe that. She did not think Rhun had died this day. As the day wore on, she had become convinced that for some reason he had not arrived in time to honor his oath to Arthur. Had it been the Goddess who delayed him and saved his life?

The thought gave Eastra hope. That Morgeuse was wrong about Mordred did not mean she was wrong about everything. The Goddess might yet have a plan for *her,* and for her child.

In the morning, Eastra washed in the river and redid her braids, then went off into the bushes to change her clothing. Morguese did nothing, sitting on an old log and staring into space.

After they ate more of the dried meat they always carried and drank the last of their wine, Owain asked Eastra, "Where to now, Princess?"

"I would like to find Arthur," she said. "I would like to pay my respects to the high king ere he is buried."

"Arthur's not dead," Morguese spoke softly, her voice flat and bitter. "He should be, but he's not."

"What are you saying?" Beli asked. "We were told he was mortally wounded when he . . . killed Mordred."

Morgeuse laughed, a harsh mirthless sound. "He will never be high king again, but he is not dead."

"How do you know?" Eastra asked.

Morgeuse shrugged. "I *know.* He is my half brother, and the tie between us is close." She glanced at the cloak-wrapped body. "That's why Mordred was so special. He had the power from both of us." She gave a pathetic sniff.

Eastra and Beli and Owain all looked at each other. Morgeuse would never understand how flawed her son was.

"Where is he, then?" Eastra asked. "Where is Arthur?"

"They plan to take him back to the priory at Avalon, in the hope the monks there can heal him. But there is naught they can do. They have not the skill to save him."

Eastra gazed at Morgeuse thoughtfully. "Who could save him? Could you do it?"

"Of course." Morgeuse sniffed again. "If I wanted to."

"He's your brother," Eastra coaxed. "Your kin. Now that Mordred's dead, he's all you have left."

"Oh, I have other children, but none of them have the power. They're all slow and cow-brained like Urien."

This almost made Eastra laugh. She felt giddy. Arthur was alive. And so was Rhun, she was sure of it. As certain as Morgeuse was that Arthur lived, she felt the same way about Rhun.

She looked at Owain. "I've never heard of Avalon. Is it far?"

Owain shook his head "Clear on the other side of Britain. But if we start out now, we will easily find them before they reach the place. They must be carrying him in a litter or a cart and can't make much speed."

He was too late, Rhun thought bitterly. He'd known it the entire journey, but as he began to meet the few stragglers traveling south, his fears were made real. They told of the victory of the Saxons, the terrible losses the Britons had suffered, of Arthur wounded and dying. But that was the part where their stories grew vague. Some said Arthur was dead already, but no one had seen his corpse. There was talk the Saxons had carried it away, or the Picts. But there were also tales he was not dead after all. One man, limping and his right eye a crusty, ruined mess, said Arthur had been taken to a house of holy men and they were going to heal him.

Rhun did not know what to believe. Whatever happened to Arthur, it was surely out of his hands. His purpose, his goal, was to find Eastra. He assumed she would be in Cerdic's camp. He had to find her and tell her he loved her and wanted her to be his wife, if she would have him. But would Cerdic allow such a thing?

Mentally, he flogged himself for all the chances he'd had and wasted. If only he'd wed her while they were in Gwynedd, she would never have left. She would be safe now at his father's fortress, their babe growing in her belly. A wave of longing went through him at the thought. What if he were never allowed to see his child? Cerdic might decide to marry her off to one of his thanes. And all of this might happen because he'd been such a stupid, selfish fool.

He rode along the old Roman road, thinking these grim thoughts. It could not be that much farther to Eburacum; the trickle of weary soldiers had increased to a steady stream. At least the Saxons had shown mercy by allowing the British survivors to return to their homes. They clearly thought they had broken their enemies' will to fight and that the Britons would not dare make war against them for a long while.

Rhun recognized a few of the men, but he could hardly bear to face them. He felt like a traitor, and he experienced their puzzled, sometimes accusing, looks like physical blows. At least he had not met any of the Companions. Of course he had not. They were dead, every one of them. Except him.

He grimaced at the thought, and when the next group of travelers approached, he hunched over and looked away as the cart and handful of riders passed by.

Then someone called his name and he looked up despite himself. He found himself staring into the stunned face of Tristan. He had been one of the youngest of the Companions, and always in awe of Rhun. He appeared to have aged years. His dark eyes were smudged with shadows of weariness, his dust-smeared face gaunt and grim. The two soldiers with him were not much better off. They looked barely past boyhood and were obviously dazed by what they'd been through.

Tristan motioned for the others to halt, then said, "Jesu, I can't believe it's you. Where were you? Arthur held out hope until the very end that you would come with some of Cynglass's warriors. Or a troop of Cymry archers, at least."

Rhun gritted his teeth. "My father imprisoned me," he said. "He would not let me leave his fortress until he thought it was too late for me to reach the battle in time. He was worried I would be killed." It sounded like the lamest of excuses. He wanted to hang his head and look away.

"Oh," was all Tristan said. "Well, perhaps it's just as well. It's good to see another Companion alive." He glanced back toward the cart. "And we could use your help in getting the high king to safety."

"Arthur?" Rhun's gaze fixed on to the contents of the cart. There would be those who would try to steal Arthur's corpse. He'd already heard tales of it. "Where do you plan to take him?" Wincing, he glanced again at the blanket-covered lump in the back of the wain. To think that this still, lifeless shape was all that was left of the high king, a man he'd once very nearly considered a god sprung to life.

"Our goal was Avalon, the isle of apples, but that seems far-fetched now. He's already feverish and weak. Too much more traveling might finish him off."

"He's alive!" Rhun almost fell out of the saddle in amazement. He took a deep breath to recover himself. "By all means, you must stop somewhere." He looked around, scanning the landscape in desperation. There must be some farmstead nearby. Some kind of shelter, a place to build a fire, someone skilled in herbs and medicine. His heart sank. This part of Britain had been the site of too many battles in recent years, and most of the people had moved to safer locales. Shelter and food they might be able to find, but a wise woman or midwife, that was unlikely. And without treatment, Arthur would surely die, especially if he were already fevered.

Rhun dismounted. "Where is the wound? Show me."

Tristan also dismounted. They walked back to the wain and Tristan lifted the blanket. Rhun gave a gasp. Arthur looked as pale as death already and his breathing was shallow and uneven.

"His arm is mangled," Tristan said. "But that's not what worries me. It's the wound in his groin that's like to kill him." He lifted the high king's long mail shirt to reveal leather trousers completely caked with dried blood.

"My God," Rhun said. He wished fervently he'd paid attention to Rhiannon when she'd brewed decoctions for his brothers and sisters when they'd had fevers, or could remember what she used to clean wounds so they wouldn't fill with poison. But he knew nothing about healing. He'd always depended on wise women like Rhiannon or the army surgeons, most of whom were monks who had made healing their special calling. "Where's Geriant? Or Hywel?" he asked, thinking of the surgeons.

"Probably back there somewhere. We had to get him away." There was a note of hysteria in Tristan's voice. "We feared the Saxons would follow us and finish him off. While Arthur lives, so does the dream. The Saxons know that as well as we do."

Rhun shook his head. "But he's like to die anyway. I don't know how to aid him, what to do, except to somehow get him to shelter and keep him warm."

"I've thought that, too," Tristan said. "But I did not feel I could leave him to go and search for a place to bed down for the night. Besides, he was not that bad until the last mile. He even spoke to me, encouraging me." Tristan looked as if he might weep. This was obviously too much for him. And what other horrors had he seen during the previous day? Who could blame him if he was so stunned he could not think clearly? Rhun had seen it often in the aftermath of particularly fierce, bloody battles.

"Stay here," he said firmly. "I'll go look for a place to spend the night."

"But what if someone comes? We can't leave the road with the cart. Nor can we carry him to safety very quickly."

Rhun scanned the horizon, looking for anyone on the road behind them. The hilly nature of the landscape made it impossible to see very far. "I'll be as fast as I can. If anyone comes, draw your swords and prepare to fight."

Tristan nodded.

Rhun took a deep breath. Surely this was why God had not allowed him to take part in the battle of the crooked glen—Camboglanna—as the previous day's conflict was already being called. He was meant to save Arthur's life instead of fighting at his side. But if that was God's purpose, why had He not given Rhun a better chance of succeeding?

It seemed hopeless, yet he remembered Rhiannon's words: while there was life, there was hope. Once again he must put aside his longing for Eastra. How could he not, when his dying king had been practically thrown into his path?

He focused his thoughts and began to search the area as rapidly as he could. No sign of farmstead or bothy or any sort of habitation on this side of the road. He retraced his steps and started to search the other side. After he'd gone a short way, he halted. Wasn't there something odd about that pile of stones in the distance?

He rushed to the place, pushing through the underbrush nearly hiding it, then took a step back and stared. Of all things, an old, square temple of worked stone. The faces of the old, Roman-style gods stared blindly from their niches in the walls. He ducked his head to enter. The construction seemed solid, although the place smelled sourly of the droppings of some animal that had used it as a den. It would suffice for their purposes, providing shelter and hiding them from the road.

He left the temple and retraced his steps to the road. Then, in the distance, he saw them. Riders. Four of them. They were bearing down on the cart and the three soldiers guarding it. He began to run.

He was about a hundred paces away. It looked as if he would reach Arthur and the others at the same time as the riders. His sword bounced against his side, and he wondered how long he should wait before drawing it. His hand crept to the hilt.

Then he saw something that made his steps slow to a dazed, stumbling rhythm. One of the riders had long, pale yellow hair. It glinted in the sun like a helmet of light. Could it be? Rhun shut his eyes and opened them again, wondering if he were trapped in some sort of dream. A dream that had seemed like a nightmare, but now promised to turn as magical and wonderful as any dream he'd ever had.

He started running again. As he neared the cart, Tristan was shouting, but Rhun did not noticed what he said. Beside the wain, he halted. "Eastra," he whispered.

Her eyes were fixed on him also, as they drank in the sight of each other. She reined in her horse, and he ran to her. He reached up and dragged her off her mount, then twirled around with her in his arms. "Eastra, my darling, my love."

He heard her laugh, wild and exuberant, sounding like the most beautiful music he'd ever heard. Then he put her down and looked at her stomach, then back at her face. "Is it true?" he asked. "Do you carry my babe?"

"It's true," she said, then laughed again.

For the first time, Rhun looked around. He wanted to share their wonderful news with the whole world. Then he saw Beli and Owain . . . and Morgeuse. The sight of her amazed him as much as seeing Eastra, but in a different way. He started to open his mouth to say something sarcastic about her gloating over Arthur's defeat. But then he saw how ravaged and pale she looked and the words froze in his throat. She was not gloating. Nay, she looked as if she had been weeping for days.

Eastra touched his face. "Morguese's going to help us," she said. "She's going to heal Arthur."

He shook his head, more puzzled than ever. "But why? Has she changed her mind about wanting him dead? What's happened?"

"It's a long tale," she said. "What matters now is that she says she can keep Arthur from dying." She looked around. "We need some sort of shelter, a place for her to work her magic."

"I've found it," Rhun said. "And it's more perfect for our task than you could ever have imagined."

The next few moments were busy ones. The cart was hauled closer to the temple, then the six of them—Tristan, the two footsoldiers, Beli, Owain, and Rhun—all carried Arthur down the slope to the temple hidden in the trees. Eastra had already swept it out with a branch and put down blankets on the cold stone floor. There was no hearth, but Owain started a fire near the door and lit a small oil lamp that he'd carried in his pack. Morguese, moving at the slow, lethargic pace with which she'd done everything since Mordred's death, set out the bags of herbs, bottles of oils and essences, and bowls and utensils she used for her spells.

When she was finished, she waved them away. "Leave me," she said.

Rhun hesitated, as did Tristan. With more force, Morguese repeated, "Leave me!"

Eastra took Rhun's hand. "Come," she said. "We can talk while she works her spells."

"But what if . . . she does something to him?"

Eastra looked at him quizzically. "If she betrays our trust and kills him, then it's no worse than the death he would have suffered anyway. His wound is mortal. Nothing but sorcery can save him."

Rhun nodded. It was true. Still, it bothered him to leave his king alone with Morguese, who'd openly plotted his overthrow. It bothered him even more when Eastra told him about the scene by the river. "By the saints! Mordred was her son! But Arthur and her . . . why that's . . . that's incest!"

Eastra nodded. "So Arthur said. But it's over now. Mordred's dead. Arthur's debt is paid. And Morguese . . ." She sighed. "Morguese has no one left to love. That's why she's doing this. I think she once loved Arthur and that's why she tricked him into bedding her. And then when he rejected her and rejected the child they'd conceived, all that love turned to hate. She's spent the last twenty years of her life plotting his defeat. But when Mordred died, it changed something in her. She remembered her love for Arthur. She doesn't want to lose him as well as her son. I believe she will do her best to heal him."

"Well," Rhun said. "You're a woman, so perhaps that makes sense to you, but it makes none to me."

"But you will trust my judgment?"

"Of course." He leaned near and kissed her. It began as a light, gentle kiss, then quickly turned to something more. The very feel of her body in his arms turned him to fire. Soon they were one writhing, panting beast, pressed against the back side of the temple.

He finally broke away. "This is madness," he murmured.

"Why?" Her voice was teasing.

"Because Arthur may be dying and here we are, like a pair of animals in heat!"

"There's nothing wrong with passion. Indeed, our lust may well add some power to Morguese's spell. Although I do agree we should find some secluded spot so we can continue in privacy."

That their lovemaking could give life to a dying man—it certainly was a strange notion. But it sounded plausible when Eastra said it. And Rhun did not think he could keep his hands off of her anyway.

He retrieved a blanket from his saddle pack. As he passed by the other men on the way to the temple, he said sheepishly, "I thought Arthur might need it." No one commented, and he wondered if they believed him. Or maybe they were too caught up in their worries for Arthur to care what he did.

He should be praying himself, he thought as he approached the thicket Eastra had selected. With every breath he took, he should be beseeching the Almighty to let Arthur live. But then would that not be hypocritical—to petition his God for aid, when in fact he was putting his trust in a devotee of the Goddess?

He had to confront the fact that as deep as his faith was in some ways, it had its limitations. Some things remained the realm of the old gods. As high king, Arthur belonged to the land, the Great Mother herself, and only She could heal him.

This thought contented him, but perhaps it didn't matter anyway, he thought as he pushed aside the concealing branches and beheld Eastra in all her naked glory. For a time, he simply stared at her, memorizing each lovely plane and curve, every facet of her beauty. His gaze lingered on her slightly rounded belly, the lavish abundance of her breasts, the deep rose of her nipples. She no longer looked like a maid, but an incarnation of the Goddess herself, ripe and lush and glowing with the splendor of the new life inside her.

He spread the blanket on the ground, then caught her up in his arms and pulled her down so they lay side by side. "What happened to you?" he asked between kisses. "I remember you as a shy maiden, not this bold, free-spirited, lustful woman."

"After months of being treated like a princess, I finally realized I was one. I had value and power, and I could change things instead of letting life pull me along like a leaf carried away on the current." She nuzzled his ear. "Do you *like* your Saxon princess?"

"Mmmm, it's what I've always wanted . . . I think."

"You *think?*" She slapped him in mock anger.

Then he rolled over on top of her and the playful mood vanished. Pushing down his trousers, he was soon deep inside her. His rhythm was urgent, rough. Eastra clutched his shoulders and gave in to the fierce, primal sensations. He was like a proud stag mounting a doe. She trembled and moaned, hungry and yearning for every thrust inside her. Her womb, already ripe with life, contracted and pulsed.

Her mind was filled with visions. She saw the great horned god of the hunt silhouetted in the light of the full moon. And in the moon was a woman's face, the Lady. As she floated down upon the silvery light the stag god's shadow moved to meet the light and became a man. They were joined, their bodies merging, becoming one. Male and female, unique and wonderful. And in their joining, the power was unleashed. Eastra felt it inside her own flesh. She was the Goddess, the giver of life, and Rhun worshiped her as only a man could, offering her his strength, his dark, wild essence, his seed.

The waves of pleasure subsided, and with them, her strange, moonlit dreams. She opened her eyes to see Rhun, his face flushed and slit-eyed with contentment, his nostrils still flared as he took long, deep breaths to recover from his climax. "This must be a dream," he said. "I can't imagine this is happening." He focused his gaze on her. "I can't believe you are really here." He reached out and stroked her cheek. "I should have been more gentle. I didn't hurt you, did I?"

She shook her head, still dazed and wondering herself. "It was . . . magical . . . like the night this babe was conceived. Morgeuse said that the child was special, that it was blessed of the Goddess."

Rhun shook his head, then gave a kind of shudder. "No matter that it might be a kind of blasphemy, I will be pleased to be away from Morgeuse and her enchantments. I want our lives to be simple and real once again. No sorcery, no spells, no curses. Just you and me, a man and a woman who love each other."

Eastra nodded. "I would like that, too."

"Perhaps, when this is over . . ." Rhun sighed. "The thing is . . . I want Arthur to live, but if he does, who is not to say it will not begin all over again?"

"I don't think that will happen. Morgeuse said she could heal him, but he would never be high king again."

"What does that mean?"

"I don't know, but I have hope it means this war is finally over."

"Now that would be a miracle."

She smiled at him. "I believe in miracles. Don't you?"

Twenty

The wind blew ripples across the lake, patterning its surface. Across the water, its form half obscured by wreaths of mist, the isle of apples appeared to float, a dreamy mirage of green. Morguese stood on the near shore facing the gathering. She wore a sheer white gown, and the breeze caught the gossamer fabric and made it billow and dance around her. Her long hair—which had turned completely white a few days after the battle of Camboglanna—drifted in tendrils around her pale face. She had lost flesh, and to Eastra, who had seen Morguese dance in Urien's hall, a creature of flame and heat and sensuality, the northern queen now appeared as a lovely, bloodless wraith. It was as if with Mordred's death all the life and passion had been leached from her, leaving behind a transparent shell. And yet Eastra was also reminded of the Goddess's incarnation as the Lady of the Moon, cool and silvery and full of ancient power.

Morgeuse raised her arms. In her left hand was Arthur's sword. The huge ruby set in the hilt glinted like a glowing red eye. Eastra heard a ripple of awe and half dread pass through the crowd. Excalibur seemed like a living thing, and she wondered with the others if the weapon were protesting being torn from the hand of its rightful owner. She thought of the bier draped in royal purple slowly being lowered into the crypt in the chapel at the priory. *The king is dead,* the people had whispered, despair in their hearts.

Eastra's attention focused again on Morgeuse, a pale specter on the shore of the lake. Morgeuse began to speak in a voice of power and authority, belying her ethereal form. "We come here today to say farewell to Arthur, high king of Britain. His body has been returned to the earth, the Mother. Now we bid farewell to his spirit, sending it back to the otherworld. The king is dead, but his spirit, his memory, will never die!" She raised the sword higher. The ruby in the hilt glowed, and ripples of light seemed to run down the length of the shaft. "Someday Arthur will return to reclaim his kingdom, to carry his sword into combat for the sake of all Britain!"

A soft sigh of satisfaction swept through those watching—widows and families of the Companions; Arthur's footsoldiers and auxiliaries, some wearing bandages or leaning on crutches; the monks of Avalon; servants and retainers of the royal household; common folk who had walked long distances to pay their respects to the high king; and Guinevere herself, looking clear-eyed and composed.

"I, his sister, his closest living kin, have vowed to keep his memory alive." Morguese's voice rose rich and true, throbbing with emotion. ". . . and to watch over his sword until he shall come again." She turned slowly and, at the same time, brought the sword to her lips and kissed the shimmering blade. Then she raised it once more. With a strength that seemed impossible for a mortal woman, she threw Excalibur into the air. It whipped end over end, making a kind of wild, haunting music as it flew over the water, then slowly descended in a graceful arc near the island. Before it reached the water, a gauntleted hand reached up and caught it, hilt first, and snatched it down into the depths.

Eastra blinked, then gasped in wonder, as did everyone around her. The people began to whisper and point, shaking their heads, their eyes wild and disbelieving. Eastra met Morguese's gaze and caught her faint smile. The awed mur-

muring of the crowd grew louder, finally becoming a rhythmic chant. "Arthur is not dead," they intoned. "The king
still lives. He will come again! He . . . will . . . come . . .
again." Their voices swelled, exuberant and elated. Then,
as the rejoicing people watched, Morguese raised her arms,
and it was as if her body had turned to light, as if she were
glowing. The mist rose around her, like a nimbus of silver.
The light faded, the mist slowly moved away—and Morguese was gone.

Eastra shivered, caught up in the mood of wonder and
amazement like the rest of them. Then, remembering
Rhun's instructions, she quickly left the stunned gathering.

The aura of enchantment and mystery, of powerful forces
at work, followed her as she made her way into the forest.
She heard voices whispering around her, subtle and keening
like the wind soughing through the treetops. From the thick
foliage, she could feel eyes watching her, and were there
not faces—gnarled, grimacing faces—peering out from the
curving patterns of the rough bark of the elm and oak trees?

She hurried onward, trying to shake off a primitive sense
of dread. It was as if Morguese had called upon forces that
had slept for centuries, ancient powers living within the
earth and in the depths of the lake. She felt them swirling
around her, unsettled and restless, and she thought again
of her brother Cynebeold's tales of the spirits of the fen,
waiting to pull unsuspecting mortals down into their murky
realm. She shuddered, then glanced down. The ground
looked solid and ordinary, green turf brightened with purple loosestrife and white forget-me-nots, green-gold
bracken and fern. But she was still uneasy, and she hurried
on.

At last she saw the glint of water through the underbrush. As she approached the lake, her breath caught in
her throat and her muscles went tight with dread. She was
not certain what she feared to see, why she felt so anxious.

But, in fact, the scene that met her eyes was perfectly
peaceful. At the edge of the water iridescent dragonflies
and drab mayflies circled the white water lilies and the

purplish pink blooms of the flowering rush. The smell of the marsh came to her, strong and earthy, and clouds of tiny insects wafted over the still, green water. Across the way, the island of apples appeared very ordinary, a tangle of vegetation, in places turning the brown-gold of autumn.

She stared hard at the island, amazed that it looked so different from this side of the lake. The sense of enchantment was gone, leaving behind only the gentle, mellow beauty of water and green and growing things. Then she heard a sound behind her and turned. Rhun walked toward her. His chest was bare, his hair wet, and he was drying himself with his tunic as he approached. "Well," he asked, grinning, "did it work? Were we convincing?"

Eastra shook her head. "If you only knew. It was magic, pure magic."

His expression sobered. "Aye, there was more than a little of that at work. Something sent the sword to my hand as a lodestone draws iron. When I pulled it into the water, it seemed alive, quivering and singing in my hand."

"Where did you put it?"

"I buried it on the island. It's all wrapped up and protected in a wooden box. If Arthur ever wants it, it should be there for him."

Eastra nodded. "And Morgeuse—she disappeared afterward, vanished, as if she were no more substantial than a moonbeam. How do you suppose she accomplished that?"

"I don't know. I don't *want* to know." Rhun shook his head, then smiled again. "Come here. I've had enough of sorcery and spells this day. I want to hold a real living woman. You can warm me up."

"Ooooh, you are cold." She shivered as he embraced her.

"Aye, but not for long." He bent his head and kissed her. In moments he did seem to warm. She ran her fingers over his chest and looked up at his face. Her golden warrior, her beautiful, wonderful Rhun, a flesh and blood man to hold her and love her and chase away her uneasy memories of spirits and ancient things.

"We'd better go join the others," he said after they had kissed some more. "I don't want anyone to think too much on my absence during Morgeuse's performance."

Reluctantly, Eastra nodded. As they walked back through the woods, she asked, "How soon will Guinevere leave?"

"Soon. Arthur's already gone north, to an isle off Caledon. The Picts who live there have no quarrel with him, and they're so closemouthed and secretive, they'll guard his true identity as well as it can be guarded."

"Does he regret he will not be high king anymore?"

Rhun shook his head. "He said it's time he stepped down anyway, to let some other man guide Britain's destiny. He believes he accomplished at least part of what he meant to do. Besides, he deserves some peace and happiness. He has given over nearly his whole life to this cause. In many ways, it's a blessing Morgeuse could not heal his sword arm. Since he can't lead men into battle, he can't be high king. Now he can have a chance at a normal life.

"Besides, as she told him, he will have much more impact on the future as a dead, martyred king than he could ever have as a living but maimed man. Already the bards are composing songs about Arthur's bravery and glory, about his wondrous deeds and how someday he will return from the dead to guide Britain to greatness."

Eastra nodded. "Except for her blind spot about Mordred, Morgeuse really does seem to have the sight. It's almost like a bard's tale, the way everything has worked out. I'm certain Guinevere is delighted with this plan. She told me she never wanted to be queen. Now she can turn her full attention to her own passionate cause. Did you know she's been taking orphans into the royal household for years? Irish and Saxon children, as well as British ones. She knew they'd either die or be enslaved, so she took them in and has been raising them as if they were her own. When things got so ugly with rumors about her and Lancelot, she went back to her father's fortress in Dumonia and took the children with her. Now Arthur, Guinevere, and those poor orphaned children can all live in peaceful, happy obscurity on their northern isle."

"And what happens when those children grow up and go out into the world?" Rhun asked. "Will they tell the true story of Arthur and his quiet retirement in the land of the north?"

"If they do, who would believe them? The legend the bards are creating is much more enthralling than the true tale, so that's what people will remember. Speaking of bards," Eastra added, "have you had any news of Bridei?"

"Well, he wasn't killed at Camboglanna, that's for certain. He wasn't even there. I guess at the last moment, before they marched into battle, he took off. Someone asked him where he was going, and he said something about 'going to claim his heritage.' "

"What does that mean? We know he didn't go back to Gwynedd."

"All I can think of is that he went to Manua Gotodin. Because Rhiannon is a princess of the Brigantes, he may have some notion they will welcome him as kin and even offer him some position of authority."

"Do you think that will happen?"

Rhun shook his head. "Although one of the princes there may offer him a place as a lesser bard, I can't imagine anyone would give him any position of importance."

"Poor Bridei," Eastra murmured.

"Poor Bridei!" Rhun snorted. "There are a lot of stories about my brother, that he was an ally of Urien and Arthur's other enemies from the beginning. That even when we were in Londinium, he was plotting with them."

"I don't believe that. I don't think Bridei would betray you, not if he thought it would mean your death."

"But then who did betray us?"

Eastra chewed her lower lip. "Perhaps now I can tell you and you won't be angry. The attack on us may have been my fault. I felt sorry for the slave girl who waited upon me while we were staying at Aurelius's house. I told her I had once been a slave myself and I also told her who

I was, to give her hope she might someday be free and
have a decent life."

"And you think she carried the information that you
were Cerdic's niece and Arthur's hostage to our enemies?"

Eastra nodded. "It's possible, isn't it? After all, the slave
girl was a Pict. She had the blue markings on her hands
the same as the ones the Pictish warriors wear on their
faces, and they were Arthur's enemies."

"But the Picts were not allied with the Saxons at that
time. So I doubt very much you caused the attack by talking indiscreetly with a Pictish slavegirl. Perhaps we will
never know who betrayed us—although I could ask Cerdic
about it when I meet with him."

Eastra clutched Rhun's arm more tightly. "Are you certain you should do that? What if my uncle takes you prisoner, or even kills you? You're the last of Arthur's captains.
If he got rid of you, there would be no one to lead the
British cause."

"I don't think Cerdic is concerned about that. If anything, he needs to find a way to restore relations with my
people. Although they would not fight him in pitched battle, there are still any number of British chieftains who
consider Cerdic their enemy. If he truly wants his people
to enjoy some years of peace, he must deal with those men,
come to some agreement with them. I mean to offer to aid
him in setting up treaties and restoring trade relationships
with those chieftains. They know me, both as Maelgwn's
son and as one of Arthur's Companions, and I imagine they
would rather bargain with one of their own than with Cerdic."

Eastra gazed at him in surprise. "You would do that—
offer to smooth the way for Cerdic so he can gain even
more power?"

"Why not? He has shown himself to be a gracious victor. He did not pursue the fleeing Britons and slaughter
them. Nor has he immediately marched into British territory and begun confiscating land and property. For all that
the treaty between Arthur and Cerdic failed, I think the

intent of it remains attainable. There must be some way for us to divide up this isle so that there can be peace."

"But what about . . ." Eastra touched her stomach. It seemed to grow bigger day by day.

"That you carry my babe gives me more leverage in dealing with your uncle, not less. I can argue I am ably capable of being impartial in my negotiations because I will soon have a child who carries Saxon blood as well as British. My bond with you is further proof that I am the ideal man to mend the rift between our peoples."

"If only Cerdic will see it that way," Eastra said.

Rhun hugged her. "We will make him see it, you and I. Together we represent the future, as Arthur was the past."

She pulled him down to kiss her one last time before they walked back to the priory.

Londinium, A.D. 544

"They're coming, they're coming!" The excited serving woman rushed down the peristyle and into the garden. "Lord Rhun and the Saxon king."

Petra, who worked for wages rather than being a slave— as did everyone employed in Eastra's household—came to stand beside Eastra. Eastra did not move from her seat beside the beds of dog roses and lilies that filled the courtyard with their fragrance, but waited for the fair-haired babe at her breast to finish suckling. Then she sat him up on her lap to burp, cooing, "Your papa has come, little Ceawlin. Won't he be surprised at how big you've gotten?"

Ceawlin stared at her with solemn blue eyes, then screwed up his face and turned bright red as he filled his diaper.

"Oh, dear," Eastra said, laughing. "Now I will have to change your swaddling before your father arrives. Although it would serve him right if I left the mess for him. He needs to learn there is more to being a father than one night of pleasure. Doesn't he, my sweet, my darling little one?" She leaned back to look at her precious babe, then kissed him on his perfect tiny nose.

"I think you will have to change as well," Petra said. She pointed to the bright yellow streak on the skirt of Eastra's gunna.

"Oh, my!" Eastra laughed again. "I will be glad when he is old enough to eat solid food."

"Don't wish him to grow up too quickly." Petra took the baby and, wrapping him carefully in a blanket to protect her own clothing, put him over her shoulder. "For now you can keep him safe from danger, spoil him and pet him as you wish. But all too soon he will be wanting to go off with his father and be a warrior."

"Perhaps this peace will hold and he need never carry a sword," Eastra said wistfully.

Petra shook her head. "You can dream, my lady. But you know in your heart that men being the way they are, war is inevitable."

Petra whisked off the babe to change him and Eastra hurried to her own room to exchange her soiled gunna for a clean one.

By the time she was presentable, Rhun and her uncle had arrived. Hearing their heavy footsteps and deep voices in the entryway, she ran to greet them. She bowed to her uncle, then embraced Rhun.

Eastra led them into the atrium, which she'd refurbished with more substantial and comfortable native-made furniture. Cerdic immediately sank into one of the big, wooden chairs by the brazier. This one had wolfsheads carved into the armrests. Rhun took a seat in a chair with a dragon motif. She chose a cushioned stool for herself and pushed it close to where Rhun was sitting. A servant brought ale and the two men sipped it, not speaking, but seemingly content to simply rest and quench their thirst.

Eastra studied the tapestry on the wall, a present from Rhiannon and featuring a crimson dragon and a golden stallion—the symbol of her Saxon heritage—on a background of purple and white flowers. How strange it was, she thought. Who would have imagined a year ago that she would be living in a Roman-style house and her uncle and Rhun would be relaxing together like a pair of hunting dogs come in from the chase? It still amazed her that Cerdic had accepted Rhun so readily. Perhaps it was his coloring and build, which were so much like a Saxon's. Or perhaps it was that over the years, Cerdic, like she, had grown comfortable with British ways and customs and could now see the similarities between the two peoples more than the differences. Cerdic and Rhun had been together almost continually this past year, trying to forge a treaty between the British chieftains and the Saxons. Eastra had taught Rhun her language, and that had further aided the negotiations.

"So," she began when her curiosity got the better of her attempt to appear as a dutiful hostess, "how did you fare in your meeting with Cynglass and Powys and Urien?"

"Well enough." Cerdic nodded in satisfaction. "We've set up the boundary line along the old Roman road that leads from Isca Dumonia all the way to Lindum. It cuts the south of the island nearly in half, expanding Saxon lands substantially."

"But it leaves most of the forested, wild places to the British," Rhun added. "Which is as it should be."

"Do you think the peace will hold?"

Cerdic shrugged. "At least during my lifetime. Oh, the British chieftains will still raid and fight among themselves, but that's not my concern."

Eastra looked to Rhun. He shrugged. "Aye, Cerdic is right. My people will fight each other and the Irish will raid, and life will go on as it always has."

This did not really satisfy Eastra, but she did not comment. Although she doubted she would ever become as complacent and accepting as Rhiannon, she was trying to learn to deal with the fact that men simply saw the world differently than she ever would.

Cerdic sat back in his chair and sighed. "Well, niece.

You have done well for yourself. This is as fine a dwelling as I've ever been in."

Although startled by the compliment, Eastra managed to say, "I'm pleased you like it. When Aurelius and his family sailed for Less Britain, I knew it would fall to ruin unless someone kept it up. The stone walls can be cold and damp in the winter, but the garden is so lovely it more than makes up for the other less comfortable aspects of Roman living."

"Ah, Aurelius," Cedric smiled wolfishly. "A pity he had to leave so abruptly and abandon so much of his wealth."

Eastra considered Aurelius's fate. Who would have guessed he was the one who had arranged for she and Rhun to be attacked on that Londinium street over a year ago? But that was no odder than the fact that it had been Cador—one of Arthur's most trusted captains—Aurelius had conspired with. Cador despised the Saxons and wanted no part of a truce with them. He had done all he could to bring about the battle that had ended up costing him his life, including sending the false message that Mordred was dead.

Crafty Aurelius had sensed that Arthur's fall was coming, but he made the mistake of throwing in his lot with the scheming Cador rather than the Saxons. When Cedric reached Londinium last autumn and heard Aurelius bragging about his part in Arthur's downfall, he had made some inquiries and discovered the whole murderous plot. He was not pleased and offered Aurelius the choice of leaving Britain or losing his life.

"I wonder what happened to Aurelius's daughter," Rhun mused. He looked at Eastra. "You remember her, don't you? The one who kept throwing herself at Bridei?"

"I remember her," Eastra answered. "According to the servants here, Aurelius ended up wedding her off to some Saxon armorer who has his shop not far from here. The story is that by the time her father found out she was with child, she was too far gone to attract a better match."

Cedric looked at Rhun. "Your brother's get?"

"I don't think so. He swore he did no more than flirt with her."

Eastra shook her head. "I think she was already pregnant when we stayed here. That's likely why she was so desperate to seduce Bridei. It was her last chance at a royal husband." She felt a twinge of gratification to think that the haughty Roman British Calida had ended up married to one of the people she despised and a lowly armorer at that.

Petra came in carrying Ceawlin, and Rhun took his son in his arms. At first, Cerdic tried to feign disinterest in his grandnephew, but there was no mistaking the pride in his voice as he said, "A fine, brawny suckling. He will make a formidable warrior someday."

"Not if I can help it," Eastra answered.

"Oh, he'll be a warrior," Cerdic said. "He's got the blood for it from both sides. A warrior and a king—high king of the Britons."

Eastra could only shake her head and laugh. Over the babe's downy, golden head, she met Rhun's gaze. The look of tender love on his face made her breath catch. How she adored him, her glorious dragon prince.

Cerdic bent near to offer a rough, scarred finger for Ceawlin to grab. Behind him, Rhun mouthed the words, "I love you."

Eastra mouthed the words back. And little Ceawlin gave a hiccuping giggle of delight.

Dear Readers,

THE DRAGON PRINCE is made up of about equal parts history, legend, and imagination. First the history: There really was a king named Maelgwn the Great. He had a long reign over the kingdom of Gwynedd (northwest Wales) and sired several sons, including Rhun, who was said to have filled the power void left when King Arthur died, and Bridei, who is associated with the northern part of Britain.

There is much less documentation for Arthur, although Nennius, writing in the 1100's (nearly 600 years after Arthur's time) lists several important battles, including "the fight at Camlann in which Arthur and Medraut were killed." Camlann is thought to be a later form of Camboglanna, and Mordred is a variation of Medraut.

As for the legend, I've always thought it ironic that the tale of King Arthur has been preserved and embellished primarily by the very people who historically were his enemies. The Saxons eventually conquered and populated most of Britain, and through a quirk of language became the English (from the name of their fellow Germanic tribesmen, the Angles). They took King Arthur as their own and raised him to the level of a mythical folk-hero, a symbol for the most idealized concept of kingship and heroic nobility. He is certainly a larger than life character, and I found the fantasy of a "forever king" so compelling that I decided to add my own twist to the story and not kill off Arthur but instead provide a semi-magical explanation for his disappearance.

The rest of this story sprang solely from my imagination, incorporating a belief in the spiritual energy of the earth, the eternal cycle of rebirth and renewal, and the powerful magic of love.

Happy reading!

Mary Gillgen

The Queen of Romance

Cassie Edwards